Praise for Bárbara Mujica's *Frida*

"Mujica's Cristina is a vivid creation."
—*The New York Times Book Review*

"A delicious blend of fiction and biography."
—*Grand Rapids Press*

"Mujica's Frida is a brave, foul-mouthed child,
simultaneously defiant and winning."
—*The San Diego Union-Tribune*

"Absorbing."
—*Book* magazine

"The best kind of fictionalized biography:
rich, vibrant, and psychologically astute."
—*Kirkus* reviews

"Brilliantly crafted, this book resonates with historical
and psychological insight."
—*Library Journal*

"The novel paints a detailed picture of Kahlo and her milieu."
—*Publishers Weekly*

BÁRBARA MUJICA is a novelist, short story writer, critic, professor of Spanish at Georgetown University, and a regular contributor to the *New York Times* and the *Los Angeles Times,* among others. A two-time nominee for the Pushcart Prize and winner of the E. L. Doctorow International Fiction competition, she is the author of the novels *The Deaths of Don Bernardo* and *Affirmative Actions,* and a collection of short stories. Ms. Mujica lives in Washington, D.C.

frida

A NOVEL

Bárbara Mujica

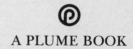

A PLUME BOOK

PLUME
Published by the Penguin Group
Penguin Putnam Inc., 375 Hudson Street, New York, New York 10014, U.S.A.
Penguin Books Ltd, 80 Strand, London WC2R ORL England
Penguin Books Australia Ltd, Ringwood, Victoria, Australia
Penguin Books Canada Ltd, 10 Alcorn Avenue, Toronto, Ontario, Canada M4V 3B2
Penguin Books (N.Z.) Ltd, 182-190 Wairau Road, Auckland 10, New Zealand

Penguin Books Ltd, Registered Offices: Harmondsworth, Middlesex, England

Published by Plume, a member of Penguin Putnam Inc. This is an authorized
reprint of a hardcover edition published by The Overlook Press. For information
address The Overlook Press, Peter Mayer Publishers, Inc., Lewis Hollow Road,
Woodstock, New York 12498.

First Plume Printing, January 2002
10 9 8 7 6 5 4 3 2 1

ART CREDIT—Front (detail) and back cover art: "Las dos Fridas" (1939) by
Frida Kahlo © 2002 Banco de México Diego Rivera & Frida Kahlo Museums
Trust. Av. Cinco de Mayo No. 2, Col. Centro, Del. Cuauhtémoc, 06059, Mexico,
D.F. Instituto Nacional de Bellas Artes, Mexico City, D.F., Mexico. Photo credit:
Schalkwijk/Art Resource, NY.

Ⓟ REGISTERED TRADEMARK—MARCA REGISTRADA

The Library of Congress has catalogued the hardcover edition as follows:

Mujica, Bárbara Louise.
    Frida : a novel / Bárbara Mujica.
    p.   cm.
    ISBN 1-58567-074-X (hc.)
    ISBN 0-452-28303-5 (pbk.)
1. Kahlo, Frida—Fiction.   2. Rivera, Diego, 1886–1957—Fiction.
3. Painters' spouses—Fiction.   4. Women painters—Fiction.
5. Mexico—Fiction.   I. Title.
PS3563.U386 F75 2000   813'.54—dc21   00-055730

Printed in the United States of America
Original hardcover design by Bernard Schleifer

PUBLISHER'S NOTE
This is a work of fiction. Names, characters, places, and incidents either are the
product of the author's imagination or are used fictitiously. Except for obvious
historical figures, any resemblance to actual persons, living or dead, businesses,
companies, events, or locales is entirely coincidental.

BOOKS ARE AVAILABLE AT QUANTITY DISCOUNTS WHEN USED TO PROMOTE
PRODUCTS OR SERVICES. FOR INFORMATION PLEASE WRITE TO PREMIUM
MARKETING DIVISION, PENGUIN PUTNAM INC., 375 HUDSON STREET, NEW YORK,
NEW YORK 10014.

To Mauro, with love

Part I

CHAPTER 1

Frida! Frida!

I KNOW WHAT YOU WANT TO HEAR, DOCTOR, BUT I'M SORRY, YOU'RE NOT going to pry some sordid confession out of me. You psychiatrists are all alike. You want to make me say that I despised her, that I resented her always being the center of attention, but you're wrong. In fact, I hated it when people looked at me, which they did often because, to tell you the truth, I was the prettier of the two. *He* told me that.

But this isn't fair. Believe me, in spite of everything, I loved her.

Look, from as far back as I can remember, she was kind to me. She protected me. I always looked up to her; she was the smarter one, the more talented one. I was quiet. She was dynamic. I was prettier. Maybe she didn't think so, but . . . well, I mean, she had to realize that everyone admired my looks, even if she pretended not to. After all, she wasn't stupid. *He* always said that I was gorgeous. Of course, he was a liar, a sweet-talker. But even so, I was the one he liked to paint. I was his favorite model. She didn't like it when I posed for him, but I did it anyway. All the time. In the nude.

The point is, it's not as though I wanted to get even with her. That's not why I did it. She had her strong points and I had mine. She was clever. I was beautiful. *She* wasn't beautiful. How could she be? A lame girl with a mustache and one leg shorter than the other? Sometimes she teased me, but that was to be expected. I mean, since she was the bright one and I was so dim-witted. Anyhow, she teased everybody. I wasn't special in that sense. Let's say I wasn't the exception. I was never the exception.

It's not as though I didn't know what I was doing. I knew, but I thought she wouldn't care. She was so wild and eccentric. Rules never mattered to her. Other people's feelings never mattered to her. So I thought, well, okay, since she doesn't give a damn about anybody, since she thinks it's fine to go ahead and do whatever you want and to hell with what people think, I'll just follow her advice.

You see, she was the leader. I was the follower. I was always the follower.

Let me give you an example. You were asking about our childhood, so let me tell you.

This happened a long, long time ago, when we were little. Such a long time ago, and still I picture it so vividly, as though it's etched in my brain. You see, I'm an artist too. No, I don't mean I'm an artist the way she was. I can't paint pictures on canvas, but I engrave images on my mind. Well, I guess that's not worth much, is it?

This is what I see: Frida, crouching behind a pillar, surveying her enemies. Estela, the commander, whispering to María del Carmen, the chief strategist. Estela gives the signal, and battle lines form. There are maybe forty girls in the courtyard. About fifteen of them group into attack teams. The others continue jumping rope or playing hopscotch, engrossed in their games. Now Frida is peering out from behind the post, taking stock of the hostile forces and biting her lip.

She was an adorable child. Not like me. I was tubby and kind of dull. I guess I have to admit it. In those days, *she* was the pretty one, although not for long. She was a delectable little girl, with a tea-and-cream complexion, full, rosy cheeks and pudgy arms. She was about six then, and she had chin-length, fluffy, dark brown curls that framed her face, which was still soft and babyish. Mami always sent her to school with a white bow in her hair, and in her gingham pinafore, she looked like an angel.

The school building was a Spanish colonial-style structure, with an interior patio surrounded by a colonnaded arcade. It had just rained—one of those quick, sudden downpours that fall in April on the Central Plateau—but now the sun was shining, and the pools that had formed on the patio tiles were glistening in the brightness. In the center of the yard, schoolgirls were giggling and jumping into puddles, each one vying to make a bigger splash than the others.

Frida wasn't paying attention. Her eyes were glued on Estela and María del Carmen, who had hooked elbows and taken their positions at the head of their troops. They were going to try to goad her into coming into the open. But Frida didn't wait for the taunts to begin. She thrust out her jaw defiantly, like this, then stepped away from the column.

"Frida!" I whispered. "Frida, don't go!" I was shrinking in the shadows.

"Shut up!" she scolded. "Don't be a sissy!" She was always calling me a sissy.

I cowered behind the column, waiting for her to move forward, into the line of attack. Suddenly I felt wetness, and the skin between my legs smarted. I shifted position, and the urine trickled down my legs onto my new white socks with the lace trim. I knew Mami would be furious.

Frida stood facing Estela. She was squinting, probably from the sunlight. Her lips were trembling, but her feet were firm, and she stared right into the eyes of her adversary.

Estela grinned, and as if on command, the girls in the hostile brigade began to chant:

¡Frida, Frida	Frida, Frida
Fue servida	Was served up
Al Diablo	To the devil
Por comida!	For dinner!

¡Frida, Frida	But even he didn't want her,
Escupida	Frida, Frida,
De su boca	So he spat her back up,
Por judía!	Because she was Jewish!

It was horrible! Horrible! We were Catholic! We had made our First Communion, every one of us, but in that horrid school, the girls were always calling us Jewish because of Papá.

I wanted Frida to turn around and walk away, but instead, she tightened her jaw to keep it from trembling. The children who had been playing started to gather around her. Soon they had formed a large, jagged semicircle. Frida lifted her head and folded her arms. The knot in my stomach was growing tighter. I started to sob.

For an instant Frida's chin quivered, but she blinked hard and managed to hold back the tears. Some of the children were snickering and pointing. A kind of phosphorescence was enveloping the yard. Frida swallowed hard, then took a deep breath.

"Shut up!" She hurled the words at Estela as though they were a spitball.

The children began to sing even louder.

"Shut up!" shouted Frida again, but this time her cry was inaudible above the chant.

"¡Frida, Frida!"

"Shut up! Shut up!"

The singing began to die down.

"What a stupid song!" she screamed. "An idiot must have made it up!"

Some of the girls started to giggle. A few took up the chant once again, only this time more softly.

I could hardly see what was going on. I peered out from behind the column and stood on my toes, but I was smaller than the girls who had formed a barricade around Frida, and I couldn't see over their heads. I felt like pushing through the line in order to get a better view, but I knew that the others would make fun of my wet drawers and socks, and besides, they might turn on *me* just for being her sister. So I stayed hidden.

Estela and Frida stood staring at each other, not more than a foot apart. No one moved. The tension had been mounting for a long time—weeks or even months. And now, finally, the standoff. And now, finally, the showdown. The other children stood watching, waiting. They were frightened yet excited, hoping that maybe something terrible would happen.

"You don't belong here, you're not one of us," hissed Estela. "You're foreign!"

The children recoiled as though a bogeyman had dropped from the roof into the middle of the courtyard. Every eye was on Frida. I wanted to kill Estela, but what could I do? I stayed behind the pillar.

"I am not!" Frida countered.

"Yes, you are, FREY-DA!" Estela pronounced the name with a guttural German *R*. "You have a foreign name!"

Frida hesitated a moment. It was true she spelled her name the German way: F-R-I-E-D-A. And it was true our father was a German Jew of Hungarian origin.

She looked straight at Estela. "My name is Magdalena Carmen Frieda Kahlo y Calderón. That's the name I was baptized with in church!"

"You're foreigners! Your father speaks Spanish with an accent. When he says *república* or *revolución*, he sounds like a pig grunting."

"I'm not a foreigner. I'm a Mexican!"

"Mexicans are Catholic!"

"I'm as Catholic and Mexican as you are! I go to church every Sunday! I go to the Church of San Juan, just like you, so you should know!"

Not that there's anything wrong with being Jewish, doctor. Years later, Frida would brag about being Jewish. But at the time, in post-revolutionary Mexico, anything foreign was considered bad. Are you Jewish, doctor?

"Your father's name is Wilhelm!"

"My father's name is Guillermo!"

"Not his real name, FREY-DA. His real name is Wilhelm!"

"Wilhelm, Wilhelm," the children chanted, "her father's name is Wilhelm!"

The light caught Frida's hair, causing the top of her head to shimmer like a halo. In the brightness she looked like a seraph, all gossamer and sparkle. She brought her delicate baby fingers to her lips and stood staring at Estela.

"My mother says your father is one of those foreigners brought in by Porfirio Díaz," said Estela. "She says foreigners ruined the country, but now, with the Revolution, you're all going to be hanged!"

"Your mother is a stupid fucking whore!"

Frida had caught Estela off guard. The girl's parents were sympathizers of the revolutionary Emiliano Zapata and his agrarian reform, but they were decent people, not riffraff. In those polished bourgeois surroundings, you didn't hear that kind of language. Certainly not from a young lady. Certainly not from a six-year-old. Estela caught her breath. I have to laugh! The expression on her face when Frida said those words.

A ripple of disbelief washed through the yard. The girls giggled. "Did you hear what Frida said?" they whispered. "She said f——! She said whore!" Even the peasants didn't use those expressions. The peasants were reserved, dignified. Only lowlifes spoke like that. Frida was breaking all the rules, and that took daring! I was proud of her.

The children looked from Frida to Estela. Their faces were anxious, expectant. Some of them were nodding and smiling at Frida. They seemed to be on the verge of going over to her side. Estela had to regain the upper hand, which clearly she had lost to this dirty-mouthed little brat.

"Your father worked for the Díaz government. My mother says—"

"Your mother's full of shit! Your mother's so mean she's got spiders coming out of her cunt!"

"FRIDA KAHLO!"

The teacher's bellow cut the air like a thunderclap. The children scattered as if repelled by some powerful magnetic force. In an instant, Miss Caballero swooped down on that precious, foul-tongued little girl, my sister, grabbed her by the ear and pulled her out of the patio.

"What kind of language is that? Who ever heard of a decent little girl using such language? It's disgusting!"

Frida wriggled loose, but the teacher grabbed her by the ruffle of her pinafore and yanked her back.

"You!" She said it with revulsion. "You, who look like God's little angel! You have the mouth of a street cleaner! You talk as though you were being raised in the gutter instead of in a decent home by a respectable, devout Christian mother. You should be ashamed of yourself!"

She was pulling Frida along the arcade toward the door that led to her classroom. I was scampering along behind.

Suddenly, Miss Caballero turned.

"And you!" she said, pointing a sausagelike finger at me. "You're

here too! Naturally. Wherever Frida goes, you go. You stick to her
like a shadow. But you'd better be careful, Cristinita. She's a troublemaker, and she'll get you into trouble too." I stood there, looking up
at the teacher. My legs were sticky, and my wet pants made my skin
itch. I started to squirm. Miss Caballero took me by the hand, then
sniffed. The urine was beginning to smell.

"Oh no, not again," she moaned. "Have you wet your pants
again, Cristina? Both of you are repulsive little wretches!"

That's what she called us: *repulsive little wretches.*

She grabbed Frida by the ear and me by the arm and yanked us both
into the classroom. "Here," she said to me, "take off those wet pants and
give them to me. I'll wrap them up in paper so your mother's laundress
can wash them. Now, come here and let me rinse you off."

Instead of taking off my underwear, I shrank back and squatted
under a table. She lunged for me, trying to pull up my skirt.

"I can do it myself," I whimpered. I didn't want her to touch me.
I especially didn't want her to rinse me off and touch me . . . down
there.

"Don't be silly," she snapped.

She clutched my arm and tried to drag me out, but I bit her
thumb as hard as I could, then wriggled into a corner. She let out a
sharp little yelp that communicated more surprise than pain.

I tried to twist out of my panties without lifting my skirt, so that
Miss Caballero wouldn't see my bottom. I had heard people make
remarks about Miss Caballero, but I was too small to understand the
innuendo. Even so, I knew from how they lowered their voices when
they talked about her that she must be strange. Some of the comments had to do with her name—*Caballero,* "man" or "gentleman." I
thought maybe it was because her hands were so big. They looked
like a man's.

I don't know exactly what Frida thought of her. I think she found
her both repugnant and fascinating. She liked to play tricks on her,
to put her to the test the way children do with a person in authority,
but she also liked to hang around her, to watch her. She adored it
when Miss Caballero paid attention to her, but then Frida always
liked to be the center of everything.

The teacher was a fair-skinned mestizo with heavy features and a firm mouth that conveyed both resoluteness and frustration. Rumor had it that she wore a wig, although since none of us had ever seen her without the thick black braids that encircled her head, we couldn't be sure. She always dressed in black, in outfits that looked as though they were reconstructed ball gowns left over from some bygone era. In spite of her rough demeanor, her body was round, soft, sensual. Her hands reminded me of bunches of ripe bananas, the plump red kind. I had the impression that Miss Caballero could be nice if she wanted to; she just didn't want to. Even as a small child, I sensed that something was holding her back, preventing her from showing the affection she kept locked inside.

Miss Caballero finally pinned me between the table and the wall. She grabbed me and held me fast with one hand. With the other, she poured water into a basin. Then, with a wet cloth, she wiped my legs and buttocks.

"Here, hike up your skirt," she ordered. I was afraid to disobey. I gathered up my pinafore and held it at the waist. I wanted to die.

Frida should have helped me. I mean, she could have screamed or thrown something at Miss Caballero. But maybe she didn't because I hadn't helped her out when Estela and the others were taunting her. Maybe her silence was some kind of revenge. Anyhow, she just stood there watching as the rag went up and down my thighs and in between my legs, up and down and in between, over and over again.

"Come on," snapped Miss Caballero, "open your legs so I can get you clean." I widened my stance and bent my knees. Miss Caballero continued her wiping. Frida just stared. That was one time when she should have opened her mouth, but she just stared.

When she was done, Miss Caballero rinsed the rag, then wrung it out.

"Now," she said to Frida, "you take off your panties and give them to Cristi."

Frida shot me a look of contempt. "Why should I?" she said.

"Because I'm telling you to."

"So? Why should I be the one to go home without underwear? She's the one who wet her pants!"

"Because you're older," snapped Miss Caballero. Frida considered this a moment, but didn't grasp the logic.

"What does being older have to do with it?" She thrust out her jaw.

"Do it!" snapped Miss Caballero.

Slowly, Frida took down her bloomers and handed them to me. "Stupid baby!" she hissed.

"Never mind!" retorted Miss Caballero. She helped me with the underwear, then she went on, "You think you're so grown up, little Frida. Remember that time in science class? The time I was explaining how the universe worked?"

Frida looked at her shoes.

Miss Caballero kept on talking. "We turned out the lights," she said, "and I held a candle in one hand and an orange in the other and I showed you how the Earth revolves around the sun and how the moon revolves around the Earth. Remember?"

"Yes," said Frida. She knew what was coming. She pursed her lips and waited for the teacher to humiliate her.

"What happened that day, Frida?"

Frida didn't answer.

"You got very excited, didn't you?"

Frida shot her a spiteful look, but said nothing.

"Come on, you remember, don't you, Frida?"

"Yes."

"Yes, ma'am."

"Yes, ma'am." Frida knew she was licked. Her face was turning red, and her jaw was tightening.

"And what did you do, Frida?"

"I wet my pants."

"That's right. You wet your pants." Miss Caballero smiled, satisfied. She had won.

But on the day of the science lesson, it hadn't been such a clear victory.

As soon as Estela had spied the little puddle under Frida's chair, she began to chant: *Frida wet her panties! Frida wet her panties!* Soon the whole class was singing: *Frida wet her panties!*

A decent teacher would have hustled Frida out of the room and cleaned her up quietly. Instead, Miss Caballero dragged her up to the front of the room and tried to pull up her dress. But Frida was too wriggly for her, too wriggly and too quick. Miss Caballero tried to hold her in place with the sash of her dress, but Frida squirmed away. As she did, she elbowed the basin that the teacher had set out to wash her. Wash her in front of the whole class! The basin crashed to the floor. It sounded like cars colliding. Frida darted for the door, knocking slates and picture books to the ground. The noise must have dizzied her, because she tottered and hit the edge of the shelf where they kept mixed tempera. A bottle of red fell and shattered, spraying bloodlike droplets everywhere. She could have sprinted to safety, but she stood there, mesmerized by the patterns the paint was forming on the floor. Her ruffled white socks were drenched, and her legs were spattered.

Suddenly, she stooped and immersed her pudgy six-year-old hands in the paint.

"Stop!" shrieked Miss Caballero, but Frida was already rubbing paint on her dress, her arms, her face. Even her eyelids were dripping with the thick, red, gooey liquid. She had . . . how do you say it? Meta—metamorphosed into a ghoul. In my five-year-old mind, blood was trickling from her lips, and an otherworldly gleam was radiating from her eyes. The hazy beams streaming through the window seemed to transform her into something enormous and sinister.

"Come get cleaned up this instant!" commanded Miss Caballero. Frida snickered. She held up her hands and wiggled her fingers like the legs of a crab. It was grotesque. I was terrified, and I was so mad at Frida I wanted to pummel her.

At last Miss Caballero gave up. Frida went home that day covered in red.

Frida had humiliated Miss Caballero in front of the whole class, and so whenever she got the chance, the teacher started in about how my sister had once gotten so excited during a science class that she wet her pants. What Miss Caballero wanted was to cut Frida down, to make her feel like a fly on a piece of turd.

Let's see, where was I? I'm so old now I can't keep my mind on anything. Ah, yes, I was telling you how Frida always protected me. Well, I had put on my sister's clean underwear. Frida held out her hand to me, and I took it and nestled my head against her shoulder.

The other children had lined up outside the classroom door and were waiting to come in. "Stay here," said Miss Caballero. She straightened her skirt and walked to the door. At her signal, the girls began to file into the room and move toward their seats.

"Come on, Cristi!" whispered Frida. "Let's get out of here!"

The building was a renovated Spanish-style house that had been transformed into a school. It was a two-story affair constructed in the form of a squared-off U with a patio in the center. On the ground floor, the sides of the U contained two classrooms, a storeroom, a small office, and a tiny chapel. Living quarters for the owner of the school and Miss Caballero were on the second floor. There were no hallways; all the first-floor rooms opened onto the courtyard and all of the second-floor rooms opened onto the balcony above the arcade. Each of the classrooms had two doors on the patio side. As Miss Caballero stood guiding the children through one door, Frida darted for the other, pulling me behind.

I was terrified. "We can't leave. Mami will kill us."

"Mami won't know!"

Miss Caballero noticed us and took off in pursuit, but before she could catch up, we had reached the unlocked gate and slipped out into the street.

Frida and I knew every crook and cranny in Coyoacán. I don't know if you've ever been there, doctor, but it's a picturesque colonial town about an hour to the south of Mexico City. Baroque churches, plazas, *tianguis*—that is, native markets. Hernán Cortés once lived there while he was fighting the Aztecs. Now it's pretty built up. Tourists, of course. Tourists who come to see our house. Frida's house, I mean. They come to see it because Frida lived there, not because I lived there. The town is still surrounded by open fields and ranches, but now it's a suburb of Mexico City, that sprawling, ravenous monster. The capital is bustling and filthy and crazy, of course, just like any big city, but Coyoacán is still sort of old-fashioned. It has a kind of small-town warmth, a quaintness, a sense of history.

Anyhow, we darted down a cobblestone path, then cut onto an unpaved road leading to the Viveros de Coyoacán, a large, tree-filled park with a narrow, sleepy river winding through it. Street vendors were selling brightly colored toys made of wood, gourds, or papier-mâché, and I asked Frida to buy me a *balero,* a cup-and-ball gizmo that we used to play with when we were kids.

"That would be just dandy, wouldn't it," she snapped. "Mami would know the second we walked into the house with a *balero* that we'd been fooling around in the streets! Really, Cristi, you're so dumb." She always used to say that to me: "Really, Cristi, you're so dumb."

Frida's plan was a simple one. We would go to the park and play until it was time for Conchita, our nanny, to pick us up from school. Then we'd wait in the little stationery shop across from the school gate, far enough away to avoid Miss Caballero's vulturine eyes but near enough to see Conchita coming up the street to get us. As soon as we saw the maid, we would run to meet her, then just go home with her as usual. Mami would never know the difference.

I wasn't too convinced, but I trudged along behind Frida, dragging my feet in the dust. We passed a *pulquería,* a bar where they served *pulque,* a fermented milkish drink made from agave juice. In those days, the walls were all brightly painted with figures from Mexican folklore—a bandit-hero assaulting an emaciated landowner, a brassy whore counting her money. I wanted to get away from the place, but Frida was enthralled by the colors and by the obscene songs the rowdy construction workers were singing inside.

Frida took a coin out of her pinafore and bought me a quesadilla—a tortilla with cheese and chili sauce—from a street vendor. She didn't know his name, but she considered him a friend because she had bought from him many times before.

"Don't get cheese on your pinafore, or Mami will know I bought you a quesadilla in the street," she said sharply. "We're playing hookey," she confided to the man. He smiled and held out another quesadilla for her.

"I have only one centavo," she said.

"It doesn't matter," he answered. "This is my gift to you."

We ran to the park and played for what seemed like a half hour or so. The whole time Frida nagged me about not dirtying my dress, not muddying my shoes, not getting grass stains on my socks, so that Mami wouldn't know where we'd been.

Frida was watching the sun's movement in the sky. When, according to her calculations, it was time to go, she led me back through the dusty streets to the school.

One look at the stationery shop and I felt my blood turn to sawdust. The store was closed for lunch. Since businesses usually shut their doors at two o'clock and didn't reopen until five or six, that meant school had been dismissed long ago, hours ago. I looked down the street. The florist was closed as well, and so were the bakery and the *tortillería*. No children were waiting by the school gate. The streets were empty.

"Let's go!" ordered Frida. "They'll be looking for us."

"Now we're really going to get it!" I cried. "And it's all your fault."

Frida didn't answer. She just grabbed my hand, and we bolted down the street toward home.

CHAPTER 2

Frida Dancing

IT'S ALWAYS SEEMED TO ME THAT THE REASON FRIDA WAS SO DAMNED patriotic, so more-Mexican-than-thou, was because of those experiences we had in school. To Frida the Mexican sky was the purest, most exquisite in the universe—even though the air above Mexico City is usually the color of filthy socks or shit-tinged urine. But you couldn't say that to her. No. Otherwise, she'd accuse you of having sold out to the Yankees. She'd accuse you of being a capitalist pawn or of sucking the cock of the European intellectual elite. She had a mouth as foul as a drunkard's piss. But I don't need to tell you that. You know that already. She'd mow you down just for saying that the sky gleamed less brightly in Mexico than in, say, California. She was like that, you see. Fanatical about everything. For Frida the Mexican sky was blazing liquid amber, a turquoise jewel, a mantle of crushed sapphires. Not just a mass of grimy air. Not just what it was. To Frida, nothing was ever what it really was. She lived in her own imaginary world. Of course, *he* found that charming, but to tell you the truth, she could overdo it. She could get on your nerves. But maybe it wasn't her fault, because when you're endlessly being teased, endlessly being called a Jew and a foreigner, it's easy to turn into a zealot. On the other hand, she provoked people. Sometimes she was so blunt and confrontational that she brought out the worst in everyone around her.

Or maybe not. After all, who am I to try to explain things? You figure out what was going on in her head, for God's sake. You're the doctor!

All I'm saying is, well, I think you know what I'm talking about because you're a foreigner yourself. You know what it's like to feel like an outsider, although you can't begin to compare what we went through with the situation that exists now. Anyway, you're a respected person, a psychiatrist. We were just impressionable little girls, and for us, always being called aliens, Hebrews, immigrants—all that took its toll. On Frida, especially, because she was the aggressive one, the one who was always in the middle of the fray. That's something else that he loved about her, her feistiness, although sometimes I think she played that role just to keep his attention. I mean, she was feisty all right, feisty by nature, but later on, that feistiness got to be part of her act. And he was an actor too. The revolutionary. Muralist for the masses. It was all part of his persona.

For her, showing she was as Mexican as anybody and more Mexican than most became an obsession. You know, Frida was born in 1907, on July 6, to be exact, but she always said she was born in 1910, the year the Mexican Revolution started. She wanted to be a true daughter of the new Mexico, down to the date of her birth.

Sometimes she would close her eyes and proclaim, all exalted, "I'm as Mexican as the eagle that spreads its wings of snow and ash and sails through the air, grazing the stratosphere with its powerful beak!"

"And dropping shit all over my murals!" *he* would answer. And we'd laugh and laugh.

Those long Indian dresses she wore, people said they were to hide her crippled leg or to disguise her limp, but that was only part of it. She wanted to make a point of her *mexicanidad*—her solidarity with the common people of Mexico—even though we had as much Indian blood flowing in our veins as the ocean has honey. No, that's not really true. Mami's father was an Indian from Morelos. The point is, Frida wanted to be identified with the revolutionary cause, especially since *he* was so important in the movement. And the other thing is, she liked to stand out in a crowd.

What do you mean I'm digressing again?

Ah, yes, I was telling you the other day about how Frida always protected me. Always. Even when we were little. I was telling you about the day we ran away from school.

When we realized how late it was, we took off toward home, praying that Mami hadn't heard what had happened and gone totally berserk. Unfortunately, Miss Caballero had sent an attendant home with the news that we had escaped. *Attendant*—that's the name we used so we didn't have to call them servants, so we could pretend we were democratic and respected everybody, so we could convince ourselves we didn't consider them just Indians who jumped and hopped at our bidding. This "attendant's" name was Arturo. Miss Caballero always said he had the face of a calf that just had its throat slit.

On the road, Arturo ran into Conchita, who was on her way to pick us up.

When Mami heard we had escaped from that hell they called a kindergarten, instead of thinking things through and just waiting for us to come back, she sent Manuel, the houseboy, all the way to Papá's studio in Mexico City to give him the news.

I can just imagine Manuel, so ancient and gnarled, bursting into Papá's darkroom and announcing, "The children are missing!"

I can imagine Papá, with that half-crazed look of his, staring at Manuel and trying to force the information into his brain. I can conjure up the scene as if I had been there. Papá is looking at Manuel with dazed eyes, trying to assimilate what he's saying.

"Señor! The little girls are missing! They left school, and no one knows where they are. Miss Caballero sent a messenger to the house. The señora is frantic!"

Papá is mute.

"Your daughters, Señor!"

"My daughters?" Guillermo Kahlo begins to process the message. Diamonds of sweat form on his brow.

You have to understand that in those times, a missing child could be a dead child. We grew up during the dictatorship of Victoriano Huerta, who came to power in 1913. Huerta's men were known to snatch little ones off the playground in order to coerce or punish their families. Zapata sympathizers, like our parents, were ready

targets. The Huertista big shots made a show of their respectability—
after all, they had wrenched power from the rebels and returned
order to society, hadn't they?—but they had goons to do their dirty
work, and these men knew no mercy. They would just as soon slice
the throat of a cherubic three-year-old as that of a goat. Children
were easy pawns in the power game.

I'm sure that when Papá finally assimilated Manuel's message, he
dropped whatever pictures he was developing and ran out the door,
probably leaving chemicals all over the counter and forgetting to put
on his hat.

What kind of a father was he? What does that have to do with the
story? What I'm trying to explain to you is how good Frida was to
me, so you'll quit implying that I—that I did what I did because I
resented her . . . or hated her. I know that's what you're getting at.

What difference does it make about Papá?

All right, I'll tell you about Papá. Let me think a minute. He was
a strange man. As a father, he was detached, forbidding even. But
deep in his heart, he loved us, especially Frida. For him, Frida was
everything, maybe because she was like him, brilliant, driven, crazy.
For him, Frida was the last hard-boiled egg at the picnic, the last
aspirin in the medicine cabinet, the last pitcher of punch in the ice-
box. Frida the imp. Frida the troublemaker. Frida was the one who
went with him on his walks. They would examine flowers or collect
stones together, organizing them by size and color. Sometimes I'd tag
along too, but I always felt out of place, like a chicken in the wrong
coop. Papá hoped that Frida would be a scientist someday, or maybe
a doctor. He would sit her on his knee and stare into space looking
unhinged and otherworldly, like a saint witnessing the Resurrection.

As for me, he thought I'd become what I became: nothing.

So, I'm sure the thought of Frida in danger zapped him like a
bolt of lightning, leaving his poor brain completely scrambled.

In the meantime, Frida and I were cautiously approaching the
house, which looked, from a distance, like a gigantic cake smothered
with blue icing. The beams and window frames were cinnamon sticks
and chocolate candies. It was a sprawling house in the old Spanish
colonial style with narrow shuttered windows that opened to the

street. Inside, interconnecting rooms enclosed a large patio, where terra-cotta pots held geraniums and flowering cacti. A few years before Frida was born, Papá had the house built and painted it a deep royal. From as far back as I can remember, everyone called it the Casa Azul.

My sister had put up a brave front on the way home, but I could see now that she was really frightened.

"Maybe we could sneak in and go to our room," she whispered to me, "and pretend we were there all the time."

"You think it would work?"

"Maybe." She tried to sound convincing, but we both knew that Mami had probably torn up the house looking for us. In my mind, I could see trinkets crashing against walls, while Mami cursed the Apostles, Miss Caballero, and especially the lunk of a husband that had given her such wayward children.

"Let's try to find Conchita first," suggested Frida.

We slipped around the side of the house and into the kitchen. Conchita wasn't there, but Inocencia, the cook, was down on her knees praying to the Virgin of Guadalupe at the small altar by the pantry: "Poor children . . . villains . . . assassins . . . *Virgen Madre* . . . bring them home . . ."

"This looks bad," whispered Frida.

I started to whimper softly. Frida brought her index finger to her lips, signaling me to be quiet. "Chst! Shut up, you baby!" she hissed.

The cook continued to pray, tears rolling down her heavy brown cheeks.

Frida snuck up behind her, then touched her gently on the shoulder. "Inocencia!" she said softly.

Startled, the cook recoiled, then opened her eyes wide. "Fridita!"

Frida giggled, and I smiled hesitantly. Inocencia, still on her knees, hugged us and began to wail: "*¡Oh, gracias a Dios!* Thank God! Oh, Holy Virgin, thank you!" She dragged her ungainly body to a standing position, then poured us some juice and put tortillas on a plate.

"Where have you been?" she pretended to scold. "Your poor mami is crazy with worry. You have to go right now and tell her you're safe."

I was wolfing down tortillas, but Frida just stood there, biting her lip.

"Why don't you just tell her we've been here with you all the time," she proposed after a while.

"Ah, no. Doña Matilde would have my hide. Anyhow, she'd never believe it. They've searched the entire house, and your mami sent two of the boys to look for you in the streets. They even sent Manuel to town to get your papá."

"They sent for Papá? Oh, no!" wailed Frida. "We should go throw ourselves in the river and let the boys find us. That way we could say we were drowning and thank God they saved us just in time. Mami would be so happy to have us back, she'd forget to scream."

"Never mind," chided Inocencia with pretend gruffness. "You'd better just go tell your mami you're home safe and face the music."

"Come on, Inocencia," said Frida, "help us out." She cuddled up to the cook and kissed her on the cheek. Frida was good at sweet-talking people into doing what she wanted.

"Let's go, Cristi," she said, nudging me. "We're going back to the river."

But I was too engrossed in clumsily spreading avocado over a warm tortilla.

"Come on, dummy! Will you stop eating? No wonder you're such a tub!"

I snatched a piece of avocado peel and threw it at her. "Leave me alone! It's your fault we're in trouble. I'm going to Mami."

That really raised her hackles. I certainly wasn't Mami's favorite—she preferred the older girls, Matilde and Adriana—but she tolerated me better than she did Frida. If she had to choose one of us to believe, she'd opt for me over my cheeky sister.

"So we're in trouble," snapped Frida. "So what? Lick your wounds and stop sniveling."

I was already tearing toward the door.

"Stop, stupid! Think a minute. We can get ourselves out of this. We'll just say we were kidnapped by one of those government guys they're always talking about, the ones that snatch you up and carry you off in big black cars. Let's see. They were tough . . . and mean. And they had guns as long as a bull's prick. Only we managed to escape through the window. Boy, after a scare like that, Mami would be thrilled to have us back. Unléss, of course, you ruin everything."

I started to howl. "Mami! Here we are, Mami!"

Mami was giving instructions to one of the servants in a different part of the house, and she wasn't sure whether she had heard me cry or whether her imagination was playing tricks on her. Years later she told me that she had been hearing children's voices all that morning—ever since Miss Caballero's messenger had come. She had heard giggling in the wardrobe, only to throw it open and find it empty. She had heard moaning in the kitchen, only to have Inocencia search cupboards, bins, and hampers to no avail. The whimpers and whispers were driving her to hysteria.

"¡Señora!" Inocencia burst into the laundry room. "The little ones are back! Fridita is in the kitchen, and Cristinita is on the patio!"

"They're back? Are they safe?"

"Yes, Señora. They're safe, praised be God."

Mami dissolved into a kind of religious paroxysm, ranting and screaming. "Oh, Blessed Virgin, thank you! Thank you!" I could hear her carrying on from my spot in the patio, next to the door. When she had impressed the Virgin sufficiently with her gratitude, she darted outside and eyed me, hunched near the house, sobbing like Mary Magdalene. She grabbed me by the arm and, with one resounding thwack, sent me sprawling. I must have let out a scream, because the servants came running. But Mami refused to let them get near me. Instead, she commanded imperiously: "Go find Frida. She's in the kitchen."

However, Frida was not in the kitchen. Nor the bedrooms. Nor the *sala*, nor the laundry. Frida was nowhere to be found. Mami was trembling, not with fear now but with rage. She was so livid that only the very tip of her nose, which resembled a barely ripe strawberry, showed any color at all. Finally, old Inocencia, who had waddled out the gate into the street, spotted Frida about half a block away.

"There she is, Señora!" she called. Conchita took off after Frida and brought her home kicking.

"What is the meaning of this? Where have you been?" Mami grabbed Frida by both shoulders and shook her until she teetered. "We've been wild looking for you! Where have you been?" Her frenzied shrieks reverberated through the patio. Her face was tight, twisted, unglued. I thought of those concave or convex fun-house mirrors that distort your features and make you look like Pinocchio or a pear-faced fiend. I thought of Mami with a huge, hourglass-shaped head, tiny shoulders, and a bloated waist. I bit my lip to keep from laughing. I don't even want to imagine what might have happened to me if I had cracked a smile at that moment. Maybe I wouldn't be here telling you this story!

Mami was quiet now, but she was as tense as a string on a finely tuned guitar. She raised her hand to slap my sister, but Frida shifted her weight, slipping out of range. It was terrifying, but at the same time hysterically funny. Mami, so staid, so self-righteous, swatting the air as though she were after an elusive fly, like one of those American cartoon characters that became popular much later: the cat that keeps trying to smack the bird, zip! zip! zap! like this. She lost her balance, great big solid, stolid Mami, and nearly went down on the floor. But the instant she regained her bearings, she raised her hand again, and this time she knocked Frida squarely on the ear.

I knew it smarted. Even though I wasn't the one to get cuffed, I felt as though I had been knocked in the skull with a bat. My head, neck, and shoulders were throbbing. But Frida didn't cry. She just looked Mami defiantly in the eye.

"You little brats!" howled Mami.

Frida crossed her arms. "It wasn't Cristi's fault," she said, feigning calmness. "It was mine."

You see, this is what I was telling you. Frida always did her best to protect me. She stood right up to Mami and told her that she was the one who had been bad.

"Lucifer himself has built a nest in your soul, you wicked little thing!" That's what Mami said to her. Can you imagine a woman talking like that to a six-year-old, doctor? It's no wonder Frida turned out the way she did.

No, I didn't mean that. I didn't mean that Frida turned out badly or that she wasn't as sweet as a mango deep down inside. She *was* sweet. Well, not exactly sweet, but good. That's precisely what I'm trying to tell you. She always took credit for everything.

"It was my fault!" she repeated. "I got into a fight at school. I don't want to go back there, Mami. I hate Miss Caballero!"

Did Frida really hate Miss Caballero? I'm not too sure about that.

"What fight?" demanded Mami. "What were you fighting about this time?"

"Nothing," said Frida, sticking out her chin.

I started to explain: "They called us—"

Frida shot me a look that said shut up. "Nothing," she repeated. She was not going to tell Mami that they had called us foreigners and Jews in school again. She was not going to give her something more to throw in Papá's face.

Mami was suddenly calm. "You'll send me to an early grave," she said simply. "Everything I put up with for you two, and you can't do enough to make me miserable! Blessed Mother, what did I do to deserve such children?" But she wasn't yelling. Her heart was no longer in it.

Papá had entered the patio and stood, morose and silent, looking at his wife and daughters. Without greeting him, without even turning to face him, Mami acknowledged his presence.

"Your father came back from work because he thought you were in danger," she said. "He made the trip all the way back from town. He closed his studio. And he's been sick again. He had a seizure early this morning. But even so, he came home. And you, you were just playing pranks!" But she still wasn't yelling.

I felt guiltier now. Papá rarely came home for the afternoon meal. Instead, Manuel made the long trek to the city every day with a lunch basket. I knew that for Papá to travel all the way back to Coyoacán, he had to be frantic.

"Go on," Mami said to him as she left the patio, "tell them how bad they've been. Tell them how you're going to punish them."

Papá stood staring at us with those uncommunicative, demented eyes.

Frida ran to him. He bent down awkwardly, and she threw her little arms around him and kissed him on the cheek. "Come on, Cristi," she said.

I followed my sister's example and kissed him, but then I ran off toward our bedroom. I guess I thought it would be better to leave them alone, to let Frida reinvent the story in her own way. Naturally, she would be the star. But she would play the other roles as well. For the part of Estela, she would make her voice abrasive, like nails scraping across a slate. For Miss Caballero, she would puff out her cheeks and make her fingers fat with rags. How would she portray me? Would I be in the story at all? In the end, she would vanquish her enemies brilliantly. Frida was a master of histrionics. The heroine! The savior!

I crawled into my bed and went to sleep.

The next morning Frida said to me, "You know, Princess Frida Zoraída came to see me last night."

I was only five. I believed in Princess Frida Zoraída. "You think someday she might come visit me?" I asked.

"Of course not," she said. "I'm the one she's friends with."

Frida was sitting on a little upholstered chair, a miniature of the ones in the parlor, looking out the window that faced Allende Street. She seemed forlorn. Neither of us had had supper the night before because Mami was so mad, she didn't let Inocencia feed us. I had the impression that Frida wanted to cry, but she would never cry in front of me.

"All of a sudden," she said, "I heard her voice."

"Her voice?" I whispered. "What did she say?" Frida had all the luck, I thought, because a real princess—Princess Frida Zoraída— came to visit her whenever she needed a friend.

She had had to strain her ears, she said, but finally, as if from the center of the Earth, Princess Frida Zoraída beckoned to her: "Frida! Frida!"

"I got up and went to the window," Frida told me. Princess Frida Zoraída's sweet, high, bell-like voice tinkled melodiously, like an oriental glass mobile in the breeze. "Come, Frida! Come and play!" called the princess. Her voice wasn't human. It was otherworldly.

"Is it you, Princess Frida Zoraída?" whispered Frida.

There was no response.

"Is it you, Princess Frida Zoraída?" she asked again.

The answer came in the form of a song, faint and ghostly.

I'm hiding in your mind!
Now open the door!
Don't ask me how.
I'll tell you no more!

"I was so excited!" Frida said. "I breathed on the windowpane, and when the glass got all steamed up, I drew a door in the mist. And then I felt myself fly out that door and cross the plain around Coyoacán. At last I got to the Pinzón Diary. There was a huge sign that read Lechería Pinzón, and I circled it again and again. Finally, I zoomed in through the O of Pinzón."

She flew and flew until she got to the center of the earth, where Princess Frida Zoraída was waiting for her.

The princess was a little girl identical to Frida. She had the same dimpled chin and mischievous eyes, the same chubby cheeks, the same frilly white bow. But instead of a pinafore, she wore a long red-orange robe adorned with round, peso-sized mirrors, sequins and beads, and a purple braided rope trim. Purple felt boots with upturned points covered her plump little feet.

"Come!" she said, with a voice like shattering glass. "Come dance with me."

She took Frida by the hands and kissed her on the cheek. Then she began to dance, floating weightlessly, bobbing this way and that. As she held Frida's fingers, her purple-booted feet wafted in the air.

"Dance!" she urged. "Dance!" Frida turned and hopped, and Zoraída followed her movements as gracefully as a balloon. Her dainty feet never touched the ground.

"That's wonderful!" said Princess Frida Zoraída, laughing. "You're so graceful! You're so beautiful! I love your pretty pinafore!" Frida smiled and kissed her.

"I felt so warm all over," she told me. "I felt better right away. I forgot all about Mami and those little brats at school."

"I love your gown," Frida said to Princess Zoraída. And then she added, "I had a bad day at school today." She always told Princess Frida Zoraída all her problems.

"What happened?" asked the princess, stroking her cheek softly with her fingers. "Tell me everything."

"The children were teasing me. Especially Estela and María del Carmen."

"They're nasty girls."

"Do you know what they called me?"

"What did they call you?"

"A foreigner and Jew! Am I a foreigner and a Jew, Princess Frida Zoraída?"

"No! Of course not! What a ridiculous idea."

"They say that because Papá was born in Germany, we're not really Mexicans."

"How stupid! You should get even with those girls."

"That's what I thought. So, you know what I did?"

"Tell me!"

"I insulted them! I called them terrible names."

"That's wonderful, Fridita! You did the right thing. You did just what I would have done."

"And then, when Miss Caballero started to scold me, I ran away and hid in the park!"

Princess Frida Zoraída burst into laughter that sounded to Frida like a million sparrows chirping and a million wind chimes tinkling. She and Princess Frida Zoraída held each other and laughed and danced around and around.

"It was wonderful, Cristi," Frida said. She walked over to the window and stared out.

"Is she still there?" I whispered hopefully. I got up and stood next to her, searching Allende Street for signs of the princess. But only the oaks, standing tall against the colorless sky, broke the monotony of the cobblestone sidewalk.

Did Frida make it all up just to make me jealous, or did she really believe what she was telling me? I don't know. It's possible that in her little girl's mind, Princess Frida Zoraída really existed. Frida had such a vivid imagination that I don't think she was ever able to distinguish between fantasy and reality, even after she grew up. Anyhow, what's real? Does any of us know? Sometimes I'm not actually sure what happened between Frida and me. Sometimes I don't actually know if I did what you say I did.

CHAPTER 3

Peg-leg Frida

FRIDA WAS ALWAYS A WONDERFUL ACTRESS, AND SHE LOVED TO PERFORM. That's why, the night she woke up screaming, I thought she was just putting on a show.

The shrieks of a child in pain. A shard of glass in the gut. A sliver of ice in the gullet that cuts off your breathing and paralyzes you, leaving you helpless to call out in the darkness. How can any mother bear it? When my Antonio and Isolda were little, sometimes they would cry out like that, and I would panic because the nightmare of Frida's screams would scud back to me in jagged fragments. But on the night I'm describing to you, I was still a long way from being a mother. I was just a little girl, and my first thought was that Frida had had a bad dream or a gas bubble and had inconsiderately let out a yelp in order to rouse the household. It wouldn't have been the first time. In fact, it had gotten to be a habit of hers, screaming in the night to bring everyone running. Mami in her ruffled nightcap and Inocencia in her frayed shawl would stumble into the room bleary-eyed and, like zombies, submit to Frida's every command so that the poor little victim, the poor, suffering little darling, could get back to sleep.

"Inocencia, a cup of *yerbabuena!*" The maid would waddle into the kitchen to brew the soothing tea.

"Mami, the new doll!" Mami would pull it out of my arms and rest it on my sister's chest.

Usually, Frida and I slept in the same room, but all that week she had had a cold, and so Mami put me in bed with Adriana and Matilde.

My big sisters must not have heard anything, because neither of them budged. I listened for Mami's footsteps in the patio, but no one else seemed to be stirring. Maybe I dreamed it, I thought. I snuggled next to Adriana and tried to fall back to sleep.

I was just dozing off when another cry shattered the stillness. This time I bolted out of bed toward the room I usually shared with Frida. My first thought was to tell her to shut up, to stop making a racket. But then I saw that Mami and Papi were already there. Mami was trembling. Papá, still groggy, was staggering toward Frida's bed.

I think a low-grade anxiety had been gnawing at Papá for days. Frida had been ill with a fever, a headache, a sore throat. It was just a cold, he kept saying. Papá had six daughters—the four of us and two others by his first wife. Of course, Mami had seen to it that our half sisters were packed off to a convent as soon as she married him. She wanted them out of the way so there would be no reminders of that other woman. Later on, we all became friends, but that's another story. Even though Papá had always remained on the periphery of our upbringing, he knew that fevers and sore throats were common in small children. But then the nausea and vomiting started. And then the diarrhea.

"It must be a stomach virus," he had said. That was in the afternoon.

"I guess so," answered Mami. She was cutting a mamey, and as she pierced the russet-colored rind, the sweet yellow juices ran over her hand. "But I think we should call the doctor just the same."

"Call him if you want." Papá searched Mami's face for a sign of serious concern. He thought that women were mysterious beings, like cats, and that they had secret ways of knowing things. Mami bit her lip and continued to slice the fruit with steady, even strokes. Maybe he thought her eyes looked apprehensive, maybe he wasn't sure.

"You don't suppose it's anything more than a stomach virus, do you?" he asked. I think his voice quivered, but it was so long ago, I

can't swear to it. You reinvent these things in your mind. You relive
them so many times that after a while you aren't sure whether they
really happened the way you think they did or whether you've made
the whole thing up, embellishing the scene just a tiny bit every time
you conjure it—adding this detail or that—until your mental image
is totally different from reality.

Mami didn't answer, but she didn't send for the doctor, either.
Money was tight, and doctors were expensive. I guess she thought it
could wait one more day.

That evening Frida went to bed at the regular time, but she had
complained of stiffness in the neck and spine during the day. I still
thought she was carrying on just to get attention, but there was something about the way Papi stroked her hair and tucked her in that
made me anxious.

"I don't feel well, Papá," she kept whining. She gasped, short of
breath. Her voice was small and cracked. Papá looked at her pinched,
frightened face and winced as though he had a gnarl of snakes in his
stomach. "Oh God," he whispered. "Even though I don't believe in
you, please make this be nothing more than a cold." His eyes met
Frida's, and I felt—well, why not say it?—I felt jealous. Don't forget
that I was only five, after all, and to me it looked as though Frida
might be playing one of her dying-orphan roles just to get Papá to sit
with her.

"I know, Friducha," he said, "but tomorrow we'll call the doctor
for sure."

He turned out the light. He was so absorbed in his thoughts that
he didn't see me there, cowering in the shadows. No sooner was he
out the door than Frida called again.

"Papá," she whimpered when he sat down beside her. Her eyes
were glazed and feverish. "Cristi was horrible to me today."

I hated her. I have to admit it. At that moment I hated her.

"No, I'm sure she wasn't. Cristina's just a baby. She does silly
things, but she doesn't really mean to bother you."

"Yes, she does! She's nasty!"

"I'll tell Mami to talk to her." Typical! He never sat me on his knee
or stroked my hair and asked me if Frida's stupid accusations were

true. He just said dumb things like "I'll tell Mami to talk to her." He let Frida get away with everything just because she was the favorite.

Frida started to wail. "She took my doll!" That was a lie! I hadn't touched her doll. Sometimes I did take her toys, but not that day, because I hadn't even been allowed in the room. But did Papá think to ask me if it was true?

"All right. Tomorrow we'll make her give it back," he said.

"I want it back now!"

"Cristina's sleeping now. We'll have to wait until tomorrow."

Frida's little fingers curled into a fist and her body trembled with rage. "I want it now!"

I was dying to call out, "I don't have your ugly doll!," but I didn't want them to know I was eavesdropping, so I kept quiet.

Papá looked exhausted. With Frida's illness, her crankiness had increased to the point that even he had to admit she was unbearable.

"Go to bed now, Friducha."

"It's not fair! I want it now!"

For the second time, Papá turned out the light, then lumbered toward his study. "You know what I am?" he said to the invisible creatures that inhabit the night. He spoke in a voice so low it was almost inaudible. "I'm some sort of ancient reptile who should have died centuries ago." I peeped through the keyhole—it was the old-fashioned kind, large enough for a wrought-iron house key—and watched him scan his record collection without registering the name of a single disk, then again, more carefully. He made a selection, turned on the Victrola, and slumped into a fat, comfortable chair. Moments later, strains of a Beethoven sonata filled the room and trickled out the keyhole. He closed his eyes and tried to listen, but Frida started moaning again. He sat up and leaned toward the door as if he had heard her, even though I knew he couldn't have. Her voice wasn't strong enough to carry over the music. And yet again, the wince as if he had snakes in his stomach. It's true I was just a young child, but I sensed his anxiety. I know now that he was straining to suppress the questions that had been tormenting him just below the threshold of consciousness: What if Frida's illness wasn't just a cold? What if something was seriously wrong with her?

I saw him doze in his chair, wake suddenly, then doze again. He resisted going to bed. I guess he felt that somehow, as long as he sat upright in that chair, he was less vulnerable to the demons that pursued him. His financial worries had already left him drained, and this new fear was gnawing him to bits. Finally, barely able to stand the oppressive weight of his eyelids, he forced his head erect and lugged himself to the door. I darted for a decorative table that stood outside the study and hid under it, and from there watched him trudge back to his bedroom.

The windows that opened to the patio were covered with heavy curtains. One curtain had been pushed aside and the pane left slightly ajar, perhaps to let in some fresh air. Standing on top of a watering can, I could see in just slightly, and I could hear, with difficulty, my parents' muffled words.

Mami was lying with her head propped up, reading the Bible.

"Does it help?" asked Papá. I don't think he intended to sound sarcastic, but Mami didn't answer. She closed the book and rolled over on her side. He got into bed next to her, kissed her on the ear, then put out the light.

I peered into the black room. They were done talking. I was getting sleepy and it was senseless to stand there in the dark, so I made my way back to my sisters' room and crawled under the covers next to Adriana. But I couldn't drift off. I kept thinking of Papá in his bed, twisting and turning like a cat with nettles. I imagined him staring into the asphyxiating blackness, straining his ears to detect a cry or a moan or any other indication that Frida's state was worsening.

I sank into a terrifying nightmare in which Papá was having an even more terrifying nightmare. Then, suddenly, both our nightmares were aborted by a terrifying reality: Frida's scream. It lacerated the night and sent pains shooting through my head. But I didn't move. Instead, I lay there, imagining Papá's gargantuan efforts to pull his hand up to the edge of the blanket and to push it away with unwieldy, leaden fingers. Another cry, this one shriller and closer than the first, yet a million miles away.

I didn't actually see Matilde and Adriana sit up in bed, but I sensed their movements, quick and automatic, as though Frida's voice had activated springs in their hips. But I was out the door before them, racing barefoot to Frida's bed.

"You should have brought the doctor," Papá was saying. "It was a mistake to wait."

Mami shot him a ferocious look.

"My leg!" wailed Frida. "My leg hurts! It's awful!"

"Which leg?" Mami pulled back the blankets with disturbing efficiency.

"This one, the right one. All this part here." Frida pointed to her calf.

Papá watched Mami lift Frida's nightgown to the knee and massage the leg. She looked somber, but she wasn't crying and she wasn't hysterical. She didn't act as though we were in the midst of a crisis.

"Here?" Mami asked, massaging more vigorously.

"It hurts!" screamed Frida. "I can't stand it! It hurts, Mami! It hurts so bad I want to cut it off!"

Papá shuddered and squeezed his eyelids shut. "I'll send for Dr. Costa," he stammered.

"Send for him at once," commanded Mami. She turned to my sister Matilde. "Tell Inocencia to come, and you," she said to Adriana, "go boil water."

"I don't think it's necessary to wake the servants," whispered Papá.

"Just Inocencia and Manuel. Manuel will have to go for the doctor."

Before Matilde could call her, Inocencia appeared at the door with a rosary in her hand. She looked like a fleecy, spectral sheep in her crumpled white nightgown. Her braids crossed the top of her head and flopped over on either side, like ears. Frida almost smiled. "Inocencia looks funny," she simpered through the sobs.

"Holy Child of the Holy Father," whispered Inocencia. "What is wrong with little Frida?"

"Bring some liniment. The child is in terrible pain."

Mami massaged with determined hands. When she got tired, Inocencia took over. But Frida continued to wail.

"Frida, Fridita," murmured the cook. "Come on, little one. You're always so brave. Don't cry now."

Papi and I accompanied Manuel as far as the sidewalk. A phosphorescent moon hung inert in a heavy black sky. I strained to see if there was a face in it. There wasn't. It was dead matter.

Dr. Costa took his time in coming. Manuel told us that he had had to bang on the gate forever before a servant appeared with a light in his hand.

"The doctor is asleep," the servant said.

"Of course he's asleep," Manuel answered. "It is the middle of the night. Everyone is asleep. But this is an emergency. Wake him."

The domestic resisted, but Manuel stuck to his guns.

"Little Frida Kahlo is sick. The child of Don Guillermo and Doña Matilde, on the corner of Londres and Allende."

When the doctor finally appeared in our doorway, he was rumpled and groggy, but he hadn't forgotten to bring his black bag. About forty-five minutes later, Manuel arrived. Costa had come in his chauffeur-driven automobile, leaving Manuel to walk. He was a bastard, all right. But Frida always loved doctors. I think she loved anyone who spent time looking at her, examining her, hanging on to her every word. As for me, I hate them. Well, not all of them. Not you.

The doctor examined her carefully but reached no conclusions. All he said was that she would have to go to the hospital in the morning for some tests.

"She can't be moved," Mami said. "She's in too much pain." But both she and Papá knew that they had no choice.

Matilde and Adriana stayed home. For some reason that I don't understand even now, my parents insisted that I go with them. Maybe they thought that my presence would calm Frida during the long ride from Coyoacán to Mexico City. Maybe they brought me along to help keep her amused. I remember that the hospital air was bitter with pestilence and formaldehyde. Everything was green. Green walls, green floors, green chairs. I was growing nauseous. At least the wimples and habits of the nurses were white.

Papi looked dazed. Who knows what he was thinking. Back then, people were afraid to articulate, even mentally, the name of the dreaded childhood disease for which there was no cure. He was pallid, overcome, I suppose, by a kind of larval terror. I knew just from looking at him that his mouth tasted like ashes.

"I am truly one of the Chosen People," Papá said out loud. "Everything in my life is putrefying."

Mami was reciting the rosary. "Hail Mary, full of grace . . ." Her voice rasped like a wooden stick against a grate.

"Stop it!" Papi said in a loud whisper that made people turn around to look.

"Stop it? I'm praying to the Blessed Virgin for the health of our daughter!"

"Have faith in the doctors."

"I have faith in God."

"I don't," said Papi under his breath. He looked woozy. He sank onto a wooden hospital chair. I thought he had forgotten about me, but all of a sudden he said, "You know what I'm thinking about, Cristina?"

"What, Papi?"

"I'm making noisy pictures in my head: waves bashing rocks, biblical tempests, traffic accidents, erupting volcanoes, snarling tigers. That sort of thing. Can you guess why, Cristi?"

"Why, Papi?" I asked him.

"To drown out Mami's praying."

"But Mami's praying for Fridita."

He didn't answer. Mami's voice droned on: *"Dios te salve, María, llena eres de gracia; el Señor es contigo; bendita tú eres entre todas las mujeres . . . Dios te salve, María . . . salve María . . . salve María . . ."*

"Do I love this woman?" Papi said.

"What?" I asked.

A man, a total stranger, was standing in front of us, looking dour.

Papi was suddenly hyperalert. I noticed a ginger-colored stain on the man's white jacket, a black hair that extended about a quarter of a centimeter from the inside of his left nostril, and several flecks of yellowish dandruff on his collar. I realized he was a doctor. Somewhere, a baby wailed and birds screamed raucously. Something metal fell to the ground with what would have been a brain-shattering clatter if the object had been nearer. A nurse walked by carrying foul-smelling flowers. A rachitic old man hobbled past on the arm of an adolescent boy. Papi looked at his fingernails.

"We have examined Frida and arrived at a diagnosis," said the doctor.

"Holy Virgin," whispered Mami. Papi and I said nothing.

"I am sorry to have to tell you that the child has infantile paralysis."

I didn't know what "infantile paralysis" meant, but I flinched at the word *sorry*.

"Otherwise known as poliomyelitis, or polio."

I looked from my mother to my father. Everyone knew what polio was—a horrible disease that made children so weak they couldn't walk, couldn't ride a bicycle or throw a ball or even play jacks. A dreadful thought crossed my mind: Ha! Now she won't always be best at everything! No, wait. It wasn't a real thought. I mean, it wasn't something I sat and meditated on. It was just . . . sort of a flash. Then it was gone, but I felt miserable—guilty and treacherous. But you can't blame me, really. After all, I was just a baby. I didn't understand things, and Frida was always taunting me. It didn't last, I didn't dwell on it, it was just a streak of consciousness that vanished in an instant.

I didn't know what to do. What sort of reaction was expected? Should I cry? Should I hang on to Mami or stage a temper tantrum? My parents weren't offering much guidance. Mami was clutching her rosary, but her eyes were dry. I was surprised, astounded, at her reserve, although I suspected the dam would break once the doctor was out of the room.

"Your daughter has paralytic polio," the doctor continued. "This is a viral disease, and there is no cure. During the active stages of the malady, Frida will have to stay in bed to avoid straining her limbs. Hot packs may help relieve the pain."

"Is she going to die?" I whispered. My voice sounded tiny, even to my own ears. My words shivered in the air like robins in the snow.

"We're all going to die," said the doctor matter-of-factly.

At that moment I wished Papá were a sturdy, muscular man who knew how to punch. I wished he spoke Spanish without an accent.

Mami opened her mouth, but it took her a moment to force out
the words. "How long . . . how long will the active stages last?"

"Impossible to tell. You will have to be very careful about her
fluid intake. Plenty of liquids, do you understand?"

He said "do you understand?" as though he were talking to a
two-year-old. Papi looked at the doctor as though the man were an
imbecile.

"You must maintain her intake of liquids in order to prevent
dehydration. That means loss of water. Dehydration could result in
fecal impaction. That means the bowels are blocked by dry, hard
material, and the patient cannot eliminate waste."

"This man is used to talking to Indians," said Papi under his
breath.

"And afterward?" asked Mami. "I mean, after . . . the active stages?"

I held my breath. What if the doctor did not foresee an afterward?

"Please answer the question," said Papi. I think he meant to
sound commanding, but his voice trembled. He was pinned, you see,
between his urgency about Frida's condition and his resentment of
the doctor's stupefying arrogance. On the one hand, he wanted to
draw as much information as possible out of the man, but on the
other, he wanted to bloody his lip.

"Afterward," (and I think he added "if there is an afterward," but
I can't remember for sure), "Frida will have to exercise as much as
possible in order to limit her paralysis. Dance. Jump rope. That sort
of thing."

His voice droned on, but I was no longer really listening. My
mind was stuck on the words *if there is an afterward* . . . Yes, I'm certain he said that. Well, pretty certain. How can I tell you what I felt
at that moment? Frida had always been victorious in all our rivalries,
and yes, I had been jealous. There were moments when I despised
her. But at that age, it's natural for sisters to hate each other. What I
mean is, I never wished she were . . . dead. I swear to you. *I didn't
want her to die!*

"I would like to speak with our regular doctor," Papi was saying.
His accent was thicker than usual.

"Of course. He's with Frida. You can go in to see her now."

Frida was sitting on a chair, her legs crossed demurely at the ankle. Her face was still contracted with pain, but she had clearly charmed Dr. Costa's young assistant, Dr. San Pedro. He was sitting across from her, engaged in conversation, as enthralled as if he were talking with a fascinating and worldly woman. Dr. Costa paid no attention to them. He stood looking out the window, smoking and passing gas.

What more can I tell you? At school Frida had always protected me. Now, Frida could no longer go to school, and I found I didn't need a protector. I could manage on my own. I stayed out of trouble. I made friends. I fascinated my classmates with stories of Frida's awful disease and of our family's heroic struggle to keep death from the door. Now sometimes *I* was the star of the show. Not often, but once in a while.

But Papá . . . The other day you were asking me about Papi, about what kind of a father he was. All I can say is that Frida's illness changed him. Until then he had lived in his own world, lost in melancholy and the vapors of solitude. He and Frida would go out for walks—sometimes I would tag along too—but even on those special escapades, when the two of them would share their love of rocks and birds and insects, he always floated several feet above her, amiable yet somehow detached. But during the nine months Frida was confined to bed, he became more attentive—at least to *her*.

Frida was growing thin and solemn. Her withering right leg hung from her body like a dead snake. She seemed horrified yet fascinated by her transformation. Sometimes she scared me, the way she sat for hours, studying her face in the mirror, comparing her sallow cheeks with the chubby moist cheeks in the portrait Papi had taken of her only months before. She seemed to take a perverse pleasure in watching her body lose flesh and her eyes sink into their sockets.

"We're doing everything we can," Papi told her.

"That's what Mami says."

"The doctor promises that eventually you'll be able to walk again."

"The doctor farts like a pregnant dog."

Papi pretended to frown.

"Every time he comes, he stinks up the room."

"He's a good doctor, and he's trying to help you."

"I know, but he smells like a chamber pot!"

"Frida . . ."

Frida giggled, and Papá winked and squeezed her hand.

We all knew that Frida was struggling to make him believe that she was still the same mischievous little girl, but the fact is, she was becoming dejected and withdrawn. Sometimes, when he came home from work, Papi would catch her deep in thought, staring out the window into the drenched sky. She was like an iguana. She'd sit and stare at things for hours, eyes open, expressionless.

What do you mean, how did I feel about it? How did I feel about what?

Well, I wasn't happy to see my sister meta—metamorphose into a . . . a creature.

The physical part? You mean her physical transformation? Well, no, I *didn't* take pleasure in watching her shrivel up like that. How can you even suggest such a thing? It's true that after always being the tubby one, the less attractive one, it was nice to be seen as pretty and healthy and cute. But I felt guilty, because now there could be no doubt about it, I was the adorable one. I was the little beauty. I felt as though I had stolen something from her. It was scary. We all thought she might die, and I was terrified that she was turning into a skeleton right before my very eyes. I thought that somehow I was to blame, because sometimes, not often, but once or twice, when we were very little, I had wished that she would disappear. And then, suddenly, she actually seemed to be wasting away before my very eyes. Deteriorating. Vanishing. But no, I swear to you, when she got sick, what I wanted most—I *swear* to you—what I really wanted was for her to get better.

The thing is, she not only looked weird, she acted as though she lived in another dimension. I mean, Frida had always had her imaginary princess, Zoraída, but now she seemed to be wandering over the edge. She conversed with a bunch of invisible people—the only people, it seemed, who could make her happy. Papá said not to worry, that they were probably warm, whimsical souls who gave her comfort and made her laugh. And it's true that sometimes, when Frida became absorbed in her prattling, she would suddenly giggle. But when Papá questioned her about her new friends, she became sulky and taciturn.

Most of the time she stayed alone in her room. She couldn't even hobble to the window to trace a door on the pane, but even so, she could conjure up Princess Frida Zoraída just by closing her eyes, breathing as deeply as possible, and reciting the magic words:

> Zoraída, Zoraída
> Come to see
> Your little Frida.
> Don't be slow.
> Don't delay.
> Come right now
> So we can play!

"You know," she told me, "Princess Frida Zoraída has a withered leg too."

"How do you know?" I asked her.

"I saw her. She came to me out of the mists just last night." She rolled her eyes and looked into space. Such a little performer.

But she wasn't lying. Frida really did bring forth the princess out of the mists. Out of the mists of her own loneliness. According to her, the princess wore the same red-orange robe as before. Only her shoes were different. Instead of the pointed booties, she wore a ballet slipper on the left foot and a heavy orthopedic contraption on the right. On her right leg she wore a brace.

"She invited me to dance," said Frida, "and when I told her I couldn't dance anymore, she said, 'Of course you can!'"

I was spellbound.

"My leg's bad. Can't you see?" Frida told her.

"So is mine! Can't you see?" said the princess.

Then Princess Frida Zoraída took Frida by the fingertips and kissed her sweetly on the cheek, and the two of them soared, their ugly shoes floating in the air like sparkling, silver-black zeppelins.

Mami obeyed the doctor like a captain taking orders from a general, and she commanded Inocencia with military precision: "Get the tub and fill it with warm walnut water. That will relieve the pain." Inocencia would prepare the medicinal bath. "Now have Frida soak her leg for half an hour." Inocencia would wash the leg. "Now make compresses with hot towels and apply them to the muscles of the calves." When Inocencia grew tired, Mami and Papi would take turns on the stool beside the bed.

Frida submitted without complaint. I'm sure she savored their attention. On the other hand, whenever I'd babble on about school, she'd become irritable. She didn't want to hear about Estela's mean pranks and María del Carmen's idiotic submissiveness. She was no longer interested in Miss Caballero's obsession with clean underpants. She had no patience with my tales of the girls' shifting alliances. I suppose that, percolated through me, all the stories sounded alike. Sometimes the neighborhood children would come to visit, bubbling with news of parties and First Communions and best friends. Frida would listen a while, visibly bored. Then she would turn away and grab her leg, grimacing and moaning.

I don't doubt that she was really suffering. But it was as though she welcomed pain as a distraction from the jabber of her friends. I don't know. Maybe she resented that school and life went on as usual without her.

Frida was bedridden for nine months. Nine months! Nine months are forever in the life of a six-year-old. In nine months a six-year-old becomes seven, and the pudgy baby face turns into a firm, distinct profile. I remember when my Isolda was six. And when the six-year-old has polio, the transformation is even more dramatic. The child's face vanishes altogether, and a thin, wan mask appears in its place. Instead of from those radiant eyes with their mischievous glint, Frida saw out of dull, faded disks. Instead of full and mirthful, her lips were thin and pallid. Worst of all, her cocky, six-year-old self-assuredness gave way to the excruciating shyness of the seven-year-old who knows she is different.

Nine months . . . the time it takes for a baby to grow in the womb and emerge into the sunlight. The time it took Frida to become an invalid.

The day finally did come when Frida was able to stand again, but . . . Look at this family portrait, doctor. It was taken in 1914. This gangly little girl shirking behind the bushes is not the same child who up and told off the class bully the year before. Look at her, doctor! She's changed. She's weak and gloomy. She doesn't want to walk in the garden or swim or ride the new red bike Papá bought for her. All she wants to do is linger in the shadows. She prefers Princess Frida Zoraída to her playmates. She mopes around instead of making the huge effort it's going to take to regain her strength.

But Papá wasn't going to let his favorite child wither and die. "I'm not Job," he told Mami. "I'm not going to let God take away everything."

"I thought you didn't believe in God," Mami said dryly.

"I don't," answered Papá. "That's why I'm not going to let him get away with this."

He turned to Frida. "Come," he said. "We're going to walk."

But Frida didn't want to.

"Doctor's orders."

Frida whined and carried on, but Papá was unrelenting.

"This time you are not getting your own way," he croaked. Whenever he got upset, his accent grew gelatinous. "You vill kum RRRight now!"

Frida didn't laugh often, but she had to laugh at Papi's sticky R. He sounded as though he was gargling.

"Yes, Herr Kahlo."

"Don't call me Herr Kahlo!"

"All RRRight, Herr Kahlo! I vill kum RRRight now, Herr Kahlo!"

They both burst out laughing. Papi didn't like to be teased about his accent, but this was a good sign. At last, Frida was regaining her spunk.

They wouldn't let me come along on their first few walks, but Papi must have realized that it was good for Frida to have someone to play with, or rather, someone to show off to.

In the beginning, we'd just stroll in the garden. Frida would have to rest under the big cedar tree every five or ten minutes, but soon she was hobbling after a ball that I'd toss first in one direction, then the other.

"I'm going to climb that cedar!" Frida said one day.

"Ah no, I don't think you're quite ready for that, *lieber* Frida," said Papi.

"Listen, Herr Kahlo," said Frida in mock defiance. "If I want to climb the tree, I'll climb it."

"You vill not!" teased Papá, egging her on.

"I vill so, Herr Kahlo. I vill do vatever I vant!"

"Okay, let's see."

Frida jumped at the cedar, wrapping her legs around it and holding tight with her knees. Then, inch by inch, she pulled herself upward.

"Bravo!" shouted Papi.

"BRRRavo yourself, Herr Kahlo!" shouted Frida. "You sound like you're choking!"

Papá took us to Chapultepec Park, where Frida rowed on the lakes. She even learned to wrestle and box, and once, when a bunch of relatives were over, she gave one of our male cousins such a clobbering that he ran into the house crying with a bloody nose.

Dr. Costa didn't think that wrestling was such a good idea.

"Hopscotch!" Frida snickered when he suggested that this game might be more suitable for a little girl.

"Hopscotch!" echoed Papi. He tweaked Frida on the elbow. "Vat an alt-fashioned, prejuticed man," he whispered. "Ve vill see about hopscotch."

Papi didn't have money to buy new equipment for his studio, but somewhere he found the cash to buy Frida a slew of boys' playthings: skates, balls, and a horn to go on the bright red bicycle that she finally learned to ride. She never offered to share those things with me, and frankly, I didn't care. I preferred dolls.

Sometimes, on fragrant, mild, fall afternoons, we would go to the park, and Frida would jump on her bike and tear around like a demon, forcing strolling lovers off the path, terrifying smaller children, upsetting picnic baskets, and giving chase to dogs. She also became a really good swimmer and would race even the boys. She would play soccer with anyone—cousins, neighbors, even the street urchins who hung around the *pulquerías*. And when she skated! When she skated, her skirts billowed out behind her like a kite straining to soar. What a sight!

Frida was making headway, but it wasn't all uphill. The polio had left her legs uneven. Her limp weighed heavy on her seven-year-old mind, so Papá showed her how to layer socks to fill out her calf and saw to it that the doctor ordered a specially constructed right shoe with a built-up heel. With Papá's hand firm under her elbow, Frida learned to walk steadily, then evenly, then gracefully. Sometimes she would go with Papá on his photographic excursions. They would trek for miles, and Frida would come back with pebbles and pieces of bark she had gathered in the country. She and Papá would sit in the patio after supper, celebrating the beauty of fireflies or the grace of frogs. Papá, who had always been so taciturn, seemed to open up to Frida. I think he shared his most intimate thoughts with her. Once in a while, when Papá was out with Frida, he would have one of those seizures, and she would shoo people away and stand guard over his equipment until the crisis passed. That made them even closer. Papá and Frida were best friends. Was I jealous? I don't know. I think I just accepted it.

Papá never had a son. Well, he did—Mami had a baby boy, but he died almost right away, and I think Papá saw in Frida everything a son might have been, everything that *he* might have been if his life had turned out differently. And when Frida got sick, well, he just wasn't willing to abandon the dream.

Papá had been a student at the University of Nuremberg, but he had an accident. He took a bad fall and injured his head, and that brought on those epileptic fits that plagued him for the rest of his life. Poor Papá! He had to give up his university career, and then his mother died. Not long afterward, his father married a woman Papá considered a pompous shrew. Papá's world was coming unglued, and he felt the only solution was to get out of Germany. He was nineteen and adventurous, so he borrowed some money from his father, booked passage to Mexico, and never looked back.

We had seen them in the streets of Coyoacán—Estela, María del

Carmen, Aurora, Inés—all the nasty little girls from school. They lined up to stare as we sauntered down the street holding Papá's hands. Papá was so handsome. Or maybe he wasn't. It's hard to be objective about your own father. But, no, he *was* handsome. People said he was one of the handsomest men in Coyoacán. Fair-complected, with brown wavy hair. The girls, sometimes they would jeer. Sometimes they would point at Frida's heavy shoe and chant, "Peg-leg Frida."

"Just keep valking," Papá would mutter. "Pay no attention."

Papá would chase them away, and Frida would hold her tongue. She couldn't say the awful things I knew she was thinking in front of Papá.

But then, finally, Dr. Costa said she was strong enough to return to school. There she was in enemy territory, and she couldn't rely on Papá to protect her. She had to defend herself by her wits.

The girls took sides. Some admired Frida. She had battled an ogre and was still standing. They admired her not only for her unbelievable recovery, but also for her skill at sports, her graceful step, her audacity, her spunk, and, of course, her colorful vocabulary.

But others resented all the attention she was getting. Suddenly, Miss Caballero couldn't do enough for her. "Here, Frida, let me strap on your book pack! Come, Frida, let me help you up the stairs!"

María del Carmen complained about Miss Caballero's fawning, but Estela knew it was dangerous to tease Frida in the school patio because the teachers were keeping a close watch on things. They were afraid of Mami.

But Frida and I sometimes played in the park.

On a damp, cool afternoon, Frida was riding her bicycle and I was picnicking with a doll. What we didn't know was that Estela and her bunch were spying on us from behind the bushes.

As Frida rode up the path, her dress billowing in the wind, a stone scudded out from behind a bush and landed in front of the bike. Startled, Frida screeched to a stop. A barrage of sticks and pebbles flew at her face and head, one of them scratching her eye, just below the lower lid.

A gaggle of children materialized from behind the vegetation.

Stunned, Frida looked from one to another, then lurched forward on her bike. Inés and Anita caught her by the skirt and knocked her off balance. The girls formed a barricade and began to chant:

¡Frida Kahlo	Come, let's see ya
Pata de palo!	Peg-leg Frida!
¡Un pie bueno	One leg's good
El otro malo!	The other's just wood!

As usual, Frida's defense came from the lip.

"Bitches!" she screamed. "I shit on your stupid songs!"

"*¡Frida Kahlo!*" chanted the girls.

"Get out of my way!" yelled Frida. "You came through your mothers' assholes instead of through the holes between their legs!" You see, at six or seven, Frida knew all about those things, and so did I. We had older sisters.

The girls were too accustomed to Frida's mouth to be shocked. They kept on singing: "*¡Frida Kahlo! ¡Pata de palo!*"

Frida placed her good foot on the left pedal and glared at them. Estela was leading the chorus, using a stick for a baton.

Frida shifted her weight and took off, ramming into María del Carmen and Inés, who fell into the dirt.

"You idiot!" shrieked Inés. "You ripped my pinafore!"

Anita tripped after Frida, trying to grab her skirt. But Frida was far down the path, chanting gleefully:

Inés, Anita!
Carmen, Estela!
Too damn ugly
To catch a fellah!

"Trash!" hissed Estela. "I know how *you* catch fellows! You let them touch your—"

"You should see her wrestle!" interrupted Anita. "My mother says it's disgusting. She gets down on the floor with the boys and everything."

"She'll never get married, though," shrieked Inés in Frida's direction. "Who's going to want to marry a deformed girl?"

But beyond the curve, Frida was still singing:

Inés, Anita!
Carmen, Estela!
Too damn ugly
To catch a fellah!

CHAPTER 4

War!

IT WAS A BAD TIME TO BE A FOREIGNER. MEXICO WAS IN THE THROES OF revolution, and the masses were out to get Díaz and his band of alien cronies.

Porfirio Díaz was in power from 1877 until 1880 and then again from 1884 until the Revolution. At first, he hadn't seemed so bad. He was gung-ho progress, and he pushed Mexico ahead faster than ever before. Industry prospered. The government extended the railroads, improved the harbors, constructed new public buildings. Telegraph lines sprang up everywhere. For the first time ever, you could go down to the telegraph office and send a message anywhere from Oaxaca to Chihuahua. And the national budget was balanced for the first time in decades. So what was there to complain about?

For a lot of people, the answer was simple: the foreigners. They were everywhere. They ran everything. Díaz had these fancy French ideas. He thought that society was like some giant animal, subject to the same scientific laws as any other living organism. He thought society was like, say, a baboon or a puma, and if it got sick and didn't perform the way it was supposed to—I mean, if it didn't shit regularly or learn to hunt by the time it was two—you could bring in a doctor who would get it going again. The doctor would train it so it would always do what it was supposed to, see? Or else he'd give it a shot, or zap it with electricity, and in no time it would be jumping through the right hoops in the right way. Díaz brought in these *científicos*, scientists, whose job it was to organize the country. Doctors for an ailing society, if you see what I mean. But Mexico didn't have the cash to carry out their projects, so Díaz went courting the foreigners. Like Pearson and Son, for example. Pearson and Son was a British firm that designed a drainage canal system for the capital, which we needed. And the American, French, and British companies that laid thousands of miles of railroad track, mined silver and gold, and pumped tons of oil. Sure, all those things were good, but before we knew it, foreign firms were gobbling up our land, our mineral resources. You Americans were the worst of the bunch!

Well, I was just a baby when Díaz and the *científicos* were running the country, but all during the time I was growing up, during the Revolution and afterward, that's all people talked about—how bad the foreigners had been, how we had to get rid of all that alien influence. And of course they were right, the foreigners squeezed all the juice out of Mexico and left it like a shriveled lemon. Still, there were people who said that the foreigners transformed Mexico, that they propelled us into the twentieth century. But really, the foreigners were bad. At least, the ones who cheated Mexico were bad, the ones who came and left, or else stayed at home and pumped money out of the country, the ones who sat on their fat Anglo-Saxon asses and deposited their profits into Swiss or English or American bank accounts, while our people sweated in the mines and fields to keep them afloat in whiskey and bourbon. Not foreigners like us. No, I don't mean that. We weren't foreigners. But Papá was born in Germany, as Mamá's relatives never let him forget. They would sit in the patio and sip sangría and make fun of his accent. They'd toss out snide remarks about money-guzzling foreigners and watch his reaction out of the corner of their eyes. Then they'd give one another knowing looks when they thought they'd made a hit. Although who knows how much Papá took in. He'd usually respond with that sharp little lunatic laugh he had. Was he agreeing with them or mocking them? Or was he just not paying attention? Anyway, foreigners like Papá weren't the problem. Foreigners like Papá came and stayed here, they worked and made a real contribution.

Why did Mami marry him? Did she ever love him? Maybe. He

was a good catch. He was handsome. What they said about Mami—
I'm really ashamed to tell you this—what they said about her was that
she was getting old. She had been engaged to another man, also a
German, and he had died, so she was kind of, how do you call it? She
was kind of on the rebound. Papá was a young widower, and he had
two little girls. Well, Mami's time was running out. Girls got married
in their teens back then, but Mami was already twenty-four—past her
prime—and so, when she met Papá . . . What I mean is, they were
two people who needed to get married, attractive people, but both
with serious drawbacks. Her age, his kids. You know what? I don't
want to talk about this. I'll tell you about it another time. No, you
won't have to wait long. I'll tell you about it before you leave today.
I was talking about Porfirio Díaz, so please don't ask any more
questions until I'm done.

· The thing is, the Mexican masses were growing poorer and
poorer, and everyone said it was the foreigners' fault. Half of the
rural population lived like slaves. They owed so much to the rich
hacienda owners that they had to work for free to pay it back. And
most people couldn't tell the difference between a foreigner like Papá
and the bloodsuckers who were gobbling up our resources and leaving our people to rot in the fields.

Díaz thought he was very sophisticated. He thought he was a
French éclair, even though he was just a plain old Mexican tortilla—
a mestizo from Oaxaca. The thing is, he had studied law. Me, I never
studied anything, because Frida was the smart one, so she was the
one they sent to school. I've learned things on my own, though. I've
done my best to improve my vocabulary so that I don't sound like a
mule driver who grunts at asses all day. I always try to say things the
best way I can. When I was young, I tried to learn a new word every
day. Surprised, aren't you? Well, I don't blame you. After all, everyone says I'm the dumb one. Anyhow, Díaz made a splash fighting
against the dictator Santa Anna and against Maximilian when the
French were running Mexico. What they say about Díaz is that he
had incredible energy, and yes, he was ambitious. The funny thing is,
in spite of tangling with the French in the days of the emperor, he
came to think of France as the cradle of culture. I mean, for him,

the French were the last drop of *pulque* in the glass. Actually, I should say the last drop of champagne or cognac, or something more . . . elegant. *Pulque* is for common people, like me. Díaz worshiped Europeans. In fact, he wanted to be one of them so badly he ordered all kinds of fancy powders and pomades from Paris in order to lighten his skin, as if a slug could stop being a slug just by dragging itself through a puddle of white paint.

He thought of himself as so goddamn . . . how do you say it? . . . cosmo . . . cosmopolitan that he couldn't be bothered messing with the rabble. Instead, he cozied up to the rich landowners and let them take over the communal properties that had belonged to the Indians. He also kissed the butts of the priests, which was a bad thing, because as you know—well, I suppose you know—there had been laws on the books limiting the power of the Church ever since Juárez threw out the French.

How can you say that? Of course we're good Catholics! We're not against the clergy. I mean, at least, I'm not. I believe in God and everything. Frida, on the other hand, she hated priests. Men who don't fuck, that's what she called them. Men who wear dresses, men who pull their clothes on over their heads, like women. It's a good thing they weren't allowed to wear their habits out in the street after the Revolution, because Frida would have sneaked around and pulled up their skirts. "Hey, padre, what's that useless noodle you've got under there? Ever use it?" She loved to tease priests. As for *him*, even though he went back to the Church at the end, he never believed in anything except his own talent and his own importance. He didn't need God, he thought, because he *was* God.

But getting back to Díaz, another bad thing he did was mess up public education. He didn't think it was important. So the peasants and the workers grew more and more miserable, and resentment grew against him, his *científicos*, and his foreigners.

In 1910 Díaz had elections and lost to Madero, but not right away. Madero was the son of a rich-bitch landowner and the grandson of a politician, and he had studied abroad in California, I think, and in France, but he wasn't a snob. He wanted change. He'd been reading the revolutionary newspapers and he was willing to get his hands dirty. My sister Adriana still remembers going to political rallies with my father. Papá had nó use for politics, really, but he was a photographer and liked to take pictures of important events—protests, speeches, stuff like that. Madero drew huge crowds. It was like a circus, with vendors selling peanuts, cotton candy, political cartoons like the ones by Posada that show all the priests and rich people as skeletons—all dressed up, but with their skulls showing and their eye sockets empty. Well, Madero was getting so much attention that Díaz was growing nervous. So he did what he always did in tough situations, he threw his rival in jail. But Madero maneuvered his way out, and before you knew it, he was plotting a revolution.

He picked a day, and on that day, small revolts broke out all over Mexico—brushfires that were easily put out by Díaz's forces. But in Chihuahua, Pancho Villa—an ex-bandit who got his start by murdering his sister's lover—put Díaz on the run. After Madero was elected president of Mexico in 1911, Díaz kept on running, and in fact ran all the way to Paris, where—at last in the lap of civilization—he eventually died.

Honest presidents don't last long in Mexico. The rebel leaders were used to making their own rules and they sure weren't going to take orders from Madero. Also, he made a big mistake. He tried to get rid of Victoriano Huerta, that ambitious, ruthless son of a bitch who had been general under Díaz. Huerta returned the favor by entering into cahoots with Madero's enemies and seizing Mexico City. Then he had Madero murdered.

Revolts erupted all over the place. Carranza pushed out Huerta and tried to make things better for the peasants, but real radicals like Zapata still weren't happy. They wanted land reform *right now*, and they thought that Carranza was dragging his heels. Zapata hooked up with Villa, and before you knew it, Carranza was heading out of town. But then the tide turned, and what can I tell you? For us, Zapata was a hero. He was from Morelos, like Mamá's family. Frida worshiped him like he was God, and *him, he* took his hat off when he said Zapata's name, just as if he was talking about Our Lord Jesus Christ. He lowered his voice and got all emotional, all teary-eyed. One of his most famous paintings was of Zapata. You know the one.

Zapata on a white horse. I grew up thinking Zapata was a saint, and
he was, I guess. No, I mean he was for sure. It wasn't his fault that
his rowdy, ragtag soldiers behaved like animals. Zapata himself, he
never raped anybody, he never stole from anybody.

There are stories about Zapata . . . Once, some of his soldiers
snatched up a bunch of women. You know, those women who tagged
along with the government troops. The soldiers took them prisoner
so they could come back and enjoy them. Sort of like going to a party
and stuffing some cakes into your bag so you can savor them later.
And then afterward, who knows, maybe they were going to kill them.
But then Zapata came along and discovered the women and asked
them, "Why are you here in this encampment? Are you Zapatistas?"
The women were terrified, because they weren't Zapatistas at all, they
were for the government—not that it would make much difference to
a starved soldier; in fact, to most men one ass is as good as another,
since when it comes to humping, they don't care what political party
you belong to. But these women, they were afraid to say that they
weren't Zapatistas, that they belonged to men who were fighting for
the other side. "They're just government whores," one of his troop-
ers said. "We're saving them for later." But Zapata set the women
free. "Go back to your men," he told them. "We have no business
with you. You're not the ones who are fighting against the forces of
liberation." Zapata's men, they were just poor peasants, and they had
been exploited for so long they felt they had the right to get whatever they could out of the war—a piece of land, a piece of bread, a piece
of ass. It was because of them that Zapata was called Attila of the
South. His men pillaged villages, burned shacks, stole livestock,
raped women. Sometimes they murdered entire families. They left a
trail of blood and spilled guts all over the countryside. But you have
to realize that these people had been exploited since the time of the
Spaniards. Frida always said you couldn't blame them for what they
did, because worse things had been done to them, and who knows if
the government supporters just made up those stories, or at least
exaggerated the facts. After a while, soldiers kill just for the joy of
killing. For example, they'd round up all the pregnant women and
hang them by their feet. They'd split open their bellies with their

knives. Then they'd take the dead babies and feed them to the dogs. If they could find the husbands, they'd make them watch. People who saw it firsthand told me. Most of them can't talk about it without gagging or dissolving into tears, even the men.

Carranza made his way back to the capital, and in 1917 became the first president to be elected under the new constitution. But then he was murdered too.

What the Revolution did was make us appreciate our Mexican heritage. With Díaz, we were all supposed to look to Europe for models. In the schools, they taught European history, European art, European philosophy. But it was all a bunch of bunk, because we're not Europeans. The revolutionaries, they put an end to all that. They were full of nationalist fury. It started with "Death to Porfirio! Death to the *científicos*! Death to the foreigners!" Once Díaz and the *científicos* were out of the way, there were still the foreigners to deal with, because lots of them remained in Mexico to suck our blood. Carranza had balls. He told you Americans to stay out of Mexico's affairs in no uncertain terms. There was one dispute after another with the U.S. government, and he even took sides with his own rivals, Huerta and Villa, against your military. In fact, in 1919—a date that's sacred to every Mexican schoolchild—he almost provoked a war with Uncle Sam when he expropriated foreign-owned oil. You did have it coming. You thought we were your plaything. You thought you could do whatever you wanted with us and we'd be too dumb even to notice.

I remember when I was a kid, under the new revolutionary government, everything Mexican was good, everything foreign was out. Instead of European styles, women wore native costumes. Fancy ladies came over to play canasta with my mother dressed in *veracruzana* dresses. In painting, sculpture, architecture, music, dance, in every aspect of our culture, there was a new appreciation of our Mexican past. Of course, *he* was a big part of it. His murals, they celebrated our culture. He was a major force. Through his art, he was educating the masses to appreciate their birthright. He was a superstar, a hero of the Revolution. That's the first thing I knew about him, that he was a national hero.

I'm getting off the subject. I always do that. I, uh . . . Anyhow, what the new government wanted was to revive the pre-Columbian styles. They paid painters—Orozco, Siqueiros, and of course, *him*, the great Diego Rivera—to cover the walls of public buildings with murals based on popular themes. We worshiped him because he was everything we wanted to be: a good Mexican, a good communist, and a servant of the people. Well, I wasn't really a communist, but Frida was. The government wanted to get through to the masses that the new Mexico was for everybody. It pushed revolutionary, Mexican messages through records, films, art. Mariachi music became more popular than the Charleston. Children learned to dance the *jarabe tapatío* in school. *¡Viva México! ¡Viva lo mexicano!* was the cry.

What do you mean what's the point of all this? You mean, all this that I'm telling you? The point is, as I was saying, that it was a bad time to be a foreigner.

But when Papá moved to Mexico in 1891, it was a good time to be a foreigner. And that was fine for Papá, because he was foreign through and through. He looked foreign, he acted foreign, he talked foreign and he felt foreign. He was a slim, handsome, brown-haired man, with an enormous mustache that was pointed at the ends. The pictures in the family album show a sensitive mouth and intense eyes, which I remember as being hazel. Even then, he had that haunted look, like a clairvoyant or an oracle. His parents, Jakob Heinrich Kahlo and Henriette Kaufmann, were Hungarian Jews who had settled in Baden-Baden, where he was born. My grandfather was a jeweler and also sold photographic equipment.

Ever since Papá hurt his head, he had epileptic fits. He had to give up his studies, and he didn't know what to do exactly. A little while later, his mother died and his father remarried a woman Papá always referred to as "the bitch *hund*." "Oy," he would say to Mamá whenever she got carried away. "Don't carry on like dot. You remind me off ze bitch *hund*." We always had dogs at home when I was growing up—tiny Mexican *escuincles*—but never females, because they reminded Papá of the bitch *hund*. All Papá wanted was to get away from her. That's how he wound up in Mexico.

He was nearly penniless when he arrived. Fortunately for him,

Mexico had a small but thriving German community, and he found
work in a German-owned glassware store called Cristalería Loeb.
Later he worked in La Perla, a jewelry store also owned by Germans,
and it was there that he met my mother, Matilde Calderón. His first
wife was a Mexican woman who died giving birth to Papá's second
daughter, my half sister Margarita. The night of her death, Papá
turned to Mamá for comfort. She comforted him so well that, three
months later, they were married.

Tongue-waggers said she was anxious to find a man and lucky to
have caught one with so much potential. As I said before, she had
been involved with another German who had—I don't know why, but
he had committed suicide. That left scars on her emotions as well as
on her reputation. A girl with a history is hard to marry off in Mexico
even now, and it was worse back then.

The pictures of Mamá in the family album show a stern-looking,
dark-complected woman with large brown eyes and a protruding
chin. She was the oldest of twelve children and very Catholic. My
maternal grandmother was the daughter of a Spanish general and
had been raised in a convent. She was rigid, fanatical, really. Papá was
the German in the family, but Abuelita is the one who always reminded me of a Prussian army general. She was very superstitious. She
thought that evil spirits lurked everywhere, so she wore crucifixes all
over her body to ward them off.

Once, when I was pretty small, seven or eight, she gave me a
pretty gold crucifix and told me never to take it off. It would keep
away the spooks, she said. It would scare away the demons. Just like
garlic, only stronger. Well, we all went to a fair one Thursday morning, and of course I had on my cross. There was a rickety Ferris
wheel, and vendors selling balloons and cotton candy, also handmade
shawls, mantillas, homespun cloth, fancy combs, lace, penny booklets—the kind that run stories in installments—prayers, pictures of
the Virgin, pictures of naked women, tortillas, beans, enchiladas,
every kind of cheese, pigs, cows, sheep, goats, dogs. You can't imagine the activity and the noise. People everywhere, some buying, some
selling, some riding the Ferris wheel, some just looking. I was so
excited that I started to turn somersaults—after all, I was just a little

girl—and the cross fell off my neck and onto the ground. I retrieved it right away, but even so, my grandmother started shaking me and slapping me until my lip bled, screaming who did I think I was that I dishonored Jesus Christ that way. Who could I be but the daughter of a Jew who had raised me to disrespect our Lord and Savior! She made me kiss the piece of metal with my bloody lip. Then she told me to kneel and say ten Hail Marys right then and there. My sister, she would have told Abuelita to shove her stupid cross—Jesus forgive me—right up her ass, but I just sat there. Abuelita stood over me, her hands on her hips, her feet planted in the ground like two oaks. "Do it!" she commanded. But I refused to move. Abuelita was standing over me, her braids tied up in knots like rodent ears, carrying on like a madwoman while people walked by and pointed their fingers at us.

"Pray!" she ordered once again.

But I just sat there on the grass, my legs straight out in front of me, refusing to get up on my knees.

"Pray!" she thundered. She pulled a lace hanky out of her bosom. She unknotted it and took out a silver rosary, then got down on her knees to pray herself. She was going to show me how it was done, you see. Everywhere, people were scurrying around, from the pig stall to the Ferris wheel, from the tortilla vendor to the merry-go-round. Balloons hovered above the balloon vendor like a flock of brilliantly hued birds. Abuelita was oblivious to it all. She just knelt there and said the rosary. After a while, I had to pee, but I was afraid to tell Abuelita, and I was just as afraid to get up and walk away. I began to feel like a wineskin ready to burst. I was really suffering.

"Abuelita . . ." I began.

She kept on praying.

"Abuelita . . ."

"Well?" she said finally.

I looked down at the ground. I could feel the tears welling up in my eyes, and I was terrified that liquid flowing out of one part would stimulate liquid to flow out another.

"Well?" she said again.

"Nothing," I whispered.

She went back to her rosary. I spread my skirts around me as decorously as I could, then inched down my bloomers and let go. Whoosh! What a feeling! Not only was I relieving myself, I was defying Abuelita! I felt like a pony breaking loose from the stable or a prisoner making it over the wall. The pee was warm and smelled of ammonia, but it didn't sting. It flowed smoothly, like tamarind water out of a jug. And all the time I was going, Abuelita was praying the rosary.

I said a silent prayer of thanks to the Virgin myself as I dragged my bottom along the grass, careful to keep my skirt dry. Abuelita was too engrossed in her rosary to notice. And all the time, happy fair-goers scuttled this way and that, to the prize heifers or to the shooting gallery, to the balloon man with his colorful flock or to the organ grinder with the dancing monkey.

Mamá learned piety from her mother, so you can imagine. Her father, Antonio Calderón, was a photographer, and from him she learned the attention to detail that made her absolutely obsessive about housework. Everything had to be perfect, every object had to be in place. Whenever she came back from shopping or canasta or church, she would check the pictures on the walls. "Rufina!" she would shriek at the parlor maid. "I told you not to dust the frames. Now they're all crooked! Ay, how can I live in this house where everything is always such a mess!" Then she would run her finger over the walls, the ledges, the objects in the sitting room. "There's dust here!" she would snap at Rufina. The maid would mumble *Sí Señora*, but you could tell she was thinking about something else, probably about her boyfriend down in Oaxaca.

Mamá was even more finicky about her appearance than her house. She loved clothes. To go to church, she wore an adorable black jersey suit with a quilted collar and bows at the throat and at the belt. It had piping down the front, and a skirt at midcalf—what they called the "deluxe poor" look. Displays of wealth were out of the question after the war, but you couldn't expect Mami to dress like a peasant. No, *veracruzana* dresses weren't for her, except for special occasions. And her accessories were always perfect. Black leather gloves, a thin-brimmed hat that cast a dramatic shadow over her eyes, and exquisite, thick-heeled pumps with a Mary Jane strap. Even when she wore traditional Indian garb to show her solidarity with the masses, she insisted on quality. Bound seams. Lined bodices. Perfectly embroidered roses along the hem and at the collar. And, of course, matching jewelry. Frida got her passion for clothes from Mami. Actually, Mami and Frida had more in common than either of them cared to admit.

My grandfather Antonio was a dark man with Indian features, a goatee, and a full mouth. He wore a downturned mustache, which made him look like those caricatures of Zapata that became popular after the leader died, after it was no longer fashionable to worship him, after so many people forgot what he had done for them. My abuelito Antonio never spoke much to us. He never spoke much to his own daughters, either, according to my mother. Mami always said he was as quiet as a shadow, as quiet as nightfall. But he managed to support his family. They had a little house, shabby but presentable. They were what they used to call "poor but decent"—*decent* meaning you could have them over for supper provided no one else was coming.

My mother never had much schooling, but she was a shrewd woman. I don't think she knew a thing about the surrealists or Freud or the Russian Revolution or any of the other fancy nonsense that Frida and Diego were always jabbering about—they liked to make themselves feel superior—but she could count money like an adding machine. As I said, Mami liked to have everything in its place. That's why she got rid of my half sisters, María Luisa and Margarita. It wasn't just that they might be a bother or a constant reminder of the other woman. It was that they were in the wrong place. For years I hardly knew them. I thought of them as Cinderella's wicked stepsisters. Me being Cinderella, of course. Ha! That's a laugh! *She* was Cinderella. *She's* the one who got to marry the prince. Anyhow, eventually, we all got to be friends, real sisters, but that was much later.

Mami's next task was to make a Mexican out of Papi. He was so German. That's what Mami always said, that he was as German as a Wiener schnitzel. After he took a new wife, Papá also took a new name, Guillermo. He couldn't go around being Wilhelm, could he? According to Mami, he tried hard to be Mexican. But he was always an outsider. Every detail of his life reminded him that he was an immigrant. His heavy accent with its ugly, guttural German *R*

irritated and embarrassed him, but he couldn't get rid of it. Spicy
Mexican food upset his stomach. But what exasperated him most was
his own rigidity, which contrasted with the total disorder of Mexican
life. And then there was the religious thing. Papá was no fanatic. In
fact, he never practiced his own faith. But he just couldn't warm up
to Catholicism. To him, Mami's infatuation with images of Christ on
the cross was morbid. It was one thing to turn the other cheek or to
transform water into wine, he said, but to expect people to kneel
down and worship you while you dripped blood all over the place,
that was too much. Papá hated Mami's collection of crucifixes, and he
didn't understand why she had to stockpile images of the wounded
Jesus—blood trickling from his forehead, blood gushing from his
side, blood spurting from the holes in his hands. Blood! Blood!
Blood! *Blut! Blut! Blut!* It made him nauseous, he said. He couldn't
look at those pictures before dinner. In time he became an atheist,
and then Mami's icons drove him crazier than ever.

His attitude toward work and time was German. He was obsessively punctual and meticulous. You could set your clock by watching
him leave for work in the morning. He was not the kind of man to
take siestas, or even to come home for lunch, as Mexican men always
did back then, and usually still do.

As time went on, Papá became more and more withdrawn. Maybe
he thought that he had made a mistake by coming to Mexico, by set-
tling in this beautiful but chaotic and inefficient land. Maybe we were
asking too much of him. Maybe the struggle to become one of us was
just too great. At any rate, he spent more and more time alone in his
room, reading, executing two-part inventions on the piano, listening
to music or playing chess with his only friend—a thin old man that
no one knew much about. His name was Neftalí and his hands shook
when he picked up the chess pieces, but he was a shrewd strategist
and had the gift of concentration, and he was a good match for Papá,
who seemed to enjoy his company, even though the two of them
hardly exchanged a word. I remember his coming over every so
often. He had sallow skin and hardly any hair. His breath stank of—
I don't know what—tobacco and rotting fish, maybe. Old Don
Neftalí, he and Papá could sit at the table for hours deciding on a

play or waiting for the other one to move. And all that time, neither spoke. Don Neftalí respected Papá's need for silence. I think that's why Papá liked him.

With the exception of Frida, none of us seemed to matter much to my father. He wasn't hostile, just aloof or indifferent. Frida used to say he was the archetypal brooding German romantic, teetering a hair's breadth from insanity.

But even brooding romantics have to earn a living. It was Mami who urged Papá to take up photography, I imagine because it was her father's profession. She always said that if it hadn't been for her, Papá never would have made anything of himself. It was my grandfather Antonio Calderón who lent him his first camera. With it, Papá launched a career, taking pictures mostly of landscapes, ruins, buildings, interiors. Later, he sometimes took pictures of crowds and political events. Not for the papers, and not for the government, either. For himself, because he thought they were interesting, from an artistic point of view, I mean. He was very precise, very meticulous, and in photography, those qualities paid off. He composed his pictures with so much care, paying attention to perspective, angle, lighting. All the things that made Frida a great painter later on, those were things that had made Papá a great photographer. And since precision demanded the best equipment, he began to import fine German cameras and lenses. It's not surprising that he attracted the attention of Díaz's *científicos*, since those boys really appreciated European talent and technology.

The centennial of Mexico's independence from Spain was coming up, and the *científicos*, who knew the government wasn't popular and their own asses were on the line, thought that a big to-do for the occasion would bolster Díaz's reputation and boost public morale. The secretary of the treasury decided to publish a series of deluxe art books celebrating Mexico's heritage, and so he started looking around for someone to do photographs of native and colonial architecture. Papá was perfect for the job.

Papá was so proud of the pictures he took for those books! Mami kept framed copies of some of the best ones in the parlor. Popocatépetl at sunset, her irregular, volcanic head stretching up

into the shadowy mists. The Cathedral of Puebla, its angular bell tow-
ers standing like two giants. Tasco's sunny colonial streets. Stucco
houses. Seductive balconies. Red tile roofs. Wrought-iron gates. The
centennial celebration was one of the few things that he showed any
enthusiasm for. He had had to travel all over Mexico. "I hot to vait
two hours to take it, until the sunlight vas exactly perfect!" he would
boast. Every photo had a story. I learned more about Mexican history and geography from those pictures than I did from textbooks.
Papá devoted four years to that project, from 1904 to 1908. He used
the best imported cameras and prepared nearly a thousand glass
plates himself.

The government paid him well. No sooner did he receive his first
commission than he had a new house built on the corner of Allende
and Londres Streets, in a smart neighborhood of Coyoacán located
conveniently near the main square and the market. That was our
house, the house that Frida and I grew up in. Then, later, it was hers,
hers and Diego's. Now it's a museum. The Frida Kahlo Museum.
Nobody cares that I once lived there.

Like other traditional houses, ours had no corridors. Each room
boasted a stylish French door that gave access to a large patio. With
her impeccable taste, Mami furnished the living room with smart
Parisian furniture, since that was the style among comfortable,
upper-middle-class Mexicans, which is what we were. I'm talking
about the time before we got poor. About the time before it became
unfashionable to be a foreigner. About the time before Papá lost
nearly everything.

Next to the parlor were a traditional dining room and a large
kitchen. The master bedroom was located adjacent to the dining
room, an arrangement that seems strange to me now that I look
back, but then we all thought it was normal; we were used to it. Along
the outside walls tall windows with gray shutters opened to the street.
The house's colors, a bright blue called *azul añil* with red trim, might
have shocked the gentry in a somber northern city, but they weren't
unusual in Coyoacán. The town was full of brilliantly hued buildings—block after block of pink houses next to yellow houses next to
lavender houses. It was like a kaleidoscope, a palette on which a

painter had experimented with every imaginable combination.
Maybe that's where Frida got her dazzling sense of color. Me too: I've
always loved luminous colors. It's because I grew up surrounded by
color—red like liquid sun, green like crushed emeralds, blue like a
baby's eyes. Sturdy cedars occupied the dirt-filled gaps in the cobblestone sidewalk. They shaded the houses and softened the appearance
of the street.

Papá was not a political man. What he liked was to sit and think.
He meditated on a lot of different subjects, but Díaz's policies were
not one of them. He was making a good living from the government,
and he was satisfied. "Zo zis regime is corrupt, zo vat else is new? It's
corrupt, zo? At least it's quiet," he said. "Quiet is gut. The next one
will be corrupt and noisy."

But once the Revolution erupted, it was impossible not to take
sides. You were either for the rebels or against them. Still, Papá
couldn't make up his mind. "Who needs this aggravation?" he said to
Mami. "Vhy can't zey leef vell enouf alone?"

When Díaz fell, fighting between Zapatistas and Carrancistas
broke out in Coyoacán. Because abuelito Antonio was an Indian from
Morelos, Zapata country, our family cast its lot with the Zapatistas.
Mamá opened the house to Zapata's men. She allowed them to climb
through the windows on Allende Street into our living room.
Inocencia and Concha and Rufina cut up old sheets for bandages,
and Mamá washed the soldiers' wounds with soap and iodine. Mamá
wasn't the nurturing type. I'm sure the smell of blood, sweat, and shit
made her nauseous, but she considered it her patriotic duty to help
the men who were fighting against that tyrant who had sold out to
the French, to the British, to the Americans, and to every other foreign power that wanted to take a bite of our country.

There wasn't much food to share except for tortillas. The markets
were closed. It was dangerous to go out. Soldiers were battling in the
plazas and alleys, and snipers hid behind every gate. I was very
young. Sometimes I'm not sure how much I really remember of the
Revolution. Is it possible I've heard so many stories that what I think
I remember is really scenes that somebody described to me? Or
scenes from books? Or films? They talked about the war all the time

while I was growing up, all the way through my teenage years and beyond. Diego and Frida, they both had such stories to tell, although when the fighting broke out, Frida was just a child like me. But the way she talked, you'd think she had been out there on the front lines, a pistol in each hand. I'm not sure how many of the pictures in my head are memories and how many are inventions. Sometimes I'm just not sure of things. Not like Frida. Frida was always sure of everything.

There are certain images, though, that have stuck in my mind. Certain terrible memories that haunt me. Things that must be true, because I see them so vividly. I must have been very tiny when this happened: In front of our house—oh God, it was awful—a child ventured out onto the road. He was a little boy who lived a few houses down. Frida used to play soccer with him sometimes. He had straight black hair that fell into his enormous black eyes, and a sweet smile. Sometimes he would play naked in his patio—he couldn't have been older than four or five—and Frida would squirt water at him to make his little prick stand up. Then, when it did, she would shriek with laughter. Well, this little boy—his name was José Luis—he wandered into the road, and . . . oh, God . . . I remember it as though it happened just seconds ago. A sniper blew his head off. I saw it. I saw it through the window. Oh, Jesus, that poor little boy . . . that poor little angel. His erect torso stood in the middle of the road for nearly a minute before it collapsed, still quivering, not five meters from our front door. Blood spewed from his arteries. It formed thick, sticky pools that were lapped up later by marauding dogs. The mother was hysterical. His pitiful, grief-stricken mother—Doña Ramona—such a gentle women . . . her only child. She couldn't fetch him right away. The soldiers were shooting at anything that moved. Finally, she couldn't bear it any longer. She crawled out over the cobblestones to collect first the pieces of the skull, then the trunk. Miraculously, they didn't kill her. It might have been better if they had.

There was another incident. A donkey meandered out of its corral and caught a bullet in the eye. It lay braying and squealing in agony until a sniper shot it in the head, less to put it out of its misery than to shut it up. That was another scene I witnessed from my window, and somehow, even though it was just a donkey, the death of that animal affected me nearly as much as José Luis's. Poor beast. He carried on, eeey-aw eeey-aw, it was enough to break your heart. He was just an innocent victim. Why did they have to kill him? I was just a baby, and I didn't understand the politics of the Revolution. I just saw the blood mixing with dust and debris as it ran over the cobblestones and seeped into the cracks, seeped into the ground, where it would nourish the huge leafy cedar tree in front of our house.

I guess that's what it was all about. Some people had to die in order to nourish the soul and spirit of Mexico. Some people had to die in order to ensure our future. But poor little José Luis and that poor, unsuspecting animal . . . Sometimes none of it makes sense.

CHAPTER 5

Prepa

THE IMAGE IN THE MIRROR WAS DECEIVING. IT SHOWED A SLENDER BUT shapely young girl with thick, black, curly hair, evenly cut bangs, and heavy eyebrows so elongated toward the bridge of her nose that they almost touched, giving her a somber, severe look. Frida frowned, forcing her brows into one straight line above her dark eyes. She looked like the kind of girl who would study hard, satisfy her teachers, make her parents proud—the kind of girl whose exemplary conduct prompted comments like "Oh, Señora Kahlo, you must be so pleased." Frida knew how to give that impression. She knew how to make adults say, "What a perfect little lady. If only her younger sister were more, well, more like her!"

She didn't wear a uniform—none was required at her new school—but her plain white blouse, tailored sweater, and dark blue pleated skirt reminded you of the outfits girls wear to public school nowadays. You know, those silly navy jumpers and cardigans. On her legs she wore thick black stockings. Her shoes were those sensible boots that keep your feet dry and are easy to walk in and don't give you blisters. The right one was stuffed with socks and rags that kept it from wobbling. On her head she wore a black straw hat with a wide brim and white ribbons that circled the crown and dangled behind. "The perfect little lady!"

Frida studied her reflection in the mirror. She pursed her lips to give herself a decisive look. She crossed her arms. She pulled herself up to her full height—a little over five feet two—and glowered at the other Frida, the one in the mirror. She took off her hat then put it on again, arranging the ribbons so that they fell exactly down the middle of her back. She took a hand mirror and checked the rear view. She wet her bangs with saliva and ran her index finger across her forehead to make sure they were perfectly even. Then she opened her underwear drawer. From among the bloomers she pulled out a tube of lipstick she kept hidden and applied a bit of color to her lips. Next, with her finger, she touched the stick lightly and daubed her cheeks. Just a smidgen. Not so Mami would notice. Just a dab. Again she studied her reflection, turning one way and then the other to see herself from different angles. No. The effect was all wrong. She wiped off the color, pulled out a new tube, and tried again with another shade. She struck a majestic pose—chin high, shoulders back, feet in fourth position—like a Degas ballerina. Frida loved to pose. She was always looking in the mirror and posing. That's why, when she became a painter, she did so many self-portraits. She adored looking at herself in the mirror. She was fascinated with herself.

I don't mean it as a criticism. I know what you're thinking, but I'm not reproaching Frida. I'm just saying that . . .

I don't think she saw me. I think she forgot that I was there.

I snickered. "You look like an ape-woman!"

She wheeled around as though I had shot a rubber band at her. Ping!

I brought my hands up under my armpits and scratched my sides. "Ape-woman!" I grunted. "Ape-woman! Ape-woman!"

Frida stuck out her tongue, then burst into laughter.

"What's the matter, Frida? Don't you think you look like an ape-woman? Well, you do."

A comb flew out of her hand, but I ducked. She made a face, stretching her lips into a grotesque apelike smile with her fingers. "Ugh! Ugh! Waaaa!" she growled at the mirror. "Me, ape! Me, ape!"

I was sitting on the bed, my feet pulled up under me, watching my sister get ready for her first day at the Preparatoria.

"I look like a real bore!"

"No, you don't, Frida," I said. "You look cute."

"Cute! I don't want to look cute. Puppies look cute. I'd rather be an ape-woman!" Frida stuck out her bust and began to strut. "Carmen Frida Kahlo, sexpot extraordinaire of the National Preparatory School!"

I laughed. I didn't want to put her in a bad mood on the first day of school. Then, if things didn't go right, she'd say I jinxed her. But I didn't think it was such a good idea for Frida to play the siren at the Prepa. I was fourteen already, and I knew that kind of stuff could be dangerous.

"You'd better watch it, Frida! They're all boys there. If you swing your butt around too much, you'll get yourself into trouble. And you'd better watch that mouth of yours."

Frida struck another pose in front of the mirror. She ran her tongue over those full, sensuous lips of hers and puckered. Then she opened her mouth and stuck out her tongue like she was French-kissing an invisible lover.

"Darling," she panted. "Darling!" She opened her mouth again and began to move her lips as though in ecstasy. "Oh!" she moaned. "Oh, darling, don't stop!" She squinted at herself in the mirror and ran her hands over her body. "Ah! Ahhh ahhhh ohhhh ahhh!" Then she got up close to the glass and pretended to lick.

I was laughing so hard I had to cross my legs to keep from peeing. "What are you doing, Frida?"

"I'm watching my mouth, you ninny! Didn't you just say, 'You'd better watch that mouth of yours'? Well, I'm just following directions, like a, you know, like a well-bred thirteen-year-old." She struck a dignified pose. "As behooves a well-bred thirteen-year-old," she corrected herself. "I'm just showing how obedient I am."

Frida bowed her head, pretending to be submissive. She was good at pretending to be a sweet, docile little thing. That's how she got her own way. Or else she'd play the feisty rebel. Whatever worked with the person in question. Depending.

She took a running leap and landed cross-legged on the bed. She began to bounce in a sitting position. "Frida is a good girl!" she chanted in a kindergarten singsong. "Frida is a good girl!"

"You're not thirteen, you liar. You're fifteen."

"I'm thirteen! You want to make an old lady out of me, you little bitch!"

"Come on, Frida! I know how old you are. I'm your sister, for God's sake! *I'm* fourteen, and you're eleven months older than I am."

"Not for God's sake, for Papá's sake. He's the one who gave Mami a good screw, and then you popped out. Or did you think you were a child of the Immaculate Conception, like the Baby Jesus? Anyway, what difference does it make if I take off two years? I lost two years of school when I was sick with polio."

"You only lost one year!"

"Well, who cares? I'll still be one of the youngest at the Preparatoria. Or, if not one of the youngest, one of the only girls."

"That's right, Frida. You'll be very special." That's what she wanted to hear, that she'd be exceptional, extraordinary. The last enchilada in the pot. The last drop of water in the desert. She *was* a phenomenon of sorts, but she had to keep hearing it.

"Damn right, I'll be very special. They'd better watch their staid old asses!"

Actually, I knew Frida was nervous. I was nervous, too, even though I wasn't the one who was going. I could feel little bees buzzing around in my stomach. Not wide-winged butterflies, just frenzied little bees. The National Preparatory was a huge school, and she would be one of only a handful of girls. Not only that, she'd have to take the streetcar into the city every day by herself. She was used to trekking around Coyoacán with me or Conchita or Papá, but this was different. Now she would be in unknown territory and on her own. Just thinking about it made me jittery.

The National Preparatory School—the Preparatoria—was not only the best secondary school in Mexico, but a symbol of a sort of— how can I put it?—a sort of sock-it-to-'em spirit that everybody had after the Revolution. You have to understand how important the Prepa was, what it represented, in order to see what it meant that Frida, our own Frida, my sister Frida, had been accepted as a student.

The Prepa had been a Jesuit *colegio*, a kind of prep school for rich boys who studied Latin, French, theology, that stuff. When Juárez became president, he took a machete to the European tradition, and the Prepa became a high-powered secondary school with courses like a university's. The idea was to prepare the best kids, *la crema de la crema* as they say, to run the country. Only things got messed up when Díaz came into power, because the *científicos* took over and made the Prepa into a European-style lyceum. After the Revolution, José Vasconcelos, the minister of education, turned the Prepa into the finest high school in the country. It became a magnet, attracting the best teachers and the most promising young people in Mexico. The students were all glassy-eyed with their own importance. It was up to them to create a brand-new nation! And Frida was going to become part of that select group. Tra-la! The next Isabel la Católica! The next Marie Curie! We all knew that Frida was headed for greatness. Nobody doubted it. Especially not Frida.

Papá had the Prepa in mind for Frida from the beginning. She was smart, smart enough to be a doctor. She was always picking up rocks and leaves and things. Not me. Rocks are dirty. I'd rather gather flowers. Anyhow, Papá was a kind of amateur artist. Sometimes, during our walks, he'd sketch or paint in watercolor, and Frida would poke around the riverbank. She'd snatch up plants or animals to bring home to dissect. Papá had bought her a microscope, and she was always looking at little pieces of fly wing or dandelion fuzz. Did she really find that stuff so fascinating, I wonder, or did she just like the way Papá fawned over her when she brought him the little slides she had prepared? "A mind such as Frida's," he would say, "ought not to be wasted." Only he said "vasted."

Mami wasn't convinced. She thought that ever since Frida got polio, Papá was raising her like a boy. And now he wanted to send her to a boys' school to study a man's profession. The Prepa had just opened its doors to girls, but hardly any attended. Decent girls from nice families didn't need the kind of education the Preparatoria offered, as far as Mami was concerned. I guess she thought that Frida was already a handful—high-strung, overactive, and big-mouthed— and in the company of a bunch of boys (even if they were from the best families), she would only become more of a roughneck than ever.

Papá rarely put his foot down, but this time he did. His own university career had been cut short, and he had no son to fulfill his thwarted ambitions. His economic situation was worse than ever and money was unbelievably tight, but sending Frida to work was out of the question. She would go to the Preparatoria and then to the university, and she would become a doctor.

Mami never expected her to pass the entrance exams, but she did, and Papá felt vindicated. He rocked back on his heels and started to crow. "I told you so! Frida is as schmart as any boy!"

"RRRRight, Herr Kahlo," Frida teased. "I ahm schmart, und I vill show tsem all!"

The Preparatoria was a grand-looking structure located near the Zócalo—the main square—called the Plaza de la Constitución. You've seen it, haven't you? The cathedral, National Palace, and government buildings are all nearby. The Cathedral of the Virgin was the grand old lady of the neighborhood. She sat solidly on one side of the Zócalo like a fat, elderly matron, tattered but gaudy, waiting for countless grandchildren to pay their respects. The avenues fan out from the Zócalo to the far sections of the city, and smaller streets crisscross to form a kind of crude gridiron. Then, like now, little stores were tucked into every available space—food stores, dress shops, restaurants, bookstores, furniture stores, cleaners, *tortillerías*, pharmacies, sweet-smelling *perfumerías*, and mechanics' workshops stinking of grease.

Frida loved the freedom going to the Prepa allowed her. In those days a young girl almost never went out unaccompanied, but Frida wandered around like a boy. She made the trip alone on buses and streetcars, sitting next to peasants in *serapes* and matrons going shopping. The streetcar was a fairly democratic mode of transportation. Sometimes I would go downtown with her, but I didn't care for the commotion. Throngs of people filled the plaza and streets at almost all hours. Men wearing suits and carrying briefcases brushed past rustics in baggy white pants and ponchos. Organ grinders cranked out tunes. Street vendors sold toys, decorative papier-mâché parrots, chewing gum, postcards, ices, succulent chunks of spicy meat called *carnitas*, and statues of the Virgin. Sometimes a peasant riding a horse darted in front of an automobile. My stomach stampeded every time we had to cross the street. But Frida was fascinated by the bustle of the city. She loved to hang around the newsboys who roamed the plaza. She picked up their jargon and even mimicked their swagger. From them she learned a bunch of colorful swear words, like her mouth wasn't dirty enough already.

Frida was one of only thirty-five girls in a school of about two thousand students. On the first day of classes, she wrote her name on the roster in the perfect penmanship she had learned in elementary school from Miss Caballero: Carmen Frieda Kahlo y Calderón. In those days she still spelled her name the German way.

"I was doing my best to make a good impression," she told me. "But the minute I met the girls' prefect, I knew I was going to wind up pissing on her petunias. An old biddy with a rod up her ass. Her name is Dolores Angeles Castillo. She took us up to the top-floor arcade overlooking the largest patio and started giving us orders, probably so we'd get the idea from the start that she was the chief mobster, kind of the *madrina* of the pack. I mean, she looked like she'd have you mowed down if you didn't jump when she opened her mouth. She wouldn't do it herself. She'd just nod her head at one of her goons, and he'd pull out his weapons and bam bam bam! You're dead!"

"This is where you are supposed to be when you are not in class," Miss Castillo told the girls. "During recess and during your free periods."

"I hated her!" Frida said. "I looked around for someone with a conspirator's face, someone who might be willing to help me take her on."

But her classmates must have been too intimidated to make eye contact. One was a bossy-looking girl with a long, ratlike nose, who reminded Frida of Estela. She was tall, sinewy, and dark, and she stood up straight, clutching her book bag in front of her, obviously impressed by her own height. Another, a prissy little thing with a flouncy blouse and a full skirt, reminded Frida of Inés. She was fair-skinned, with jet-black hair tied back in a knot and a cool, condescending look.

It must have been like tumbling into a ravine, scraping against juts of memory that cut. It had been a long time since her schoolmates had teased her about her withered leg and about not being "really Mexican," but now the chants were grating in her head— *¡Frida, Frida! ¡Frida, Frida!*

"I shot that ratlike girl a look that said *Don't mess with me!*" Frida said. "But she was too busy licking ass to notice."

"You are to be up here at all times, except when you are in your classrooms," concluded Miss Castillo. "Is that understood?" It was not a question.

"Yes, ma'am," said the rodent-girl and the one who was dressed for First Communion.

"Suck-up," Frida whispered under her breath. Ha! That's my Frida! Putting her best foot forward.

"Excuse me, Señorita Kahlo," said Miss Castillo. "Did you say something, my dear?"

"No, nothing," she mumbled dutifully.

"But I had already decided not to hang around with those mealy-brained, brown-nosed nitwits," she told me. They were too *cursi*—showy, affected, snobby, and vulgar. She would find her own friends, perhaps among the boys. Or she would go it alone.

The Preparatoria was a beehive. On one bench, boys reviewed French verbs—*je parle, tu parles*—on another, boys struggled with the intricacies of the Quiché language. In an arcaded patio, twenty or thirty students reached to the sky, then touched their toes as a drill master yelled *Arriba . . . dos . . . tres . . . cuatro! Abajo . . . dos . . . tres . . . cuatro!* Everywhere, impassioned student orators trumpeted causes, accosting passersby like vendors hawking their wares. *Buy my brand of political reform! Abandon Western civilization and embrace your own heritage! No! Embrace Western civilization but tell the gringos to stay the hell out of Mexico! No! Try a little revolutionary reform! No! The Revolution was a flop! The Revolution was a triumph! The Revolution never happened! Free love for sale! No! Let's get back to Catholic morality! ¡Viva la Raza Cósmica!* The *Raza Cósmica* was the brainchild of Vasconcelos, who was pushing the idea that in Latin America all the races of the world would mingle to form the "fifth" or "cosmic" race, which would bring peace and prosperity. The progressives were convinced that Vasconcelos was a genius. The conservatives were convinced he was full of shit.

The Preparatoria was full of the sons of illustrious men, adolescents who knew that someday they, too, would be famous. Every day Frida came home with some fabulous story about people you read about in the newspapers. She knew Salvador Azuela, whose father

had written the most important novel of the Mexican Revolution.
She hung around with Salvador Novo and Carlos Pellicer, who would
become celebrated poets, and with Xavier Villaurrutia, who would
revolutionize Mexican theater. Even then, they were dizzy with their
own importance.

"Carlitos wrote this *silva* just for me!" Frida told me. "Tomorrow
we're going to do a reading of Sal's new one-act!" On and on. She
never asked me how I had spent my day. She was so smug, so self-
absorbed. They all were. They were always in a kind of . . . a kind of
. . . orgasmic delirium. It was as if every time they had a new idea, a
firecracker was supposed to burst in the sky, ignited by the heat of
their brilliance. They were always arguing with one another, trying to
show the others up. They faced off with their teachers too. They were
busy, so busy, reinventing the country. They experimented with new
literary forms and new political ideas. They called protests. They set
off bombs. They defaced walls. They played pranks. You have to realize that Mexico was in the throes of rebirth, and the students were
caught up in their own roles in the transformation. They were drunk
with pride.

It wasn't long before Frida had found her niche. At first she
would come home and tell me everything that had gone on that day.
But then she started staying late for meetings or going to cafés with
her friends. She didn't have time for me anymore. She didn't have
time for any of us.

But what really changed everything was Alejandro.

According to Frida, the first time she saw Alejandro Gómez Arias,
he was talking to another girl—a beautiful, light-haired with a soft,
voluptuous body and full, seductive lips. Frida had seen her that first
day, when Miss Castillo told the señoritas to keep away from the boys
at recess, and had decided that she was utterly *cursi*. "She's an *escuincla*!" she told me. "She's an *escuincla* from top to bottom! She probably pads her brassiere."

Escuincle is the name of a hairless Mexican dog, but it was also
slang for *kid*. Frida called the girls she considered stuck-up or stupid
escuinclas. In fact, she called me an *escuincla* all the time.

Getting back to Alejandro and his friend, at that moment, she

loathed them both. He—she didn't know his name yet—he seemed
enthralled with this dumb little girl. He kept leaning forward as if her
spit were honey. "He looked like he wanted to lap it right out of her
mouth," according to Frida. "I couldn't stand the sickening way she
was oozing all over him."

She didn't feel like standing around and watching them, but for
some reason, she found herself dawdling in the corridor, pretending
to wait for someone, checking her watch, glancing up and down the
hall—and, occasionally, at the boy and his adoring little *escuincla* pup.

He was handsome—dark-complected, with soft, gentle eyes and
a ready smile. His nose was wide but not heavy; his lips were ample,
his chin firm. He wore his black hair combed back off his broad forehead. You could tell he had breeding just by his clothes—his immaculate, perfectly pressed dress shirt, his fashionable, striped tie and
double-breasted suit. Besides, he had the well-mannered poise of a
young man of good family. He must have been about eighteen then.

Snob! That's what Frida thought when she first saw him.

He was so absorbed in his conversation that he didn't notice Frida
standing there. It must have driven her mad. Frida was used to
attracting attention. She was the youngest, the smartest. Everybody
knew who she was. But this boy seemed oblivious to her presence. He
took a notebook out of a bag and jotted down something the girl was
saying. She squeezed his hand, then ran off down the hall. She
turned back and waved, and he returned the gesture.

Then, unexpectedly, he pivoted and looked straight at Frida. "I
felt my feet tingle" was how she described it. "I felt as though my arches were swarming with ladybugs. I tapped my shoe. I had to get them
off! But then I felt them scurry up my foot to my ankle, then to my
knees, then up the back of my thighs and right into my cunt!" I'm
sorry, but that's the way she talked. She wriggled and looked away.
The ladybugs seemed to be crawling up her spine. She glanced at her
watch. She tapped her foot again, this time to convey that she was
growing impatient with the person she was pretending to wait for. She
looked down the corridor and sighed, then looked at her watch again.

"I know that the hall must have been buzzing with students at that
hour," she said to me, "but somehow it seemed empty and still. I was

sure I wasn't fooling him a bit with that waiting-for-a-friend routine, but I didn't know what to do. I was trapped! He must have seen me watching him out of the corner of my eye." She giggled and paused for effect. Frida liked to draw out her stories. She liked to make them very dramatic in order to suck people in and hold their attention. "I'm not going to look up," she told herself, but then she did look up, and there he was, his eyes twinkling teasingly, his smile radiant.

I like to imagine it. Even now, after all these years, I like to close my eyes and imagine it. Alejandro . . . his incredible cheekbones, his muscular arms flexing under his jacket, his broad chest, his exquisite tie, and his special fragrance—a touch of almonds, cinnamon, musk . . . And Frida, all starched and buttoned, but with those flirty hips, that extraordinary way of moving, that goading smile. It's like a scene from a movie.

"*¿Qué hubo?*" he said. "What's up?" He spoke as though he'd known her forever. Frida couldn't take her eyes off his lips.

"I'm waiting for my friend, Adelina Zendejas," she lied. "But I guess she's not coming."

"Listen," he said, "I want to ask you a question. What do you think about the jellyfish?"

"What?"

"You know, the jellyfish!"

"What the hell are you talking about?"

"I'm talking about jellyfish."

"What about jellyfish?"

"Well, do they have immortal souls or what? What I mean is, is salvation a possibility for jellyfish?"

Frida looked at him like he was mad. Then she bit her lip to keep from laughing, or maybe crying. Was he making fun of her? Did he think she was a baby? Or stupid, just because she was a girl? He hadn't treated the *escuincla* that way. He had clung to the *escuincla*'s every word and even taken notes! Frida didn't like to be teased.

"Get lost!" she snapped.

She moved away quickly, losing herself in a crowd of students. It wasn't until she was sure she was out of his sight that she allowed herself to react. By the time she got to class, she was giggling convulsively. The ladybugs were still scurrying all over her body.

Later on in the day, she saw him again, this time in the middle of a group of boys. She recognized some of them—Miguel Lira, Alfonso Villa, Jesús Ríos y Valles. They were caught up in an animated conversation. Jesús, with conspiratorial gestures, confided something in the others, and they howled raucously.

Frida was walking with her friend Carmen Jaime, one of the few Prepa girls she considered worth knowing. Carmen was a quick-witted rebel who dressed in sloppy men's clothes and a black cape. She spoke in a kind of code that forced the listener to reinvent her thought process. Instead of *birds,* Carmen said *plumed flowers.* Instead of *fish,* she said *scaled vessels.* Instead of *it's windy,* she said *the gods are sneezing. Flowers* were *petaled butterflies, animals* were *quadrupeds in multicolored coats, to sleep* was *to meet Morpheus,* and *to die* was *to swim the Lethe.* She was a nonstop reader, and she knew Spanish literature backward and forward from *El Cid* to Unamuno. She also knew about philosophy—everything from ancient Greek to modern German to Oriental. Sometimes she would come over to the house and Frida would shoo me out of the room. "You're too dumb to understand this stuff," she'd tell me. "Go play with your dolls." At that moment Carmen was initiating Frida into her private language.

"Who's that?" whispered Frida, nodding at the group of boys.

"That? You mean the divine spirit Miguel Lira, he whose voice is a lyre, for which reason he is known as El Lira—not La Lira, of course, even though *lyre* is a feminine noun, because that would mean he was either a neck breather or a pillow biter, if you know what I mean—but El Lira. You mean him?" Carmen's tone was always matter-of-fact, not exalted. She said things like that as though she were giving the maid the grocery list.

"No, the kid next to him."

"Alejandro? You don't know Alejandro?"

"Who is he?"

"The sparkplug!"

"What?"

"The energy source! The sun! The blessed Apollo in his golden chariot! The leader of the pack."

"What pack?"

"What pack? Our pack—the Cachuchas! Come, my juvenescent sprig! I'll introduce you."

Frida liked the way the boys greeted Carmen. No flirting. No *piropos*—those flowery compliments that compare women with angels, dewdrops, roses. Instead, they treated her with a kind of rough camaraderie that made it clear they wouldn't watch their language just because she was around.

"Frida," said Miguel. "Frida Calo. I've already met her. *¿Qué hubo, Frida?*"

"Calo, Caló. Are you teaching her your *caló*, Carmen?" asked Alberto. "If you are, and she gets to be good at it, we'll call her La Caló!" *Caló* means slang, but Frida didn't find Miguel's jokes very funny. We were both sensitive about our name. All those nasty remarks we had to put up with when we were little girls.

"It's Kahlo," interrupted Frida. "With a *K* and an *H*. K-A-H-L-O." There was an uncomfortable pause while she waited for someone to remark that her name was foreign.

Alfonso was the one. "What kind of a name is that?" he asked. "It's not Mexican."

"A German name, Señor Aldea," said Frida mockingly. Get it? I don't know how good your Spanish is, doctor. I mean, we've been speaking Spanish all the time, but I don't know if you're getting the subtleties. Anyhow, Alfonso's surname, Villa, means "town" or "country house," and *aldea* also means "town."

"And just because my name's German doesn't mean anything," Frida went on. "My father's German, but *I'm* Mexican." She waited for someone to make an issue out of it, but no one did.

She wondered who would be the one to bring up her leg. Whoever it was, she had already decided to tell him to go to hell and mind his own goddamn business. "So I've got a short leg," she was going to say. "I've heard *you've* got a short prick! Want to compare?" Or else "Would you like a kick right where it hurts so that you can see there's nothing wrong with this limb?" She laughed under her breath.

"What happened to your leg?" asked Alejandro.

Damn! she thought. Why did *he* have to be the one? Frida

considered not answering. She chewed her smart-assed comeback for a while and swallowed it. She wasn't laughing anymore. It didn't seem so funny anymore.

"I had polio when I was six," she said finally.

"I'm sorry," said Alejandro.

"Don't feel sorry for me," she said angrily.

"I meant I'm sorry you had polio, not I'm sorry for you."

I imagine Frida looked away at that moment. I imagine she felt like crying, but she tightened her jaw to keep her lips from trembling.

"Listen," he said. In my mind, I can hear his voice, deep and serious. I can see his face, solemn, earnest, reflective.

"Yes?" said Frida.

"Have you thought about what I asked you before?"

"What?"

"Have you thought about the jellyfish?"

Frida let out a yelp. "You dope!" Both of them burst into laughter. Frida took off after Alejandro, chasing him around the patio and threatening to wallop him with a book.

Listen, there's something you have to understand. In spite of our . . . differences, Frida told me everything. At least at first. Sometimes even later. And then, after she got married and started having problems with Diego, it was like we were kids again. We'd talk for hours. Actually, she talked. She was the one with things to tell. I was Frida's confidante. I was her best friend. Not just then. All during our lives. Whenever she had a problem, it was me she'd turn to. I was Frida's best friend. Then and always.

What do you mean, what was I doing all this time? You asked me to talk about Frida, not about me. Frida's the interesting one. No, doctor, it's not what you're thinking. I'm not resentful. Not at all. It's just that I was always the one who had to take care of whatever had to be taken care of, because Frida was always too busy with her exciting life. When Mami got sick, I was the one . . . Never mind.

Ah, you're right, I did do a few interesting things. She's not the only Kahlo who slept with the great Diego Rivera.

Well, to answer your question, I was still in school in Coyoacán. There was no talk of sending me to the Prepa. That would have been out of the question. There wasn't money to send both of us, even if I could have passed the entrance exams, which I couldn't have.

Frida hooked up with the Cachuchas. That was the name they gave themselves. They were a loosely knit band of troublemakers that included the cleverest students at the school. Alejandro Gómez Arias was their leader. *Cachucha* is a kind of cap. They took their name from the little red caps they wore to school.

Back then, you would never have thought that some of these kids would grow up to be big-shot intellectuals, but Alejandro became a famous lawyer and journalist; José Gómez Robledo became one of Mexico's first professors of psychiatry; Manuel González Ramírez became a lawyer and a writer; and Lira, well, you already know, he became a poet; Carmen Jaime, the only girl in the group until Frida joined, wound up a scholar in the field of seventeenth-century Spanish literature. And, of course, Frida Kahlo. Everybody knows what she became.

The Cachuchas were a nightmare for Vicente Lombardo Toledano, the head of the Preparatoria. Poor Don Vicente. Frida used to do imitations of him in front of one of those little mirrors that made you look like Pinocchio. She would croak like a bullfrog: "Those damn brats! Those goddamn brats! I'd like to throw the lot of them out!" It was true, you know. He wanted to get rid of them. Not only were they disrespectful and cocky, but they sowed chaos. Once they rode a donkey through the corridors of the school, and once they set off a round of firecrackers in the main patio. I remember when they dropped a bottle from a third-floor window right in front of Elías Galdós, the Latin teacher. It hit the ground like a bomb, exploding about three feet in front of him. Sparkling slivers of glass shot geyserlike into the air and onto the pavement. I wasn't there, of course. I'm just repeating what Frida told me. *Sparkling slivers of glass. Geyserlike.* See? I'm not so stupid. I still remember. It was only by the grace of God that Galdós didn't get his head knocked off. He could have been blinded. Frida used to tell me these stories at night, sitting on the bed and laughing so hysterically that she'd have to dash for the chamber pot. That is, when she still had time to talk to me. Before she got so busy with her friends she almost forgot all about her sister.

It was as though these stunts proved her group's superiority over the riffraff—the rest of the student body. I pretended to think they were hilarious, but the truth is, it was sort of disgusting, their attitude. As though it didn't matter that an old guy could have died of a heart attack. Just as long as they got their laughs, see? Just as long as they started an uproar and got everybody looking at them.

One night I said to her, "You know, you think you're the last piece of toilet paper in the outhouse, but you could have killed that old guy. Then how would you feel? If you had to go to his funeral and watch while they lowered his casket into the ground? If you had to think about the worms crawling into his mouth and chewing up his tongue and his brains and his guts?" When she was young, Frida was terrified of death, but at the same time, she was fascinated by it. The whole idea of the corruption of the flesh enthralled her. Corruption of the flesh. A hot topic with the priests. Frida loved it. I mean, when she was still a Catholic. When she still went to church, she loved to hear them talk about corruption of the flesh. I thought I'd bring it up, just to make her squirm.

After a while Frida began to feel bad about teasing poor old Galdós, and in an act of contrition, she went to the cathedral and lit a candle to the Virgin. I went with her. She started out by explaining to Our Lady how sorry she was, how she felt like of turd in the gutter, and then, somehow, she got off track and started talking about how Galdós had it coming because he was such a damn snob, one of those highbrows who think their shit doesn't stink because they always cross their *T*'s and dot their *I*'s and can spell words like *Oberammergau* and *Massachusetts*, but when they go to mass they sit in the back row and jerk off, and then she started to laugh hysterically. She was laughing so hard that people turned around and glared at her. So we got up and left. And that was the end of her penance.

Whenever there was a speaker at a student assembly that they thought was boring, the Cachuchas would gang up and shoot spitballs at him. Conservative professors who lectured on what these kids considered outmoded topics were prime targets. But how did they get to be the authorities on what was interesting for the rest of the students and what wasn't? That's what I want to know. What I mean is, how did they get to be the arbitrators—the arbiters—of good speeches?

Of course they were all leftists. We all were, even me. Even though, to tell you the truth, I didn't know much about it. I just sort of repeated what Frida said. The thing is, we were all carried away by the revolutionary rhetoric of the new government, and well . . . no. It's not true that I didn't understand it. The Revolution taught us to be proud of who we were, proud of our heritage, proud—well, I said all that before, didn't I? But it wasn't really ideology that united the Cachuchas. It was more the members' passion for mischief.

Frida loved being a Cachucha comrade. She loved being one of the boys. And she loved Alejandro. Or maybe not. Was it really love?

After a while, Frida never came home after classes. On cool autumn afternoons, she and her friends would walk to the Ibero American Library, a few blocks from the school. The library was a favorite hangout of the Cachuchas. They all loved to read, and the shelves were full of books in Spanish, English, French, German. The library lured them like a lodestone away from those predictable lectures, those repetitive experiments. Pretty soon, they were spending more time at the library than at the Prepa. I never went. Why would I go? I practically never went to the city in those days. I just stayed at home and helped Mami hem dresses or polish silver. Money was so tight that we had to let some of the servants go, so there was more work for me. Frida didn't have to worry herself about those things.

At the library they would read and draw, argue and gossip. "We debated Hegel today," Frida would tell me, as if I knew who the hell Hegel was. Sometimes they'd be inspired by the works of those European writers—Hugo, Wells, Dos . . . Dostoyevsky, or the one who wrote about the submarine before it was even invented—Verne—and they would describe fantastic imaginary voyages to far-off places. They would scale the Great Wall of China or travel down the Volga or visit the crypts of Notre Dame.

Frida was always reading. She had been reading Papá's books for years, and she knew a lot about German philosophy. Me, I never read that stuff. Not that anyone ever suggested I give it a try. Not that anyone ever suggested I might be bright enough to understand Hegel. But her friends, they read everything. She got to know

Russian writers, Pushkin and Tolstoy, she was always talking about them. She read them in translation, of course. She was brilliant, but not brilliant enough to learn Russian. *He* knew Russian. They use a different alphabet, you know. The Russians, I mean. Each student had a special corner. The librarians were all *chochos*, so thrilled to see young people devouring literature. Naturally, they gave them more or less free rein.

The building was nice. Frida showed it to me once or twice. It had been a church, and it had an elegant, high nave, which was sort of humanized by a maze of bookshelves. The walls were decorated with murals by Roberto Monte Negro y Nero, who founded the Museum of Popular Art. Colorful flags of all the Latin American nations brightened the main room. It was nice.

I remember one scene Frida described to me. The Cachuchas had gathered in a corner and were sprawled out on chairs and tables and the floor. Carmen, seated on her black cape, was reciting a poem by the Spanish Golden Age poet, Góngora. It was one of those poems we all had to memorize in school.

Mientras por competir con tu cabello,	*While, to compete with your hair,*
oro bruñido al sol relumbra en vano;	*gold burnished in the sun gleams in vain;*
mientras con menosprecio en medio el llano	*while your white brow looks with scorn*
mira tu blanca frente el lilio bello;	*upon the lovely lily in the field;*
mientras a cada labio, por cogello,	*while each of your lips is observed*
más ojos o que al clavel temprano;	*by more eyes than follow the early carnation*
y mientras triunfa con desdén lozano	*and while, with hearty disdain, your graceful*
del luciente cristal tu gentil cuello:	*neck triumphs over glimmering crystal:*
goza cuello, cabello, labio y frente,	*enjoy throat, hair, lips and brow*
antes que lo que fue en tu edad dorada	*before not only what was in your golden youth*
oro, lilio, clavel, cristal luciente,	*gold, lily, carnation and glimmering crystal*
no sólo en plata o viola troncada	*turns to silver and pressed violet*
se vuelva, mas tú y ello juntamente	*but you too shall turn, along with them,*
en tierra, en humo, en polvo, en sombra, en nada.	*into earth, smoke, dust, shadow, nothingness.*

They started arguing about it. Miguel kept saying that the poet wasn't really saying anything new. Miguel always said things like that. Then he said something like "He's playing with images." "But," Jesús

answered, "I wouldn't say that he represents no philosophical position." And Miguel interrupted: "Góngora is not interested in taking a
philosophical stance. What he wants to do is renovate Spanish poetry
by invigorating conventional love rhetoric." Or maybe it wasn't
Miguel. I'm really just making this up, the way I imagine it was. You
like the way I'm imitating their voices? I heard these arguments so
many times. I heard them in person when Frida's friends came over,
which wasn't often, because we lived so far away. And I heard Frida
recreate them. She was better at it than I am. She'd do the dialogue,
with everybody's gestures. One was pompous, one was earnest, one
was vehement.

According to her version of this story, she was seated on the floor,
engrossed in the discussion. Alejandro was leaning against a bookcase
about a foot behind her. And then, without warning, he leaned forward and, with his fingertips, touched her arm lightly.

When she told me this story, I was sitting in the patio in the dark.
I felt a shiver go up my arm, and suddenly, my bloomers felt full of
ants. I squirmed. I wanted to rub myself to make them go away. I'm
sure I turned red. I was afraid to look at Frida because I thought she
might realize what was going on, even though she couldn't see my
face in the blackness.

Then he touched her hair. Frida jerked away, startled. Alejandro
moved closer and pinched her gently. This time she turned. He
winked at her and smiled, then signaled her to follow him.

He left first. She waited about ten minutes, then pulled herself up
nonchalantly and walked out, leaving her books on the table.

Frida loved to tell me about her, uh, experiences. I'm only
eleven months younger than she, but at that age, eleven months is
a long time. Eleven months makes a big difference. I had never
done anything with a boy, and when she'd tell me how Alejandro
looked at her, how he touched her, I lapped it up. I'd get excited,
just as though it were happening to me. And afterward, afterward
I'd go into a corner of the patio, a corner hidden by shrubs,
and. . . I'm sure Frida knew how those stories affected me, and
she liked to embellish them, stuff them with details, just to make
me fidget.

He was waiting for her in the hall.

"Come here," he said. He led her into a small room used for storage. "Look," he whispered. "I bought you this on the street."

He stuck his hand in his pocket and pulled out a colorful papier-mâché trinket—a little painted toucan attached to a chain.

"I thought you'd like it." He leaned over and fastened it around her neck. "I bought it from Lucho, the old vendor who stands in front of the cathedral. It was the prettiest one."

"I could feel his breath on my cheek," she told me. "It was like caramel."

The ladybugs—the same ones she had felt that first day she saw him in the corridor of the Prepa—were beginning to crawl again, only this time they were creeping from her elbows to her armpits, and then . . . I could feel them too.

She stood up on the tips of her toes and put her arms around his neck.

"Fridita, my little Prepa girl . . ."

"I'm not such a little girl, Alex."

"How can I describe his voice?" she said to me. "Warm and bright, like sunbeams. Sweet and delicious, like candy." I closed my eyes. I could hear Alejandro's voice. I felt as though I was going to swoon. "I was warm and yet I was quivering," she whispered. "My lips were very, very close to his."

"Go ahead!" she begged him.

His kiss was gentle, chivalrous even.

"No," she breathed, "kiss me like this!"

She pulled herself up farther, pressing her torso against his, thrusting her tongue into his mouth. He drew her to him and gave her a long, deep kiss. But Frida wanted more.

Frida was like that. She always wanted more.

"Tell me what he did next!" I pleaded.

"What will you give me if I do?"

"My—my clown puppet, the one with the papier-mâché face!"

"I don't want your stupid puppet." She laughed. "Puppets are for babies. I'm not interested in your clown."

She was tormenting me.

"I don't know, then. What do you want?" Papá had bought me the puppet in the street. It had a beautiful red lace collar and a brightly painted face. It was a treasure, but I was willing to part with it in exchange for the rest of Frida's story, even though Papá would have been heartbroken to know I had given it away. Papá was . . . how can I say it? . . . sensitive. And, even though I wasn't his favorite, he did buy me that gift, a gift he really couldn't afford.

"Your gold locket!"

"Oh no, Frida! Not the locket!"

"Yes, the locket! I'm going to put a piece of Alejandro's hair in it."

"But Frida," I whimpered. "I can't give it away. It was a First Communion gift. I've had it for years. Mami would kill me."

But Frida knew how to get what she wanted.

I think Alejandro must have been taken aback. He was a prankster, but he was from a good family. He was the kind of boy who would make a ruckus in school, but knew better than to go too far with a girl. He chuckled. "Hold on, little Frida. Take it easy. Don't rush."

But Frida was in a hurry. "Yes," she said. "Let's rush! Let's rush!"

He kissed her again. She closed her eyes and saw spiderwebs of brightly colored light against a phosphorescent blackness, sparkling gossamer threads of blue and turquoise and red and rose. Every centimeter of her body seemed to tingle.

That's how she described it to me. "Spiderwebs of brightly colored light. Sparkling gossamer threads." Or maybe she didn't. Maybe I made it up later.

She grabbed his hair and held it tight in her fist.

"Kiss me," she implored. "Really kiss me this time!" She nibbled at his lips. Then she opened her mouth. She bit and sucked as though she wanted to devour him, as though she wanted to cram all of him into her, as though she wanted to swallow him whole, to keep him inside her forever. She hung on his neck, forcing him to hold the embrace while she writhed against him.

Oh, God, even after all these years, I can feel their passion.

"My, but you're a voracious little thing!" Alejandro must have felt as though he were in a tight space with a live bomb.

"I'm a hungry tiger!" growled Frida. "I'm going to eat you all up!"

"Frida, please . . ." His voice was glutinous; at least that was the way she described it. It excited her to think that she had made him speak in that choked, throaty way.

"Alex, darling," she murmured. "This is so wonderful!"

She brought her hands up under his jacket and caressed his back. The cloth was moist and smelled faintly of lemon and shellfish. She buried her head in his neck in order to breathe in his aroma, then pulled at the knot of his tie and began to unbutton his collar. She licked his chest. His skin tasted sweet and salty on her tongue.

His breathing was heavy, tight. "I felt as though I was hallucinating," she told me. Ideas were weaving in and out of her glistening spiderweb. Ideas that were visible, almost tangible. Ideas that seemed to pulsate with Alex's strained inhaling. Ideas that had color and form and movement. One strange, beautiful, frightening idea worked its way through the core of the web: I did this to him. I made him lose his breath. I can make him lose his restraint, his willpower, even his common sense. He loves me. He loves me.

That's what she was thinking. I know it.

"I can feel how you want me!" she whispered in his ear.

She moved her hand downward, past his waist to his lower buttocks. She felt the curve of his cheeks, the crack between them, the firm, tense muscles of his upper thigh. She massaged gently with her fingers until he was almost in tears. He must have been rigid. She must have felt him pressing against her through his trousers.

"Touch me!" She began to pull her blouse out from her skirt.

"Frida, no! I can't! You're just a baby!"

"I'm not such a baby, Alex. I'm not thirteen, the way I told you. I'm really fifteen."

"No, you're not! You're just a baby!"

"I lied that time!" She had told everyone she was younger than she really was, and now it had caught up with her.

"You're lying now!"

"No, I'm not. I'm telling the truth!"

"How do I know that?"

"Because you're you, and I would never lie to you, Alex. When I said I was thirteen, the whole crowd was there. It was different!"

She took his hand and placed it under her shirt. "Feel me!" she begged. "Feel me, Alex. I want you to touch my tits! Put your finger in my brassiere! See? It's loose! You can stick your fingers right in there!"

But Alex's hands were down around Frida's waist.

"Why would you lie about your age?" he asked her.

"Because when I had polio, I lost two years of life. So I just don't count those two years."

Ha, Frida! You ruined your own party! She must have been chafing. Here she wanted her boyfriend to feel her up, and he wanted to do some kind of investigation!

"But that doesn't make sense!" he insisted.

"What difference does it make?" She tried to place his hand on her chest, but the spell had been broken.

He pushed her away gently. "I can't do it here," he whispered.

"Yes, you can!" She propelled herself forward, butting his chest gently like a baby goat. Lifting aside his shirt, she passed her lips over his nipple, then took it in her teeth and squeezed deliciously.

"Oh, Alex," she moaned, "let me suck you, mi amor! Let me! Let me!"

"I was shivering from the roots of my hair to the soles of my feet," she told me. But she wasn't. She was lying. The spell was broken and it was all over. Well, maybe for her . . . but for him, it was all over.

"No, Frida, no!" he kept saying. "Not here! We can't do this here!"

Frida pulled back. She had to. He wasn't going to go any further, and that was that. "I had to hold on to a storage cabinet for balance," she told me that night in the darkness of the patio. Her voice was low, as if she were confiding a delicious secret instead of admitting defeat. "I was dizzy, and my body felt heavy and liquid. I had the impression that it would melt into a puddle and seep through the floor. Oh, Cristi," she moaned. "Even though it didn't happen, it was wonderful. Because it was a start! I knew that Alex and I were a couple!" What she thought was that all the girls would die of envy.

She held out her hand to Alex, and he took it and kissed her fingers, one by one. Then he kissed her palms and her wrists.

"I love you, Alex," she said.

He smiled. It was the same dazzling smile that had disarmed her that first day.

This should be the end of the story. At this point, balloons of many colors should waft gently upward into the sky and violins should play a—I don't know, a waltz! But Frida never knew when to stop.

"Alex," she said softly.

"Hmmm?"

"Remember that girl you were talking to the day we met?"

"What girl?"

"You know! That light-haired girl."

"I don't remember."

"Yes, you do! I think her name is Raquel."

"I don't know."

"Yes, you do. There are only thirty-five girls in the whole school. You must know who I mean."

"I'm not sure, Fridita. What about her?"

"What were you talking to her about?"

"I swear, I don't remember. I have no recollection of her at all. But—"

"But what?"

"But I do remember something about . . . a philosophical, no . . . a theological problem . . . a question of grave importance."

"Oh? What question of grave importance?"

"Something about, let's see—what was it now? Something about jellyfish."

Frida threw her arms around him. "You're such a damn tease!" She poked his stomach with her finger.

So you see, at least this story has a happy ending.

"Come on," he said, nudging her toward the door. "We have to go back."

"Okay."

"You go first. I'll wait ten minutes, then I'll follow."

"No, let's go together."

"But then everybody will know."

"So?"

"But you don't want the others to think . . ."

That's exactly what she wanted. Nothing pleased her more than to shock. She loved to see people's eyes open wide and stare at her in disbelief. It made her feel superior.

"I couldn't believe he was still hanging on to those bourgeois ideas," she told me. "The common people, the Indians, they don't feel shame about these things. Love, sex, having babies, for them it's just natural. So why shouldn't it be the same for us? What do you think the Revolution was all about? Shaking off this veneer of European gentility!"

"Please," I told her, "don't turn this into a political sermon."

She was annoyed and she . . . got . . . up got up and . . . went into the house. The . . . the next day . . . when . . . when she came home from school . . . she was wearing it . . . the locket . . . my gold locket . . . the one I got . . . for my First . . . my First Communion . . . with a few strands of Alex's hair inside. I'm sorry . . . I don't know . . . I don't know why . . . why I'm sniveling like this . . . why . . . suddenly I feel so . . . so . . . I almost . . . never cry . . . Anyway . . . here it is . . . the locket . . . see? I'm wearing it now. I took it back after she died. I always wear it. I first got it so many years ago . . . when I was just a little girl. I always wear it. It re . . . reminds me of . . . Frida.

CHAPTER 6

Pranks

OUR SISTER MATY WAS WORSE THAN A CAT IN HEAT, AND THERE WAS nothing Mamá could do to keep her at home. Wilberto Luzárraga, the boy my parents had picked out for her, had excellent revolutionary credentials, but he wore Prince of Wales suits and tied his shoelaces in perfectly symmetrical bows, so of course he wouldn't do. The guy who caught her eye was a tomcat named Paco who came from nowhere and who (Mami thought at the time) would never be able to pay the bills, but he had luscious brown eyes and a mustache like Zapata's, even though he was just a kid, really. Maty was always threatening to run off with him, and Frida egged her on.

"I'll die! I can't live without Paco!"

"Then go to him! Go to him!" Frida urged.

"She's sleeping with him," she told me on the side.

"How do you know, Frida?"

"She told me."

I must have looked as though I'd just seen Pancho Villa walk into church naked, because Frida snickered.

"You're such a baby, Cristi. What do you think a girl with tits like Maty's does with her boyfriend? You think they shell peas together or embroider pillowcases? Of course they're fucking." At the time, Frida was only about seven.

It's true that Maty always had her eye on the boys. After the war, when it was safe to go out, Mami and my sisters and I would go to the *tianguis*—the Indian markets—on Friday mornings. People were thrilled to be able to leave their houses. They poured into the streets early Friday mornings to purchase grains and vegetables in the sprawling conglomeration of stalls. Vendors sold everything—brightly colored pottery, papier-mâché ornaments, baskets, embroidered blouses, *serapes,* woven blankets, corn starch for rashes, and charcoal for stomach aches. Mamá loved to go to the market. She would go instead of sending the maids, although she usually took Inocencia along to help carry the packages. She'd cinch her waist and strut into the *tiangui*—a coquette in spite of her devotion to the Holy Virgin Mother—and haggle till she got her price.

Maty could have been as sly as Mamá when it came to bargaining, if only she'd been able to keep her mind on what she was doing. But she'd lose interest. She'd start out dickering with the chicken man, for example. *You call that scrawny bird a chicken? It looks like it died of consumption, poor thing! I can get one twice as fat for half the price at Don Tito's!* But then some handsome young dandy would catch her eye, some guy who had come to buy blankets, or maybe horse feed or saddles, and she'd forget all about the chickens she was supposed to be buying. Adriana, my second-oldest sister, was good only for helping Inocencia lug parcels, and of course, Frida and I, the two little ones, mostly scampered around getting into trouble.

The markets were hotbeds of Zapatista propaganda. On Fridays a centavo would get you a ballad sheet with revolutionary *corridos*— folk songs—edited by the printmaker José Guadalupe Posada. We'd look at the hoity-toity society matrons depicted as smiling skeletons wearing enormous flowered hats and burst out laughing. Later, back home, we'd hide in Mami's *armario* and sing at the top of our lungs:

Si Adelita se me fuera con otro	If Adelita ran off with another
La seguiría por tierra y por mar,	I'd follow her over land and over sea,
Si por mar en un buque de guerra	If by sea, in a warship
Si por tierra en un tren militar.	If by land, in a military train.

Maty didn't sing. She wasn't interested in politics or *corridos*. She was interested in men. And ever since that rogue Paco had weaseled his way into her life, all she talked about was running away with him. *"Quiero realizarme en el amor,"* she'd say. "I want to find fulfillment in love." And she'd roll her eyes like Claudette Colbert.

Frida and Maty planned the escape. They didn't include me in the project. I was just a kid, and a stick in the mud to boot. Maybe they were afraid I'd tell Papá, and I would have, too, because the idea of Maty running away and living with someone who wasn't one of us, that scared me. It didn't matter who the guy was. It didn't matter that he was poor. That wasn't the thing. I was too young to care about his background or his wallet. I was just frightened by the idea of Maty going away. I thought I'd never see her again, and I was almost right. I didn't see her again for a long, long time, because after she took off with Paco, she was too embarrassed to show her face again in Coyoacán, and both of them went off and hid in Veracruz. It was years and years before they came back.

The night she left, Maty crawled into bed at the regular time, but she didn't go to sleep. She and Frida had tied some clothes and money into a bundle and stashed it so well that not even Rufina found it—Rufina, who cleaned the floors of our rooms with toothbrushes in order to pick up any incriminating evidence we might have left lying around. She didn't miss a thing, that Rufina. Dirty books. Torn-up love notes. Cigarette ashes. Her vulture's eye saw it all, and then she'd run to Mami in order to tattle. But not even Rufina found Maty's pack, and to this day I can't imagine where they hid it. Maybe they buried it with Frida's dirty laundry, or maybe they stuffed it into a pillowcase. Frida was a regular Houdini when it came to making things disappear.

Of course I'd seen Houdini. Not in person, but in the newsreels. You're just like Frida. You think I don't know what's going on.

Anyhow, after everyone had gone to bed and the house was so quiet you could hear a moth fart, Maty came tiptoeing into our room. She threw off her nightgown and under it she had on a long, faded black skirt, a white shirt, and a shawl.

"Why is Maty dressed?" I whispered.

"Shut up, turtle brain," snapped Frida. "We're serving the cause of true love." As I told you, Frida was only about seven at the time, and Maty was about fifteen. Helping Maty escape made Frida feel grown up, important. It was an incursion into the adult world of love affairs and high adventure. Something I wasn't ready for yet, according to Frida, because I was just a baby. She was always calling me a baby, even though I was only eleven months younger than she was.

I rubbed my eyes and wondered if Frida was going to tell me that this had something to do with Princess Frida Zoraída. I had figured out a while before that she didn't exist, but you never knew what kind of shit Frida was going to come out with. Frida was flushed with excitement. She kept jumping around as though she had sparklers under her feet. She hovered over Maty, whispering and twittering, her hand over her mouth to keep from making too much noise. Maty, on the other hand, was strangely reserved, and her upper lip quivered when Frida pulled about a dozen coins out of a wadded-up stocking and handed them to her. Frida took some things out from under the cushion of a chair: her prized embroidered handkerchief, a gold cross, a pocketknife, and her favorite colored stone, which she had picked up on a walk with Papá. She pressed them into Maty's palm, then pranced over to the window and cranked it open very slowly, taking care to keep it from squeaking. Sometimes that window whined like a pig in labor, but who knows, maybe Frida oiled it. Before I knew it, Maty was hiking her leg up over the sill. In the flicker of the oil lamp, the skin above her boots looked like fine ivory, and I cringed to think of Paco's rough, granitelike hand on her body. I looked away from her open thighs and wanted to cry. Or maybe not, maybe those ideas didn't come to me until I got older and thought back. Anyhow, before I knew it, she was on the other side.

I felt despondent, as though someone had died. What do you mean you're surprised?

It's true that up until now, I haven't talked much about Maty, have I, doctor? After all, the one you're interested in is Frida. But when I was little, Maty and I were very close. Maty was my big sister, my friend, and my guide. She was the one I curled up with when I felt myself being washed down the drain in a whirlpool of piss. But I was very little when she left, and during most of the period I've been describing, she was gone. Frida, on the other hand, was always there, always at the center of things. During my whole life, Frida has been at the center of things.

To get back to the story, everything was beginning to fall apart. I began to think that if Maty could leave, so could Mamá or Adriana or Frida, and I'd be left alone. Frida was darting from one side of the room to the other, giggling and waving. To her, it was all just another prank.

Paco emerged from the shadows like a specter. He carried a lantern that gave off a dim, eerie light; it perverted his face, giving it a diabolical cast. Maty gave him her hand, and they both disappeared into the night.

The end. There's no happily ever after, and Maty doesn't turn up again for quite a while. Actually, maybe I should say "To be continued," because we didn't lose her for good, thank God.

You mean you don't see the point? The point is that Frida was always up to antics. Helping Maty run away had nothing to do with true love. There was no romantic motive, no violins in the moonlight. Frida just liked to push things to the limit. She liked to see how much she could get away with. She was like that from the time she was a very little girl, and it was the same, years later, at the Prepa.

I'm coming to that. Wait a minute. I can't tell you everything all at once. Let's see . . . school . . . Wait, let me catch my breath.

As I told you before, the Prepa was a very special place, and celebrities were there all the time. I mean, celebrities were nothing out of the ordinary at the Preparatoria. The faculty included some of the most famous men in Mexico, and big shots like José Vasconcelos showed up periodically. Even the president of the republic made an appearance once in a while. The kids were pretty blasé about visiting luminaries, but when Lombardo Toledano announced that the actor Camilo Ramón Echegaray was coming, the student body went wild. Echegaray wasn't a movie actor. He was a theater actor and reputed to be the best on the Spanish stage.

You have to understand that at the time there were hardly any original Mexican plays. Most of the productions at the Palace of Fine Arts or even local playhouses were Spanish. The classics, mostly. Lope de Vega's *El Caballero de Olmedo*, that sort of thing. Once in a while someone would put on a regional musical, but even when the plays were Mexican, the actors were nearly always from Spain. They pronounced their *C*'s and *Z*'s with a Castilian lisp and declaimed like orators, even when they played bumpkins or clowns.

Well, Papá took Frida to the theater to see Echegaray in action. I didn't go. In fact, I wasn't invited, but to tell you the truth, I didn't care. I had been to the theater before, and I hated those old-fashioned Spanish plays. If it had been a musical with lots of *corridos*, I might have felt differently.

Frida thought that Echegaray was an ass, which was too bad because Papá had spent money on the tickets, and money was scarce. Poor Papá. Frida actually whistled and booed after the performance. She told me about it, proud as a duchess in an eight-horse carriage.

Carmen had seen the play, too, and she called Echegaray "a braying quadruped." "Why doesn't Lombardo Toledano invite a Mexican poet or a Mexican playwright instead of that colonialist?" she huffed.

The Cachuchas put their heads together and came up with an idea to show Lombardo Toledano what they thought of his guest. On the morning of Echegaray's presentation, while the students were filing into the auditorium, Angel Moreno snuck three large pigs from his uncle's farm into an empty classroom.

"They were beautiful!" Frida told me. While her friends looked on in amazement, she pulled an assortment of fabric remnants, baubles, ribbons, yarns, and paper flowers out of her satchel and began to weave intricate garlands to decorate the animals.

"Everyone said I had an eye for color," she told me, very impressed with herself. "Only that stupid Lorenzo, you know what he said? He said I should become a dress designer!" Obviously, she thought dress designing was beneath her, although as an adult she actually wore a lot of her own creations. I can understand how someone might have thought that Frida would become a dress designer. She was so particular about her clothes—the jewelry, the colors, the ribbons in her hair. Everything had to match. Clever Frida. I have to admit it; she was good not only in math and science and philosophy, but she knew how to doll herself up in order camouflage her defects. I mean, Frida wasn't really pretty—I told you that before—but she was very particular about her appearance. She took hours to get dressed and do her hair. It was important to her to divert people's eyes from that ugly, deformed leg.

Frida created the most stylish pig fashions any of them had ever seen. One of the sows, unimpressed with her new look, began to chew on bits of crepe paper lying on the ground.

"Don't let her eat!" screamed Alberto. "She'll shit all over the auditorium floor!"

Frida laughed. "So much the better. One piece of shit deserves another!"

At the appointed time, the two Cachuchas who were standing guard by the classroom door signaled Frida and Alejandro to let out the pigs, which they herded down the corridor to the auditorium.

Echegaray was reciting great monologues from Spanish theater. He was just reaching the culminating point of Segismundo's soliloquy at the end of the second act of *La vida es sueño*—*¿Qué es las vida? Un frenesí*—when Alejandro shoved the pigs, one after the other, into the assembly hall.

The animals, aggravated with their "outfits" and frightened by the unfamiliar surroundings, squealed and shot down the aisles like escapees from an insane asylum. Pandemonium broke out. Some students dove at the pigs. Some stood on their seats. Everyone was shrieking and laughing. The clamor was deafening. The renowned Spanish actor turned the color of eggplant and began to sputter. Lombardo Toledano tried to calm him down with a glass of water, which Echegaray shattered on the lectern. "He was in a hyperbolic rage!" is what Frida told me. That's what she said: "A hyperbolic rage."

Lombardo Toledano disliked all the Cachuchas, but he especially hated Frida. At least that's what she said. Frida would rather be hated than not noticed, so maybe she exaggerated. But maybe not, because Lombardo registered a complaint with José Vasconcelos that very day. I can just imagine him wringing his hands and complaining to the minister of education: "I cannot run a school under these conditions. This girl has no respect for authority."

But Frida, brazen as a whore on a summer night, went to see Vasconcelos herself.

"What do you expect?" she said. I just see her standing there, adorable Frida, in her little middy blouse and her pleated skirt, a bow in her hair, her eyes huge and disarming. "We're supposed to be reclaiming Mexico for the Mexicans, and here Lombardo Toledano brings us this rotting carcass from Spain."

Who knows what Vasconcelos said to Lombardo about the meeting, but the next thing we knew, the director of the National Preparatory School had asked for an appointment with Papá. "I promise dot from now on, she vill go to class und behafe herself," Papá promised.

Mami was seething. "I told you that sending her to a boys' school was a mistake," she hissed. "She's not learning anything. All she does is waste her time! She'll turn out worse than her sister!"

It had happened a long time ago, but Maty's escape was still a thorn in Papá's heart. Mami brought it up because she knew it would galvanize him into taking action.

"Zis has got to schtop!" he yelled at Frida, and this time she didn't make fun of his accent because she knew he was really, truly upset, and she didn't want to provoke a seizure.

For a while, at least, her behavior did improve.

And then, in psychology class, she drew a caricature of the teacher as a sleeping elephant and passed it around the room. It broke up the class.

In French, she glued the pages of the teacher's book together so that he couldn't open it.

And one morning she and the other Cachuchas rode mules down the corridor.

One of the worst stunts was the one with the firecracker.

The philosophy teacher, Antonio Caso, was highly respected in intellectual circles, but the Cachuchas considered him a right-wing snob.

"He lectures about Plato! He lectures about Aristotle!" Frida griped. "But when is he going to talk about something relevant? He won't touch Marx and Engels!"

"Who?"

"Marx and Engels, Cristi. You're such a dunce."

Well, of course. Silly Cristi. How was *I* supposed to know about Marx and Engels? *I* wasn't studying at the Prepa. I found out about that stuff later because Frida was always talking about it. *He* taught me a lot, too, and I learned quite a bit from all the communists who hung around Frida after she was married, but at that time, I didn't know.

Anyhow, Caso delivered his lectures in the Generalito, a large hall that had once been a chapel. What the Cachuchas wanted was to shake him up without really doing too much damage. One of them, I can't remember who, suggested tying some firecrackers to a mule and letting it loose in the lecture hall, but somebody else reminded him they had already done that once with a dog.

"The idea of firecrackers is good, though," said Carmen.

The plan was to get a firecracker, a little one, and place it outside, in the window above the lectern. They'd attach it to a long fuse, one that took twenty minutes or so to burn, and one person would light it. The rest of them would go to class, except for Alejandro, Miguel, and Manuel, who would leave the school grounds to avoid suspicion. Whoever ignited the fuse would have time to make his getaway, and they'd all have alibis.

They drew straws to see who would light the match, and the job fell to Pepe—José Gómez Robledo.

"Shit!" he moaned. "How come I always get stuck with the filthiest job?"

On the designated day, Alejandro, Miguel, and Manuel made sure that Lombardo Toledano saw them leave the Preparatoria before Caso's lecture. As leader of the Cachuchas, Alejandro was always a suspect whenever there was a ruckus, so it was important for Lombardo to see him make an exit before it all started. Frida and Carmen and several of the boys went to the lecture and sat in the back, taking notes to beat the band. Gómez Robledo lit the fuse, then entered the hall and sat down next to Frida.

Everyone waited.

Frida glanced at her watch every half second.

Pepe bit his lip.

Carmen kept looking up at the window, then tugging on the collar of her baggy brown jacket.

And then, BOOM! The panes exploded, sending glass and gravel flying into the hall.

The audience went berserk. Students screamed and howled and wailed. Frida and Carmen tried to look astonished, then caught each other's eye and burst out laughing. Pepe looked down and stared hard at his notes.

Everyone else turned toward Caso. What would he do? Would he throw his papers down and run out of the room? Would he erupt in anger? Would he point a finger at one of them?

There was a long silence. Students fidgeted and held their breath. Some looked around the room to see if any of their classmates had guilty expressions.

Caso just stood there, brushing himself off and gazing out at the sea of faces. He had several small cuts on his right cheek, but most of the glass had hit his clothing and the lectern. He waited for the commotion to die down.

Finally, it did. "Ladies and gentlemen," he began. "As I was saying, Aristotelian poetics have been greatly misunderstood by generations of modern playwrights. The essence of the three unities is not . . ."

Let me tell you something about Frida. I loved her very much. She was clever and funny, and she shared everything with me. We were best friends. It's true I had a special place in my heart for Maty, but Maty left when I was just six, and she was a lot older than me. Frida was my age. We were only eleven months apart, so we were like twins. Why do you think I can tell you all these stories? Because Frida reported everything. It's true that there were times when she was so busy with her friends that she neglected me, but other times, she'd make up for it. And then she'd tell me absolutely everything. In luxurious detail. Maybe with a little exaggeration, too, but what's wrong with that? Frida really didn't know she was exaggerating. She built up things in her mind. She had trouble separating fact from fiction, but then who doesn't? Who really sees things the way they are? Only God. Every trick Frida played, she lived it twice, once when she did it, and then again when she described it to me. Or maybe more than twice, because some of these stories she told me over and over again. With each telling, the stunt became more outrageous, and she became more the star.

Nobody knew Frida better than I did. Not Maty, not Mami, not *him*!

Frida had a kind of . . . almost . . . a sickness. Or maybe *obsession* would be a better word. She always had to be at the center of everything. Everyone had to be looking at *her*. She wanted to be different, and she *was* different, but it was strange. On the one hand, we were all different, I mean all us girls, because we had Jewish blood, and to have even a drop of Jewish blood in Mexico sets you apart, even if you're a practicing Catholic. And in addition, she was—she'd kill me if she heard me say this—she was, well, a cripple. But both those things that really set her apart, being Jewish and being lame, she tried to cover up. She tried to convince the world that she was more Mexican than the Virgin of Guadalupe and more physically fit than Alfredo Codona.

You don't know about Alfredo Codona? The Mexican aerialist who was the first man to ever perfect a triple somersault. You never saw him on the newsreels? Ha! And *you* think *I* don't know what goes on in the world!

I was saying about Frida, the things that really made her different, those were the things she tried to hide. Sometimes I think she really didn't like herself very much, and so she pretended that she didn't care if other people liked her either. But that don't-give-a-damn attitude, it was just a mask.

I don't know if that makes sense or not.

No, I'm not trying to do your job. I'm just trying to give you my impression of things. I thought that's what you wanted. But if you don't want to hear it, just go away. I've talked enough for today, anyway.

CHAPTER 7

Amphibia

I'LL TELL YOU THIS ABOUT DIEGO: HE WAS THE UGLIEST MAN I'D EVER
seen, ugly enough to win an ugly contest. A mountain of suet that
had to be stuffed with a trowel into those filthy overalls he wore.
Vasconcelos had hired a bunch of famous artists to paint murals at
the Prepa, and Rivera had been commissioned to do one of them. As
you can imagine, sitting on the scaffold with his fleshy buttocks hanging over the edge, the fat man was an ideal target for the Cachuchas.

Pepe Robledo suggested that they set fire to the wood shavings
the artist left all over the floor where he built his platform, but
Alejandro thought they might try the firecracker bit again. "The
paint would splatter and leave mosquito bites all over his Allegory of
Erotic Poetry," he suggested. The Cachuchas had created such hell
for some of the other painters that they came to work armed.

Getting at Rivera wasn't so easy. The Bolívar Amphitheater was
off limits to students while he was working, and the doors were kept
locked. A full-scale invasion was impossible.

For Frida, the prohibition only made the challenge more tantalizing. Besides, she was curious about this mountainous, homely,
frog-faced painter. He seemed to be an affable type, not at all a snob.
He stopped to talk to admirers in the corridor or to wink at a pretty
girl. If he wouldn't let the students watch him paint, it was probably
just because he was afraid they'd distract him, she thought, although
the boys had other ideas.

Rivera was six feet tall and weighed three hundred pounds. In his shabby overalls and immense Stetson hat, he himself was a spectacle. His shoes were filthy and stained with paint and plaster. As if in order to prove his revolutionary zeal (or perhaps only to protect himself from the Cachuchas), he wore a cartridge belt and carried a large pistol. His hair was fine and always a mess. He had a large, round baby face, with fat cheeks and who knows how many chins. His eyes were positively amphibian—you know what I mean, like a frog's. They bulged out of his head and seemed to move separately from his face. They were set far apart and could turn in all directions in order to take in a complete panorama. His mouth was enormous, and you half expected a long, thin tongue to shoot out and snare a fly. His skin had a greenish tinge, except for his chest and paunch, which were creamy, like the underside of a frog. His shirt was always open halfway to his belly, which looked like a vat turned on its side, and on his chest you could see filaments of the fuzz that covered his whole body. After a day's work in the hot auditorium, sweat rolled down his cheeks and neck and dripped from his armpits, giving him the look of an aquatic creature just emerged from a pond. He had swollen white breasts like mounds of blubber, a thick neck, and no shoulders. Amphibian forelegs stuck out from his huge torso, and his hands were pudgy and surprisingly small, with five skinny fingers—not four, like a frog—sticking out in all directions. Frida always said that it was unbelievable that such ugly, odd hands could produce such magnificent paintings. In spite of his girth, I wouldn't say that he was lumbering. No, not really. Papá, who was slim and well proportioned, was far more lumbering than Diego. No, Diego was pretty agile for his size. He was capable of remaining almost motionless for a very long time, and sometimes, when he was working on a detail in a painting, his body would appear inert for an eternity. Then, all of a sudden, he would reposition himself, taking a gigantic step to one side or another. It was as though he leaped two or three meters at a time, you know, like a bullfrog. As I said, Frida liked him from the start, even though she was duty-bound to the Cachuchas to play the most malicious tricks on him. No, I've got it all wrong. She played tricks on him because she liked him and she wanted him to notice her. He seemed so unassuming and friendly that she couldn't help but be enthralled, and I was enthralled just listening to her.

Of course, it was an act. Diego Rivera wasn't really unassuming at all. He was as full of himself as a Spanish sausage.

You have to understand that at that time, Diego was thirty-six and already quite a star. Not the star he became later. That came with the murals he did at the National Palace and the paintings that I posed for. I told you before, I was his favorite model. Not Frida, but me. He always said that I had a softer, more . . . I had a gentler, fuller look. Frida had a harder edge. I was, well, more feminine.

Countless rumors circulated about Diego. For example, Frida told me he was part Chinese. We were looking at a picture of him in *La República*. He didn't look Chinese to *me*, but to Frida he looked like a potbellied Buddha. Carmen called him "he of the porcine physiognomy." She was a real pain, that Carmen, trying to impress everybody with her fancy expressions.

At the Prepa some people said he was part Jewish, but Frida didn't get involved in those discussions. It was still a sore subject. Other people also said he was part Portuguese, part Spanish, and part Indian. The truth is that nobody knew exactly what he was.

"I hear he's Russian," said Pepe. "Someone heard him speaking Russian with one of the teachers."

"No, he's not Russian," Alejandro corrected him. "His girlfriend in Paris was Russian."

"Two of his girlfriends!" observed Alberto.

"Two of his many girlfriends," added Adelina Zandejas, "according to my uncle's godfather's cousin, who knows Lupe Marín, his mistress."

"You mean the model?" asked Alberto. "The one who's posing for him?"

"One of the ones who's posing for him. There are a lot of them— Lupe, Nahui Olín, a bunch of them."

"You think she's posing nude?" That was Pepe. In spite of the fact that they all thought of themselves as sophisticated revolutionaries who pooh-poohed bourgeois attitudes, they'd walk from here to Oaxaca for a peep at a nice pair of bare thighs.

"Of course she's posing nude! Didn't you see the sketches?" That was Alejandro, who always knew what was going on. "That's the real reason they won't let us in there."

I have to admit that Frida made it all sound intriguing. I wasn't interested in going to the Prepa to study to be a doctor, but I would have given anything to meet some of the exciting people who passed through the school's doors—people like the movie stars Mimí Derba and Joaquín Coss, you know, from *El automóbil gris*. Me, I never did anything exciting. I mean, the local boys all looked at me. I had my share of admirers, big strapping boys with mustaches and worn boots and machetes to kill snakes with. But I had never met an artist or a movie star.

"I would never pose nude for anybody," I told Frida self-right-eously.

"I would. God, Cristi, you're such an *escuincla*! You're the same person with your clothes on or off, you know." I knew she was just trying to shock me, but I was annoyed anyway.

"You know," she said, "I wouldn't mind being Diego Rivera's model."

"I think you're disgusting."

"What's the big deal? I'm going to be a doctor, and doctors look at people's bodies all day, just like artists. A person can't have all those bourgeois prejudices like you and Mami and be an artist or a doctor."

"You're Catholic, aren't you?" Both Mami and Abuelita had worked hard to instill the ideals of modesty and purity in us. And a sense of decorum. "*El decoro, hija,*" Mami would harp whenever she caught me with my feet on the furniture or my finger in my nose. "*¡El decoro!*"

The mention of our beloved faith didn't faze Frida. "Yeah," she said, "but God makes pricks and tits, doesn't he?"

"Besides," I said, playing my last card. "I heard he was a communist!"

"So? I might become a communist!"

"I thought you said you were Catholic, Frida. Communists don't believe in God."

"So I'll be a new kind of communist."

From the very beginning, Diego was associated with two things in Frida's mind. Not painting, no. Sex and communism—two forbidden topics in polite Mexican society in spite of the leftist rhetoric of the Revolution. We were Zapatistas during the war, okay. But not communists. Being a Zapatista was not the same as being a communist. Communism was some foreign ogre who hated Our Savior Jesus Christ, and no self-respecting Catholic could be a communist. You could think like a communist, you could talk like a communist, you could glorify the workers and the peasants and vilify the imperialist pigs, but you couldn't actually be a communist. At least, that's what I thought, because that's what my grandmother had told me.

Like I said, all sorts of stories circulated about Diego: that when he was a little boy, his father caught him cutting open a live mouse to find out where baby mice came from; that he had humped a girl when he was nine; that he had had an affair with a mulatto woman (the wife of an engineer on the Mexican Central Railroad); that he wanted it all the time, just like a bull, and fucked every woman he could get his hands on—actresses, prostitutes, housewives, models, artists, secretaries, tourists, everybody—and that his dick was so big, he ruined the uterus of one of his lovers! And, of course, that he was a revolutionary hero, not because he had fought on the battlefield, but because he fought injustice with his brush. Liberty, equality, fraternity, truth, and tortillas in every belly. Rivera stood for all that, and was a card-carrying communist to prove it. That's what they said. So, you see what I mean, Sex and communism. The two taboos. How could Frida resist a man like that? A man who represented everything that was banned from refined conversation. Naturally, she fell in love with him. But not right away. At first it was just fascination.

Was I fascinated too? It's hard to say. I had never met Diego, never even seen him. I pretended not to be interested, but Frida was full of anecdotes. Every day she'd come home with a story. I guess, well, I guess she sort of planted a seed. She made him sound so exotic and at the same time so ridiculous and lovable, with his bulging eyes and drooping chins. I couldn't help but become infatuated.

Frida was determined to meet Diego Rivera.

She planned it carefully. He was painting that fresco in the Bolívar Amphitheater. Frida waited until late, when the building was practically empty. Diego used to begin at four in the morning, with the first glimmer of dawn, and worked practically without stopping until dusk, squinting and straining in order to accomplish as much as possible before the plaster dried. He didn't even go home for lunch. Lupe brought him his food in a large, colorful basket decorated with flowers and covered by a small cotton tablecloth embroidered with a folk motif. Frida watched her go in and out, sizing her up. Sometimes other women came too, bringing lunches or gifts. Since they were allowed into the Bolívar Amphitheater to see Diego Rivera, why wasn't she? Frida wanted to know.

"You have to help me, *mana!*" she said to her friend Agustina Reyna, known as *La Reyna*—"The Queen."

That afternoon, they waited. They waited until the students had gone home. Until the teachers had gone home. Until the director had left. Until the janitors were out of the way. And then, forming a battering ram with their shoulders, they pounded the auditorium door.

"*¡Uno dos tres, PUM! ¡Uno dos tres, PUM!*" Not a very subtle entrance.

The door began to tremble. They could hear Rivera grumbling. "What's going on here?"

"*¡Uno dos tres, PUM! ¡Uno dos tres, PUM!*"

One final thrust and the door opened.

Imagine Diego, stupefied, looking down from his scaffold. What did he see? A small, delicate girl dressed in a calf-length blue skirt, a white blouse, and a patterned sweater, a girl with fine features and dark hair. To him she must have looked like a child, except that her body was well formed and her breasts large and firm.

"What did you say to him?" I asked her. I couldn't pretend I wasn't fascinated. My very own sister, face to face with the great Diego Rivera! Did I really understand who he was? I'm not sure, to tell you the truth, but I knew he was very important.

"I asked if I could watch him work. That's all. 'May I watch you work?' That's all I said to him." She repeated the sentence to me exactly as she had uttered it to him. Her tone was steady and self-assured. I imagine she made Diego grin.

"What did he say?"

"He said he'd be delighted."

She sat down on a stool, her gaze riveted on the painter's brush. There was no one on the scaffold with him that night, but Lupe Marín sat on a chair down below, weaving.

"I was breathless," Frida told me. "His hand was so quick and sure." Segments of the wall seemed to come alive as he applied the colors—red, green, purple, gold.

The theme of the mural was creation, with specific reference to the Mexican race. The work was filled with dramatic allegorical figures—Man, Woman, Knowledge, Erotic Poetry, Tradition, Tragedy, Music, Charity. Some of them were more than twelve feet tall, and they represented every Mexican type: whites, Indians, mestizos. The lines of the figures harmonized perfectly with the curve of the ceiling and even integrated the pipe organ, which was built into the wall. Frida was hypnotized.

Lupe Marín was eyeing her and scowling. She had posed for three of the allegories, Woman, Justice, and Song. The one that held Frida spellbound was Woman, a seated nude. She looked like a peasant or a worker, a woman who had had four or five children, maybe, because she had massive breasts and a round belly, a woman who knew how to survive, who didn't put up with any nonsense, who found out what had to be done and did it. Her legs were slightly parted, her jaw heavy and her nose uneven. Her mouth was rather too toothy, and her strong arms and thighs looked like they were used to heavy labor. Frida found the figure both hideously ugly and vibrantly feminine. "It didn't look like Lupe at all," she told me. "Lupe is tall, gorgeous woman with olive skin and breathtaking green eyes. She has black hair that looks like it was combed by a windstorm and lips like a luscious plum, so ripe it's ready to split and spill its juices." Diego's Woman was earthy, heavy. Frida found it incredible that Rivera would make her look so unattractive, or that she would agree to pose for a portrait that deformed her so. At the same time, Frida was captivated by the painter's ability to transform object into idea. The painting didn't look like Lupe because it wasn't meant to; it was meant to be an incarnation of womanhood, to capture a kind of . . . let's see, how did Frida put it? A kind of vital reproductive energy. Diego's Woman was bulky and earthbound, because she was part of the life force of nature. I understand now because I posed for that kind of painting too.

"Ideas were crashing around in my head," Frida told me. She forgot the time. She forgot where she was. She felt as though she really was watching a "creation." Diego could have that kind of effect on you.

But Lupe was growing impatient. "Little girl," she said after a while, "don't you have to go home now? Aren't your parents waiting for you? Won't they be worried?"

And do you know what Frida did? She looked right into Lupe's dramatic green eyes. As I said, Lupe Marín was a truly breathtaking creature, a proper lover for a great artist. But that was no reason for Frida to allow Lupe to intimidate her.

"No," she said calmly. And she went back to watching.

Diego's hand moved with the lightness of a butterfly wing, yet his lines were firm and incisive. Such a giant, froglike man, but with such a delicate touch. He was a master technician, and yet these were not the lifeless shapes of a mere draftsman, but the robust, vibrant forms of a passionate artist.

Lupe had a violent temper. I saw it in action many times. Later, I got to know her pretty well. I can imagine that Lupe was growing irritated. This child had been in there nearly two hours. Lupe waited about fifteen minutes more, then became insistent. To her way of thinking, the girl had abused her invitation.

"It's time for you to go home!" she snapped in a tone that made it clear she expected Frida to leave immediately.

Frida pretended not to hear.

"I said," repeated Lupe, "that it was time for you to leave. Now, go!" She stood up and threw her weaving on the chair.

Frida didn't say a word. Lupe towered over her. She was an imposing figure. But Frida held her ground.

"Look," said Lupe, grabbing Frida by the arm, "I want you out of here."

Diego turned to look at them, a grin on his lips. He loved it when women fought over him, and he found Lupe's jealous fits amusing. Besides, he was enthralled by Frida's tenaciousness.

"Leave her alone, Lupita," he said gently. "She's not bothering me."

"Well," snarled Lupe, "she's bothering *me*!"

Lupe sat down and picked up her weaving. She unbraided three strands of yarn, then let her work fall to the floor. She got up and paced. She was fuming.

"Damn it, Diego," she screamed. "I want her out of here! Get her out of here!"

Diego went on painting and Frida went on watching.

Lupe sat down, crossed her arms, and sulked. "Shit! I don't know why I put up with you."

"You love me!"

"Pig! Your ego is as swollen as your belly."

"That's why you love me!" Diego answered without pausing. His power of concentration, thought Frida, was extraordinary.

Finally, Frida got up. "Thank you," she said. "I appreciate your letting me watch you."

Then she turned to Lupe and smiled. "Bye!" she said.

Lupe became suddenly involved once again in her weaving. But Frida wasn't going to let her get away with pretending to ignore her. She had stayed exactly as long as she wanted, and she was going to rub Lupe's nose in it.

"Good-bye, Señorita Marín." Frida held out her hand.

It was a standoff.

Lupe directed her gaze at the mural. "Look," she called to Diego, "you messed up that section there, right by my foot, right where the male figure starts."

Diego didn't bother examining the spot, or answering Lupe for that matter.

Frida was still standing there with her hand extended.

Lupe finally looked up.

"Nice to meet you, Señorita Marín," said Frida. Her hand and her eyes were steady.

"Bye," said Lupe. And, in spite of herself, she smiled.

Frida heaved her book bag over her shoulder and walked out of the room. Her step was firm, her carriage dignified and graceful.

This story is a family legend. Frida told it to me that very night, when she got home from the Prepa. Not just once. Over and over again, because she comes out the winner. She plays David to Lupe's Goliath. Years later, Lupe told it to me too. And so did Diego.

"You know," Lupe told Diego when Frida had gone, "that child is really something! How many little girls would have the guts to invite themselves in here like that, and then to stand up to a woman like me? Not many!"

Diego just chuckled and went on working.

Lupe liked Frida. She liked her a lot in spite of everything. And that's the strange thing about Diego's women: they started out rivals, but they wound up friends. They loved and hated one another. Just like . . . just like Frida and me.

What can I tell you about Diego Rivera? It's not easy to get to the truth about Diego, even for someone like me, who knew him so well. So many stories circulated about him. Scandal clung to him like a second skin. And to make matters worse, he was a terrible liar. It was something he had in common with Frida.

I've spent my life surrounded by famous people. So many famous people. Diego and Frida, of course, and so many others. Politicians, movie stars . . . Yes, I finally got to meet movie stars, lots of them. Artists and photographers. People like Trotsky, Vasconcelos, Cantinflas, Dolores del Río, Siqueiros, Edward Weston—the photographer who took so many magnificent pictures of Lupe. Lots and lots of famous people. I was the one who stood out by not standing out. But I was there at their parties and rallies and openings because I was Frida Kahlo's sister.

So, you want to know about Diego. What I can tell you is that he was born on December 8, 1886. We always gave him a birthday party, and we celebrated his saint's day as well because Diego loved parties. If you forgot one of his special days, he got out of control like a bee in the attic on a hot afternoon. Diego had had a twin brother, but he died as an infant. His father, also named Diego, was an enormous

man, a schoolteacher, who according to the official story was the son
of a Spaniard and of a Mexican woman of Portuguese-Jewish
descent. His mother, María del Pilar Barrientos, was the daughter of
a Spaniard and a mestizo woman, so I guess it was true that Diego
was a lot of things—Spanish, Jewish, Portuguese, Indian—but not
Chinese. Every time some reporter interviewed him, Diego invented
a different story about his background. Sometimes he said he was
part Dutch, or that his great-grandmother was Asian, or that his
grandfather was African. He was like Frida. He would say anything
to get attention.

According to him, he was a brilliant baby. According to his old
aunt Vicenta, he talked in paragraphs from birth and drew elaborate
pictures from the time he could hold a pencil. He drew everywhere,
including in the family bible, an omen, perhaps, that someday he
would become a *come-cura*, a priest-eater. I guess his father realized
that surrender was the better part of valor, because he covered the
walls of Diego's room with blackboard and told him to hop to it. The
budding Diego filled them with images of everything he saw in his
town, Guanajuato, or in his imagination: trains, toy soldiers, flowers,
birds, a dog peeing, a monster on roller skates, a pyramid, a snake
with wings and feathers.

When aunt Vicenta took him to church and told him to pray to
the Virgin, Diego pointed out that the statue was made of wood and
had no ears. When aunt Vicenta complained to the boy's father, the
elder Diego started taking Dieguito with him to his meetings with the
town Jacobins. I guess that's how Diego became a radical.

He was five when his sister María was born. Of course, Diego was
curious about where babies came from. Sex was always one of his
main interests. He began to conduct experiments. The story that he
stabbed a pregnant mouse is true. Diego got ahold of some anatomy
books and added pictures of human bodies to his repertoire. He
loved to draw crashes and train wrecks, with mangled corpses strewn
over the ground. He also made cutouts of soldiers and staged massive military campaigns with lots of carnage.

Now the facts get blurry. Legend has it that, at nine, he had sex
with an eighteen-year-old American schoolteacher, then took up with

the wife of a railroad engineer. At nine years old! In spite of his grotesque looks, women found him irresistible. Even beautiful women. Just look at Frida. Just look at me.

Diego's papá thought that with his son's taste for sex and gore and his talent for strategy, he had the makings of a good general. He enrolled him in a military school, but Dieguito threw a temper tantrum and insisted on studying art instead. Before long, he had won a scholarship to the San Carlos Academy of Fine Arts. But Diego always said he learned more from the engraver Posada than he ever did from his teachers. During those years, Posada was a hero. Even maids and peasants knew his stuff. He had a little shop right near the school where he hung his pictures. Every day, Diego used to press his fat little nose against the pane and watch him work. One day the engraver asked him in and they became friends. Diego always said that Posada was one of his most important influences because Posada created art for the people, and that's what Diego wanted to do too.

In those days, before the Revolution, students were always protesting about one thing or another, and Diego always had to be in the middle of everything. Before long he got caught up in some riots and was expelled. It was a blessing in disguise.

He picked up his paints and his brushes and left the classrooms, the rules, and the theorists. For four years he roamed the Mexican countryside, painting whatever he saw, the spectacular and the mundane, which at times were one and the same. Indians with expressionless faces, purple volcanoes against topaz skies, serene landscapes. He also painted a portrait of his mother.

"Oh my God," she cried when she saw it. "Who is that bulky, common-looking woman with the deformed body? Now I know you don't love me!" That story became a family legend.

Most of Diego's other paintings pleased not only Mrs. Rivera, but also the public. His reputation was growing. Still, how far could he go if he just kept on doing what he was doing? Europe was the heart—and the navel—of the universe. Everything was being churned up over there—politics, art, science, sex. Diego was having fun in Mexico, carousing in bars and brothels, but he knew he really wanted something else. The best teachers were abroad; Europe was like a distant, beckoning star. Papá Rivera couldn't finance a trip, and Diego grew bored and sulky. He painted less and less. He was always a hypochondriac, and he became convinced he was going blind. Señor Rivera saw that he had to find a way to challenge his son. A talent, like a precious flower, withers without proper nourishment.

At the time, Diego Senior was an inspector in the National Department of Public Health. When yellow fever broke out in the southeast, he saw his chance. He left for Veracruz to do a report on the medical situation and took his son with him, but left the boy in Jalapa, the state capital, where he would be out of danger. The new surroundings worked like peyote. Colors became radiant; forms became distinct and arresting. Once again Diego could really see the world—hues, patterns, contrasts, shapes—and he filled his canvases, this time with semitropical vegetation and delicate colonial houses. Diego Senior was thrilled. His plan was working. Next, he arranged for the governor of the state, Teodoro Dehesa, to see his son's work. As Diego Senior had hoped, the governor loved it and used his clout to get the boy a scholarship to study abroad. Diego's dream had come true, and so had his father's. Two for one, because they were the same dream.

Just before Diego left for Spain—it must have been around 1907—there was a big rally in the textile mills. The cavalry charged the workers, and soldiers fired at close range on men, women, and even children, leaving heaps of bodies on the blood-drenched earth. Diego saw it all, and it was something he would never forget. It helped make him a true revolutionary who used art to educate the people and tell their story. Much later, when he painted the murals at the National Palace, he incorporated that scene. It's on the left wall. You've probably seen it. A row of peasants facing soldiers who are pointing guns right at them. It gives you goose bumps.

Diego left a country in chaos, but he was headed for greater chaos still. I don't know too much about Spain, but I know from what Diego told me that she had lost her last colonies not long before in a war against the United States, and that set off a national disaster. Republicans wanted to get rid of the monarchy. Socialism and anar-

chism were winning converts left and right, and strikes were breaking out all over. The monarchists were shooting at people, the social-
ists passed out leaflets, the revolutionaries made bombs and burned
down factories, and the republicans drew up one constitution after
the other. It was as bad over there as back home.

Diego didn't learn so much about art in Spain, but he did learn
something about politics. He listened, he watched, and he got caught
up in the revolutionary rhetoric. He spent hours in cafés talking.
Diego was never much of a reader, but he began to skim anarchist
pamphlets. He purchased a copy of Marx's *Das Capital* and read a
few pages.

The ideas people were throwing around weren't new to him. He
had already heard them during the student protests in Mexico City
and in the mill workers' strike. "But during those first few months in
Madrid," Diego once told me, "everything seemed finally to come
together."

His imagination was going wild! He took off for the north, making his way through Belgium, Holland, and England, drinking in the
popular culture. He studied the great masters. I can't remember
their names right now . . . Breughel, Hogarth . . . I can't remember.
He met other painters, writers, activists. And he slept with lots of
women. He wasn't at all shy about talking about it. When Frida first
met him, she didn't mind hearing about his conquests. She was
proud of his success as a lover. Later, though, his affairs devastated
her. Especially . . .

I always knew that Diego belonged to other women. He was
never mine alone, although sometimes he would tell me I was his
favorite. I didn't make demands on him, like Frida. I wasn't tem-
peramental. I was—how can I say it?—a refuge . . .

Wherever he went, Diego caused a commotion. People turned
around to look at him. Frida used to call him a walking hyperbole.
How do you like that, doctor? *A walking hyperbole.* Frida knew words
like that. And that's what he was, an exaggeration. Everything about
him was excessive. His belly poured over his belt. His clothes were
outlandish. He was extravagantly filthy because he never took a bath,
never washed his things, never brushed his hair. In Brussels he took

up with María Gutiérrez Blanchard, a painter who was part French and part Spanish. He would have been a strange enough character on his own, but when he walked down the boulevard with her—a dwarf-size hunchback—the eyes of passersby popped out of their heads.

He told a million stories about those days in Belgium. He was good at spinning yarns, and he never let the truth get in the way of a good story. According to him, a fire broke out one night in Brussels, so he grabbed an armful of paintings and ran out in the street, only to realize later that he had forgotten to put on his pants! Maybe it was true, who knows? Diego was very comfortable with his pants off. María introduced him to the Russian émigré painter Angelina Beloff, and Angelina soon replaced her friend as Diego's bed partner. But neither affair prevented him from sleeping with whatever other women came along. Attractive ones, ugly ones, fat ones, thin ones— every woman from the hooker on the street to the flower vendor on the corner to the society matron in the salon. How do I know? He talked about it all the time.

Diego wound up where all aspiring artists had to wind up, in Paris. He shared an apartment with María and Angelina. That was a favorite arrangement of his—being shared by women. Since all three valued art over cleanliness, no one bothered scrubbing the floors or even washing the dishes. The stench got so bad that the neighbors called the police.

In those days, all the famous painters were in Paris—Cézanne, Rousseau, Picasso, Klee. Diego saw paintings that were totally different from anything he had seen before. "I was thrilled to the roots of my hair!" he told me. Or maybe it wasn't me. Maybe he was talking to Frida and I was just there. He wandered around the city looking at galleries. He got so excited he developed a fever. At least, that's what he said.

He started to paint. He made friends with Picasso, and his style began to develop and change. Before long, he had built quite a reputation in Paris, and people were talking about him here at home as well. When Díaz began to make plans for an art exhibition to celebrate his regime's thirty-year anniversary, he invited Diego to take part in the festivities.

The day it opened, Madero launched his revolt. Zapata led the peasant uprising in the south, and Villa in the north. Diego forgot the exhibition. He was dazzled by what he was witnessing. All those discussions in European cafés, all those abstract ideas taking form right here at home. Words made action! Diego was completely taken by Zapata. Here was a real revolutionary hero, larger than life. The man on the white horse who would appear in so many of his paintings.

He was so excited, you might think he would have stayed until the end of the war. But he didn't stay. He returned to Paris.

In Mexico, revolution was transforming the country, but in France, cubism was transforming art. Diego must have felt torn. Or maybe not. He was an artist, not a warrior. In fact, I would say that Diego had none of the qualities of a warrior. He wasn't brave, and he wasn't disciplined, except when it came to painting. He detested regimentation, and he was incapable of following orders. He loved the idea of revolution, but wars were something other people fought. When World War I broke out, he made a kind of halfhearted attempt to enlist in the French Army because that's what all of his friends were doing, but he didn't really want to go. Long marches in the mud weren't his style. Fortunately for him, the recruitment officers felt that, with his huge bulk, he was too conspicuous a target and rejected him. No, Diego was no soldier. A soldier has to be willing to make sacrifices. Diego didn't like to make sacrifices. What he liked was for other people to sacrifice themselves for him. He was egocentric and self-indulgent. I'm not criticizing, really. An artist has to be that way. Diego was too caught up in the spell of cubism to waste his time cleaning muskets. You know what cubism is, don't you? Cubism is where you reduce things to their geometric forms—rectangles, circles. Listen, you can't live a lifetime around people like Frida and Diego and not learn an awful lot, because they knew everything about art and they were always talking about it. I had to pick up *something*. I'm not as dumb as Frida used to say.

Diego painted a lot of cubist paintings, but after a while he got tired of the Paris avant-garde. As far as he was concerned, cubism had become just another school with theories and rules. He wanted to produce art that was more authentic, more *his*. Nostalgia for Mexico began to creep into his paintings. Zapata on a white horse! A lot of Diego's friends had gone off to the war, and he felt left behind. The ones who stayed in Paris were mostly foreigners, and they were starving. With bombs exploding everywhere, no one was interested in buying art. So what was the point in being there?

"*¡Bombas! ¡Bombas!*" Diego would cry, flailing his froglike arms. "*¡Bombas!* Everywhere *bombas! ¡Pum! ¡Gapum!*" He was describing a tragedy, but Frida and I would burst out laughing.

His scholarship funds were used up. They were all in the same boat—Diego, Picasso, Juan Gris, Modigliani, Lipschitz. All poor, I mean. "When one of us sold a piece," he told me, "we would *all* eat." Only sometimes no one sold a piece for weeks, even months. According to him, once he went five days without eating. Can you believe that?

Diego had friends and he had women, but he was still a foreigner among foreigners, too involved in his own work to be really one of the crowd. He painted from dawn until dusk, driving himself until he was tipsy from exhaustion. His behavior became weird. He rambled on about being possessed by spirits. He became convinced that his liver and kidneys were diseased, and went on strange diets. One day he thought his eyeballs had become too big for their sockets. Another day, he thought his heartbeat was irregular, his bowel movements were too black, his skin was full of blotches. Sometimes he felt his immense body growing, growing, growing right out of his baggy clothes. He complained that the room was becoming tight and suffocating. He ran to the window to give himself space to expand because he felt his torso inflating like an immense blob and spreading all over Paris.

People know that Diego was a great painter. What they don't know is that he was crazy. He was impossible to live with, yet women fought over him. María, Angelina, and later Marievna. Lupe and Frida.

I guess it's that women are drawn to genius. Or maybe it's that Diego was such a big baby that women couldn't resist taking care of him. Or maybe he was just sexy in spite of his flaws, and when he was in a good mood, he made you feel really beautiful and important. He threw out María and shared his room only with Angelina, who became his common-law wife. But when Angelina got pregnant, he flew into a rage. He didn't want ties and he didn't want distractions.

"I'll throw the kid out the window!" he screamed.

He found solace in the arms of another émigré, Marievna Vorobiev-Stebeleska, the daughter of a Jewish actress and a Pole who served as a Russian official. Marievna, who knew what had happened to Angelina, started their affair with two gifts: a pair of Siamese cats and a condom. Between his two Russian mistresses and their émigré friends, Diego learned to speak Russian pretty well, which is why some of the Cachuchas were convinced that he really was a Russian. It was a skill that served him to argue politics in Paris cafés and later to insult Soviet bigwigs who pretended to be connoisseurs of art.

Angelina had Diego's baby. When their son, Dieguito, was born, Diego did learn to change diapers. But the winter was too cold and the living conditions too awful, and the child died when he was two. Diego cried. In spite of everything, he cried. Marievna wound up having a baby as well—a little girl she named Marika. Diego denied he was the girl's father, but I've seen pictures, and she looks just like him. He must have thought so too, because for years he sent her money.

Things were rotten in Paris, and Diego was getting homesick. The cubists got on his nerves, and he fought with Picasso. The Russian Revolution was promising a new world order, and Diego began to think about his responsibility as a painter in Mexico, where the new revolutionary regime was in place. He left for home, promising both Angelina and Marievna that he would send for them. He never did.

Diego's timing was perfect. He returned to Mexico in 1921, just when Vasconcelos was pushing the idea that art should be used to educate the masses. He was planning a giant construction program—schools, libraries—and he wanted the public buildings to be adorned with murals that would teach Mexicans their own history, their own values. Mexican people, the Mexican landscape, the rich folklore of Mexico, those were things that stimulated Diego's creative juices. Vasconcelos invited him to participate in his mural program, and Diego, who had seen a lot of public art in Italy, could not think of a single thing he'd like to do more. That's how he came to be painting his allegory in the Bolívar Amphitheater at the Prepa, where my sister barged in on him.

Is it hard for me to talk about Diego? What a strange question. No, not at all. I spent so many years by his side. Perhaps I knew him better than anybody, even better than Frida. Hard? Well, maybe a little. After all, when you love someone . . . Yes, I did love him. He was an outrageous man, but he was so—so vibrant, like a revved-up machine. He was ferocious about everything—food, love, music, politics, art. Especially art. He attacked his mural assignments with the savagery of a wildcat. Yes, he was careful, yes, he was meticulous. But I'm not talking about technique. I'm talking about passion. His passion made him so exciting to be around, and so demoralizing too, because that passion could crush you. It could run you over and flatten you like a tortilla. But what I loved the most about Diego was that he treated me . . . like a real person. He told me about his experiences in Paris, about his little son who died, about Picasso, about the Latin Quarter.

Diego talked about himself all the time. He was completely self-absorbed. That's why I can tell you so much about him. All right, some of his stories weren't true, a lot of them were exaggerations— excuse me, hyperboles—but he talked to me as if he enjoyed talking to me, as if I weren't stupid. So you see, I can tell you what he said, even if I can't guarantee that it's true. Frida was self-absorbed too. That's why they fought, why they got on each other's nerves. They both had to be the center of attention all the time. If you want to know the truth, I think they both needed me, and I'll tell you why. Because I didn't make demands. I didn't jabber all the time. I didn't have to be the star. I learned early on, when I was just a little girl, that I would never be the star, and I was better off for it. I never tried to compete. So they both clung to me. I was an oasis.

The things Diego told me, they make for a good story. Look at how you're listening to me, hanging on to my every word. Not just because it's your job, but because you're fascinated by the great Diego Rivera.

Frida was a lot like him. She was an incredible girl. No matter how much she irritated you, you couldn't help loving her. I loved her more than any person on earth, except, of course, my own children. That's why when people say now, after all these years, that . . . that I destroyed her, I can't bear it. I just can't. I'm sorry, I don't know why I suddenly break down sometimes. It's that it's so unfair . . . I loved her so much . . . We were so close. Listen—listen to this. One day, when she was still at the Prepa—it wasn't a school day—one day I walked into the bedroom and let out a yelp.

"Frida! Your hair! What did you do to it?"

Frida, dressed in a man's suit complete with vest and tie, was admiring her new look in the mirror. Her nails were beautifully lacquered and her lips painted bright red. That was the style among the avant-garde set: men's clothes, but lots of makeup. Frida was delighted with my shocked reaction. She also liked the fact that the trousers covered her thin leg.

"Answer me, Frida!" I yelled at her. "What did you do to your hair?"

"I had it bobbed, you twit! Everyone's doing it. You should do it too!"

"Me? Never!"

"You'll get it done," she said smugly. "Everything I do, you do . . . eventually." Neither of us knew at the time how prophetic those words would turn out to be. "Anyway," she went on, "the Cachuchas love it. Especially Alex. He adores it. That's what I appreciate about him, he's not like those old-fashioned men who expect women to wear their hair in curls and faint at the sight of a dick!"

"Frida!" I must have looked horrified. Frida climbed on the bed and began to massage my back.

"Don't be such a prude, Cristina. I hate middle-class prudery. Sometimes you sound just like Mami." But her voice was gentle, not taunting.

"I don't sound anything like Mami," I said. "Anyway, Mami doesn't care anything about me. She's still crying over Maty." Frida and Papá had found her living in the Doctores neighborhood with her boyfriend, and ever since, Mami had been impossible. She wanted to see her, but when Maty came to visit, she wouldn't let her in the house. And when Maty stayed away and didn't at least try to visit, Mami got furious.

"She thinks it's my fault, doesn't she?" said Frida. "She thinks I tore the family apart by helping Maty escape."

I didn't answer.

"I hate being at home. I'd rather be at school with the Cachuchas."

"You and your Cachuchas are going to get yourself thrown out of the Preparatoria."

"Don't be stupid, Cristi. We're careful and we work together. Besides, we're a hell of a lot smarter than the teachers."

Frida really believed that. She thought she and her friends were invulnerable because they were cleverer than anyone else.

"Papá is going to kill you when he finds out how many classes you've cut." I was thinking of telling him about it myself. We had so many money problems, and here Frida was fooling around in school. I had to work. I worked for a printer, laying out the pages. Why shouldn't Frida have to work too?

"Why go to classes taught by stupid, boring teachers?" she snapped.

"The teachers are stupid and boring? I thought this was supposed to be such a hotshot school! It sounds to me like Mami is right. All you do is waste your time there."

I remember looking up at the ceiling and pouting. Frida got off the bed and walked across the room. She took something out of her knapsack with a grandiose gesture. I stared at her in disbelief. It was a cigarette! A cigarette already rolled and ready to light. When she was sure I was looking good and hard, she lit it, took a long drag, and blew the smoke out through her nose.

My eyes must have been as enormous as balloons. "You're smoking!"

Frida smirked. "Of course I'm smoking," she said. "We all smoke."

"Mami will kill you!"

Frida struck a vamplike pose in front of the mirror and watched herself take another drag. She contracted her lips into a sensuous pucker and blew smoke rings at the glass.

"Who taught you to do that? Alex?"

"Maybe."

"Are you in love with him?"

"Maybe." She picked up a pillow and threw it at me. "I guess so."

"What do you do together?"

"What do you mean?"

"You know what I mean!" I said.

"We don't do anything together, you idiot! We go to the library together. We read books together. We talk about stuff. We play tricks on the teachers."

"Do you kiss him?"

"Of course!"

"Do you let him touch you?"

Frida looked at me as though I were some kind of prehistoric toad. "What's wrong with that?" she said, shaking her head as if the question was too mindless to answer, but out of compassion for a lesser being she was going to answer it anyway. "I love it when he touches me."

"Do you let him touch you, you know, down there?" I could hardly talk because I could hardly breathe. I wondered if Frida could tell.

She made a lewd movement with her tongue. "Wouldn't you like to know, you little dimwit." She blew a smoke ring toward me. "But to answer your question, yes, I do love him."

And she did, too. Alex was the knight on horseback, the fierce revolutionary, the rebel. He was the idealist and the ideal. Zapata, Rudolph Valentino, and Don Quijote all rolled into one. Frida adored him with that girlish passion that lets you dream of utopias and enchanted isles and endless, misty moonlit nights.

That's why what followed really shocked me.

Frida was sitting on the bed now, blowing willowy smoke rings toward the window.

"Tell me your secret dream," she whispered. "Your most secret, secret dream. The one thing you want more than anything." I thought she was teasing. I thought that whatever I said, she would make fun of me. Even so, I told the truth.

"I'd like to be a movie star, like Emma Padilla." Emma Padilla was my idol.

Frida didn't laugh. Instead, she asked: "Do you know what my ambition is?" She looked me straight in the eyes.

Then, without waiting for me to answer, she said: "My ambition is to have Diego Rivera's baby!"

I was speechless. She was looking at me, waiting for me to react.

"Are you crazy?" I said finally. At the time, I couldn't imagine my sister wanting to go to bed with that fat, greasy man. I had never seen him in person, but I had seen pictures.

"He's old!" I cried. "He's thirty-six! And he's repulsive!" That was all I could think of to say. Thirty-six! Thirty-six seemed ancient to me. After a long pause, I added, "He'd squash you!"

She shrugged.

I shook my head. "What about Alejandro?"

"I still love Alex."

"Well, you can't want both of them! You can't love two different people."

"Why not? Men do it!"

I just couldn't believe that I was hearing what I was hearing.

"Does Diego Rivera even know you're alive?" I asked her. "Have you talked to him, really talked to him face to face, since that day you barged into the amphitheater?"

The answer was no, but that didn't concern Frida. I don't really know what was going through her head. Did she have a crush on Diego? Did she just want to knock me off my feet with her gall? You tell me.

She took another drag on her cigarette.

"Frida, teach me to do that, will you?" I had to change the subject. Those disturbing things that Frida was saying were making me dizzy.

"I don't know, *escuincla*, you're kinda young." But she rolled a fresh cigarette and handed it to me.

"What do I do?" I asked her.

"Put it in your mouth, stupid!" She showed me how to light it, and I inhaled deeply, the way Frida had. The cheap black tobacco produced an awful stink and the smoke stung going down my throat. I tried not to cough, but that only made it worse. I began to sputter. My chest hurt. My eyes burned. Tears ran down my cheeks. I could feel my face turning splotchy and my nose starting to run.

Frida was laughing hysterically. She sat down on the bed and threw her arms around me. "Poor baby," she cooed between jags of laughter. "Poor baby." She kissed me on the cheek.

Now I was laughing too.

"Stick with me, kid," said Frida, patting me gently on the back. "I'll teach you everything."

"Yeah," I said, putting out the cigarette and resting my head in Frida's lap. "That's what I'm afraid of."

CHAPTER 8

Doldrums

IT DIDN'T TAKE FRIDA LONG TO FIGURE OUT HOW TO SNEAK INTO THE amphitheater without banging down the door, and the shenanigans that followed made for fables and legends. What I want to know is this: Why did they tell this story over and over? Why did these three people—Lupe, Diego, and my sister—people who had done fascinating things during their lives, find such pleasure in sitting around and telling stories about when one of them was a schoolgirl? Especially when that girl stole the other woman's lover! Does this make sense to you? Frida would tell the story, then Diego would elaborate, then Lupe, then Frida again. Why?

One day Diego's lunch was missing. He was furious. Lupe insisted that she had left it right by the scaffold, but it wasn't there, and Diego carried on as though he was facing a calamity of tragic proportions. That's the way he was. He transformed any minor inconvenience into a catastrophe. Inconvenience to himself, that is. If *he* inconvenienced *you* by sitting on your sofa and crushing it, or forgot to show up at the dinner party you had spent three weeks planning, that was just an excusable oversight, an insignificant slip-up.

"Here's another lunch," Lupe said. "One of your admirers must have left it." She pointed to a small, plain basket sitting in a corner.

"No one has been here yet today," complained Diego. "Not Teresa, not Leonarda, not Flavia." Diego had a whole harem that came to watch him work, and what would you bring a fat man you were crazy to impress? Food, of course. They always brought food.

"Those women love me!" he sniveled. "Not like you! You say you care, but you're trying to starve me."

Lupe shrugged. Diego was a man of appetites. When he was hungry, he wanted to eat. When he was tired, he wanted to sleep. When he was horny, he wasn't interested in talking about it, in pondering whether it was appropriate or not, or even whether it was possible or not. No. If he wanted to do something, then he expected to be able to do it.

Lupe handed him the basket. "Here," she said. "One of those bitches you go to when you're not with me must have left it."

He stuck his hand in and pulled out a luscious-looking slice of watermelon, but his sensitive artist's fingers knew immediately that the texture and weight were all wrong. "What's this?"

"It looks like a slice of watermelon," said Lupe.

"It has nothing at all to do with a slice of watermelon," snorted Diego.

Of course. A piece of papier-mâché feels nothing like a slice of watermelon.

"You're right," Lupe said, taking back the reins. "It doesn't look like fruit at all."

They investigated the wicker and found a covered platter with enchiladas made of real tortillas filled with pebbles and rags and floating in a muddy sauce, a thermos of something slimy, papier-mâché sweets, a rotten banana.

Frida, watching from her hiding place in the balcony of the amphitheater, burst into hysterics. Diego, ravished and humiliated, grabbed the basket and hurled it in the direction of the laughter with such force that it splintered against a wall. Pebbles and mud flew about wildly. Then he sat down on the floor with his face in his hands and started to sob like an orphaned child. Lupe shrugged again and walked away in disgust.

Diego got up and faced the balcony. "Who's there?" he shouted.

Frida didn't say a word.

"Who's there?" he shouted again. And then, inexplicably, he threw back his head and roared with glee. He hooted and snorted until he shook. Lupe laughed too, and Frida, with feigned meekness, stood up and let herself be discovered.

"You!" said Diego. "You again!

I don't know exactly what happened then, but I suppose Frida gave back the lunch Lupe had packed and they all sat down and ate together.

You know, this is terrible to say, well, maybe not terrible, but sort of pretentious—sometimes I think that Frida was the dumb one. Not dumb in book learning, but Frida was so childish, the way she'd get all giddy when she told about her days at the Prepa, even after she was a grown woman. It was as if she was holding on to her girlhood, living in the past. Maybe to escape all the pain. I hate to think of Frida in pain. Especially since I was sometimes the cause.

For a little while after that, the tricks continued. Once Frida spent hours on all fours rubbing the steps of the amphitheater with a bar of soap. The idea was that Diego would skid and go kerplop like the guys who slipped on banana peels in music-hall skits. Did she want him to break his neck? Is that what you do to a man whose baby you want to have? Actually, Diego didn't fall. Like a frog that moves and waits, moves and waits, he made his way step by step. But the next day elegant old Antonio Caso came ambling down the stairs, and pum! Landed hard on his ass!

It continued for months. One day she filled Diego's hat with mud. Another day she tried to mix up his paints and left a dead iguana in his pocket. Kid stuff. Stupid stuff. And then, something happened.

On November 23, 1923, a rebellion against President Obregón brought the government to a halt. It was a messy time. Obregón was trying to carry forward the agrarian reform the revolutionaries wanted, but the landowners were battling him tooth and nail. You Americans made it hard for him too, because you were afraid you were going to lose your oil holdings. By Christmas, the fighting had spread all over the city. Obregón sent in the troops, seven thousand people died. Vasconcelos resigned, although later he agreed to go back to his old post. Students all over Mexico protested in support of the minister of education, and the Cachuchas were in the middle of everything, screaming, throwing bottles, marching, scribbling graffiti. Except for Frida. Frida stayed at home.

"It's chaos out there," said Mami. "You're not going."

Frida protested that her friends were risking their lives, but Mami wouldn't budge.

Frida sulked, but for once she obeyed. She yearned to join her schoolmates. She felt lonely and useless and even guilty because we were nice and comfortable here in Coyoacán while her friends were getting their heads bloodied in the streets. Besides, Frida loved to be in the middle of the fray. She wandered from room to room, looking for something to do. Sometimes she read books. Books on oriental art, on impressionism, on Indian totems. For someone who thought of herself as a revolutionary, she didn't keep up much with events. She never looked at the newspapers. Sometimes she helped Mami with the chores. We had only a few servants left, and there were always errands to run, clothes to mend, meals to prepare, plants to care for. Mami was such a perfect homemaker, and she taught all of us girls to be good homemakers too. Even wild, rebellious Frida. With her eye for detail and her artist's touch, she loved to fill space with objects, colors, forms. She could turn a room into a masterpiece with a few flowers, an exquisitely placed doily, a piece of pottery or a papier-mâché ornament. She adored Mexican handicrafts and knew how to combine a traditional French love seat with a gaudily painted wooden chair so that they looked as though they were made to go together. She rearranged our bedroom, carefully choosing the right position for each painting, vase, and knickknack, and she hissed at me when I moved anything. But redecorating didn't fill her life, nor did the endless social obligations of a middle-class Mexican family—visits to the neighbors, outings and receptions, parties, First Communions, weddings, and baptisms. Frida went, but she was bored. Her mind was elsewhere.

She wasn't thinking about Diego Rivera. No. She was thinking about Alex. She had forgotten all about wanting to have Diego's baby.

She wrote to Alex nearly every day. She spent hours and hours penning poems, decorating pages with sketches. She never showed the letters to me. Sometimes she hardly even spoke to me, except to complain that I was a stupid *escuincla* who didn't even know the difference between, who knows, Marx and Santa Claus. It was as though she blamed me for all the awful things that were happening. She would snap at me to leave her alone, accusing me of trying to read her letters, steal her cigarettes, ruin her clothes. And then, on rare occasions, she would cling to me, call me her *muñequita preciosa*, her precious little doll. She would tell me stories about the Cachuchas, about the tricks they had played. She would say that she loved me, that she would always take care of me no matter what.

We would go to church together and take communion. "I'm praying for Alex and all the Cachuchas," she told me. She would go to confession, then come home crying because she had forgotten to mention some important sin and taken communion anyway. Other days, she would say that she was beginning not to believe in confession. "Why should I tell my secrets to some guy in skirts?" she would say. "Why should I tell him about Alex and me, when he's never even been with a woman and doesn't have the teeniest idea what it's all about?"

It got to be January, and Frida still hadn't registered for the next semester. There wasn't much time left, but Mami said she couldn't sign up for classes until things calmed down in the city. Hardly any of the Cachuchas came to visit, but rumors reached Frida that Alex had started seeing Agustina Reyna. "La Reyna, how could she!" Frida sobbed into my lap.

January came and went, and the crisis continued. Frida didn't return to the Prepa that semester, and in the days that followed, she seemed to grow more and more forlorn. What could I do? I tried to comfort her, but to tell you the truth, she wasn't very nice to be around. Besides, I was busy with my own friends.

At last, Frida made a decision.

"I don't care what Mami says," she told me. "I'm going to the city. I have to see Alex."

CHAPTER 9

Revelations

SOMETIMES I FEEL AS THOUGH I'VE LIVED MY ENTIRE LIFE THROUGH Frida. She was the one who had adventures; she was the one who experienced magnificent emotions. I wore life secondhand, just as I wore Frida's old clothes. My very first taste of love was Frida and Alex. I had infatuations, and boys would wink at me and tease, but the delicious secret aches, the volcanoes spewing lava in my breast, the feeling of dissolving into liquid in his arms, that wasn't about me and anyone, that was about Frida and Alex. My first kiss was when Alex kissed Frida. Wherever I went, she had been there before. The great love of my life had been her lover first. Sometimes, even when they're close, sisters go through life independently, each reaching toward her own destiny. But not in my case. The simple truth is, without Frida, there is no Cristi.

When it came to love, I knew everything and I knew nothing. I'm talking about when I was fifteen or so. I knew the mechanics of what went on between men and women, of course. Even though Abuelita thought that dogs should wear diapers so you couldn't see their privates, with a sister like Frida, how could I not know what fit into what? But how it felt to be with a boy, all that, I experienced through Frida.

The day she met Alex in the city was full of bad omens. The atmosphere was heavy and menacing. Tufts of sooty cotton blanketed the sky. The wind slapped against a tree, causing the branches to flail crazily. A wooden box danced around in drunken circles, then crashed against the side of a church. How do I know? Because she told me, of course.

Countless times. Or maybe I've reconstructed the scene in my mind so
many times that it's as though I actually lived it myself.

Alex sat down on the edge of the bed. Frida huddled next to him
and buried her face in his chest. A mother called to her little boy:
"Pancho, come in! It's going to start!" A vendor called to his helper:
"Hurry, get the stuff in the cart! I felt a drop!" Alex took Frida's chin
in his hand and tilted her face upward.

"Don't worry, little princess, it's just rain." It's as if I was there, it's
as if it were me. I've lived that moment so many times in my mind,
in my dreams. What did that hotel room really look like? How could
I know? And yet I can see it—simple, with traditional, rustic wooden
furniture, a washbasin, an oil lamp. The reek of mildew. The warm,
moist air.

He kisses her tenderly, first her forehead, her eyebrows, her eyes.
Just like in a movie. Frida feels his fingers move down her arm. His
thumb circles the back of her elbow, and she shivers with pleasure.

"Alex," she whispers. "Alex, protect me from the storm!" Like
Emma Padilla in . . . what's the name of that film?

"What can I do to protect you from the storm?" he says. "Can I
make it stop raining?"

"Alex!"

"You're safe here. The storm won't bother us here."

"I love you, Alex. Tell me you love me!"

Alex runs his lips lightly over Frida's cheek, then kisses her on the
mouth. She clings to him, pressing her mouth against his, thrusting
her tongue between his teeth. He brings his hand up under her
blouse and caresses her back. Things they never show in the movies;
at least, they never showed them back then. But I can see it all when
I close my eyes. Frida feels the warmth of his touch run through her
veins. She unbuttons her blouse and slips it off.

Maudlin, isn't it! Go ahead and say it. Cristina Kahlo loves a
mushy love scene. I suppose that if someone told me about fucking
in a cheap hotel today, it wouldn't produce the same effect, but don't
forget that when Frida told me this story, I was fifteen years old. An
impressionable age when it comes to love and brassieres and stuff.
And those are the images I've carried with me all these years.

"Alex," she pleaded. "Tell me that you love me!"

The first drops of rain were lashing the window. The tufts of cotton had turned murky and shroudlike.

Frida pushed herself up on her knee so that her breasts were even with Alex's lips. Swaying gently from side to side, she ran her nipples over his mouth.

"Kiss me," she insisted. "Kiss me."

She felt heady with pleasure, and yet a ball of pain the size of a marble was beginning to form under her sternum.

"That's good, Alex. That's beautiful, Alex. But tell me that you love me!"

Frida unbuttoned his shirt and pulled it off. She kissed his back, his shoulders, the moist hair of his chest.

"Tell me that you love me!"

"My little Frida. My little Prepa girl."

"Not my little Frida! Not my little Prepa girl! Frida, I love you. Say it, Alex, say it." Oh God, what was Frida feeling? Fear fusing with the pain, causing the ball under her breastbone to expand, press upward, obstruct her breathing.

"Alex, what's the matter?"

"Nothing, Frida. Nothing, my little princess."

She had to ask him. She didn't want to, but she had to. Uncertainty was killing her.

"Alex, it's true you made love to La Reyna, isn't it?"

"Fridita," he murmured. "You promised we wouldn't talk about that again."

Men can be so heartless, so treacherous.

"I'm not mad! Really, I'm not!" Frida told Alex.

"Frida, please," he kept insisting. "It was just an accident, something that happened. I don't want to talk about Agustina Reyna any more."

"No, okay. She's an adorable girl, and if you love her . . . well, then, I love her too. I love everyone that you love."

They lay there for a long while. Then Frida started up again: "Alex . . ."

"Mmm?"

"You think we'll go to San Francisco someday? Now that I'm work-ing again, I can save money." Frida planned to work after school and during vacations when she went back to the Prepa. Only, the truth is, she wasn't going to be saving up to go to San Francisco. She was going to help Papá put food on the table because his business was in sham-bles. At that time, she was kind of between jobs. She was helping out Papá in the studio, but that practically didn't count because she wasn't bringing in any extra money. She had had a decent job at a pharmacy, but they fired her for bungling the books. At the end of the day, she was always short. She was supposedly great at math, but some-how she couldn't make the figures work. Still, she wanted to work, because she felt guilty. After all, why was it that we never had enough money? Frida's health, her medical expenses, her schooling . . .

Alex didn't answer. He took her hand in his and kissed the palm, then the back, then the wrist. "You know what I like about working at Papá's studio?" she whispered. "It's easier to sneak out to see you."

Alex smiled and touched her breasts with the tips of his fingers. Frida had wonderful breasts, smooth and firm. No wonder she liked to paint herself in the nude. She loved to stand in front of the mirror and look at her body. Such a little girl, such heroic breasts.

Something was wrong. Alex was going through the motions, but at the same time, he was pulling away. Frida shifted her weight against him and he fell back on the bed. She wriggled on top of his body. He was stiff and ready, but somewhere else.

The storm was taking on Old Testament proportions. Knots of water slapped against the window. The panes trembled and moaned.

"I hate having go to a hotel," complained Alex. "I'm not com-fortable in this hole."

"Well, we can't go to my house in Coyoacán. It's too far, and besides, my mother's always there. She doesn't even want me to be your girl-friend. Imagine what she would do if she knew we made love."

Alex laughed.

"And we can't use your house. Even when your parents are gone, there are the servants. Is that it, Alex? Is that what's wrong?"

"Nothing's wrong," he whispered, pulling her toward him. A spider of light ignited the sky. Seconds later, a clap of thunder reverberated through the streets. Water pounded the ground merci-lessly, and the wind threatened to tear the houses from their very roots.

Frida let her skirt drop to the floor. Then she untied her clunky, ugly shoes and pulled off her hose. Carefully, she folded her clothes and laid them on a chair. She hid her shoes under her skirt and blouse, folding the cloth around them so that they wouldn't fall and wouldn't show. Alex was unbuttoning his pants.

Frida made love with genuine artistry, as though she were an experienced courtesan and not a schoolgirl. She was proud of her finesse. She bragged all the time.

Alex closed his eyes and moaned. "Let me," she cooed. "I know what you like. Little Frida knows what you like."

They moved with the precision of two accomplished dancers, ris-ing and falling, soaring, leaping, breathing in cadence with the rain. That's how Frida described it.

When it was over, they lay in each others' arms, listening to the drops thwack the pane. The winds had subsided. There was no more thunder. The water fell in orbs, not daggers. Alex closed his eyes. When she was sure he was asleep, Frida turned over and peered out the window at the saturated gray sky.

She felt horribly alone.

"When I was a little girl," she told me, "and I felt the way I did then, lying there next to Alex, I could conjure up Frida Zoraída." A tear welled up and trickled out of the corner of her eye. She wiped it away with her hand, so that Alex wouldn't see it. What difference does it make if he sees me cry? she thought. Besides, he's sleeping. But she patted her cheeks one more time, just to make sure they were dry.

CHAPTER 10

Breaking the Rules

THREE YEARS HAD PASSED SINCE FRIDA HAD SNUCK INTO THE BOLÍVAR Amphitheater to watch Diego work. Diego had long since abandoned the Prepa, and Frida was no longer the same little girl who had rammed her way through the door and confronted Lupe Marín. She was still fun-loving and adventurous, insolent and foul-mouthed, but she was a woman now. She had the frank, audacious look of a person who knows the rules and has decided not to play by them.

Diego's allegory had set off a storm of controversy. Comedians told jokes about it. The newspapers printed caricatures. Pedro Henríquez Ureña, the famous intellectual from the Dominican Republic, sang its praises. Antonio Caso, in spite of his conservative leanings, called Diego a genius. Alex said it stank, but maybe he was just jealous. Another student said that Rivera's Woman, for which Lupe had posed, was the ugliest female he had ever seen. Society ladies said it should be whitewashed, and conservative students vandalized it.

Frida adored the work because of the way Diego combined everything he had learned in Europe with an energy that was vibrantly, authentically Mexican. Even though it had been defaced, in her mind she still saw it in its purest, most magnificent form.

But Frida didn't have much time to think about Diego's murals. She was going to have to concentrate on finding a new job, because our financial situation was critical: we were in danger of losing our house. I had given up my job doing layout and taken a position in a dry-goods store. Frida worked in a factory for a while, which made her proud because she had become a communist, and she liked being surrounded by workers. But then she got tired of it. She took a course in shorthand and typing at a secretarial school so she could work at an office, but that didn't pan out either. In those days, secretaries were almost always men, and when you went to apply for work, if a man wanted the same job, he would probably get it. Even though the old rules were supposedly crumbling. Even though the Revolution had supposedly done away with the old taboos.

Frida was unbearable. She was frustrated because she couldn't go on to the university with her friends and because she couldn't find the right job. As usual, she took it out on me. How was it, she wanted to know, that I—the stupid one, the useless one, the pudgy one—had work and a boyfriend and she had nothing? The boyfriend part was what irked her the most, because Alex had become practically invisible. Eusebio Vega, a local boy with sturdy thighs and broad shoulders, had started coming to visit me on Sundays. Frida called him a dumb ox and said he was perfect for me because he couldn't sit through a movie without falling asleep, but I think she was just jealous because her own world was collapsing.

"What have I got to lose?" she said when we heard about an opening at the Ministry of Education library.

She left for the city at the crack of dawn. The morning was translucent, and the cries of the street vendors must have brought back memories of other lovely mornings she had spent with Alex.

"The personnel desk of the library was piled high with papers," she told me. A slow-moving clerk took his time finding the correct forms, then dozed as she filled them out in triplicate. Mexican bureaucracy! Even the Revolution couldn't kill it. A lazy moth posed on the windowsill, flapping its wings listlessly.

What do you mean I'm making this part up? The part about the moth, you mean? Well, so what? That's the way I see the scene. I'm doing the best I can. I wasn't there, you know. I have to tell you the story the way Frida told it to me. What if I *am* embellishing? I'm just trying to—Do you want to hear this part or not? Okay, then, please don't interrupt. I get confused. I forget where I was.

Frida read over the list of irrelevant questions, then answered them one by one. And then . . . then . . . See what happens when you interrupt me? You make me lose my train of thought. Well, finally she finished, and she shoved the forms in the clerk's face. The man was annoyed at having been disturbed, but he took a set of official-looking seals out of his desk and stamped the papers one by one.

"We'll call you," he told her, motioning to the door.

But Frida, she wasn't one to be put off. "Wait a minute," she said. "I need a job now, not next year. When will you call me?"

"Listen, señorita," said the clerk, "the decision depends on the chief librarian, and he's not here."

Frida was vexed. "Where is he?" she snapped.

"He hasn't come in yet."

"When will he come in?"

"How would I know? He doesn't give me his schedule. I'm just a clerk." A typical Mexican *funcionario*. One tiny spoke in a huge bureaucratic wheel. His only job was to hand out applications and collect them, see? Nothing else. But Frida expected him to offer her a job on the spot. Brilliant Frida. She could tell you all about Freud and Marx and Darwin, but she couldn't figure out that a simple clerk could only do a simple clerk's job, namely, hand out applications.

"Well, I'm not going to wait for you to get in touch with me," she said. "I'll come back later."

"Suit yourself, but I doubt it'll do any good. Come around one, if you want." Frida didn't mention it, but he probably went back to sleep.

At one o'clock, she was standing in front of the clerk. "He was slumped over his desk like a dead man," she told me.

"Where's the director? Has he seen my application?" she wanted to know. The clerk raised his head and forced open his eyes.

A young girl—perhaps a student or an office worker—came in and crossed the room without saying a word. She picked up a stack of papers and walked toward the door.

"The sunrise pales in comparison with your smile," called the clerk languidly.

The girl laughed. "Go back to sleep, Grandpa."

"Ay, the angels in heaven are in mourning because the prettiest angel has come down to earth to visit the library!" he said.

The girl giggled tolerantly and shook her head, then disappeared out the door.

"Imagine!" Frida said to me. "Here I am waiting for a response in a practically life-or-death situation. After all, we're in danger of losing our house! And this jackass just ignores me while he flirts with this little pigeon-head."

She cleared her throat to remind the clerk that she was still there.

"What? Oh, the director. Well, he came in," said the man, "but he hasn't had time to look at the applications."

"Let me talk to him," insisted Frida.

"You can't talk to him, señorita. He's the chief librarian!"

"I was forming a spitball of obscenities in my mouth," Frida told me, "but for once I thought twice about launching it. I knew that if I alienated this moron, I'd never get the job. So I asked politely if I could at least see the director. No, I couldn't, he said. Why not? I wanted to know. 'He left for lunch,' the clerk told me. I was ready to grab the guy by the balls and squeeze! 'For lunch!' I said. 'It's only one o'clock! The library doesn't close for lunch until two o'clock!' 'Look,' said the clerk, 'come back this afternoon. I'll give him your application myself.'"

It sounds to me like the guy was trying to be civil, even though Frida was being a pain in the butt.

When Frida arrived at four, the chief librarian was not back from lunch yet, and when she came at seven, he had already left for the day.

"Tomorrow for sure," said the clerk.

"Damn!" screamed Frida. "I know what'll happen when I come back tomorrow. The son of a bitch won't be here yet. And then when I come back later, he'll have left for lunch. And it'll go on and on for weeks!" Astute Frida. Taking it out on the clerk.

Now the story gets hazy. The reason is that she didn't tell me this part right after it happened, like she did the first part. This part I heard later, from her, but also from Alex Gómez Arias, then afterward, from Diego, from Tina Modotti—a girl who became Frida's friend later—and from lots of other people, none of whom was there, obviously. I guess they had heard different versions from Frida and

from one another, then dressed up the tale according to their own
particular inclinations. I also heard it from Frida, but not right away.
Not the day it happened. By the time she told me, she had probably
reworked it hundreds of times in her mind. Who knows the truth
about anything, anyway?

I guess the next thing that happened is that an attractive woman
came out of one of the smaller offices and said, "Can I help you?"

Frida described her in detail, although, as I said, not right away.
She was stylishly assembled and perfectly manicured, and apparently
she had heard the whole encounter and sized up the situation. Her
dark blue midcalf dress fell straight from the shoulder, obliterating
any suggestion of bust or hips. It had a boat neck, the plainness of
which was offset by a long necklace that nearly reached her waist.
Her hair was ear-length and permanent-waved. Her stockings were
a new shade of tan rather than the conventional black. She looked
like anything but the typical library worker.

"I'm the assistant acquisitions librarian," she said. "I heard you. I
thought there might be a problem."

"Damn right there's a problem!" growled Frida. But then she
lowered her voice. "Look," she said, "I'm sorry, but I've been trying
to file a job application all day, and—"

"Come with me," said the woman.

Her name was Leticia Santiago, she said. She had been working
at the library for five years and she knew how frustrating the bureaucracy could be, but she also knew how to cut through the red tape.
She led Frida to a small office toward the rear of the building. On the
wall there were photographs of several paintings—two Gauguin
Tahitian nudes, a Picasso acrobat, and Diego Rivera's Woman. Frida
was delighted.

"Oh!" she said. "Do you like Rivera?"

"Yes," said Leticia. "I do. Do you?" She smiled at Frida and
touched her curls. The bob had grown out long before, and Frida
now wore her tresses tied back in a ribbon or hanging loose in
ringlets on her shoulders.

"Yes."

"I thought that there was something strange about the way

Leticia was looking at me," Frida told me when she finally shared this story. "Her words were friendly, but her eyes were as black as ink and weirdly forbidding. I began to fidget."

"Look," said Leticia, "I'll take charge of your application myself. You have nothing to worry about. By ten tomorrow I'll have it all straightened out."

It sounded perfect. Why question a stroke of good luck? Still, Frida hesitated.

"Is something wrong?"

Frida didn't want to anger this woman. She thought quickly. "Uh, forgive me for asking, but the pay?"

"You will be satisfied with your salary, I assure you," said Leticia.

Frida forced her doubts out of her mind and allowed herself to be ecstatic. A job! This was the first good thing that had happened in weeks.

"At last," she told Papá. "I'll be able to make a real contribution. And the work is interesting. I'll be helping in the Acquisitions Department." But she didn't say anything about Leticia either to him or to me.

Papá felt awful. He hated that Frida had to work. He didn't want her to give up her studies the way he had done. He kissed her on the cheek.

The next morning, she got to the library early, but Leticia was already there. According to Frida's detailed account, the librarian wore a knee-length yellow dress with a dropped waist and a white scarflike tie around the neck, complemented by both a choker and a long string of pearls. On her head she wore a white turban. How could Frida remember all those particulars? I guess because clothes were as important to her as they were to Leticia. Or maybe because Leticia herself was so fascinating.

Frida found Leticia's attire both attractive and fiercely intimidating. In comparison with Mami's conservatively fashionable friends or the schoolgirls from the Prepa, who were still wearing their skirts three inches above the ankle, this woman was a real radical. Frida was obsessively meticulous about her appearance, but now she felt suddenly dumpy. Her skirt was dragging, her stockings were too dark, and her sweater was too plain. But, she thought, with her undersize right leg, she could never get away with wearing such short skirts and light-colored hose.

Leticia led her to her office and explained her job. Frida watched the woman's dark red lips move as she spoke. Her lipstick was perfect.

"Have you understood everything, dear?"

"Yes, I think so." Leticia was a large woman, and as she bent forward to pick up the fiches on the desk behind Frida, her breast brushed lightly against my sister's shoulder.

"Now, on this one, what you need to do is look for the subclassification." She touched Frida's hand as she pointed to the appropriate place on the card.

"Didn't you squirm?" I asked Frida. But for her, there was no moral dimension to sex. Whatever was interesting, whatever felt good, was okay. She had already thrown out her bourgeois biases, even before she joined the Young Communist League.

"Do I make you nervous?" whispered Leticia.

"No, not at all," said Frida. "But I think I can do it by myself now."

"We can all do it by ourselves," murmured Leticia, "but it's so much nicer when you do it with someone else."

Here the story gets even more muddled. According to Alex, the librarian took Frida by the waist and pulled her close, and Frida was too stunned to resist. According to Diego, Frida was drawn to Leticia's sweet, flowered scent and actually made the first move herself. In Frida's version, Leticia suddenly traced a line over her mouth with a forefinger and said, "You have a little mustache. It's adorable." Then Leticia ran her finger over Frida's brow. "And I like the way your eyebrows come together. They look like the wings of a bird." The fuzz on her lip and her heavy eyebrows had once made Frida self-conscious, but she learned to love them, even to highlight them in her paintings. The people she cared about thought they were attractive; although, to tell you the truth, I never did.

Leticia took Frida's face in her hands and kissed her lightly on the lips.

"Darling, have you ever made love to a woman?" she whispered. "It's so much nicer than doing it with a man. A woman understands

what a woman likes." She began to stroke Frida's body softly, apply-
ing pressure in the most sensitive places.

Is this story making you uncomfortable? Would you like me to
stop? You said you wanted to know everything, and I'm doing my
best to accommodate. Are you sure you want me to go on? Well, just
tell me if you want me to change the subject. With Frida, there's so
much to talk about. If you don't want to hear about this, I can tell you
about something else.

"See?" said Leticia. "Not like a man! A man grabs you, but a
woman is gentle. Come, darling, let me. Isn't it lovely? Now, you do
the same to me!" With one sweep of the arm she pulled off her loose-
fitting dress. She stood directly in front of Frida in her underwear
and stockings and high-heeled shoes, her dangling necklace pointing
provocatively toward the V between her legs. Her breasts were large
and round, but her brassiere was designed to minimize. Her crepe de
chine undergarments were gorgeously embroidered.

How did I feel about it? I don't know. I didn't like it. I didn't go
to any fancy schools where I learned stylish, revolutionary ideas. I
wasn't part of the dissident movement that rejected convention. I was,
well, shocked. Yes, why not say it? I was shocked when I found out
about Frida's—you know—unorthodox activities. I was a good Catholic
girl, and all I wanted was to get married and have about six kids,
although it didn't work out that way . . . but that's what I was hoping
for. Later, I became more accepting, tolerant, let's say. I mean, Frida
was right. Why shouldn't you do what makes you happy? Why not
take love where you find it, no matter who offers it? What does
morality have to do with any of it? You should be able to have a relationship with anyone you want, as long as you aren't hurting anyone.
The problem with the relationship *I* had was that I hurt someone.

"Come now, precious," Leticia kept telling Frida in her low,
throaty voice. "Modern girls don't need men. They can take care of
their own needs."

"Her breasts were like two fleshy melons that she was offering,"
Frida told me.

What did I do? I started to cry.

"Leticia's hands were as soft as silken gloves, but her knuckles were hard and delicious," Frida went on. She was torturing me. My sister was torturing me. "It was wonderful!" she murmured over and over again. She wanted to make me squirm. She found it funny that I thought what she was doing was disgusting.

Carrying on an affair with Leticia Santiago was easy. Leticia had her own office, and besides, she knew every secret nook in the library. To simplify matters further, she had an apartment on Aguascalientes Street, right above a mechanic's shop, where she lived with her very accommodating sister and a maid who shared her inclinations.

Still, there wasn't a clerk or a secretary at the library who didn't know that Leticia Santiago was a lesbian; she was subject to continual vigilance and gossip. And soon her name was linked with Frida's. It wasn't long before Mamá got wind of the scandal.

The volcano erupted one evening when Frida came home from work, less than a month after she had met Leticia Santiago. The instant Frida walked through the door, Mami grabbed her by the hair and nearly shook her senseless. My God, it was awful. I hid behind Inocencia in the kitchen. Mami slapped her across the face, she pummeled her, she kicked her, she yanked her ear, she bit her hand, all the while screaming, screaming, screaming, Slut! Disgrace!, screaming, screaming, Tramp! Oh Holy Virgin! Oh Mother of God!, screaming, screaming, Bitch! screaming, screaming, Pervert!, Worse than Maty! Worse than Maty!, screaming, screaming until her lungs were ravaged and she was overcome with a fit of coughing.

It never occurred to Frida to lift her hand in self-defense.

Finally, Mami swooned and fell into a chair. Rufina and Manuel came with smelling salts. I fanned her and patted her cheeks. It was around this time that Mami started having seizures similar to Papá's.

I had no idea what was going on. Frida hadn't confided in me about Leticia yet. I couldn't imagine what she could have done to provoke such hysteria. Papá just watched with sad, sunken eyes. For days he said nothing to any of us.

Finally, he knocked on our bedroom door. "Come, Fridita," he said. "I have another job for you. This one will be better."

Fernando Fernández was a commercial printer who had known Papá for years, and out of friendship, he offered Frida a paid apprenticeship.

His studio was full of prints, but the ones Frida liked the best were by the Swedish impressionist Anders Zorn. His exuberant, vivacious bathing peasant girls were so innocent and free of guilt that they seemed to mock the staid, middle-class mores that Frida now loathed more than ever. "I am like those girls," she said. "I don't care what others think. I could splash in the nude at Xochimilco, and I wouldn't care who saw my naked body."

But it wasn't entirely true. The episode with Leticia had left deep scars. Others now saw Frida in a different light, and I don't think she was entirely comfortable with her new image.

Fernández wanted her to learn to sketch, and he set her to copying Zorn. She produced draft after draft. "He says I have enormous talent," she told me. She worked long hours to master the technique. "He says I could be a professional artist."

But Frida didn't want to be a professional artist. She still wanted to be a doctor, even though she knew she would probably never get to the university. "Actually, I'd probably be a terrible doctor," she conceded, "because the idea of sticking my finger up people's asses all day for a living nauseates me."

Fernández kept encouraging her. "He says I'm a remarkable girl," she said. I knew where it was headed. He was flattering her, leading her on, and Frida was ripe for an affair, because after the mess with Leticia, she had to prove to herself that she was still attracted to men. Fernández was middle-aged and a friend of Papá's, but according to Frida, he had a beautiful, sensitive mouth that quivered ever so slightly under his mustache.

The romance with Fernández didn't last long, but Frida learned how to draw.

Did Papá ever find out? He never said anything, but shortly after Frida left the printer, he grew more taciturn than ever, and then something happened. Did he think he was being punished, or was he punishing himself for allowing Frida to go to work and get involved with Leticia and then with Fernández?

In spite of all our money problems, Papá had managed to buy a brand-new Zeiss lens, thanks to Mamá's scrimping. He ordered it directly from the Zeiss-Abbe workshop in Germany and gave instructions that the manufacturer should hold it until a German visiting Mexico could deliver it to him personally. It would have been crazy to send it by mail because the Mexican postal system was as unpredictable as a pregnant pony. Months passed before the right courier came along, but finally, a German reporter doing a story on Obregón delivered the treasure.

Papá was thrilled. He checked his lens for imperfections. He turned it around in his hands, over and over. He held it up to the light and cleaned it carefully with a soft cloth, then put it in its box and carried it into his study.

The next morning he removed it from its case one more time to admire it, just as he was getting ready to leave for work. And then something hideous occurred. Papá's vision went blurry, and his hands began to tremble. The lens slid from his fingers, went rolling over the worktable, and crashed onto the floor. Papá just stood there, staring at the cracked glass, the perfectly ground crystal that he had waited almost a year to hold, to caress. It seemed to me that his eyes, weepy but for once focused, wanted to leap out of his head and grab the glittering splinters. Weeks, months, even years later, Papá was still trying to figure out the reason for the grotesque accident. Had he been startled? Had he bumped into the table? He didn't remember. Had he had a mild epileptic seizure? All he recalled was a sudden, inexplicable weakness of the wrist, the eerie feel of the glass sliding out of his hand, and the terrible sight of the lens moving across the table, then falling, falling, falling through the air. In his mind's eye, he saw it shatter, a million fragments flying upward in slow motion.

Only the lens hadn't shattered. Not really. It had only looked that way to Papá. When he finally got his bearings, he realized that it had only cracked, which somehow made it worse. If it had been demolished, he could have swept up the pieces and wept. But there was the lens, seemingly whole, seemingly good, yet utterly useless.

Papá picked it up as lovingly as if it was a dead baby. He wrapped it in a piece of flannel and put it back in its case. Frida and I had both witnessed the accident, but neither of us spoke. Mami was in another part of the house, or maybe she had gone to church, I can't remember. Both of us knew that this had to be our secret, our secret with

Papá. Both of us understood, even though Papá said nothing, that we must never breathe a word to anyone. Papá got his things together. Then he left for work as though nothing had happened.

He couldn't tell Mami. How could he tell her that all of her sacrifices had produced only a fractured lens? Poor Papá. I think he felt as though the lens had cracked of its own free will—a kind of occult reprimand for going broke and ruining Frida's chances of becoming a doctor. I think he felt as though everything—fate, his father, his own weak body, political events, even the objects in the house—were conspiring against him. I think he thought that, from the day he had fallen and cracked his head to the day he had dropped and cracked his lens, a steady succession of disasters had turned him into a failure.

And the morning wasn't over. Once out on the cobblestone street, Papá began to feel lightheaded again. The air was dank. He must have been thinking about what he would do at his studio in Mexico City. There was no work. Maybe he would try to appear busy, polishing lenses and cleaning his equipment. Perhaps a customer would appear. He had a sign on his door that read GUILLERMO KAHLO, SPECIALIST IN LANDSCAPES, BUILDINGS, INTERIORS, FACTORIES, ETC. It was always possible that someone would want him to take a picture of . . . of what? A refinery? A plot of land? If asked, he would do a portrait, although he didn't care to take pictures of people, except in crowds. With crowds, it wasn't the individual that mattered but the complete scene. "Why should I take pictures of people and try to make them look attractive?" he used to say. "Why should I make beautiful what God has made ugly?"

Maybe Papá was mulling all this over as he walked down the street. Maybe that's what made him dizzy—his exasperation, his feelings of inadequacy. At any rate, all of a sudden he reeled. In his mind's eye, he must have seen the trees in front of the house growing larger, their branches stretching out toward him, toward his lens case. He must have seen the sidewalk growing longer; each cobblestone, a mountain; the yellow-edged curb, a precipice. If he slipped, he would fall for an eternity. At one point or other, he surely remembered that somewhere beyond was the street, but in his state of mind he must have seen it as a vast, open valley with no beginning and no end. Papá could usually feel his seizures coming on, so he would have known what was happening to him. He would have recognized the signs—rubbery legs, difficulty in breathing.

How long did he lie there on the ground? Perhaps a moment or two, perhaps longer. When he regained consciousness, he was crumpled on our doorway, a servant standing over him with his epilepsy medication and a glass of water. Mami was giving directions: "Don't move him. Watch the equipment bag. Don't let anyone touch it. Now, now . . . gently take him to the bedroom. Be careful now . . . be careful." Frida and I watched from the window. We had seen seizures before, but we were scared anyway. When they got him into the house, I started to cry.

Papá rested. Was he aware of Mami flitting around the room? Did he know why he was still at home instead of on his way to the studio? Probably not right away. At first he was disoriented, but slowly, slowly, he got himself together. At some point, with a sick feeling, he must have remembered his lens, his cracked lens.

Mami was busy straightening his things. She was fussing with his lens case. "Leave that alone," he barked at her. He looked as though he had been seized by a fit of nausea.

Mami lifted an eyebrow. "What?" she said.

"I'm leaving now," said Papá.

"I don't think so," Mami said calmly.

"Yes," he said. "I'm going."

"Why don't you rest a while?" she suggested.

"I don't want to rest a while," he said wearily. "I want to leave."

Mami tried to get him to wait another few minutes, but Papá was anxious about the lens. He was afraid she would find it. He pulled himself into a sitting position, then breathed deeply. Mami was fidgeting with the clasp on the lens case, and Papá's eyes were glued to her fingers.

"What's in here that makes you so nervous?" Mami asked. "Pictures of your sweetheart?"

"I don't have a sweetheart," Papá said sourly.

"*Gracias*," answered Mami.

He pulled himself out of bed and smoothed out his clothes.

Mami said good-bye without affection and promised to have Manuel take him his lunch when it was ready.

"I suppose you won't want to come home," she mumbled.

But Papá said, as he always said every time she suggested it, that it was too far to come home for lunch. Then he clutched his lens case and his equipment bag and opened the door.

"God is getting even with me for being an atheist and a bad father," he whispered to me as he left. Little did he know. God was just getting warmed up.

CHAPTER 11

September
17, 1925

SEPTEMBER 17, 1925. WHEN I REMEMBER THAT DAY, I SEE A RIOT OF crows. I see shattered glass and rivers of blood, wolves devouring maggot-infested meat, swords piercing writhing bodies, battered roses, muddied corpses, dissected embryos, urine-splattered crucifixes, feces, vomit, tears, death. I see death. I can't bear to think about it, and yet I think about it all the time. Even now. Even though it happened nearly forty years ago.

It was supposed to be a wonderful day.

I had stopped seeing Eusebio, not because I didn't like him anymore, but because I had met Antonio Pinedo. I thought my parents would adore Pinedo, especially Mami. He had a job. He kept his nails perfectly trimmed and went to mass. I was young and still at an age where I thought you could make people love you by doing what they wanted. Pinedo was taken with me because I had a full, soft figure and demanded very little. I had set my mind to making him marry me, so I flirted relentlessly, and he fell into my trap like a grasshopper into a spiderweb. After that business about Frida and Leticia Santiago, our name had been pretty much dragged through the mud. Even the servants were embarrassed. I figured it was up to me to redeem the family honor and supposed that while I was at it, I could earn the everlasting gratitude of my parents. September 17 was the day I thought Pinedo was going to talk to Papá, but as it turned out, fate changed the reel. I wasn't the star of the show that day. Frida was.

The afternoon was gray, and maybe that was a sign. But maybe not. Most September afternoons were gray, and anyhow, Frida didn't care about the atmospheric pressure. She and Alejandro had reconciled, and she was positively giddy when she left for the city to be with him. Alejandro was attentive, more attentive than he had been in months. The two of them wandered hand in hand through the Zócalo district. Street stalls had been set up for the Mexican National Day celebrations, and vendors hawked their wares with the kind of jubilation reserved for holidays.

"*¡Cómpreme este muñeco, señorita!*" "Buy this doll from me, miss!"

"*¡Cómpreme este títere, señor!*" "Buy this puppet from me, sir!"

A brightly colored miniature parasol caught Frida's eye, and Alex bought it for her.

"It's for a doll," he told her, "and since you're a little doll, I'll buy it for you!" Alex paid for the trinket and gave it to Frida, and she stood on her toes to kiss him on the lips. The vendor cheered them on. "*¡Andale, hijo!*"

"See?" said Frida. "These people are never embarrassed by love. Only stupid middle-class people like my mother make a big deal about things that are perfectly natural!"

Strangely, I have a clearer recollection of Frida's afternoon than my own. I wasn't there, but we had long hours to talk about it afterward. Long hours while Frida recovered. But it's more than that. When something happened to Frida, I reinvented it, relived it my mind over and over again, until it was as though I had been there.

The two lovebirds made their way through the streets, stopping to buy a taco or a *churro*. A light rain forced them to take refuge under a nearby awning, but after a while they ventured out again. Afternoon showers are an almost daily phenomenon here, don't forget. No one really pays attention to them. Frida and Alex started toward the plaza and ran into some school chums. They lingered to chat a while, then examined the wares in front of the cathedral, silvery and spectral in the rain.

"It's getting late, *mi amor*," said Frida with a sigh. "I have to get going."

"Parting is such sweet sorrow!" declaimed Alex melodramatically.

Frida laughed. "Shut up, you lunkhead. Can't you at least find a Mexican poet to quote?"

"*Como hermana y hermano / vamos los dos cogidos de la mano . . .*"

("Like sister and brother / we'll go hand in hand . . .")

"I don't recognize it, but it sounds like shit!"

"It's not shit! It's Enrique González Martínez. You said to quote a Mexican poet."

"Yeah, but I don't like this brother and sister stuff. I'm not your sister, I'm your woman!"

Alex grabbed her around the waist and kissed her on the neck, and they took off in the direction of the trolley.

"God, you're in a hurry to get rid of me," complained Frida.

"Don't call me God, just call me Alex!"

She poked him in the ribs and he tweaked her cheek.

They reached the trolley, and he helped her board. But all of a sudden, Frida wailed and jumped down.

"What's the matter?"

"My parasol! The little parasol that you bought for me. I must have left it at one of the stands where we bought food or something. Come on, let's go back and look for it."

They retraced their steps, and when they didn't find it, they returned to the vendor who had sold it to them.

"Come," said Alex, "I'll buy you another. I can't let my little *chamaca* be unhappy, can I?"

But the parasols were all gone.

"I'm sorry, señor," said the vendor. "Maybe the señorita would like something else. Here's a nice *balero*."

The man showed them a carved wooden cup with a wooden ball attached by a string. He swung the ball around a couple of times, then caught it in the cup to show how easy it was. Alex paid for it and they took off.

A gaily painted wooden bus stopped on the corner. Buses were a curiosity, a novelty in Mexico City. They hadn't been running for very long, and they attracted crowds of people—something like a roller coaster at an amusement park. Sometimes Frida would take me to the city just to ride the bus.

"Come on," said Frida. "Let's take this. You can transfer to the trolley later on."

Alex and Frida darted toward the door of the clunky vehicle.

The driver had decorated the dashboard with images of the Virgin of Guadalupe and faded pinups with fixed plastic smiles. A rosary dangled from the rearview mirror.

A bench ran along either side of the bus, which was packed, although Alex and Frida finally found seats toward the back. Across from them a woman in a *rebozo* nursed an infant, and a worker in a large sombrero pulled out a cigarette and lit up, jovially offering smokes to his fellow passengers. Toward the front, a housepainter with splattered overalls closed his eyes and waited for the bus to move. Between his feet, he balanced a can of paint, and in his hand he held a packet of gold-colored powder.

The driver was a young, mustachioed mestizo with a kind of nervous aggressiveness. He pulled out cockily into the busy street. He seemed to think that since the bus was bigger than the automobiles and carts, the other drivers would just have to watch out for him. Like a hotheaded knight rushing into the fray, he pushed ahead without checking for danger. A car swerved to the left to get clear. The driver bore down on the horn.

They were nearing the San Juan Market, at the corner of Cuahutemotzín and Cinco de Mayo. A two-car trolley from Xochimilco was approaching. The bus driver was about to turn onto Calzada de Tlalpán, but the oncoming train was in his way. He slowed down for a second, then gauged his distance and decided he could make it. The train proceeded slowly but steadily, as if the trolley engineer was challenging the bus driver for the right-of-way. The bus driver forged ahead. And then it happened. The trolley bulldozed the bus, hitting it right in the middle and ramming it against a wall.

The bus didn't break right away. Curiously supple, it yielded to the pressure, bending and contorting crazily before it snapped. Suddenly Alex found himself nose to nose with the worker with the cigarette, and Frida found herself in the lap of the nursing mother. It happened instantaneously, yet things seemed to be moving in slow motion. Objects floated lazily above them—a newspaper, a wedding band, a baby blanket, a pinup, a paintbrush, keys, cigarettes, a ball of yarn, gold-colored speckles. And then, with an excruciating crash, the vehicle shattered. People were hurled onto the tracks in a tempest of wood and metal. Meanwhile, the trolley moved forward slowly, deliberately, as if to claim victory over its adversary.

Alex was thrown under the train. He opened his eyes to find a metal chassis above his head and mangled bodies all around. Two or three people were dead. Others were nearly dead. Somewhere, a baby was crying.

In an instant he sized up the position of the rods. If the train moved forward another centimeter, it would slice him to pieces. Cautiously, Alex worked his way out from the pinched space. The front of his coat had disappeared, but he seemed to have no serious injuries. He looked around for Frida.

He found her in the street, bathed in blood, totally nude. Her clothes had been torn off by the force of the collision. The housepainter's packet had burst and covered her with specks of gold, giving her an eerie, carnivalesque appearance.

"*¡Miren a la pequeña bailarina!*" shouted a man. "Look at the little dancer!" He must have thought she looked like a circus performer, all covered in red and gold. Or maybe she reminded him of a dancer because her body was so slight and delicate and graceful.

Shattered glass and rivers of blood. Exposed entrails. Crushed skulls. Twisted metal and twisted limbs. The stench of bile and terror. Screams. Sobs. Sirens.

Blood oozed from Frida's body. An iron handrail had pierced her pelvis from one side to the other. But she didn't know what had happened to her. Maybe she was hysterical, or delirious, or numb. "My *balero!*" she kept crying. "Where's my *balero?* Don't tell me I've lost that too!"

Alex watched in horror as Frida groped for her toy, oblivious to the rod that impaled her. He tried to calm her, to keep her from moving. He threw what was left of his coat over her and picked her up. Frida continued to twist and cry, "My *balero!*" The huge piece of iron moved with her body.

A familiar-looking man came running up to Alex.

"Is that Frida Kahlo? Oh my God! What's that thing she's got sticking into her? We have to get that out!" He grabbed the iron rod.

Alex was frantic. "Who are you?" he screamed.

"I work at the school. What difference does it make? Here!

Put her down! Someone call an ambulance!"

The man pinned Frida's body in place with his knee and yanked. Frida shrieked with pain. Blood gushed from her wound. Together the man and Alex carried her to a nearby billiard hall and laid her by the window. Alex stroked her hand, but Frida didn't even know he was there. She was in too much agony.

They didn't hear the Red Cross ambulance come because Frida's wailing blocked out the siren. Alex helped the medics ease her onto a stretcher and transport her to the hospital on San Jerónimo Street. All the time he was praying, "Please don't let her die, dear God. Please, please don't let her die." He was a revolutionary, of course, but at moments like those, you forget about politics and just pray. By the time they got to the hospital, he was exhausted and nearly hysterical.

A weary nurse with a large mole above her lip took his arm. The mole seemed to expand and contract as she spoke, and Alex had to focus on that mole in order to keep from collapsing at her feet. All the nurses wore ankle-length white tunics tied at the waist and a wimple with a red cross on it. In the rarefied air of the hospital, they seemed like specters that floated in and out of ill-defined spaces, nodules of light that appeared and disappeared, angels who guided dazed pilgrims to safety.

"Come," she said. "You can't stay here. They have to get the young lady ready for surgery."

"Will she be all right?"

The mole remained motionless.

"Tell me, will she be all right?"

"It's in God's hands," she murmured finally. "If he wishes to save her, he will work through us."

"I wanted to squash that mole, and with it, that voice that seemed to come from an apparition," Alex told me. He was screaming at the nurse in his mind: "Stop talking about Jesus and tell me if Frida's going to be all right!" But he didn't say it out loud. He was too upset, too consumed with fear. He just sat down and waited.

The doctor's prognosis wasn't encouraging: multiple fractures, deep wounds.

"Have her parents been notified?" Alex asked when he got his wits about him.

"Not yet. There hasn't been time." The doctor sighed. "We'll do everything possible, of course, but it'll be a miracle if she survives."

Frida's pelvis had three separate cracks in it, and her spinal column was broken in several places. Her collarbone and two of her ribs were smashed. Her right leg was shattered, her right foot dislocated, and her left shoulder thrown out of joint.

A nurse appeared to tell the doctor that Frida was in the operating room. Alex turned toward the wall and did something that he seldom allowed himself to do. He cried.

The hours are endless when you're waiting to see whether or not someone will die. The air teems with demons. The angels wrestle with them as best they can, but sometimes they lose. Often they lose. The hospital had once been a convent, and its rooms were dark and cold and full of supernatural murmurs. All around, people were scurrying, whispering, giving orders, but Alex felt enveloped in an immense silence. He closed his eyes. Images of Frida, the sunny adolescent, the tease, the seductress, erupted into a clutter of mangled bones.

A nurse touched his arm.

"Will she be all right?" he asked wearily.

"For the moment, I'm concerned about you."

"There's nothing wrong with me."

Alex looked up at the nurse. The insignia on her collar identified her as a nun. In postrevolutionary Mexico, nuns were forbidden to wear their habits, although some of them did. Except for the insignia, the garb of a nursing sister was no different from that of her lay colleagues.

Alex had been so anxious about Frida that he had forgotten his own condition; now he became aware of a dull pain working its way from the top of his head to the base of his skull. But he had no idea of the seriousness of his injuries, or that he himself would be confined to bed for months.

When Frida awakened, Death was sitting by her bed. That's what she told Maty. "It's not just that I can feel it," she said. "I can see it. Death dances all over the room. Sometimes it rides a bicycle around my bed. Sometimes it takes a guitar and plays a cheerful tune. An enticing tune, one that makes me want to go to Death and embrace it." All during her life, Frida found death attractive, alluring. Even when we were very young, when she still found it frightening, even then, death fascinated her.

"I begged her not to talk like that," Maty told me, "but she said that Death wasn't scary the way it had been when she was six or seven, that it looked like a skeleton, *her* skeleton, and that it wore her clothes—her blue skirt, her white blouse, her sweater. She said the skull had a little red rose painted on it. Very pretty. Very lively. According to her, Death has a sunny disposition, and Death is a girl, so we should say 'she,' not 'it,' when we talk about . . . it . . . her." Maty was very upset by that conversation, as you can imagine, but I could see what Frida was trying to do. The doctors said she might die, so she was trying to look death in the face, to come to grips with it.

One good thing about the accident is that it brought the family back together. Mami still hadn't forgiven Maty, but we all were rallying about Frida, and we had to pull together. Maty, Adriana, and I went to the hospital nearly every day, and Mami and Papá went when they could, although not right away. Mami was so upset when she heard what happened to Frida that she went to pieces, and Papá was having so many problems with his health that it was hard for him to get out.

The first time I saw Frida after the accident, I nearly fainted. She was encased in a coffinlike structure, her torso caged in a stiff plaster cast and her legs pinned into a kind of swing. Maty was afraid to touch her, and I was scared even to get close. She looked like a mummy. I was afraid that she was already dead.

"You'll be getting out of here soon," Maty kept saying.

"But who knows where I'll be going! Maybe back to Coyoacán, maybe under the ground. At least I won't die a virgin. The rod that went into my belly took care of that!"

"Ah?" said Maty. "I heard another version of how you lost your virginity." She forced herself to laugh, and then they were both quiet.

"Mami and Papá send their love," I said to break the silence. "Papá's been having seizures again. He'll come as soon as he can."

"I want to see Papá."

"I know. Don't worry, he'll come. You know that Adri passed out when she heard what happened to you?"

"It's true," said Adriana. "Alberto said that I was in no condition

to make the trip to the city, but I came anyway. I wanted to see you."
Alberto was Adriana's husband.

"*You're* in no condition!" snapped Frida, suddenly hostile. "That's
pretty funny. I'm the one who almost died! I'm the one who had a
rod stuck in her gut."

"I'm sorry," whispered Adriana, blinking back tears.

Frida was instantly repentant. She grew pensive, then weepy.
"You're the only ones who really love me," she sobbed. "You, my sisters." And then she said something that made me really angry!
"Especially you, Maty. You're the only one who bothers with me. You
and my Cachucha friends. They've all been here. But it's funny . . .
When you ran away with Paco Hernández, Mami said you were the
black sheep, that you were a good-for-nothing, but you're the only
one who hasn't abandoned me. You're an angel, Maty."

Where does Maty come to be the angel? I was thinking. *I'm* the
one who's been putting up with Frida's nonsense for the last seventeen years. Her arrogance, her airs. I'm the one who shared her
room, although I moved into the other bedroom after Adriana got
married. I'm the one she always confided in. I'm the one who helped
her through all those terrible times with Alex. She always told me
that *I* was her best friend, her *cuate*. And now *Maty* is the one who
loves her the most?

"How could I abandon you?" Maty was cooing. "You were the
one who helped me run away! You were the one who closed the window so that nobody missed us for hours! You were only seven years
old, remember? Anyway, one black sheep deserves another, and,
according to what Papá tells me, Mami says you're the blackest sheep
of all. Even blacker than me!" They both laughed in sisterly collusion.
I felt like vomiting. Suddenly, I was happy that Mami still wasn't talking to Maty, even though she and Paco had gotten married, and she
was now a respectable señora.

Frida ambled on about Death, *la pelona*, "old baldy," we call it—
or her—in Mexico. And then she started to whine about Alex. He
hadn't come to see her, although she had written to him. He hadn't
even answered her letters.

"So that's it," I said to myself. "That's why she's being nasty to me." I was the one who knew about her ups and downs with Alex, you see, and I guess she was sort of embarrassed. After all, she had chewed my ear off about their "reconciliation."

"Alex was hurt pretty bad in the accident too," I reminded her.

"Not as bad as me, though," she retorted. "I was hurt the worst. And now nobody bothers to come to see me except for you all and the Cachuchas and *la pelona*."

"The doctor says that the longer you keep *la pelona* at bay, the better your chances of sending her packing," said Maty soothingly.

"You know, Maty," said Frida, "sometimes I think she'll be with me always."

Look, doctor, I understand that she had just been through a trauma. Yes, goddamn it, of course I know what a trauma is! You're just like Frida. You think I'm stupid. Look, all I'm saying is that she had a real bent for the melodramatic, and she was playing her role to the hilt.

Of course I felt sorry for her. What do you think I am? A demon? She was my sister, and she was suffering. I'm just saying, even then, in that awful state, she knew how to manipulate.

Anyhow, from the hospital Frida wrote long, detailed letters to Alex. She described her pains, the doctor's diagnosis, the treatments. She complained about the nurses. She said she understood that with twenty-five patients per nurse, it was impossible for them to do better, but still, she thought they should pay more attention to her. I saw some of the letters. She spoke of the visits of her schoolmates or of friends from the Communist Youth Organization. She complained of her boredom and her terrible luck. She told him how she cried when they told her how much pain he was in. I don't know if that's true. I never saw her cry over anyone else's pain.

Poor Frida. You have to admit, she was a remarkable girl. She went through so much, and yet she kept going, kept struggling. I suffered to see her suffering. She was so frail, but she had a will of iron and a spirit like a geyser. I loved her so much. In spite of the fact that she made me so angry and hurt me so deeply, I loved her more than anyone. Really.

Portraits

WHEN FRIDA WAS RELEASED FROM THE HOSPITAL, MAMI WAS SO RELIEVED that she offered a mass of thanksgiving, which we all dutifully attended, except Frida, of course, who couldn't be moved, and Papá, who was too traumatized to deal with God. Then Mami took out an ad in the local newspaper expressing her appreciation to the Red Cross. Everyone remarked that it was a nice gesture, although Elena Cabrera Andrade, Estela's mother, went around saying that Matilde Kahlo was always looking for a way to get her name in the society pages.

Frida was impossible. "Paint my nails for me, Cristi. No! Not like that, you moron!" "Read me this story, Cristi. Dummy! You don't even understand what you're reading!" "Cristi, bring me my mirror." "Cristi, bring me a glass of water." "Cristi, bring me the note that came from Alex. I know you're hiding it."

She was convinced that I stashed away Alex's daily letters because I was jealous of their magnificent love affair. The truth is, Alex never wrote. Or not very often. Anyway, I was having a magnificent love affair of my own. Pinedo and I were going to be married, so it wasn't as though I had nothing to think about except Frida and Alex.

At first, the Cachuchas came to see her, but then fewer and fewer were willing to spend two hours on the trolley to make the round-trip visit to Coyoacán. Frida didn't like being alone, so she'd call for me to come sit by her bed. But then she'd get nasty and complain that I didn't pay enough attention to her. It's true that she was as bored as a plank full of carpenter ants, but that was no excuse for barking at me all the time. I wound up looking for excuses to get out of the house so I'd have to spend as little time with her as possible.

As for the wedding, Mami was a disappointment. I mean, mothers are supposed to go all gaga when their daughters get married, aren't they? They're supposed to shop and make guest lists, plan menus, put announcements in newspapers, all that stuff, aren't they? Announcements like, you know . . . "The noted European photographer Guillermo Kahlo and Mrs. Matilde Calderón de Kahlo announce the marriage of their daughter Cristina to . . ." I thought she would be harping at Papá about dress fittings. But no. She had to attend to Frida. Well, of course. Frida had been in a serious accident.

It just didn't seem fair, because Frida was the one who had always been the troublemaker. Along with Maty. Maty was no bargain either, according to what Mami had been saying for years. But now, all of a sudden, everything was different. Maty had gotten married, and Mami let up on her. In fact, now Maty came to the house all the time, and she and Frida were the two new best friends. I should have been the star, since I was the one getting married. I was doing everything right, wasn't I? I was playing by the rules. But Mami treated Maty as though she were the prodigal daughter, and as for Frida, Mami couldn't do enough for the poor little invalid.

Frida wrote to Alex almost daily—long, pleading letters in which she itemized her ailments and begged him to visit and to write. "Oh my darling Alex, I spent the whole night vomiting! Please come to me." Or else, "Oh dear, beloved Alex, my stomach is so inflamed I can hardly fart! I'm dying to see you!" And then, long, detailed descriptions of all her operations—one on her arm, one on her spine, one on her uterus. Really, for such a smart girl, she was pretty stupid. What I mean is, what man wants to read stuff like that? Is it really wise to tell your lover that it hurts when you take a crap? No wonder Alex practically stopped answering. He did come to visit once, but Rufina told him Frida wasn't home. After all those years, Rufina was still mad at Frida and Maty for putting one over on her the night Maty ran away with Paco. Rufina took vengeance on Frida every chance she got. That's why she told Alex that Frida had gone to visit I don't remember who. Imagine, after he had spent a whole hour on the trolley. Frida was furious. "That maid hates me!" she sobbed. "She hates me!"

To tell you the truth, we were all getting tired of Frida's complaining. Frida was hurting, yes, but she was also playing for sympathy. She moaned incessantly, but the truth is that she was making a lot of progress. Mami was convinced that the Virgin was lending a hand because, you know, the Virgin loves a sinner. Just like Jesus. That's why he went into the den of thieves, remember? And don't forget Mary Magdalene.

Before we knew it, Frida was sitting up, then standing, then walking. Sometime in December, she decided she was well enough to make a trip to Mexico City. Mami didn't want to let her go, but finally, she gave her permission—not that Frida cared one way or another about Mami's permission. The condition was that I go with her. About that, Frida wasn't one bit happy. The last thing she wanted was me tagging along, because her reason for going in the first place was to see Alex.

"As soon as we get to the city, I'll dump you somewhere," she said. "Then we can meet up at El Lazo Roto for lunch."

She left me off near the Zócalo and pointed out the place where we would eat. "Now, don't wander off and get lost so I have to spend the whole afternoon looking for you," she scolded. I hated it when she talked to me that way. As though I were a four-year-old. As though I were an idiot. She didn't think I was capable of going for a walk and finding my way back. She thought I was too dumb to keep track of where I was going.

"He's not here," the maid told her when she knocked on the Gómez Arias' door. Frida waited a while in the parlor, then took off for the Ibero American Library. But Alex wasn't there, either. She walked around the Prepa. She peeked into the cafés and shops where she knew he hung out. She couldn't find Alex, but Agustina Reyna was buying a book at the Librería La Mancha, and I guess it was impossible for Frida to pretend she hadn't seen her. Anyhow, the two of them showed up together at El Lazo Roto, where I had been waiting for a good fifteen minutes. Not that I'm picky about time, but the point is, I didn't get lost.

It was an uncomfortable situation. After all, I wasn't supposed to be there. For one thing, I wasn't a Cachucha, and therefore wasn't bright enough to carry on an exchange with such superior people. For another, what they wanted to talk about was Alex, and for that, I was definitely in the way. Neither of them made any effort at all to include me in the conversation, so I just sat there stupidly eating my *arroz con pollo* and looking at the table.

Agustina was fumbling around for something to say. Neither of them wanted to be the first to mention Alex.

"So, will you be back with us next year?" ventured La Reyna. "Will you finish up at the Prepa, then enroll at the university?"

"I don't know," said Frida. "I don't think I'll be able to continue at school."

Agustina tried hard to look disappointed. "That's too bad. But you could make up your tests." Because of her accident, Frida had missed the fall round of examinations.

They chitchatted a while. Frida talked about her accident, about how she had already lost the habit of studying, about our medical expenses. "As soon as I get back on my feet, I mean, really back on my feet, I'm going to have to get a full-time job to help my parents," she told Agustina.

There was an uncomfortable pause, and then Agustina made a move.

"What were you doing at the library this morning?" she asked slyly. I didn't think it was a very subtle question.

"What do you mean?" asked Frida. We both knew what she meant.

"Were you looking for Alex?"

"No . . . ," stammered Frida. "I . . . I just wanted to see who was there."

"You know," said Agustina, "you ought to try to forget Alex. I'm trying to forget him myself."

The remark caught Frida off guard, and for once she was slow on the comeback.

"You know," added La Reyna, "Alex isn't a gentleman at all. He said some horrible things about me. He said I was almost as big a tramp as you!"

Now, I've certainly been candid about Frida. I've recognized her faults. I never said she was perfect, or even close to perfect, but Agustina's words left me flabbergasted. How could she say a thing like that about my sister? It was a cruel thing to say, and poor Frida, she was stunned. Agustina looked at me and smiled as if she had just made some innocuous comment like "I think it's going to rain," or "The cathedral looks pretty all lit up." I know that Frida wanted to cry, but she held it in. I could almost feel her saying to herself, "I won't cry here, I won't cry here." My own chest was constricting and my back ached horribly. You see, that's the way it was with Frida and me. When she suffered, I suffered. When she felt pain, I felt pain.

Yes, it's true that sometimes I'd grow impatient with her. When you live with a person who's as demanding as Frida, you're bound to grow impatient. One thing has nothing to do with the other. You can love a person and still get annoyed at her. The point is, when Frida was miserable, so was I, and sitting there that day in El Lazo Roto with Agustina Reyna, we were both miserable.

"You know what else he said?" Agustina went on.

"She doesn't want to know what else he said," I interrupted. Frida squeezed my hand in gratitude, but Agustina had no intention of letting up.

"He said that you were a worse slut than Nahui Olín, that woman who used to model for Rivera. He said that what you gave to him, you also gave to Lira, and to who knows how many others: Lira . . . Fernández . . ."

Frida looked mortified. Maybe she was upset that Alex knew about Fernández. As for Lira, that was the first I'd heard about it.

"He even said that the worst accident he ever had in his life was you, but that he was finally recovering. So I guess," said La Reyna, savoring the effect her words were having on Frida, "that Alex has ruined both our reputations, so both of us had better forget him."

That afternoon we returned to Alejandro's house together, but the maid turned us away.

It's true that I sometimes criticize Frida, but what you have to understand is that we were so close that it was impossible for us not to get on each other's nerves. After we came back from the city, Frida became . . . I don't know the right word . . . melancholy, I guess. Nowadays, they say *depressed*. You're the one who knows about this sort of thing. Is *depressed* the right word? I don't know whether it was because she really adored Alex and couldn't bear to lose him, or because she couldn't stand rejection of any kind, but she sank into a funk as gloomy as purgatory. It was awful. I couldn't think of my *novio* or my wedding or anything but Frida. I forgot about the dress, the lace, the music, the invitations, the flowers I had dreamed of for months. There wouldn't be any money for any of it, anyway.

As I told you, Frida had made a quick recovery in spite of all those operations. In just a month she was out of the hospital, but after that visit to the capital, she started having relapses. They say that a person's state of mind affects her health. Is that true? It must be, because Frida's poor little body seemed to be coming apart like a sand castle slapped by a wave. The doctors hadn't taken X rays. They had seen no need, since her spine seemed to be mending nicely. Now they discovered she was a wreck inside. She was in constant pain, and she had to have one medical procedure after the other. There was no money left, and Papá couldn't pay for the treatments the doctors said that Frida needed. Instead of real medication, they gave her plaster corsets, which helped for a while, but then the pain started all over again.

I shouldn't mention it, but I had dreamed of a nice wedding, with an embroidered dress trimmed with Mexican lace. I would have used Maty's if she had had one, but Maty had been living with Paco for about eight or ten years when they finally got married, so what was the point of making a party? Adri used a hand-me-down from María Luisa, and I would have used it too, even though I didn't care much for my half sister. The thing is, it had a big stain on it, and who wants to start married life with a stain?

I know I told you that I forgot about the wedding, that I was too wrapped up in Frida even to think about it, but I guess it would be more accurate to say that I put it out of my mind. You're right, I didn't forget about it entirely. I mean, no woman forgets about her own wedding. Looking back, I guess it was a bad omen, all these problems.

Frida wasn't very interested in my romance. Nothing I did ever interested her until I—until I fell in love with someone that she loved too. That got her attention.

Frida continued writing to Alex to no avail. And what made her feel worse was that I had a fiancé who walked me home from work and came to call every Sunday. I was basking in my *novio*'s attention. I knew that eventually I would be a bride, and a bride is always the star, at least for one day. Did I rub Frida's nose in it? Did I gush just to make her feel bad? I honestly don't know. What I can tell you, though, is that during those months Frida was as dejected as I had ever seen her.

Most of the time she had to stay in bed, but whenever she could get up, she puttered around the house, and that's how she discovered the one thing that would bring her relief: Papá's paints.

"Cristi, do you remember those chimerical mornings when we were little, and we accompanied Papá on his painting expeditions?" she once said to me. I was embarrassed to tell her I didn't know what *chimerical* meant, so I kept my mouth shut. It didn't matter, though, because Frida wasn't waiting for a response. She just kept on talking. "Sometimes I'd help Papá set up his easel and paints, but to tell you the truth, I didn't pay much attention to his work. How about you, Cristi?"

"Me either," I mumbled. Actually, most of the time I didn't go. Most of the time it was just her and Papá.

"But I should have, because now I feel like trying my hand at painting. Do you think I could do it, Cristi?"

All I knew was that the only time Frida had had any training in art was when she was working for Fernández. Papá had never tried to teach her painting because he wanted her to be a doctor. Even when it looked as though she'd never return to school, he still held out the hope that she'd somehow get her medical degree.

"Can I have these?" she asked Papá, holding up some containers of color. "It looks as though you haven't used them for years."

Papá's answer surprised me. "No, Frida," he said. "They're mine."

"It's the German in him," she whispered. "He always starts out by being obstinate, but he'll come around."

And sure enough, after a few days he agreed to lend them to her, but just for a while. "All right," she said, "just for a while," although both of them knew she'd never return them.

The pains in her back and legs prevented Frida from sitting for long periods, so Mami hired a carpenter to construct a special easel that hooked onto the bed. That way, Frida could paint lying down. Then Mami hung up a mirror so that Frida could use herself as a model. Mami thought painting would be a nice distraction for Frida. To tell you the truth, I think everyone was happy to have her occupied and quiet.

The funny thing is, Mami had fought with Frida like a hyena after the Leticia Santiago affair, but now she bustled around her room, straightening up, freshening her flowers, gathering her dirty clothes for the maid to wash. It was Mami who bathed her and fixed her hair. It was Mami who smoothed down her sheets. And now Mami had ordered this wonderful new easel for her. Frida asked me: "Is it possible for a girl to love and hate her mother at the same time?"

What made Mami so attentive? Guilt? The realization that Frida might die? Maternal duty, pure and simple? I can't tell you. I don't know. Anyway, you're the one who's supposed to figure it all out.

At first, Frida painted a few hours a day, then for mornings and afternoons at a time. Toward the end of summer, 1926, she completed her first self-portrait, which she sent to Alex as a gift. It wasn't that good, to tell you the truth. It was sort of stiff, not at all like the things she did after she got more practice. She painted herself as a Renaissance lady—the kind we had seen in books—with a distant gaze and a velvet dress. Anyhow, it worked. Alex not only accepted the painting, but once again became Frida's *novio*.

You know, Frida could be arrogant, but she was also very fragile. What I mean is, she wasn't all that sure of herself, in spite of that cocky attitude. Sometimes, when she was painting, she would suddenly start to cry, "It's no good! I don't know what I'm doing! If only Papá would teach me!" But Papá was too busy with his own problems to worry about Frida's new hobby.

One day she couldn't get the colors quite right in a self-portrait. "This stupid painting," she screamed. "I hate this stupid painting!" I just stood there and watched her. I knew better than to intervene. I

had just had an argument with Antonio about the date of our wedding—he was tired of the postponements—and the last thing I wanted was a tussle with Frida. "Damn it!" she howled. "Damn! Damn!
Damn! I can't do anything right!" All of a sudden she took the brush
and starting drawing black X's all over the picture.

At that point, I had to open my mouth. "What are you doing!" I
demanded. After all, those paints and canvases cost money. She had
used up Papá's old cache weeks before, and he had had to go out and
buy new materials for her, which she was now wasting. And just when
Papá was telling me there wasn't any money for a wedding!

Frida just kept on painting X's. Then she took her brush and
started to scribble, mixing all the colors together until they were a
black-brown mess. A mess the color of shit! That's what she had done,
you see, she had covered herself with shit! Shit in her eyes, shit in her
hair, shit in her mouth, shit on her forehead.

"Stop it, Frida!" Now I was screaming.

But she wasn't through, and what she did next mortified me. She
pressed her open hands against the wet canvas, then smeared the disgusting concoction of colors all over her eyes, her hair, her mouth,
her forehead.

She was crying, really sobbing, and the tears poured down her
face, making channels in the muck.

"Please stop it, Frida," I begged. I was terrified. "Stop it! Stop it,
please!" I wasn't yelling anymore. I was trying to calm her, but she
wasn't even conscious of my presence.

"Oh God," she moaned. "Oh God. I can't do anything right. No
wonder no one loves me!" Then she stuck her hand right into the
paint on the palette, the red paint, and started spreading it all over
her cheeks, over her corset, her sheets, her pillow, everything. Her
entire face was covered with red and brown and black, every part
of her face except her teeth, and even they were tinged with red. It
looked like blood was dripping from her mouth. It was as though she
was bathed in blood. She was transforming herself into a ghoul! All
of a sudden, an image flashed into my mind. Miss Caballero's class.
The time when the teacher had tried to embarrass Frida in front of
the other children, and Frida had wriggled free and covered herself

with paint. And now it was happening again! I let out another scream, and Mami came running, but before she could attend to Frida, she had to attend to me because I was hysterical. She called for Inocencia, who brought me a *hierba luisa* with something in it and put me to bed. I think I slept all the way through supper.

But in spite of everything, Frida kept on painting. Mostly she painted her favorite subject: herself. No, that's not fair. Frida was stuck in bed most of the time, so it was normal for her to use herself as a model. After Frida was able to spend more time sitting up, Maty would come and sit for her, or Adri would. She painted portraits of me and Mami too. Everyone said her work was lovely. Everyone said she had talent. She began to think that maybe she could even earn some money as a painter. But she really didn't trust our judgment, and she was right not to. After all, we were all friends and family. What did we know about painting? "Who can I ask?" she kept saying. "Who would give me an honest opinion?" On the one hand, I think she honestly wanted to know whether or not her work was worth anything. On the other, I suspect she was frightened by the idea of asking an expert. Who wouldn't be?

"Well," I said to her, "you used to know a famous painter."

Frida bit her finger and thought about it a while. "No," she said finally, "I could never ask Diego Rivera."

"Why not?" I insisted. "You said he was nice, that he wasn't a snob."

She stood there a while without speaking. "He's the only person whose opinion I could trust absolutely," she said finally.

But she didn't look him up, and we didn't talk about it anymore that day, or the next either, as I remember. About a week or two later she brought it up again.

"I really need an impartial evaluation," she said. "I know you and Mami mean well, but I can't trust your opinions. You don't know the slightest thing about painting. And neither do I."

I thought it was kind of miraculous that Frida admitted that there was something she didn't know anything about. Especially art. After all, she had read a lot of Papá's books, and she had spent a lot of time at the library. You would have thought she would consider herself some kind of an authority.

"Well," I said, "go find an expert. Go find Rivera."

"I don't know whether or not he'd remember me. After he finished painting the amphitheater, I only saw him a couple of times. Once at one of Tina's parties. He was carrying a pistol and all of a sudden started shooting streetlamps out the window. He even shot Tina's phonograph! It was scary . . . and funny! But he was with another girl. Maybe he didn't even notice me—even though he did grab me around the waist and put his hand on my ass."

Frida was talking about Tina Modotti, the mistress of Edward Weston. You know, Weston, the American photographer. Tina had come to Mexico with him and stayed here after he left. Well, Tina was part of the avant-garde crowd that some of the Cachuchas hung around with after they finished the Prepa. A few of Frida's old friends started taking her to Tina's parties. Tina knew all the artists. She slept with most of them, including Diego, and she gave these wild orgies at her house. All the top talent went, and Frida, too, not only because she liked the artsy crowd and wanted to be one of them, but also because she was sure of not running into Alex there. He had a new girlfriend now, and he had changed. He had become very, very serious.

"Who cares if Rivera remembers you! He probably doesn't, because he was probably too drunk or crazy to know whose ass he was feeling, but it doesn't matter, Frida, just go find him. Ask him! What have you got to lose?"

Frida didn't answer. She just stood there, but after a while, a satisfied little smile began to form on her lips, and I knew she had made up her mind.

CHAPTER 13

Encounters and Couplings

THERE ARE A LOT OF BOGUS STORIES ABOUT FRIDA AND DIEGO. REPORTERS were always writing about them, and whatever they didn't know, they just made up. They'd come down here to interview us. All of us. Me too. They were interested in everything about Frida—her old letters, her little dogs, her doll collection, her dirty hankies, even her sisters. And then Diego wrote this book a few years ago. Let's see . . . it's 1963 now and Diego died in 1957 . . . It must have come out in '58. He describes how he met Frida, but just like everyone else, he leaves out one important detail, which is: I was there.

Only, I was invisible. This is what happened: At the time, Diego was painting the frescoes at the Ministry of Education. Wonderful frescoes, Frida said. Paintings that celebrated our Mexican heritage by depicting Indians working in the fields that had been returned to them by the Revolution, Indians holding meetings and deciding their own destinies, Indians in school, learning to improve themselves. Tra-la-la! Frida was always singing the communist tune in those days, always on the soapbox pushing the communist line. What were they learning, those Indians? Were they learning Spanish, the language of the conqueror? Were they learning the farming methods invented by Europeans? Now people are asking if all that "improvement" of the Indians was such a good idea, or if all we really did was wipe out their culture, but back then, no one asked. Especially Frida. She was too carried away with the Party slogans. She had just joined the Young Communist League. Well, where was I?

Frida had about three or four paintings she wanted to show Diego. They were heavy canvases, and her back was still giving her problems, so I offered to go with her and help carry them. No matter what they say, I always tried to help Frida.

We had a nice trip in the trolley. Frida was a little jittery, but she was chipper and talkative, and she kept telling jokes about Diego's looks. But as we got closer to the Ministry of Education, she started to clam up. She was growing more and more tense, and then, all of a sudden, she said to me, "Listen, Cristi, I don't think you should go the rest of the way with me. Why don't you give me the paintings you're holding, and I'll go see Rivera alone." I was stunned. After all, I had taken the morning off from work to accompany her, and now she was telling me to get lost. It seemed pretty rude to me.

"And what will I do while you talk to Diego Rivera?"

"You could just wander around."

"I don't want to just wander around," I said.

We kept walking toward the Ministry of Education. When we were a few meters away from the entrance, she turned to me.

"Give me the canvases," she commanded. "Then go into that little shop and buy yourself some pastries and something to drink, and I'll meet you there as soon as I'm done talking to him." She pointed toward the Pastelería Agua Mansa. "You like to eat," she added. She was being sarcastic.

I handed over the paintings and she took off, walking as fast as she could, which wasn't very fast, since her spine and leg were bothering her and the paintings were bulky. I let her get pretty far ahead of me, then followed her into the Ministry at a distance.

Why do you think she didn't want me to go with her? Because I was the prettier one and she didn't want Diego to see me? Because she didn't want him to know that she was an invalid who needed help carrying her paintings? Or was it just nerves? Maybe she was afraid he would tell her to shove off and she didn't want a witness, or maybe she thought he'd take her for a baby if she showed up with her sister. Anyhow, I crept along until I pretty much caught up with her. She

was too wrapped up in her own thoughts to turn around, I guess. I
was careful to be very, very quiet. I got pretty close, then ducked into
a doorway.

Diego was on the scaffold. From where I stood, he looked like an
enormous ass topped by a peanut-sized head. Frida walked right up
to him. "Diego!" she called. "Please come down. I have to talk to you
about something."

An awful thought popped into my mind: I hope he drops a brush
on her head and tells her to scram. I hope he spits at her! It was a
horrible, mean-spirited thing to think, but I was miffed because Frida
hadn't let me go with her to meet Diego Rivera. I stood there fuming
and waiting to see what would happen. What happened was nothing.
Diego looked at her and smiled, but kept on working. Lots of young
girls went to watch him paint. He was used to it, and he loved the
attention, but he couldn't stop every time a pretty face materialized
in front of him. Good, I thought. He's just going to ignore her.

But Frida never gave up.

"I have something to show you!" she called.

Diego kept on working, but he gave her a kind of once-over. You
know what I mean. He looked her up and down. He always loved a
fresh young girl, and even though Frida wasn't, shall we say, conven-
tionally pretty—I mean, she was lame and had a mustache—she had
a kind of brazenness that made her attractive to a lot of men.

"Look," she said. "I'm not flirting with you. I have something
serious to talk to you about. I've brought some of my paintings and
I would like your opinion of them."

After a long pause she added, "I am Frida Kahlo. I met you a
long time ago at the Prepa."

Did he recognize her as the little girl who had faced down Lupe
Marín in the amphitheater years before? Maybe. Lombardo Toledano
was always complaining about her, so maybe the words *Frida Kahlo*
stuck somewhere in his brain. Or he could have remembered her
from Tina Modotti's party. Anyhow, she pestered him a while and he
finally climbed down, strangely nimble, a hippopotamus on a
tightrope.

"I'm not here to play pranks," she said. "I'm here to get your opinion on my paintings. I have to earn a living, and I want to know if you think I could become a professional painter. If I have no talent, I'd rather know it now so I can stop wasting my time and find something productive to do."

Diego looked at her paintings, but actually, I think he was looking at *her* out of the corner of his eye. He had just separated from Lupe Marín. They had never had a civil wedding, and church weddings weren't recognized in postrevolutionary Mexico, so they didn't have to get a divorce. Diego had been in Russia to paint a fresco celebrating the Red Army, and by the time he got back to Mexico, Lupe had decided she was sick of his affairs. He had been carrying on with Tina before he left, and Lupe felt he was making her the laughingstock of Mexico City. The minute he walked in the door, she told him to go to hell, and that was the end of it. Lupe was a real tiger. Diego licked his wounds and hopped into bed with Ana, with María, with Neli, Marta, Rosalía, and so on and so forth. I found out about all this much later, when Lupe and I became friends.

One peek at Frida's valiant boobs was probably enough to convince him that the conversation was worth having.

He looked—or maybe pretended to look—at Frida's paintings a long time.

"I have many more," she said. "If you want to come to my house on Sunday to see them, I live in Coyoacán, Avenida Londres, 126."

"You have talent," he said. "I especially like this self-portrait." But I couldn't tell whether he actually meant it or was just saying it to be polite, because after all, Frida was a young lady. Then he said something else, but since he was turned toward her and I was standing off to the side, I couldn't quite hear. I supposed he said something like "I would love to see the rest of your paintings, little girl, but I'm busy on the weekends." After all, he was a famous painter with hundreds of friends, and besides, he was an important member of the Communist Party and had meetings and important functions to go to.

Frida said thank you and good-bye and moved through the corridor toward where I was hiding. Diego offered to help carry her paintings, but she said no, she could manage. Of course, she didn't want him to see her out. She didn't want him to see her join up with

me in the pastry shop on the other side of the street where I was supposed to be waiting for her.

I met Frida halfway up the corridor. "What are you doing here?"
she snapped. "I thought I told you to buy yourself a cake and wait for
me over there." She nodded toward the shop.

"So? I didn't do it. So what?"

"Here, take these paintings," she ordered. She handed me the
two heaviest ones.

"Well? What did he say?"

"You should know. You were spying on me."

"I couldn't hear very well," I lied. Actually, I had heard everything but that one sentence.

"He said he adored my paintings, that my portrait is magnificent,
that I was one of the most talented young artists around, and that he
would be happy to visit me on Sunday to see the rest of my works."

"Really?" Since she exaggerated on the first part, I assumed she
lied about the second. I figured he had just made some polite excuse
or some ambiguous remark to salvage her feelings. I mean, I certainly never thought the great artist Diego Rivera would agree to
come all the way out to our house in Coyoacán just to see the paintings of a twenty-one-year-old girl.

No, Frida wasn't eighteen at the time. She was twenty-one. Don't
forget, she had been out of commission for a year after her accident,
so she just took another year off her age. So now she was making herself three years younger than she really was. If you read that she was
eighteen, that's because she always lied to reporters.

You can't imagine my surprise when that Sunday, who should
appear at our house but the great Diego Rivera! Frida was wearing
overalls and climbing a tree, and I was sitting in the shade daydream-
ing, when this enormous beast comes clumping along, clump clump
clump. He was wearing a clean shirt for once, and pants that weren't
all speckled with paint, a jacket, and his typical Stetson. He was smoking a cigar that made an awful stink, but Frida said she liked it.

"Is this where Señorita Kahlo lives?" he asked me.

"I am Señorita Kahlo," I said, just to be ornery.

Frida threw a twig down from the tree, and it landed right by those big steamboats. I mean his feet, of course.

"I'm the Señorita Kahlo you're looking for. That's the other Señorita Kahlo. Come on," she said, without introducing me. "Let's go inside and I'll show you my paintings."

That day Diego didn't stay too long. He looked at the paintings Frida had set aside for him to see, but I didn't hear his comments because I didn't accompany them to Frida's room. She made it very clear that she wanted him all to herself and didn't care to have me tagging along. I thought: Even if he doesn't like them, he'll tell Frida that he adores them because he's a real lady-charmer. He'll tell any girl that he loves her work in order to jump into the sack with her. Frida must have had the same thought, because after they came out of her room, I heard her tell him, "Please give me your honest opinion. Don't try to flatter me, because I really can't waste time on something that I'm no good at."

Frida asked him to stay for supper. He declined but promised to return the following week.

Mami was not pleased at all. It was bad enough that Frida had become a communist and ran around with the likes of Tina Modotti, that crazy woman who thought she was a photographer, but now she had become friends with this fat old painter who boasted he was a national treasure. In Mami's middle-class Catholic mind, Diego was nothing more than an oversize atheist.

True to his word, he came by the following Sunday afternoon, but this time Frida and I were both dressed for callers, I in a simple skirt and blouse and she in a tailored man's suit that Alberto Lira had given her when he'd outgrown it. She wore a carnation in the lapel; the color of the flower was identical to that of her brilliant lipstick and the polish she wore on her Dracula-length fingernails. She had pinned a matching carnation in her hair, which was slicked back like an Argentine tango dancer's, only it was too long to be a man's. The trousers hid her misshapen leg, but strangely, as if to call attention to her handicap, she had put on a ridiculous little pair of satin slippers. You can't imagine how feminine she looked, how feminine and how seductive. It was incredible how alluring she could be in a man's suit. I was a little nervous—after all, Diego was already a legend and here he was, right in my own living room—but Frida was very poised, not in the least flustered.

His entrance was like an invasion. First, his Trojan-horse belly, then a warship-like foot, two shoulders like battered citadels, lips that reminded you of fresh carnage, flaccid jowl, chins, nostrils, a second warship-like foot, a baggy posterior (deserted bunkers? empty store-rooms?)—an army of incongruous parts that seemed subject to some inner, cohering discipline in spite of their individual functions. I found him repugnant.

Mami invited him to sit down, and as he sank into the chair he swung his arm—a huge, unwieldy battering ram—and knocked over a silver tea service, one of the few remaining mementos of better times, which went crashing to the ground like ten thousand suits of armor clashing furiously. He spread his legs to accommodate his gargantuan paunch and smiled self-consciously as Inocencia picked up creamers and sugar crystals. How could this uncoordinated mass of parts be a great painter? I wondered. I felt as though our space had been violated. Yet Frida seemed hardly to notice.

I peered at him coyly. I crossed my legs and arranged my flowered skirt over my knees. Dainty Cristina. So graceful. *She* was laughing raucously. She was recalling some hilarious prank the Cachuchas had once played at school and describing the incident in meticulous detail. He turned toward her, his face as impassive as a rhinoceros's. Then he smiled, parting his meaty, obscene lips. He smelled slightly of sweat and turpentine.

"Old Mr. Bayer, the English teacher," she was saying, "he turned as red as a whore's underpants when he opened his desk and found an exquisite porcelain pot full of dog shit!"

"Frida!" snapped Mami.

But Diego was enchanted. His smile widened, and the scales of armor dropped off his face slowly, as if they had trouble detaching themselves from his skin. He no longer reminded me of a rhinoceros. The flesh beneath the coat was as smooth and fragile as the skin of a delicate fruit. In fact, settled into the cushiony armchair, he now reminded me of a huge, overripe plum, ready to split and pour forth its sweet, sticky juice. Much later—decades later—I realized that those paintings Frida did of voluptuous, succulent, mangoes and watermelons, slit and spilling their juices to the viewer, were actually portraits of Diego.

"That's disgusting, Frida," I said self-righteously. Diego's eyes were no longer on Frida. No. He was looking at me. I could feel his gaze on my ankles, on my knees, on my thighs, and I shifted nervously in my chair.

Then, all fleshy and oozy, he looked me right in the eye and grinned.

A shiver shot from my elbow to my ear, and suddenly I felt as though I were sitting there naked in full view of everyone—Diego, Frida, Mami, Papá, Inocencia, everyone. Instinctively, I lifted my hand to my chest, as if to protect myself, and once again, Diego's lips parted into what seemed to me to be a lewd smile. I looked away. My eyelids were stinging.

Frida was jabbering about her communist youth group. Something about equality. Something about the new Mexico, where workers and peasants would rule. Something about no more foreign investment. Something about the end of Yankee imperialism. Diego had turned back to her and was eating it up. Don't forget, he was a revolutionary hero, an instrument of the people. But, except when it came to painting, Diego had a short attention span, and after a while, I think, he forgot about the masses. Yes, he definitely forgot about the masses. Instead of contemplating the masses, he was examining me from head to toe. Me. Not Frida, but me. He wasn't even discreet about it. Didn't my parents notice? They were sitting only a few meters away. And what about Frida? Was she too absorbed in her story to realize? I don't know. I've never understood how he got away with it, but I guess that for Diego, admiring a beautiful young girl was so natural, so normal, that he could ogle without attracting attention. Or maybe the others just didn't want to see. Or maybe, maybe I just imagined the whole thing.

Well, that was the beginning. After that, Diego came to our house to visit every Sunday. It was a very bourgeois courtship for two rabid communists. He would bring a bouquet of flowers or a box of bonbons and would sit in the parlor and talk to Papá about the political situation. He and Frida would go for walks around the plaza, just like two old-fashioned sweethearts, except that he would be dressed in work clothes and she would be wearing jeans and a black shirt with a hammer and sickle pin. Politics was an obsession they shared. In one of the murals in the Ministry of Education, Diego showed Frida as a Communist Youth activist in a work shirt with a red star on the pocket, surrounded by bigwigs from the Party. Frida used to say that the attraction between them was electric. Once, according to her, they were walking along the street at dusk when all of the streetlamps went on. It must have been about five o'clock. The way she told it, Diego took her gently around the waist and kissed her on the lips, and the second their flesh touched, the lamps began to glow. Can that be true, or is it just another one of Frida's inventions? According to Frida, there was so much voltage between them, they could have lit up the whole city. Anyhow, I'm sure they didn't limit themselves to pristine kisses under streetlamps. I'm sure they slipped off to Diego's apartment and fucked themselves crazy, or else carried on like savages at Tina's orgies. But in Coyoacán they performed like middle-class angels with wings of gossamer, even though they looked more like an orangutan and a sparrow. There was no doubt that Diego was absolutely in love with my sister, although, to tell you the truth, whenever I was present, he couldn't take his eyes off me.

Was I flattered? Of course I was. After all, we're talking about the great Diego Rivera, painter-hero of the Mexican Revolution, and besides, there was something irresistible about Diego in spite of his bulk. Or maybe because of his bulk. He was so sensual. Fleshy and sensual. You wanted to touch him. You wanted to sink your teeth into those folds of flesh. Besides, he had such a reputation. No, I don't mean as an artist . . . that is, I don't mean *just* as an artist, I mean as a lover. He had been with so many women; at least, that's what people said. A girl couldn't help but be fascinated. A girl couldn't help but wonder: What's he giving to the others that I've never had? What does he do that other men don't do? And then it was the way he looked at you, the way he talked to you. He made you feel that you mattered, that he really admired you, that you weren't just some thing, some object with the necessary equipment to satisfy his needs.

Once I got to know him, I never felt like just the other sister. I was me, Cristina, not as brilliant as Frida, maybe, but a young woman with ideas and opinions and feelings as well as a beautiful body. He would tell me about communism, about his days in Paris, about Picasso and Juan Gris and André Breton, the poet. He would talk about the Italian frescoes, about his trip to Russia, about how he tried to sign up to be a soldier in World War I. In other words, he treated me like a real person, and that's why I fell in love . . . No! I don't mean that. I didn't fall in love with him, at least not then, while he was courting Frida, because I was in love with someone else. I was very much in love with my own fiancé. We were going to be married soon, very soon. In fact, we were married that year, 1928. So, although flirting with Diego—and I guess I did flirt—was a pleasant game, it was nothing more than that, because I would soon become Señora Cristina Kahlo de Pinedo.

In spite of all Papá's complaining about being broke, we did have a wedding. Mami finally got herself into gear and started to behave like a proper Mexican mother of the bride, fussing over lace and sending pictures to the society pages. The ceremony turned out to be just what Mami wanted: a church affair with her darling youngest daughter wearing white. All our friends came, although the festivities weren't too elaborate because of the money situation. Me and Mami and Inocencia spent days making burritos, enchiladas suizas, tamales, *chiles rellenos, empanadas,* mole, *ceviche* . . . There were vats of *pulque* and *sangria.* All kinds of *pasteles. Dulce de coco. Arroz con leche.* Frida helped too. She loved to cook. Maty and Adri also lent a hand. Even though we had to skimp and do without a lot of things, and do all the work ourselves, there was plenty of food. We had a civil ceremony as well, because Mexican law required it. Pinedo was very handsome and proper-looking at the mass, although a bit distant. Maybe he was intimidated by Frida and Diego and their artist friends. He thought they were degenerate and silly. Especially Diego. Here he was masquerading as a worker when he had ten times more money than any of us and lived in a big house with a studio and a car. "He's a phony," Pinedo said to me, and I guess that in a lot of ways he was right. We went to live in a little house on San Cristóbal Street, not too far from

Mami and Papá, and before I knew it, I was pregnant. Isolda was born in 1929, the most precious, bright-eyed little bundle you could imagine. Well, I thought, at least I did something right. You see, I was the only one of my sisters who had produced a baby.

Mami was growing more and more apprehensive about Frida's relationship with Diego. She didn't care that he was a famous painter. The arts were not something that mattered to Mami. Diego was too fat and too communist and, above all, too old. He was already forty-one, twenty years older than Frida. Besides, he was a slob and a playboy.

Mami was so beside herself that she wrote to Alejandro and begged him to do something. But Alejandro was busy with his new girlfriend, and frankly, I think he was glad to be free of my sister. They had been like a *balero*; Frida was the cup and he was the ball. Every time he'd try to get away, she'd whine and snivel and snap him back and catch him. Now he had finally cut the string, and he wasn't about to fall into that little cup again. Would Frida have gone back to him if he had begged? I don't think so. She was too happy being the girlfriend of the magnificent Rivera. She went to parties with famous people who paid attention to her because she was with Diego. It made her feel important. She wasn't about to give that up.

During all this time, Frida was painting like crazy. That's something I have to hand to Diego. He never discouraged her. Some famous men keep their wives in cages, like decorative birds. They don't want them to have interests of their own. But Diego appreciated Frida's talent, and he pushed her to paint. He wasn't exactly her teacher. I mean, he didn't give her lessons. "I don't want to overwhelm her," he told my father. "I don't want to impose my own style on her." But he was very supportive of Frida, and she was grateful for it. She would watch him paint for hours, sitting beside him on the scaffold. That's how she learned.

She did this one portrait of me where I look like I have a rod up my ass, all serious and stiff. A tree branch is leaning toward me as if it's alive and wants to touch me, and another lonely tree cowers in the background. It's a weird picture; the canvas seems to extend right into the frame, as though I'm oozing out of the painting and into the real world, which is exactly how I feel sometimes—like I'm trapped in some sort of cell that's too small for me, and I kind of pour out in spite of everybody's efforts to keep me contained.

Frida also painted a portrait of Adri about the same time. I don't like it. It makes her look like a mean old schoolteacher. I said old. Old, like me. How old do you think I am? No, don't look at the records, just guess. I'm fifty-five years old, and I feel as though I'm a hundred. Adri glares out of the painting as though she wants to nab you. She's wearing an off-the-shoulder dress that emphasizes her enormous breasts, and she looks very imposing. The kind of person you don't want to antagonize. It's funny, because Adri wasn't that way at all. Frida also did a lot of portraits of children—neighborhood kids, the sons and daughters of friends. Frida loved children. She was a good aunt to mine.

Well, Frida and Diego were becoming almost inseparable. Mami still didn't like him, but she was beginning to see that he had more than enough money to take care of Frida, and besides, he was generous. Don't forget that Papá was still trying to pay off Frida's doctor bills, and we were worried about losing the house.

One day Papá said to Diego, "It looks to me like you're interested in my daughter."

Diego laughed that deep, throaty laugh of his. "What do you think?" he said. "That I have nothing better to do with my Sundays than to travel out to Coyoacán to see a girl I'm not interested in? Of course I'm interested in her. That's why I'm here."

"She's not an easy child," said Papi. "Cristi here is much easier." I was visiting my parents with my baby Isolda, just as I did every Sunday.

Diego smiled at me. "Yes, I know. Frida is a real little demon, but I love her very much."

"Well," said Papá, "you've been warned."

"Yes," said Diego. "I've been warned."

"And another thing," added Papá. "Und anoder tink. She is expensive. Zer are doctors' bills." He explained about Frida's illnesses, about her accident. He told Diego that Frida would probably need medical attention for the rest of her life.

"Come," said Diego. "Let's talk."

The two men went into Papá's study to hash things out, I guess. I wasn't invited to go with them, and anyhow, I had to nurse Isolda. The next thing I heard, the wedding date had been set for August 21, 1929.

Frida had to outdo me in everything, didn't she? I had made a nice marriage and I had produced a beautiful baby, but I wasn't the one who was going to be the savior of the family. No, of course not. The savior of the family was Frida. Or rather, Diego. I thought I had done everything right, but I couldn't pull them out of that morass of debt that Frida had gotten them into with her sicknesses and her accidents. No, I don't mean that. It wasn't Frida's fault. But the truth was, her medical expenses were so enormous that they ate up every cent Papá made, and he wasn't making much. We would have lost the house on Londres Street for sure if Diego hadn't taken over the mortgage payments. And he not only paid for the house, he let Papi and Mami go on living there. Later, when my husband left me, I went back and lived there too. Isolda, little Antonio, and I. So we all owe Diego a lot. If it weren't for Frida . . . If Frida hadn't married him, I don't know what would have happened.

It was a very lively wedding, I heard. Not the civil ceremony, of course. The party afterward. I didn't go to either one, and neither did my mother or sisters. Mami didn't like the kind of people Frida and Diego had invited or the fact that there was no priest, and she carried on so much about it that Maty, Adri, and I were afraid to cross her. She would have taken it as a slap across the face if we had abandoned her that day and run off to Frida's bash. Don't forget that Maty had only recently worked her way back into Mami's good graces. Papá went, though.

Some wedding. They showed up at the courthouse and said their I do's in front of a judge. Very revolutionary. Very in keeping with their communist, anticlerical principles. I'm sure it made them giddy with self-righteousness to dispense with the clergy. Poor Mami. She had cared for Frida so lovingly while she was ill, and now Frida was throwing tradition into the sewer and marrying without religion, knowing how much that would hurt her.

Frida didn't even wear a wedding dress. No, a wedding dress

would have been too bourgeois. Instead, she turned the ceremony into a political statement, a declaration of her solidarity with the people. She borrowed clothes from the maid. The maid! Skirts, a blouse, a *rebozo*—that is, a kind of shawl poorer women wear hear in Mexico. She could have at least put on a *nice* Tehuana dress, a *new* Tehuana dress. She could have gone to the market and bought one, but she wore Inocencia's daughter's old rags. I'm sure she thought it was a cute move, very radical. Or maybe she just wanted to humiliate Papá because he couldn't give her the kind of wedding he had given me. Anyhow, she stuffed her shoe and wore heavy stockings so you couldn't see she was lame—she was always good at camouflaging her defects—and, for added effect, smoked during the whole ceremony. In the picture that came out in the newspaper the next day, she had a cigarette dangling from her lips, just like a whore. Excuse me, but that's what she looked like. Mami nearly fainted. Diego just wore a regular suit with no vest. "It was a joke," Papá told me afterward. "Eet vas a choke! Such business, such business. How can such business be taken seriously!"

After Judge Mondragón said the magic words and Frida and Diego were husband and wife, they all took off for the house of Andrés Henestrosa, a writer who was a good friend of Diego and Frida's. He had a nice voice, and he always sang at all the parties, especially after he got good and drunk. He was part of Tina Modotti's crowd, so that should give you an idea. So they all left, except for Papá, who went home.

For months the stories circulated about the orgy at Henestrosa's. This one got drunk and peed in a flowerpot. That one got drunk and threw up on the sofa. The other one got drunk and grabbed Lupe Marín between the legs, not that she minded. And then someone was smoking opium and someone was crazy on heroine. I didn't go. I had a baby to take care of. Isolda had a bad cough and I didn't want to leave her with the maid, and besides, I had the impression that Frida didn't really want me there with her unruly crowd. In other words, I wasn't invited. They were the elite, you see. The aristocracy of the art world— even though there wasn't supposed to be any aristocracy in Mexico. Very distinctive people. Frida did tell me about it afterward, and I admit it, I asked a lot of questions. I was curious. I had never been to a party like that, and I wanted to know what it was like. The women wore bobbed hair, greased to keep it close to the head, and mannish blazers. The lesbian look was still in with Frida's crowd, even though it was going out everywhere else. Tina Modotti wore a revealing red shift, her abundant hair caressing her body sensuously. She shouldn't have been there, because Lupe was. Lupe hated Tina because Tina had posed for some of the nudes in Diego's murals in the Chapingo Chapel, which had made Lupe wildly jealous. She blamed Tina for the breakup of her marriage, and when she saw her at Henestrosa's, she went right up to her and slapped her. "Slut!" she screamed. "Why don't you go back to California or Italy or wherever the hell you came from!" Tina had actually been born in Italy, but had lived with Weston in California before coming to Mexico with him. When she was done insulting Tina, Lupe grabbed Frida's skirt and pulled it up. "Look at those legs," she shrieked. "Wooden legs! Legs like toothpicks!" When I heard this story, I remembered how the girls at school teased Frida, how they chanted, "Peg-leg Frida! Peg-leg Frida!" and I felt sorry for my sister. "These are the legs that Diego now takes to bed with him instead of mine!" And then she pulled up her own dress to reveal her gorgeous gams. Lupe was still tied to Diego emotionally—they had two children together— and even though she said she didn't love him anymore, she couldn't stand it that he had found someone new.

Diego behaved very badly at that party. He got drunk on tequila and went around shooting things—plants, lamps, mirrors, vases, glasses. He left Henestrosa's place full of bullet holes and didn't even offer to pay for the damage. Hugo Leffert, a journalist from some-where, I can't remember where, tried to get the gun away from him, and Diego shot off his little finger! Frida usually thought Diego's antics were cute, but things were getting out of hand. This was their wedding party, and he wasn't paying any attention to her. Instead, he was firing his pistol and grabbing the women's asses, walking into walls and breaking Henestrosa's china.

"You're behaving like a savage," she told him.

Diego was indignant. Who was this twenty-one-year-old kid to tell him what to do?

"I'm your wife, that's who," she snapped.

Diego roared like a wounded lion. "Get away from me! Get out of here!"

"Fine!" said Frida. "I will!" And she burst into tears.

It was late at night, but she made her way all the way back to Avenida Londres and fell asleep in the same bed she had slept in since she was a little girl.

The next day, when I went to visit, I found her sobbing. "I'll never go back to him!" she cried. "Never! I'll live with you and help you take care of Isolda!"

But in a few days Diego came to get her, and they began their life together.

CHAPTER 14

Endings and Beginnings

THEY SAY I'M A RECLUSE. THEY SAY I DON'T LIKE PEOPLE. AFTER ALL I'VE been through, can you blame me? Ever since Frida left . . . I mean, ever since she died . . . I've felt so alone. I don't even see much of my own children. They're not interested in me. Nobody is interested in me. Now that Frida isn't here anymore, it's as though I never existed. I was someone only as long as I was standing there by her side. I was the other sister, the other Kahlo sister, the dumb one, the one who never did anything. But at least I was a living, breathing person.

I don't know why I'm telling *you* this. After all, I don't really know you. Why are you still bombarding me with questions? You're beginning to annoy me.

You want to hear about Frida's marriage, don't you? Isn't that what you said? Don't forget that I was married too, although things weren't going so well. In fact, things went badly right from the beginning. I thought I was doing everything right. As soon as Isolda was born, I got pregnant again. That's what girls were supposed to do, wasn't it? Give their parents grandchildren? None of my sisters had managed to do it, so I thought I'd be the queen of the Kahlo hive, because I was the only Kahlo girl who could produce babies. I thought that, for once, I'd be the favorite. But I guess Frida's health problems had left Mami exhausted, because she didn't really seem to have much energy left for me.

Diego and Frida went to live at 104 Reforma. It was a French-style

house, the kind they built when Díaz was in power and everyone still
believed that everything European was better. It was an elegant house
on an elegant street, because Diego was a national treasure. After all,
just because he and Frida identified with the masses didn't mean they
had to live like them. Diego was always interested in archaeology, and
he had hundreds of little pre-Columbian figurines, including one of a
man sitting astride a snake that's really a gigantic penis. Ha! Diego loved
that kind of thing. Anyhow, he explained to me that, in the Maya-
Quiché culture, the snake was a fertility symbol. See, that's what I mean.
He explained things to me. He didn't treat me as though I was too
dumb to understand. He was the only one who made me feel that I mattered, that I was beautiful, that I was actually *there*.

They had a house full of people. Naturally, there was a servant,
because even though they were communists, they still had to be waited on. What I mean is, everybody had servants, even after the
Revolution. Even though the radicals talked about people all being
the same and nobody having to kowtow to anybody else, Indians still
flocked to the cities, and women took jobs as domestics for a couple
of cents a day. Now, three decades later, it's still the same. The thing
is, having a servant didn't make you antirevolutionary. Just because
somebody picked up your shit and cleaned out your bedpan didn't
mean that she wasn't as good as you. It's just that she had her job,
and you had—well, I don't know. It's sort of complicated.

They had a servant named Margarita, and the painter Siqueiros,
his wife, and a bunch of other communists moved in with them. I
can't remember who. It was such a long time ago, and don't forget, I
was busy with my baby. What I do remember is that there were people everywhere, because in addition to the friends who lived with
Diego and Frida, other communists were always stopping in. They
slept on the floor in the dining room or in the parlor. They crowded
together on the sofas, under the tables. At first Frida loved it. It was
like a big game, like a camping trip. "We're all brothers and sisters,"
she told me. "We work together and help each other. I cook, Andrea
supervises the housework, Edit does the grocery shopping . . ."
Andrea and Edit were two of her communist friends. "And if I don't
feel well, I don't have to worry about it, because one of the other girls

takes over." But afterward, the newness wore off and the whole thing got tedious. "I wish they'd get the hell out of here so I could fuck my husband in peace!" she told me. They could have come over to my house. I wasn't fucking my husband at all, and I could have used some company.

Why wasn't I fucking my husband? Because as soon as I got pregnant, Pinedo started telling me I looked like a milk cow, and before I knew it, he was carousing all night and screwing the neighbors' daughters.

After a while, the communists did clear out, because Diego was in big trouble with the Party. He was secretary general of the Mexican branch, but some people thought he was in cahoots with the new government, which was strongly anticommunist. The country had moved to the right, you see. The international Depression was making money tight, and the government wasn't anxious to spend pesos on starving Indians and workers. Besides, a lot of people thought the goals of the Revolution had been accomplished and it was time to give up the struggle. But they were wrong. Anyone could see that the masses were still miserable and the rich were still calling the shots. The poor idolized Diego because his paintings celebrated the common people and showed their suffering. But for the communist bigwigs, pictures of peasants weren't enough. They wanted total commitment, and the way they saw it, Diego was playing footsies with both sides.

Diego adored being a Marxist superstar. He loved being the hero of the crowds, but he wasn't—what do you call it?—an ideologist, an ideologue. He wasn't above accepting a commission from the anticommunist government. He used to laugh about it. "What do I care if they want to pay me for making fun of them in my paintings?" he'd say. "I don't see what's wrong with taking money from pigs to fight for God's forgotten children." But the thing is, Diego wasn't really a very good Party member. He didn't go along with everything the communists wanted, and he had a lot of friends who weren't communists at all. Besides, going to meetings, waiting for other people to speak, taking votes, that wasn't his style. He wanted to do things his own way. He expected to show up at those Marxist powwows at his own convenience, crack jokes, chug down a few drinks, and have everybody eating out of his hand. The hard-nosed Stalinists didn't like that. They were serious boys and that wasn't their way at all. They wanted Diego to follow the rules, and when he refused, they decided to throw him out.

Wait a minute. I'm confusing things again. I'm giving you the wrong impression. It's so hard to get things right. I don't mean to say that Diego wasn't a Marxist at heart. He *was* a good communist. He believed in equality and all the things you're supposed to believe in. He believed in the beauty and strength of the people. He really believed that he was doing good, bringing the Party message to the masses through his murals. I mean, he was trying to help achieve the goals of the Revolution with his brush. He was sincere about it. The point is, he was more of a pragmatist. He wasn't above kissing the *culo* of a few conservatives, a few rich bastards, for the opportunity to educate his beloved peasants, if you know what I mean. The Calles government was pretty reactionary, but they kept feeding him assignments. They gave him a commission to paint a mural at the National Palace, and he accepted it, which made the communists think he was two-faced. They were—you know, purists, and they saw Diego as a traitor and an opportunist.

He knew they were going to throw him out, so you know what he did? He went to a Party meeting with a big pistol in his hand. He covered it with a bandanna and put it on a table, then, in an elaborate speech, he accused himself of collaborating with the bourgeois government and officially expelled himself from the Party. He paused, looked around, and waited to see who was spluttering with rage and who was peeing in disbelief and who was as paralyzed as a polecat that just got bit in the balls by a rattlesnake, and when he was convinced that they were all sufficiently shocked, he picked up the gun and smashed it on the edge of table. Pieces went flying around the room. The comrades all caught their breath, and Diego roared with glee. It wasn't a real gun at all, only a clay model!

"I really had the last laugh!" he boasted to Frida and me. Isolda and I were on one of our rare visits to the city. "You should have seen the looks on their faces! Ha! They think they can expel Diego Rivera?

No one can expel Diego Rivera but Diego Rivera!" He kept looking at me out of the corner of his eye to see what kind of impression he was making. I laughed as though my guts would pop. It had been a long time since I had let go like that, and I liked the effect my laughter was having on him. It was as though we were dancing together without touching, as though we were doing a wild, suggestive dance after which we would collapse, exhausted, into each other's arms— only without touching. It's hard to explain, but sharing that moment with Diego, sharing that laughter with Diego, inflamed me. I felt flushed, dizzy.

Frida didn't notice.

"I quit too!" she announced, making a fist. "Solidarity!"

"Solidarity!" trumpeted Diego. But he was still looking at me out of the corner of his eye.

Actually, Diego was just putting up a front. He felt lost without the Party. After he dropped out, some of his best friends abandoned him. Tina would have nothing to do with any of us. Diego had just taken over as the new director of the Academy of San Carlos, but everywhere, people were turning against him, and before we knew it, they fired him. He started working longer hours than ever, I guess in order to blot out the pain. He worked on the murals at the National Palace, the Ministry of Public Education, and the ones that, well— the ones that started us on the road to trouble—the murals at the Ministry of Health.

We were sitting in a little café in Coyoacán, I can't remember which one. Actually, I can't even remember if Frida and Diego were married yet. I think they were just married. Frida was doodling, drawing obscene pictures that made Diego roar with delight. They were both obsessed with genitals. She was smoking one cigarette after the other, and so was I. The smoke made me nauseous because I was pregnant, but even so, I kept on lighting up those cheap cigarettes, those bitter, black Mexican cigarettes that make you feel as though your lungs will burst. Now I only smoke blond cigarettes, American cigarettes. Every once in a while, Diego tried to caress my leg under the table, running his fingers up my thigh, under my dress. I'd turn away and cross my knees so that he couldn't get his hand on my crotch. I was

used to his antics, and so was Frida, but you could never tell how she'd
react. Sometimes she'd just laugh it off when he flirted with other
women, but other times she'd fly into a rage. I didn't want her mad at
me, so I just smoked and giggled as if nothing was happening.

Diego was working on the murals at the Ministry of Health at
the time—six huge nudes, allegories of Purity, Knowledge, Strength,
Moderation, Life . . . what else?—Moderation—no, I said that . . . oh,
of course, Health. We were fooling around, the three of us, when all
of a sudden Frida blurted out: "Hey Diego, why don't you use Cristi
for your wall? She's pregnant now, and her tits are really big!"

"Frida!" was all I could say. I mean, what was I supposed to say?
I just sat there, gasping.

The thing is, it was true. I was feeling very voluptuous. As I told
you before, my husband wasn't looking at me very much those days,
but when I'd walk down the street, other men would eye me and go
Pssst! pssst! *¡Llévame a Edén, mi amor, llévame al Paraíso!* Take me to
Eden, my love, take me to Paradise! I had that full, round, soft body
that men associate with submissiveness. That's what drove them
crazy—the idea that they could do whatever they wanted with me.
Not that I was so pretty, or that my hips were so ample or my skin
was so tight. It was that I was like a big plush doll they could squeeze
or lie on, like a pillow. I was pliable.

Diego chortled. "Cristi!" he said. "Why, I never thought of that!
That's a fine idea!"

Like hell he never thought of that. He'd been looking me up and
down since the first time we'd met, only back then, he wanted Frida,
so he couldn't very well come after me too. Even when they were
courting, Frida knew Diego fooled around with other women, but
her own sister? She wouldn't have stood for it. A little groping under
the table was one thing, but anything more than that . . . And now,
here she was saying I should pose for him. Was she toying with me?
Trying to shock me? I think she just liked playing with fire, pushing
people to their limits. She knew that Diego usually wound up in bed
with his models. She was always trying to catch him, then she'd fly
into a rage when she did. But now she was pretending that posing
nude had nothing to do with sex, that this was going to be a strictly

professional arrangement. I mean, she knew that Diego liked my body. He was always flirting, teasing, making comments. So why was she trying to put us both in this risky situation? It was a game she was playing. She was going to choose all the models for the Ministry of .Health, she said. Was she going to put the crotches of all her best friends within reach of her oversexed husband just to see what would happen?

"Tell me about the mural," I said, to make time. I didn't want to answer right away. I didn't want to say what a great idea, or something like that, then change my mind later.

"It's a series of allegories," he said.

I must have looked at him as though he had belched in Chinese, because he added, "Figures that represent ideas." The way Diego explained things, he didn't make you feel stupid. He didn't say it as if he were defining a word I was too ignorant to know. He just said it, you know, naturally. "Figures that represent ideas."

And then he went on: "Six nude figures, with decorations showing a hand holding bundles of wheat—ripe wheat, ripe, like you." He patted my belly. "Ripe and voluptuous, just like you. You'd be perfect."

The word *nude* stuck in my mind. I knew the painting was of nudes, but the way he said it made me feel as though he was looking right through my blouse. Frida loved to be nude, to paint herself in the nude. But I had less experience in that department, and I still had Mami's old-fashioned ideas. For Diego, there was nothing moral or immoral about nudity. People had bodies. They could either cover them with clothes or not. He loved beautiful objects, including the beautiful bodies of women, and he filled his paintings with them. He painted a lot of nudes, and he had a lot of women because he also loved sex. But he didn't paint nudes because they were sexy, but because they were gorgeous and interesting forms. Also, a body could represent something to him—an ample, shapely one like mine could be fertility, or a scrawny one could be misery.

I wasn't so sure what I wanted to do. The way Diego had been looking at me, I knew once I took my clothes off for him—I mean, I knew at the end of the session it wouldn't just be "Thanks for your help and *adiós*." I knew that . . . something might happen.

"I think you'd make a very good model," Diego said, suddenly serious. His hand wasn't on my leg anymore. I guess I was supposed to pretend I understood just because I would have to undress didn't mean he was going to seduce me. I was confused. Here he was suddenly being solemn, distant even, when I knew that what he wanted was to break into me like a plow into fresh, moist ground.

Frida was egging me on. "Go ahead, say yes," she said. "You're pretty enough. You're much prettier than I am." What I think is that Frida was excited by the idea of having me take off my clothes for Diego. She almost always went to watch him paint, and all I could think was that the two of them would be standing there, fully clothed, while I would be posing stark naked. Sort of like a gang rape, only with just eyes. Their eyes on my body, on my nipples, on my thighs. It would be even more uncomfortable because, well, this is awful to say because she was my sister, but don't forget that Frida liked girls, too. I could feel my face redden. They say that pregnant women don't become aroused, but it's not true. The thought of those four eyes kneading my flesh made me dizzy, feverish. That night, I waited for Pinedo to come home with my heart in my throat. For the first time in months, I really wanted him. He came in drunk, as usual, smelling of whores, but I didn't care. I attacked him so passionately I thought he would give up his hookers forever. At least, I thought he'd remember making love to me when he woke up. But then I knew I was wrong. Afterward, he fell off me like a concrete block and plunged into a void. Down, down through the bed, through the floor, through the earth like a lifeless mass, down to the core of the planet, so far away from me . . . so far that I knew I couldn't reach him, no matter how hard I tried. Once in a while I heard his voice, a million miles away, drifting toward the surface from an abyss. He was muttering things, things related to arguments he had had, to debts, to women. Things that had nothing to do with us.

"Absolutely," Frida was saying. "She would make an excellent model. She's so fecund-looking! Like a beautiful tree laden with luscious fruit. Come on, Cristi. Say you'll do it!"

"I don't know," I said. "I'd have to think about it. What would my husband say?"

But we all knew he wouldn't say anything, or if he did, it didn't matter. Lots of men find their pregnant wives disgusting, but still, they can't stand to think of them in another man's arms. But Pinedo . . . It's not that he wasn't possessive. It's more that he gave up on our marriage almost from the very beginning. He surrendered to the inevitable, to what he thought was inevitable. He thought that Diego and Frida and their whole crowd were degenerate. He detested Diego. If a housepainter went out drinking and whoring, that was okay. That was normal. But a painter of pictures, an artist, a man who stood around looking at naked women all day, that wasn't healthy, that was perverted. He associated Diego, and Frida too, with depravity. And because Frida and I were so close, he began to think that I was just like her, that it was just a matter of time before I started doing the things she did. "Whore!" he would scream. "You, your sister, Tina, Lupe, you're all the same! She-cats on the prowl!" When I got pregnant with Isolda, he started to run around. He couldn't stand to look at my swollen belly. It made him sick, he said. "Who do you suppose made me puff up like this?" I asked him. "Do you think I got pregnant all by myself. This baby is *yours!*" After Isolda was born, for a while he got a kick out of playing the proud papá. You know, the macho guy whose wife pops one out nine months after the wedding. But when I got pregnant a second time, he just snapped. He became unbearable. He'd ram me against the wall and snarl, "This one isn't mine! Whose baby are you carrying?" You can't imagine how those words stung. He behaved as though he couldn't stand to look at me. I knew he wouldn't say a word if he found out I was posing for Diego, because, well, he was expecting it. He was expecting me to fall, just like, you know, just like Eve. In fact, he thought I already had.

Which allegory do you think I posed for? I was Knowledge! I think Diego chose me for that one as a joke. Me, Cristina, the stupid sister! I was sitting very demurely, looking down, my knees together, holding a little flower in my hand. Frida said a flower is symbolic of female sex because it opens up like the female sex organ, but maybe her head was full of cornmeal. Off to the side, a serpent is slithering up a tree. According to Frida, the serpent convinced Eve to eat from the Tree of Knowledge, and then Eve knew she was naked and found out about sex. But in spite of all these sex organs, it's not a very sexy picture. Knowledge isn't very enticing. I just sort of sit there, looking down at the flower.

I also posed for Life, the allegory on the ceiling. It looks like I'm flying, or rather, hovering in the air, because Life encompasses all of nature, everything represented by all the other allegories. Actually, I was lying down on my back when Diego painted me. Flat on my back.

Posing nude for Diego wasn't as bad as I thought it would be. I stopped being embarrassed after a little while. In the beginning, he was very professional, very matter-of-fact. He surprised me, really, because I thought he'd be flirting with me the whole time, but that came later. I suppose Frida's presence kept him in line—that, and the fact that I was pregnant, and very, very nervous. For a long time, he hardly looked at me, except to guide his brush. I never felt he was ogling me. To tell you the truth, I liked posing for Diego. I was the most prominent of the allegories—Knowledge and Life. You have to remember that this was all happening when Pinedo was treating me like scum. He was always belittling me. Sometimes, when he was drunk, he would get really mean, and other times he would just sit and sulk. I was beginning to think he wouldn't stay with me even until the baby was born. I felt helpless, desperate, but posing made me realize that I wasn't completely worthless. If the great Diego Rivera appreciated me, I must be good for something. After a while, Pinedo began to fade out of my life. Whether he was there or not, whether he was drunk or not . . . it just didn't matter. Diego was the one who filled my mind. After the Ministry of Health, Diego asked me to pose for him all the time. After Antonio was born and I got my figure back, I got to be his favorite model. It was something I could do for him that nobody else could, because Frida—it's strange—but Frida didn't like Diego to paint her nude. She did nude self-portraits, but she hardly ever posed for her husband. Maybe it was because she was lame and her back was twisted. I already told you she was a master of camouflage, and in her own paintings she could camouflage her imperfections. But she couldn't be sure how Diego would recreate her, so she wouldn't pose for him. Or maybe that wasn't it at all. Maybe she just got a thrill out of watching him paint other women, out of tempting fate. She was almost always on the scaffold with him, and in a strange way, her presence was sort of comforting. Feelings were starting to grow inside me, disturbing feelings. But I kept telling myself, I'm not doing anything wrong. How can I be doing anything wrong? Diego's wife—my own sister!—is standing right here beside me.

When you're sitting for an artist, you don't feel embarrassed, because the work he's doing creates a kind of barrier. I mean, you're there for a purpose. You're helping him do his job. It's not as though you're just standing there for his pleasure. And his clothes create a barrier too. That's what I kept telling myself.

Frida was busy setting up her new home. She went shopping with—you'll never guess who—Lupe Marín! Lupe helped her buy pots and tablecloths and material for curtains. In other words, she did what Mami should have done. Mami still couldn't stand Diego, and it was a long trip from Coyoacán to Mexico City, so she wound up leaving Frida pretty much on her own. I guess Mami was disappointed in all of her daughters, although, God knows, I tried.

Lupe even taught Frida how to make an extraordinary *mole poblano*, Diego's favorite dish. They wound up becoming good friends. It's funny, Frida always made friends with Diego's sweethearts. Maybe it was a way of holding on to him. She made her rivals into allies so they wouldn't betray her, so they'd leave her husband alone once and for all. But it didn't work, did it? After all, who can you trust if not your own sister?

Frida didn't use her new curtains for very long, because she and Diego moved to Cuernavaca. Maybe you knew the American ambassador, his name was Dwight Morrow. He liked Diego's work and commissioned him to paint a mural in the Cortés Palace. Diego was always ranting about you Americans, about how you exploited Mexico, taking natural resources out of the country and treating us all like morons who didn't know a bull's ass from a whiskey bottle. Still, when Americans offered him dough, he took it. That's one of the reasons the communists got after him. About the time my Antonio was born, Frida and Diego moved to Morrow's house in Cuernavaca so Diego could work on the Cortés mural. The ambassador was going to be on vacation, so it worked out perfectly. The residence was a very luxurious affair, from what Frida told me. I didn't visit them because I was too busy with my baby. But I'm not surprised they accepted Morrow's invitation; Diego was fond of his comfort.

After she got married, Frida stopped painting for a while. She spent her time watching her husband work, choosing his models. But Frida was sort of bored in Cuernavaca. There was nothing much for her to do but wait on Diego and attend social events, so she started painting a bit to pass the time. And then it happened, the event we were all waiting for, the great, spectacular event that was going to represent a milestone in the history of the world, the phenomenon that Frida had dreamed of since she was a teenager.

Frida was pregnant! She was going to have Diego's baby, just as she had predicted years before.

What kind of a comment is that? Of course I was happy. We were all thrilled. After all, what more could Mami want but a few more grandchildren? And Papá didn't care much for babies, but I'm sure he would have been gaga if the babies had been Frida's. And no, it's not what you think. I was dying to be an aunt. Dying! None of my other sisters had made me an aunt and now Frida was going to. At last, we were going to be a typical Mexican family, with grandchildren and grandmothers and great-grandmothers, aunts, cousins, everything!

Naturally, Frida's pregnancy was exceptional, because everything about Frida was exceptional. When I got pregnant, the family was happy, but no one made too much of a fuss. After all, Cristina was a real woman, with breasts like gourds ready to spill their juices and thighs like wings, ready to spread. Everyone expected me to produce a healthy baby, and I did. And, of course, they rejoiced. And when Antonio was born, they rejoiced even more, because he was the first and only male heir. Mami had had a baby boy before Frida was born, but he died of pneumonia, so Antonio was special, and I felt special because I had given him life.

But with Frida, it was different. When she announced that she was expecting, they were all delirious—we were all delirious—

because we all wanted the baby so much and we knew she was crazy to be a mother. We all went to church and lit candles to the Virgin— Mami, Maty, Adri, and I, and even our half sisters from Papá's first marriage, María Luisa and Margarita, who was very devout and later became a nun.

When Frida found out she was expecting, she moved back to Coyoacán and into her old room, so that Mami could take care of her—bring her broth, straighten her bedclothes, change her flowers, just like in the good old days. She required special attention. Even I had to wait on her, although I had just had a baby myself.

But then something awful happened. The doctor told Frida that her baby was all twisted in the wrong position, head up, feet down. It was possible that it would grow the wrong way, that it would get stuck and she wouldn't be able to deliver it. Of course, he said, she could wait and see if it flipped itself around, but even if it did, there might be complications. Frida's uterus had been badly mangled in the bus accident, and who knew if there was even room for a baby to develop fully? We were all devastated. Frida cried and cried. So did I. Really.

"What should I do, Cristi?" she kept asking me.

We both knew what she had to do, but I wasn't going to be the one to tell her.

"Talk it over with Diego," I said. "After all, he's the father."

Did I really think that Diego was going to offer much advice, or was I just being cruel? It's hard to figure out your own motives, you know. Pinedo certainly had been no help when Antonio was born. I had hoped that he would fall back in love with me after the birth because I had given him a son. A son! What every Mexican man wants! But instead of turning into the attentive, adoring father I had dreamed of for my little boy, he up and left. "What kind of woman poses nude for a reprobate like Diego Rivera while she's pregnant?" he said. And then, again and again, the business about how did he even know the baby was his. Finally, he packed his bags and took off. Men don't get very attached to their offspring, do they? They're like iguanas or something. They fertilize your egg and then just forget about it. Look at my own papá. It's true, he stuck around, but did he ever love us? I mean, aside from Frida, did he ever love one of his daughters?

Frida did try to talk to Diego about what to do about their baby, but he was too busy screwing his American assistant, Ione Robinson, to pay much attention. To tell you the truth, I don't think Diego was ever very interested in Frida's pregnancies. As he saw it, pregnancy was a woman's thing, something like menstruation— nothing he should be particularly concerned about. Remember I told you about the son he had in Paris? After the little boy died, he made no bones about the fact that he had never wanted Angelina to have a child in the first place. And when Marievna's daughter Marika was born, he wasn't at all happy about it. As for the two children that Lupe Marín gave him, Lupita and Ruth, Frida paid more attention to them than their own father did. The truth is, Diego saw kids as a bother, and he wasn't very kind to Frida about her pregnancies. Most men want their women to have babies. That's the way they prove to themselves that they're men. That doesn't mean they take care of those babies, but at least they want them to be born. What Diego wanted was to be Frida's baby himself, and he was afraid a real baby might get in the way. Frida used to spoil him, cook for him, take care of his clothes, coo over him, bring him lunch while he was working, watch him paint, put up with his love affairs. She did get jealous sometimes. She would scream and carry on, throw things, rip his clothes. But in the end, she put up with it. She pretended to laugh it off. "What do I care," she would say, "as long as he comes back to his *mamita*." She would call him her *ranita*—her little frog—her *saporana*—her toad-frog. She adored him, even when he made her miserable, and he was so selfish and conceited that he didn't care if he hurt her. Or maybe he did it on purpose, just to prove he had power over her. The fact is that Diego wasn't very interested in whether Frida had the baby or not, and so she turned to me.

The doctor didn't perform the operation himself. He sent her to an abortionist, an old woman with gnarled hands and kind eyes who gave Frida a *manzanilla* spiked with something to relax her, and told me to hold her hand while she stuck a wire between her legs. Frida bled for a long time, and when it was over she sobbed into my bosom, but to tell you the truth, I think she was relieved.

Why do you ask that? I just told you she was dying to have a baby. You could tell by the way she looked for things to cuddle—little dogs, monkeys, dolls. She collected dolls. She dressed them and undressed them, she combed, bathed, and fed them, she put them to bed, she took them to the doll hospital when they were "sick," you know, broken. But you're right, there's a big difference between a doll and a baby. A doll doesn't make demands. A doll you can put down and go on vacation. A doll doesn't become your rival for your husband's attention.

God forgive me, I've never told anybody this before—you're the one who brought it up—but in my heart, I believe that my sister never wanted a child any more than Diego did. In spite of how she carried on about her lost baby. In spite of the pictures she drew of uteruses with the babies erased from them. In spite of her tears. Frida was like Diego. She wanted to be the center of everything, and a baby reduces you to, well, a slave. When he wants to eat, you have to get up and feed him. When he pees, you have to change his diaper. He's the star, not you. Frida couldn't have taken that for very long. Because, let me tell you, like Diego, she wanted to be a baby herself. She wanted to be his baby, just as he wanted to be hers. They used to talk baby talk to each other. He used to call her *Frisita chicuitita, mi niñita preciosa*—itsy-bitsy Fwida, my pwecious wittle girl—and other stupid things like that. Not being able to have a baby turned her back into a victim, and a victim is always the center of attention. That's what she wanted, for everyone to fuss over her and say *pobrecita Fridita*, poor little Frida. She loved it.

No, of course I wasn't jealous. I was the one who had two babies, wasn't I? I was the only one who gave them grandchildren, wasn't I? I wasn't jealous at all. I felt sorry for Frida, that's all. Just like everybody else.

I think those first years with Diego were difficult for her. She was a strong-willed, self-centered girl, and now she had to play devoted wife to a man who was just as egocentric as she. She took to wearing Tehuana costumes all the time—long, colorful skirts and lacy blouses.

I already told you it was the style in Mexico after the Revolution, but with Frida it got to be a fetish. She said it was to show her solidarity with the peasants, but there was more to it than that. Frida didn't look anything like a peasant. Are you kidding? With her bright red nails, drop-dead makeup, and elaborate hairdos? Do you think peasant women have the time to braid their hair a zillion times with different-colored yarn? Frida used to spend hours in front of the mirror. She loved to look at herself! If the shade of polish wasn't just right, she would do her nails over. If her ribbons weren't right, she'd take down her hair and plait it again. And her skirts and her petticoats! They had to be ironed just so. She drove the maids crazy. No, it wasn't solidarity with the Indians, or it wasn't just that. Frida was cultivating her own look. She loved it when people turned around and stared at her outfits. How do I know? She was always talking about it. "Everyone loved my Tehuana dress at the American ambassador's party!" "Everyone turned around and applauded when I walked into the Cabellos' reception!"

She wasn't fooling around with Tina Modotti and her crowd anymore. Tina had stopped talking to us, but she didn't just cut us off. She renounced us and denounced us with cries of *¡Viva México!* at some big Party bash. Well, not *us*, really, *them*. Frida and Diego. I mean, why would she denounce me? She wore a slinky dress in the colors of the Mexican flag for the occasion. Her picture was in the paper. What a fruitcake. A beautiful woman, really, but what a nut!

Well, you know that Tina had a flair for the dramatic. She'd been an actress in California, before she hooked up with Edward Weston and became a photographer. You've probably seen her pictures—the bedraggled, crushed roses that she said were the souls of workers destroyed by the capitalist system, the bare telephone wires that stretched out into nowhere. In her own way, she was as great an artist as Frida. At least that's my opinion.

Come to think of it, it's not surprising that Tina got so fired up over Diego's expulsion, because at the time, she was living with Julio Antonio Mella, a hotshot Cuban communist. They killed him. He and Tina were just walking down the street when bam! somebody pumped a bunch of bullets into him. Tina tried to get away, but they grabbed her and accused her of being involved in the murder. They couldn't pin anything on her, though.

Who is "they"? I don't know. Government goons, I suppose. *They*, like when you say *they* predict rain for tomorrow. Where was I? Oh yeah, they let her go, but the case attracted a lot of attention and left a lot of people looking bad. I mean, how could anyone mistreat poor, beautiful Tina like that? Poor, beautiful Tina with her huge, tragic, dark eyes and her flapper's bob. So, to make up for it, they offered her a job as official photographer of the National Museum of Mexico, but of course, she told them to go to hell. Very idealistic, Tina. Very naive too. Never knew when to shut her mouth, and that's how she got herself arrested again. For being a terrorist. A terrorist! Imagine! She was in jail only a couple of weeks, but it destroyed her. They kicked her out of the country. It must have been awful for her because she loved Mexico. She went to Moscow to work for Stalin, I think. Stalin, one of Frida's big heroes. Some people said Tina worked for Stalin's secret police. Finally, she came back to Mexico in the early forties. She died here, supposedly of a heart attack, if you believe that.

That's the story of our friend Tina. Our *ex*-friend Tina, I mean, because she turned her back on us when Diego got thrown out of the Party. It didn't matter to Frida, though, because she didn't need Tina Modotti any more. She and Diego were too busy hanging around rich Americans, spewing communist rhetoric while they ate caviar and Frida pretended to be an Indian.

Maybe I'm not being fair. After all, Diego had to take his commissions where they came, didn't he? An artist depends on affluent people, and Diego used those spoiled gringos to get money to advance the cause of the workers. And by wearing peasant dresses, Frida was telling the fancy foreign ladies, "Look, I have to associate with you because I need your money, but don't think I'm one of you. I haven't abandoned my own people." That's how it was, I guess.

Diego was getting it from all sides. By this time, there weren't many high-minded radicals left at the Prepa. The new crowd hated his murals, and a bunch of right-wing kids got together and trashed them. Diego was a survivor, and he managed to hang on by kissing the ass of Calles's new minister of education. He grabbed some nice government commissions, and that made things worse with the communists. A *comunista de salón,* they called him, a salon communist, an armchair revolutionary. Even after they threw him out the Party, they kept on spitting at him. The government was cracking down on leftists. Some they murdered, some they threw into jail. Diego's friends—Orozco and that crowd—were all hightailing it to California, and Diego looked around for a way to get out too.

It wasn't hard to find one, because he was the star of the Mexican muralist movement, and all the American bigwigs were after him with offers. Even though he depicted people like John D. Rockefeller as twisted, blood-sucking monsters, they couldn't wait to give him money to paint pictures on their buildings. It was funny, really. I guess they were so powerful, so rich, so smart, that they didn't feel threatened by Diego's murals showing auto workers waving banners with hammers and sickles. Or maybe it was their way of proving that they weren't such bad guys, that they really did feel for the masses whose blood they sucked with miserable working conditions and pitiful salaries.

In November 1930, Frida and Diego took off for San Francisco. I remember helping Frida pack, folding her long ruffled skirts and her shawls, pretending to be thrilled for her and Diego. I didn't know what I was going to do without her. We had never been apart—not for more than a few weeks or a month. "Oh, you'll have such a wonderful time," I kept saying. "You'll meet so many fascinating people!" But I was dying. Pinedo had left me, and I had moved back into my parents' house with my two children. Mami, her nose in the air and her rosary in her fingers, never stopped harping on my botched marriage. I felt like a dud, an ordinary girl who had attempted only ordinary things and had failed even at those. Papá looked right through me—the see-through woman, there but invisible. Was he angry with me or just not interested? Maty came to visit nearly every day, but she talked mostly to Mami, now her great ally. Adri came too, and so did some of my old friends, but in spite of the bustle of visitors, servants, and, of course, my own children, I felt lonely, indescribably lonely. I was used to having Frida by my side, to sharing her most secret

thoughts. And I was worried about her because her health was delicate and, besides, Diego could get very mean. In the U.S., she would
have no sister to run to.

It was the beginning of our new lives, our lives without each
other. I was frightened for both of us, but especially for her. My darling sister, my twin. It was as though someone had torn out my fin-
gernail, ripped it right from my flesh.

Part II

CHAPTER 15

Wonderlands

FRIDA HAD BEEN UP NORTH LESS THAN SIX WEEKS WHEN I RECEIVED HER
first letter. Do you want to read it? Here it is. Look, she calls me Kity.
It was her special name for me.

San Francisco, November 28, 1930

My darling Kity,

How you would suffer if you could see the way they treat your poor
twin in this dreadful place, the City of the World. They're such hyp-
ocrites, these San Franciscans! I feel like a performing monkey here.
They're always giving parties and luncheons for Diego, and I have to sit
there and pretend I find their stupid conversations riveting. The other
day we were at the home of Mr. and Mrs. Reginald Baker. He's the president of a bank and is thinking of commissioning a painting by Diego.
She was showing off her glittery new cigarette holder.

"Look how long it is, my dear!" she kept saying. "It was the longest
one I could find. It has sixteen diamonds on it."

"That's not long," I said. "My husband's prick is longer than that!"

Mrs. Reginald Baker turned red as a chile and everyone else just
stared as if they couldn't believe their ears. Diego roared with laughter,
but afterward he told me to be careful with these people, because we
absolutely need them. He makes me mad. First he acts as though he's
thrilled with my comebacks, then he carries on about how I'm ruining
everything. "Don't you forget," he tells me, "that we can't go back to

Mexico because the government will never forgive me for being a communist hero who fights for the people. They might even kill me, Frida. Maybe that's what you want, so you can run off with that gringo lawyer who was flitting around you. Well, don't count on it, bitch! He's a faggot!"

I don't know what's come over him since we got here, but he's more jealous than ever. He's always accusing me of making eyes at some guy, and sometimes I don't even know what guy he's talking about. What I really think is that he doesn't like it when I say something funny that attracts attention. He doesn't like me to upstage him. He wants me to keep my place. Well, I'll keep my place, all right. I'll stay right by his side and play the adoring wife, because I have nowhere to go in this huge, horrible City of the World, although sometimes I feel like running out and jumping off one of those bridges that San Franciscans are so proud of.

Let me tell you, there are a lot of us Mexicans up here. Most are farm hands who pick oranges or onions. Everything grows here, Kity. You'd be in paradise, because there's everything you like to eat. Of course, the avocados are not as good as our own, and the lemons are dry, not juicy and tart like the ones we get at home. Anyhow, most of the Mexicans who aren't pickers are servants. The rich Americans treat them very badly, and the terrible thing is, deep down, they think all Mexicans are low. I'm sure they look down on us because we're dark-skinned, even though they bow down to Diego because he's a famous painter and a genius when it comes to fitting murals into odd-shaped spaces. He incorporates the architectural elements right into the design—but I suppose I'm getting rather technical for you, aren't I, darling? Well, what I'm saying is, even though they're nice to us on the surface, deep down, they *disdain* us.

I don't know how they can reconcile treating their servants like shit and at the same time kiss up to Diego as though he's Jesus Christ with a palette. After all, we're all Mexicans, aren't we? Do you understand what "reconcile" means, precious Kity? It means "bring together" or "make compatible."

Diego is very busy. He is going to paint murals in the San Francisco Stock Exchange Luncheon Club and also at the California School of Fine Arts. We're staying with Ralph Stackpole, a sculptor who has a big studio on Montgomery Street. There's another couple here, Lucile and

Arnold Blanch. He is a sculptor and she is a painter. I avoid talking to them about art, though, because I'm afraid I might forget myself and say something that makes them mad, and we might need these people someday.

Precious Kity, I am going to say good-bye now. I hope this letter was not too tedious for you. Please give my love to Mami and Papá, to Maty and Adri, and, of course, to my darling little Toño and Isolda. I miss you very much and I love you,

Frida

No, you're absolutely wrong. I felt no satisfaction at all. Why should I have been happy that Diego was mistreating my sister?

Everyone was wining and dining Diego, taking him to parties and to picnics in the country. They even took him to a football game. Frida says American football is a ridiculous sport. Also, he gave lectures. There were a lot of Americans who believed in communism in those days because of the Depression, and when Diego talked about the role of the artist in bringing about social justice, people showed up in droves—intellectuals, artists, workers, all kinds of people. Frida went along, the silent, admiring bride, so dainty, so beautiful. She was playing her part.

She sent us postcards showing acres of orange trees, purple foothills, interminable bridges, graceful and dramatic. She sent back magnificent silks from Chinatown, which she had made into the most unusual Tehuana outfits. She sent me back these jade earrings, see? I always keep them in this box, with her letters. But was she happy? Just look at this letter.

San Francisco, February 1, 1931

My dearest Kity,

I hope this finds you all well. I am having a wonderful time, in spite of the fact that this place is very dreary. So many people are poor, not only the Mexican workers, but huge numbers of whites who stand in breadlines for hours just to get a few crumbs. In the meantime, the people on Telegraph Hill live in mansions and dine on caviar and quail's eggs. But in spite of the horror, I find pleasure in my everyday existence.

Diego is at work on the Stock Exchange mural, so I have plenty of time to roam the streets and explore. I love to take the cable cars up and down the hills. Some streets are so steep that you feel as though you're walking up a wall, as though if you turn around and look down, you'll drop like a glass ornament and shatter into a million pieces. When the trolley takes off, I hold my breath and force myself to keep my eyes open. At first, I was afraid, because I would remember my accident years ago, but now I find it exhilarating, like a roller-coaster ride. Another thing I love to do is wander around the Chinese section. The Chinese children are so lovely, all decked out in colorful outfits—some purple, some orange, some pink, some red—like candied ices. I would like to eat them up!

When I walk down the street, everyone stops and looks at me because of my beautiful Tehuana skirts. No one here has seen anything like them. Complete strangers come up and talk to me, and I answer them in English. I'm getting more and more fluent! You wouldn't believe it if you could see how well your little sister prattles gringo. Here are my favorite words: *dick, shit, pussy, ass,* and my all-time favorite, *fuck.* Repeat them a few times every day, darling, so that we'll be able to speak gringo together when I get back. With Diego's friends I don't get that much practice because everyone wants to talk with *him,* even though he doesn't even speak English. I just sort of stand there and smile.

I can't do too much walking because my right foot has been bothering me again. I don't know what's the matter with it. It's like a boat that wants to float off in its own direction. It turns outward, you see, and it's such a strain to make it go where I want it to that sometimes I just give up. But not very often! And my sweetheart, I have the most wonderful news! I met a famous doctor here, Leo Eloesser, who is sure he will be able to help me. He's a dear person. I'm going to do a portrait of him when I begin to paint again. He has looked at my back and tells me I have severe scoliosis. That means a crooked spine, darling. He also tells me I have a missing vertebral disk, which is terrible news, but the good thing is that they are very advanced here in medicine, and if Dr. Eloesser operates, I'm sure he'll leave me as good as new. And then I'll race Toñito from the *pulquería* to the park and back again!

Also, guess who else I met! Cristi, you'll never believe it: Edward Weston, the great photographer, the one who was Tina's lover for so long. I've always been curious about him. Tina talked about him so much. She once told me he was as sensitive as a rose petal, as passionate as a windstorm. [Look, here you can see that Frida drew delicate little flower petals and puffing clouds with fiery eyes!] I didn't know what to expect, especially since he and Diego had both screwed Tina, but it turned out to be wonderful, darling, because between them, Weston and Diego generate an exquisite tension. Weston is so handsome, with the most sensuous eyes. He and I did nothing but flirt in the most brazen way, and Diego just ate it up. Weston took a picture of Diego and me. I can't wait for you to see it.

Last month we went to New York, the capital of the world, the lunatic asylum of the universe, because Diego's show at the Museum of Modern Art was opening. The Americans kissed his cheeks right and left—not the cheeks of his face, of course. He showed some of his paintings of Zapata, agrarian reform, all Marxist ideology stuff, and they just lapped it up. Imagine, these fancy hags in their long, brocade dresses with rods up their asses, ooing and ahing, all pretending to be friends of the suffering peasants. They like to champion the masses, you see, because it makes them feel less guilty about their poodles with diamond tiaras and their gold-trimmed Daimlers. American guilt. You see it everywhere. In the way they adore the lustiness of Mexican art, in the way they pretend they don't notice that Diego and I aren't white. "Oh, my dear, just look at the robustness of those figures! So earthy! So authentic! So sincere!" "And do look at Rivera's little wife. Isn't she *perfect,* with her darling little native costumes!" I didn't talk to any of them, I just stayed close to Diego and let him patter away in French, oblivious to the fact that no one understands a word he's saying.

These Americans have such awful taste. You should see what Mrs. Alice Bricker was wearing, the one who invited us to her penthouse the night after the opening. A perfectly wretched draped gown with ruffles at the shoulders and a huge bow behind, pale pink. She looked like a fifty-year-old schoolgirl. And her friend, Mrs. Fitch, in her layered pajamas that turned her into a walking version of the Chrysler Building!

You can imagine how exhausted I am, precious Kity, going to one party after the other. Everyone wants to meet us. We travel constantly and I see new things every day. Imagine, the Empire State Building, a monument to modernity! Diego loves it. I'd like to get married again, way up on the top floor! Now that we're back in San Francisco, on top of everything there are important political rallies that we simply must go to, because the people worship Diego, they absolutely worship him.

Oh, darling Kity, why am I lying to you, my own sister? It's not going wonderfully at all. Diego is gone for days at a time, and you can guess why, can't you? He says he's doing research for his new mural, but the only research he's doing is between the legs of his new model, the glamorous, athletic, white-skinned Venus, Helen Wills. She's a famous tennis champion, and Diego is making her an allegory of California in his painting. He follows her around everywhere. Supposedly, he has to see her in action to get a sense of the fluidity of her movements. He's seen her in action, all right. I can just imagine what goes on at their practice sessions: "Take off your blouse, darling, and serve again! That's right, now lift your arms, turn toward me. Now take off your panties and show me your lob!" You should see the nude he's doing of her. Up there hovering on the ceiling like a winged forest nymph, like the moon goddess Artemis. What she really reminds me of is a skinned vulture.

A man like Diego has to have his distractions, I guess, but the thing is, I'm so lonely, my little Kity. If only you and Toñito and Isoldita were here with me. Diego is always surrounded by people—assistants, students, admirers, hangers-on. Everyone fawns on him, and nobody pays any attention to your poor little twin. I mean, of course they do—Diego introduced me to his entourage, and they're always inviting me out— but only because I'm Mrs. Rivera, not because they really care about me. I have to be nice to them, especially to people like Al Bender, the famous art collector who not only got a visa for Diego, but also bought a lot of his paintings. People like that keep us alive. But really, they're not interested in me. I'm just an accessory. Diego's wife. Diego's bootstrap. To tell you the truth, I don't like gringos at all, with their faces like half-baked rolls and their complexions like oatmeal.

My dear Kity, how will I survive here? I know you won't write back to me, but please save up all the news you can, so that when I get back, you can tell me everything, EVERYTHING, and we can relive those important moments I missed. Give Mami and Papi a big kiss from me, also my darling niece and nephéw. To you I send all my love,

Frida
♥ ♥ ♥ ♥

It's true I never wrote back to her. I wasn't that good at writing letters, and besides, I was busy with my children. On the one hand, I felt sorry for Frida, but on the other I thought, well, she's finally getting a taste of what it's like to be the *other* one. Yes, I admit it. I felt a certain satisfaction in knowing that, for once, she wasn't the center of attention. I was going through a very bad period, living with my kids at Mami's, with practically no social life.

Don't get me wrong, I didn't want Frida to suffer. And the part about her foot bothering her, I didn't like that part at all. But let's face it, in spite of all of her complaining, Frida was living it up—going to parties, meeting exciting people, riding cable cars, visiting Chinatown, dashing off to New York. So what if everybody's eyes weren't on her? She was still having a good time. But then I started thinking about something else—someone else—Helen Wills.

I had never seen her, not even in pictures, but I couldn't get her out of my mind. Firm and athletic, with hair like moonlight reflected in a quivering sea. White, but an outdoors type. Would her skin be the color of fine sand or the color of blond wood, smooth and varnished by lotions? I imagined her practicing her backhands and overheads, wearing nothing but her visor and her tennis shoes, raising her arms to exhibit luscious breasts, twisting to show the suppleness of her torso, Diego's eyes caressing her as she shot up against the clear, blue California sky. Radiant smile. Sparkling eyes. Gleaming teeth, all straight, the way gringos' teeth always are. And Diego, licking his lips, swallowing in delicious anticipation, while he made sketch after sketch. What about the detachment of the artist at work?

I hated her, not for what she had done to Frida, but for what she had done to *me*.

What had she done to me? It was all very confusing.

Frida didn't write for a while after that. She had started painting

again, since she had a lot of time on her hands and often couldn't go
out walking because of her foot. She did do a portrait of Eloesser, one
of her worst, in my opinion. He looks like some sort of cheap doll, his
head too big for his body and stuck onto his shoulders awkwardly,
with rubber cement. She painted Eva Fredrick, a black woman with
tight, high cheeks and a rounded body. Frida liked blacks. She said
they were like Indians—beautiful, intelligent, rich in culture, and
completely neglected by the upper class. My favorite painting from
that period is the one she did of Luther Burbank, a man who did
experiments with plants. She transformed *him* into a plant, with a
sturdy stem, wide-reaching roots, and robust green leaves. And then
there was a kind of wedding scene she did of herself and Diego, with
a banner over it, like in the old-fashioned paintings you see in hacien-
das, where she refers to him as "my beloved husband Diego." She was
getting good at that role, you see. The role of worshipful wife, I
mean. "My Diego this, my Diego that . . ." Look at this letter:

San Francisco, August 15, 1931

Dearest, darling Kity,

I have to make this short because I'm getting ready for a big
exhibition. Mine! Can you believe it? In New York! So much has happened since I last wrote. Summer here is delightful, although I haven't
been able to do as much hiking around the hills as I would have liked
because my foot has been giving me terrible problems. Your poor little
twin has such miserable luck with her extremities. How I wish I could
be beautiful and healthy like you! Diego and I have both been working
like mad, especially me, because I have to have everything ready for my
show in a week. It's all very exciting. Here in San Francisco everybody
loves my paintings, everybody wants one! I can hardly keep up with the
requests because we simply have to leave time for our social activities.
I've gotten so much better at gringo parties, darling, even though I really hate them because Americans are such bores. They all have personal-
ities like boiled white rice, speaking of which, no one here knows how to
cook. All they eat is bloody red meat that makes you want to throw up
just to look at it.

Last week we went to a dinner party at the home of Mr. and Mrs. Jerome Pattison, very important art patrons who have bought three of Diego's paintings and may acquire another. She was wearing a pencil-thin silk sheath that was about three sizes too small, with a flowing organdy robe over it that she apparently thought gave her a kind of ethereal look. Actually, it reminded me of somebody's laundry flapping in the breeze. Well, they droned on about workers' rights and other stuff they know nothing about. I was bored to tears, just sitting there and sipping my wine, so finally I said, in a very earnest tone: "You know, there was a man who had an extremely serious problem."

Everyone stopped talking and looked at me, expecting me to make some pronouncement on the plight of the unemployed.

"Yes," I said, "a very serious problem."

Every single eye was on me. The corners of Diego's mouth were twitching. I knew he was struggling not to laugh.

"So he went into a pharmacy and he said to the lady at the counter, 'I have this problem and I need to talk to the chemist.'

"'I am the chemist,' the woman said.

"'Well, it's very personal,' he said. 'I'd like to speak with a man chemist.'

"'I'm the only chemist here,' she said. 'But you can tell me anything. I am a graduate chemist and completely professional. I own this business with my sister.'

"'Well,' said the man, 'the problem is, I have a permanent erection.'

"'A permanent erection. Hmm, I see,' said the lady chemist."

You have to imagine this, Cristi. Everybody was looking at me and giggling. They'd all been drinking for hours, and they were already more than halfway to the land of Bacchus. Diego was chuckling out loud in spite of himself.

"'Can you give me anything for it?' he asked.

"'Well,' answered the chemist, 'let me consult with my sister.'"

Here I left a pause, Cristi, just to create a sense of expectation. Then I went on:

"After she had been gone quite a while, the lady chemist came back and said: 'Yes, I've consulted with my sister, and we can give you two thirds of the business, plus thirty percent of the profits!'"

Everybody just roared, Kity. You should have seen them! After that, they all started telling dirty jokes, even the staid Mrs. Pattison, with her face like porridge. I told one after the other, and Diego sat there beaming. When we got home that night, instead of chewing me out for shocking his refined, high-paying benefactors, he threw his arms around me and said I was the best thing that had ever happened to him. I love him so much, Kity, more than life itself. You just can't image how it thrills me to make him happy. From that experience, I learned that it's all in the timing. You can have them eating out of your hand if you just wait until they've got enough alcohol in their gut before you bring on the filth. Ever since then, the parties have been more fun. And it helps, too, that Diego is done with his mural and is more relaxed, with more time to spend with me. Maybe I'll get through this Calvary after all, dearest Kity.

I miss you all so much, you can't even imagine. Please remember your little twin in your prayers. I love you all,

Frida

It wasn't true, of course. She wasn't deluged with requests for paintings. She sold hardly any in San Francisco, and her show in New York was a complete disaster. Diego told me. I never told her I knew the truth, though. Never. After all, I loved her. I had to protect her.

Things get a little blurry at this point. Frida and Diego went to Detroit at the end of 1931, I think, or maybe it was in 1932. Diego had got a huge commission from this important American businessman. Ford was his name, you know, the one who makes cars. Not Henry Ford. Edsel Ford. What a funny-sounding name. Diego once bought Frida a car, and he bought me one just like hers. Ford wanted Diego to do some murals celebrating the car manufacturing business. That was right up Diego's alley, because he was going to be able to show men at work, men with grimy faces and flexed muscles, the whole industrial thing, the masses, the proletariat, the nobility of sweat. Viva Marx! Viva Zapata! Diego loved machines, machinery, anything modern, anything that had to do with progress. What kind of a name is Edsel?

Well, they arrived in Detroit, and first off, they went to the Wardell, a hotel where you can live full-time with maid and laundry service and everything, but you can also have a kitchen and cook your own dinner. Frida hated American food. She insisted on cooking Mexican meals because she said the gringos made everything taste like wet plaster. They moved into this very classy hotel with all their stuff, Diego's colors, Frida's Tehuana dresses, Diego's ocean-sized boots, Frida's medicine cabinet, Diego's booze.

"You know what makes it such a good hotel?" Bill Regginer told them. He was a guy who raised money for the Detroit Art Institute.

"What?" said Diego.

"They don't take Jews." He thought that was funny. Regginer did, I mean. He thought he was letting them in on some kind of inside joke.

But Frida felt like she'd caught an ice pick in the throat. "It never stops haunting you," she told me later. "You can never get away from it." The curse of Guillermo Kahlo, that's what I call it.

So you know what Diego did? He went to the manager and said: "I hear you don't take Jews at this place." He spoke in French. Frida had to translate for him.

"That's right," said the guy. "After all, this is one of the best addresses in Detroit. We have standards to maintain."

"Well, Carmen and I will be moving out, then, because we're both Jewish." He had taken to calling Frida "Carmen," because Nazism was on the rise and it wasn't good to have a German name. The guy's jaw must have dropped two feet under the floor. Diego was the most important artist in the world, and it was prestigious for the hotel to have him there.

"That can't be . . ." stammered the manager.

"Well, it is!" Diego laughed. "We'll go up and start packing right away, unless you change your policy!"

"The thing is, it's not really a policy—it's just that . . ." Diego had the guy in corner and was enjoying watching him squirm.

"I mean, it's not *my* policy . . . I'll have to check with—check with the, uh, I mean, there's a board—"

"Go ahead and check, but unless you've changed your policy by the end of the day, we'll be gone by tomorrow."

Well, the Depression was still on, and they needed the business that a name like Diego Rivera could bring in. The upshot is that they not only changed their policy, but also lowered the price of the suite from $185 to $100 a month. Diego considered it a triumph over bigotry.

Not long after that, they went to a dinner party at Edsel Ford's house. "Full of bitches with satin sanitary napkins and their noses pointing at the moon" is how Frida described it. They all sat around talking about who knows what. Tennis, maybe. Helen Wills had just won the U.S. Women's Singles Championship. Or maybe Chaplin's latest film, or Gary Cooper's. Frida would say things like "You saw *City Lights*? Well, shit!" And when the society ladies turned pale, she would say, "Oh, did I say something wrong? Isn't that what you're supposed to say when something is fantastic? I guess I meant 'Great'! My English isn't that good yet." Anyhow, they were at this party at Ford's, and he was famous for hating Jews. Later, during the war, he rooted for the Germans. All of the sudden, there was a lull in the conversation, and Frida piped up and said, "Oh, Edsel, I hear you're Jewish! Isn't your mother a Jew from Brooklyn?" Well, you can imagine!

Of course I wasn't *there*. I'm telling you what I think it was like, the way I imagine it.

Another time, they were attending a function at the Art Institute. There was a kind of reception line, and Frida was standing next to Diego in a silk Tehuana outfit with loads of jewelry and a ring on every finger. The society ladies would go through the line and say things like "Oh, I just love your husband's work!" "We're so delighted you and Mr. Rivera are here!" And Frida would gush, "Oh, thank you. Fuck you!" Afterward, she explained in her sweetest little voice, "Oh, I thought that's what I was supposed to say! I thought it meant something like 'You're very kind.' That's what my husband told me. Naughty Diego. He's just trying to get me in trouble!"

But if you think Frida was having a good time in Detroit, you're wrong. Her foot was torturing her, and to make matters worse, she got pregnant in the spring. Why worse? Because she was in a foreign country, where everything was different—the people, the language, the food, the way of reacting to a pregnant woman. In Mexico, an expectant mother can depend on her sisters, her mami, her maids. I would have attended to Frida, watched her like a hawk, and made her obey the doctor when he told her not to drink or go to so many parties. But she always had to be in the middle of things, and besides, she didn't like taking orders from anybody. Diego worked all the time. He had to finish those murals for Ford. Frida couldn't stand to be alone, so she went out, she pushed herself, and—this letter is from the end of May.

Detroit, May 30, 1932

Darling sister,

I don't know how to begin this letter. I would like to tell you that everything is wonderful, because I'm expecting a baby. I am! I'm expecting a baby! I should be deliriously happy, but oh, my dearest Cristi, I am suffering so horribly. I have strange thoughts, I see weird and terrifying creatures in my sleep, monsters with wings like bats and beaks like parrots that hiss and caw, that swoop down and snatch my child out of his cradle. I want to go back home, but there is no chance that Diego will finish his frescoes before September. The baby will be born in December. The thing is, I want to go now. Nobody here knows how to take care of me, and Diego doesn't show the teeniest bit of interest in my condition. Whenever I'm nauseous, which is all the time, or whenever my leg aches, he stomps out and slams the door. "You had to go get pregnant," he yells. "Now live with it!" He's always snarling at me, he's in a perpetually ugly mood. I don't see him for weeks, he says he sleeps at the Institute of Art so he won't waste any time getting ready in the morning, but who knows where he sleeps, or who he sleeps with!

Oh, Cristi, I hate this dreary city. The whole place is like a tenement basement, and it's so hot that rats and roaches lie frying on the sidewalk. I wish I could die! Pray for me, darling Cristi. Communists don't believe in God, but maybe he will come to my rescue anyway.

Your loving sister,

Frida

Something was eating at me, but I couldn't put my finger on it. This time she'll have it, I thought. Dieguito. Little Diego. I never doubted that it would be a boy. The darling of Mami's life, the apple of her eye. "Please, God, don't let me die before I see Frida's baby," Mami kept wailing. Because she was very sick, you see. The doctor had told Mami that she had cancer, and she knew she might not live to see her new little grandson. She had Toñito, but he was only mine. The new one would be Frida's. Everyone was carrying on so. "Against such tremendous odds!" "That little Frida is such a fighter, such a heroine!" And I admit it, yes, I was irritated, because Frida was in the United States playing the naughty but adorable little wife of Diego Rivera, socializing with the cream of Yankee society, and yes, she did love it, in spite of what she said, and I was stuck in Coyoacán trying to raise my two children and take care of Mami too. Well, I thought, at least this will clip her wings. She won't be the crucifix, the Holy Grail, and the altar boy's prick all rolled into one anymore. She won't be Jesus Christ in lavender pajamas for a while. She can't be the center of the social scene and take care of a newborn at the same time. She'll have to stay home and take care of herself and the baby. Poor Frida, it's true she suffered terribly because of her spine and her foot, and the pregnancy would only make her medical problems worse. I felt sorry for her. Of course I felt sorry for her. But still, I was suffering too. Mami wasn't easy to deal with in the best of circumstances, and with her illness, she was unbearable. Pills, doctors, bedpans, vomiting all day long. And complaining. Constant complaining. Oh, if only Frida were there, Mami whined, everything would be better. Her darling Frida. The whole thing was wearing me out. I was a young woman, I needed to get out. But there I was, stuck at home day after day. I was glad to do it for Mami. I loved Mami. She was my mother. I owed her care and attention. The thing is, why didn't Frida owe her those things too?

By the time I got the letter, the baby had already died. One night Frida started to bleed. Oceans of blood. Clots like islands. Diego went into spasms of grief at the hospital. The Monument Rivera suffering his monumental agony. I'm sorry. I don't mean to be nasty. I don't doubt that he was really grieving, but not for the infant. If he was going through hell, it wasn't because of the child, which he never wanted. It was the thought that Frida might actually slip off to paradise and leave him alone in that piss-filled, pus-filled city. "Perfumed *caca*," was how Frida described it, "diarrhea garnished with parsley."

After she recovered, Frida started painting again like a wild woman.

I'm sure it was hard for her, because she wasn't a very organized person. She would start a project, and then you'd say something like "Let's go shopping" or "Let's play cards" or "Let's go visit the Soliz girls down the street," and she'd forget all about work. But this time, she put herself on a schedule. She'd paint all morning, then bring Diego his lunch at the Institute because, of course, he wanted enchiladas and mole, not sawdust and dried paint. She'd cook it the night before. Good Frida. The dutiful wife. She'd sit there and eat it with him. And he'd pick off tortillas with that amphibian tongue of his and berate her. His moods were getting uglier. He criticized everything. Not her art, not her clothes, not stuff like that, but other things. Why did she have to have to go and get pregnant again? And why did she keep running to doctors? Why didn't she stop complaining about her toe?

She made sketches of fetuses, just like the first time. Sketches of dead babies, aborting mothers. It was around then that she really started collecting dolls in earnest. She had always liked dolls, she already had quite a collection. Now she became obsessed. She not only dressed them and undressed them, she baptized them (even though she was a communist) and taught them their prayers and buried them when they died. Quite a few of them died, you see. She shrouded them in sheets or old shawls and buried them. I don't know how many she left rotting under the ground in the yard of the Wardell Hotel.

This is her next letter:

Detroit, July 8, 1932

My adored sister,

You can't know how much I am suffering here. Diego works all the time and pays no attention to me. He is still mad that I got pregnant again, and he is punishing me by never coming home. He not only sleeps with every pretty model and art student at the Institute, he flaunts his affairs, making me the laughingstock of Detroit. Oh, Cristi, why do I go on living? I desperately want a baby, but every time I mention it, Diego flies into a rage and starts to throw things. Yesterday the brass candlestick holder barely missed my head. When he walks through the door, it's like a storm crashing through the apartment. Sometimes I think it's better that he spend the nights in the arms of those blond dimwits. I paint to forget, but my misery is so intense.

I'm very sick, Cristi. I'm still bleeding, and my foot burns horribly. I wish I could cut it off! If only I could go home, Cristi. You and Inocencia would take care of me because you love me. You're the only people who really love me. Diego doesn't love me at all.

Please tell that old *pícaro* God to watch out for me, sweetheart. He'll listen to you because you're pure at heart. He won't listen to me, though, because I've always been a black sheep.

Good-bye, darling. I'm counting the days until I see you again.

With love from your devoted sister,

Frida

Frida got her wish. Early in September I cabled her to come home immediately. Mami was dying.

CHAPTER 16

Dirge

SHE WAS COMPLAINING TO HER NEW FRIEND LUCIENNE BLOCH, AN ARTIST who worked as Diego's assistant and was the daughter of the Swiss composer Ernest Bloch. At first, Frida had detested her, even insulted her at a party, but then, when she realized Lucienne wasn't out to dive into bed with her husband, the two of them became as close as the two halves of a peanut. Frida's voice droned on.

"Diego doesn't want kids, Lucienne, I have to face it, he doesn't want kids and he's not going to let me get pregnant again, he told me so, just like that, words that slash like an ax, and in my present state, I'm so exhausted, darling, you can't imagine, painting all day every day, on my feet and still hemorrhaging. But I have to stay busy, Lucienne, I have to keep my mind off the baby, the loss of the baby, you're kind to come with me all the way to Mexico, darling. It's important to have friends who really love you, people you can talk to, who share your interests, that's what I love about you, Lucienne. You think Mami will be fine, don't you? Gallstones aren't really dangerous, are they? They can be taken out, that's what the doctor said, but Mami has so many of them, over a hundred of them, and she's so weak from the cancer, you don't think she'll die, do you, Lucienne? God, I can't bear it, first the baby and now this. Mami took such good care of me when I was sick. I'm still sick, my foot, Lucienne, the pain is intolerable, and my back, too, who will take care of me if she dies? When I imagine her lying inert, cold, under the earth, larvae boring into her skull, nesting in her nostrils, when I see her without any eyelids, her hair matted and dull like dry seaweed, her hair coming loose from her scalp, her scalp coming loose from her cranium, her breasts with no nipples, her desolate womb, her rotting sex, it's horrible, Lucienne, it's like someone's rubbing ice on my spine. Diego's losing weight, Lucienne. He's on a diet, that's why he's so cross all the time. He hurls things at me, paintbrushes, cigarettes, ashtrays, loaded guns, but it's not him, it's the diet, he doesn't know what he's doing. He loves me, and he'll give me a baby because he knows I need one, I need a baby, Lucienne, you understand, don't you? I'll die if I never have a baby. Sometimes I don't want to go on, but I love Diego and that's what gives me strength, Lucienne. Nobody understands except you. What am I, Lucienne? A rusty pipe, worthless, ruined. A gutted house, empty . . ."

I tried not to listen.

"Oh darling, I don't know why I cry all the time. It's as though I can't control myself, Lucienne, and the only thing that helps is work, but here I won't be able to lift a brush with everything that's happening, and Diego all alone up there in that heartless country, poor Diego, I suffer for him, my poor wittle fwoggie, you can't know the agony, darling."

Shut up! I thought it, but I didn't say it. I was ready to wrap my fingers around her throat and squeeze. She had come back for the final farewell. We all knew this was the end. Cancer had been gnawing away at Mami's insides for who knows how long, and now she was going to have a gallbladder operation which the doctor said she probably wouldn't survive. She had no more flesh, no more stamina. I don't know exactly what I felt at that moment. The drone of Frida's voice. Her incessant whining. Maybe I just wanted the whole thing to be done. Maybe I hoped Mami would just get it over with and Frida would go back to Detroit. No, of course not, of course I didn't want that. It's just that I was so drained. Sleepless nights. Bedpans. Broths. Medicines. Soothing words. "Of course you're not leaving us, Mami. You're not going anywhere. Before you know it, you'll be running after Rufina with a switch, just like you used to. You'll dance at Isolda's wedding, Mami." Never being able to do anything right, that was the worst thing. Because Mami was never satisfied. If I put yellow sheets on her bed, she wanted blue ones. If I put daisies in the vase on her dresser, she wanted carnations. It was the illness. The illness ate away at her understanding and made her say hateful things. I know that, but still, it was exhausting.

We had just picked Frida up at the train station in Mexico City. Maty's husband was driving I can't remember whose car, it wasn't theirs, Maty and Paco didn't have a car. Frida and Lucienne Bloch were sitting in the backseat. Frida had brought her friend with her because she said, she was too weak to travel alone. She and Lucienne were inseparable. Sometimes I wondered if they were lovers. Poor me, Frida was whimpering. Poor me poor me poor me poor me. I was getting a headache.

The problem, she kept explaining to Lucienne, was that she was exhausted. *She* was exhausted. Do you have any idea what it's like to take care of a cancer patient? Maty didn't help. She was too busy dolling up her little apartment—sewing ruffles on curtains, embroidering sheets, that sort of thing. Mami had given her a lot of things from the house, and she had bought some fake antiques. Frida said that Maty had terrible taste, that she was too bourgeois, but what business was it of Frida's? It was Maty's house, after all. Adri didn't help either, because she couldn't stand to be around sickness. Whenever the cat threw up, Adriana ran the other way and left the mess for me. And when Mami shit in her bed, well, Adri just couldn't deal with it. I was the one who lived with them, and so it was up to me to fuss over Mami, to make sure she took her pills, to sit by her and read, to tell her the plots of the newest films. *Anna Christi* with Garbo, for example. It had come out before in the States, but I had just seen it. I also had to wait on Papá, make sure he ate, because he'd go for days without food. And my two kids . . . So yes, I admit it, I was irritated, because the tired one wasn't Frida. I was the tired one.

It happened on September 15, two days after the operation. I was with her. I was the only one. The priest had been there earlier and performed the last rites. I closed her eyes very gently. Then I put on a black dress, threw a black shawl around my shoulders, and went to tell Frida.

The minute she saw me, she knew Mami had died. "It's happened, hasn't it?" she said. Right away, Frida began to scream like a pig at slaughter. "Mami! My beloved mother! Take me with you, Mami! Oh God oh God oh God, how could you do this to me? How could you take away my sainted mother?" The doctor gave her a pill, and Lucienne and I put her to bed. Then we went to tell Maty, Adri, and Margarita and María Luisa, too, because even though Mami wasn't their mother, they had long since forgiven her for sending them away to a convent. We didn't tell Papá, though. Not yet. He was so fragile. We were afraid that the news would bring on a seizure so violent that it would kill him. It wasn't until the next day that, very tenderly, with the help of the doctor and the priest, we told him his wife was gone.

"Go," he said to the cleric. "Take care off sings. You know vhat to do." That's all he said, but he wandered around the house like a soul in purgatory for the remainder of his life.

Inocencia, Margarita—our half sister who eventually became a nun—and I washed and dressed the body. How tiny Mami looked, her withered corpse stretched out on the bed. Such an imposing woman in life, so delicate in death. Flaccid breasts, emaciated arms. Disease and age had ravaged her form, except for her thighs and sex, which seemed to belong to a much younger, much healthier woman. How could it be, I wondered, that her malady had left some parts almost intact? It was as though she were two women, one already putrefying, one still clamoring for her place at the table.

At the funeral, Frida went berserk. She played the scene from *Farewell, My Poet,* where Catalina Trueba, who's about fifteen in the film, sees them burying her brother who was killed by some land-owning bully. She wails and wails. Then everything gets blurry, and she falls into her brother's grave. Frida didn't jump into Mami's tomb, but she was shrieking and carrying on like Mary Magdalene. Still, she couldn't pull off a scene the way Catalina Trueba could.

"My God," I said, "control yourself. We're all in pain. People are looking at you!"

"You cold-hearted bitch," she hissed. "You can't know what I feel!" And then she went on screaming, "Mamiii! Mamiii! I love you! Take me with you!"

"Just go!" I said under my breath.

I know what you're thinking. You think I was so angry that I— that I conjured up a plan to punish her, but that's not what happened at all. I was irritated, I don't deny it, but you have to realize that all this had been a tremendous strain. When your mother dies, it's as though you're suddenly an orphan. Even when you're a grown-up woman, when your mother dies, especially when you've been living in the same house, it knocks you off balance. It leaves you wobbly, as though you're just learning how to walk. All the things you said you'd do when she died . . . dance with an Indian, throw out the ugly purple bedspread, smash the French porcelain vase in the parlor—the one with the two cupids—take the fur-trimmed jacket in her closet for yourself, throw your sister into the mud . . . all those things, you can suddenly do them, and yet you don't feel a sense of liberation, because even more than before, her eyes are on you, watching you, judging you. Even though she's not there, she's there. Even though her eyes are closed, they're open. So all those unruly thoughts that you've kept imprisoned in a dark corner of your mind, you leave them there. Maybe you let them out to play once in a while, but you feel uncomfortable about it.

In the four or five weeks that followed, Frida played the part of the adoring daughter. She had missed the mess. She hadn't had to deal with the havoc caused by Mami's illness the way I had. She came in at the end of the story, but now she and Lucienne were Papá's saviors, fixing him tea, taking him to the park, telling him stories about the wonderful parties they had been to in Detroit and New York. They were quite entertaining, really. Frida told about the time she kissed a taxi driver on the cheek for teaching her how to sing the first four lines of "The Star-Spangled Banner," which had just recently become the official hymn of the U.S. A song about a dog! "Oh say, can you see, by the dog's ears . . ." Something like that. I didn't understand it at all, and neither did she, but it was really funny when she sang it. "Well, why not have an anthem about a dog!" She laughed. "I find it very democratic! Hail to the dog's ears!"

Beneath it all, Frida was agonizing. Her face had grown drawn and tight, as though she suffered from perpetual gas pains, and her eyes were wet and red. I could hear her crying when she was alone in her room. I didn't doubt her sincerity. After all, it's true that on top of Mami's death, she had to deal with just having lost a baby. She was in distress, all right, but the point is, she wasn't the only one.

"You know," she said to me on the way to Mexico City, where she was to catch a train to the States, "it's a good thing I brought Lucienne along, because you didn't take very good care of me, Cristi."

Every nerve in my body stood with musket poised, ready to attack.

"What do you mean, Frida? I had Inocencia prepare *mole poblano* especially for you."

"I don't need Inocencia to make me *mole poblano*. I make better *mole* than she does."

"Look," I said. "This has taken a lot out of me, Frida. I did my best."

"I know, darling, I know. You're exhausted, we all are. It doesn't matter. With the children, you don't really have time for me anymore."

I let it go. I didn't say a word. But then, she started up again.

"It's just that—"

"It's just that what?"

"Well, you know what I've been going through with Diego and my own health, Cristi. I have practically no energy at all. You could have at least—"

"You had energy enough to make a scene at the funeral," I snapped.

"A scene, Cristi? A scene? I was expressing my profound grief."

"We were all feeling profound grief, sister, but you were the only one to carry on like Catalina Trueba."

"My God, you're hurting me, Cristi."

"You're hurting her, Cristina," piped in Lucienne, with her awful Swiss accent that always made her sound as though her throat was full of diseased phlegm.

Frida started to cry.

I felt terrible. Poor Frida. After all, she was sick. After all, she had just lost a baby. After all, she was tired from the trip. After all, Diego treated her like shit. I knew all that.

"I'm sorry," I said.

She reached over and held my hand. We were approaching the station.

The train for Texas pulled away slowly, a giant caterpillar of metal and glass. I waved good-bye, feeling horribly alone.

CHAPTER 17

Where the Road Divides

I REMEMBER THIS FROM SCHOOL: "A GOOD TREE CANNOT BRING FORTH evil fruit." It's from the Book of Matthew. I've thought about that idea a lot over the years, because I brought forth evil fruit. At least, that's what you think. You and everybody else. But . . . No, you're right. I brought forth evil fruit. Yes, of course I did, but how? That's what I want to know. I was an innocent kid. I didn't know what was going on. I wasn't an evil tree. At least, I don't think so. All right, I wasn't a baby. I was twenty-six or twenty-seven. But the thing is, I didn't have evil intentions. I didn't even know what I was doing. Or maybe I did. Of course I did, but I didn't have an inkling where it would lead. No idea. I had no idea that our lives would never be the same afterward, that it would ruin everything, that it would destroy Frida. Maybe that in itself is evil. I mean, the fact that I didn't even consider there would be a price to pay. Because everything we do has consequences. Maybe I should have realized. Or maybe I'm lying.

Frida returned to the States. Everything was going wrong. The frescoes in Detroit caused a lot of fuss because they were communist. They were a celebration of the worker. A lot of Americans thought they were a kind of attack on the American way of doing things, on capitalism. Also, there were nudes, and Americans are prudes who think that bodies are disgusting. That's what Frida told me. She said that Americans don't even like to touch their own bodies. That's why, when they bathe, they use washcloths. The priests and the Protestant ministers all attacked the work. They're the worst prudes of all, and besides, Diego always represents the clergy as greedy pigs. People were threatening to destroy the murals, but a bunch of workers got together to protect them. That made Diego feel great. Again, he was the hero of the people. His name was in all the papers. He wasn't just supporting a cause, *he* was the cause.

No, Frida didn't write to me. She was mad at me. But when they got back, they talked about it all the time. He was the hero, the knight in armor, the crusader, the leading man, and she, Frida, was the leading lady. It's not hard for me to imagine what went on, how they ate up all the attention.

They were done in Detroit, and they left for New York, where Diego was to paint murals at the RCA Building. He was such a celebrity that they sold tickets to watch him work. Can you believe it? Every day crowds gathered under his fat but thinning ass, thinning because he was on a diet, and gawked at him painting images of greedy businessmen exploiting downtrodden laborers, peasants, workers, teachers, mothers . . . all those people united in a Marxist paradise. This is all a little blurry because, as I just said, Frida wasn't writing to me.

The deal is this: Diego was having the same problems in New York as in Detroit. A lot of people were indignant because he was taking the Rockefellers' money to paint pictures showing that American capitalists were crooks and pigs. I mean, let's face it, the Rockefellers were the princes of capitalism. And here Diego was, showing that the princes of capitalism were living off of everybody else's sweat. People said Diego's work was immoral and profane, not only because of the nudes but because communists don't believe in God. That's why Mami never liked Diego. Frida brought back newspaper articles saying that the murals were nothing more than communist propaganda—full of red flags and red shirts and red bandannas. I couldn't read them, but she translated them into Spanish for me. Frida was very clever at languages, you know. Such a brilliant girl. So talented. "Why can't you be more like your sister?" Mami used to say. And when she didn't say it, she thought it. She'd forget that Frida was a lesbian and a tramp. You don't have to be a genius to figure out that if you hire a communist artist, you're going to get a communist painting. Nelson Rockefeller might be a financial wizard, but he sounds like a bonehead to me. He's the one who decided to use his family's oil fortune—made, according to Diego, by abusing generations of poor slobs, hardworking bastards—in order to commission murals celebrating a New and Better Future. So, you tell me, if you hire a communist artist to depict a New and Better Future, what do you think he's going to paint? Society ladies dressed up like the Chrysler Building with diamond-studded cigarette holders, or a workers' heaven?

Diego just kept on painting, and Frida, well, I'm not sure what she did. She didn't paint. Frida only painted when she had nothing else to do, but in New York, there was plenty to keep her busy. It was a big city. There were stores. She went shopping with Lucienne. There were theaters. She went to the movies with Lucienne. Diego didn't go. Diego did nothing but work work work. Frida loved dime stores. She found all kinds of treasures in dime stores: dangling earrings with glass birds, a plastic comb painted with different-colored flowers, an ashtray with a mermaid seated on the edge, a hideous scarf—so hideous it was almost pretty—with brown and yellow stripes, a gadget to peel oranges without breaking the skin, a picture of Betty Boop, panties with the days of the week printed on them in English. She brought all that stuff back with her. She stole some of it, not because she didn't have money, but because she thought it was fun to snitch things from dime stores. What difference did it make?, she said. After all, the owners were rich. She gave some of that junk to me. And she went to parties. She had all kinds of high-society friends—in spite of the fact she was a champion of the worker and said she hated high society. She loved being surrounded by smart, powerful people who groveled to her because she was the wife of the great Diego Rivera. She made fun of them, but she loved being with them. She loved how important they made her feel. She bought fancy materials to make stunning dresses to go to their parties. (She had given up Tehuana costumes for the moment.) And she met other artists—painters, sculptors, photographers. What did they do when they got together? What did they talk about? I don't know. I guess they played at being superior to everybody else. And they played *cadavre exquis*. Do you know that game? Frida taught me. You fold a paper in sections, like this, and the first person draws the top of a body in the first section, then folds it back so the next person can't see it. Then the next person draws the trunk of the body in the middle section, and the next person draws the bottom of the figure. At the end they unfold the paper to see what they have. Lucienne saved some of those pictures. They're a riot, because Frida always drew something obscene—a head that looked like a giant penis with balls for jowls, breasts dripping with milk, a woman's open legs with a man's fingers in between. A riot. When she got back to Mexico, she and Diego and I would play.

Frida couldn't play all the time, because things were going badly with the mural. The crowds were getting hostile, and Rockefeller put guards all over the place. Of course, Diego had to go and make things worse. He was so used to everyone fawning all over him that he probably thought he could get away with anything. Rockefeller kissed his ass even when priests and politicians said that Diego was making a mockery of his generosity. Diego probably said to himself, "Hell, I've got the support of the masses, I've got the support of the bigwigs. I can do whatever I damn please." Anyhow, he painted a portrait of Lenin right in the middle of the mural.

That was too much, even for Don Nelson. He told Diego to change it, but Diego wouldn't. So what do you think Rockefeller did? He fired him! Just like that! He paid him what he owed him and kicked him out. Then he had the frescoes destroyed. I'm not the brainy one, but it seems pretty clear to me that in a capitalist country, the man with the money calls the shots. The guy who hires you can also fire you. I mean, Rockefeller was something of a dimwit—it took him a long time to catch on—but when he finally did, boom! The ax fell! Diego thought he was above all that because he was the great Diego Rivera, Jesus Christ on roller skates, but you can push a person too far, and he pushed Rockefeller too far.

Maybe it wasn't all that terrible, because it certainly got Diego in the news. There was a huge public outcry, and all the big shots in the art world came running to help poor, abused Rivera. Here he was, defending the rights of the workers to take over the world, and those miserly savages from Standard Oil were going to try to put him in his place. But he wasn't going to take it. No. He was going to fight back.

Not for himself, but for his beloved masses. He was the hero again. He was on his white horse again. He was the Cid, with his devoted Ximena by his side.

Maybe I'm not being fair. After all, imagine what it must be like to work day and night on something, and then some moron who doesn't really understand it comes along and throws it out. Diego really believed in what he was doing, and to be treated like that by some witless American . . . Frida knocked herself out defending Diego. She went back to wearing Tehuana dresses and stood on corners handing out leaflets. She went to meetings. She granted interviews. She insulted Rockefeller in public, although, as soon as the fracas was over, she turned around and kissed his ass all over again. She wasn't stupid, you know. She knew which side her bread was buttered on. The truth is, if you ask me, not that anybody ever did at the time, the truth is that Frida loved it. "The Americans are so stupid," she told me once. "It is so easy to win them over. You just play the poor little Mexican, all delicate and vulnerable, so hurt because everyone has turned against your husband, and they eat it up. The next day an article comes out in the paper saying, 'The lovely Mrs. Rivera, so young and fresh, so beholden to Mr. and Mrs. Rockefeller for their kindness in the past, is at a loss to explain the sudden change of heart of the great philanthropist, in whom she trusted.' And tra-la! Everyone feels sorry for you and joins your cause." That's how she talked about the Americans. "They're very moral, you know. Very decent. They always want to do the right thing, and they're ridden with guilt about everything—their success, their wealth, their treatment of Mexico. Find the right string and it's really easy to jerk them around."

But after a while, she got tired of it all. Her right foot was getting worse. Sometimes she couldn't even move it. Everybody was busy defending Diego, and she had to sit at home with her foot up, or else she'd soak in the bathtub, because the humidity was so bad she couldn't bear it. She wanted to come home, but Diego was busy on some other project. I can't remember which. And when he wasn't painting, he was screwing some model, or student, or hanger-on. So he was busy and she was lonely. I think it was around then that she painted a picture called *My Dress Hangs There*. It shows New York, the rich part and the poor part, and right in the middle of all the skyscrapers hangs one of Frida's Tehuana dresses. It means, she explained to me, that even though her dress was hanging in that big American city, *she* wasn't there, not really. She wrote letters to her friend Isabel Campos, asking for news and making fun of the American women who tried to imitate her by wearing Tehuana outfits but looked absolutely ridiculous in them with their blond curls and big, gawky frames. Isabel showed me the letters. Not then, though. Years later. But Frida didn't write to me. For months I had no news.

And then they were back. Diego finished whatever he was working on, and they took a boat to Havana, then to Mexico.

Yes, I was glad to see her. I missed my sister. I missed her terribly. We were like the petals on a flower. Pull one off and the flower is ruined. But . . . How can I explain it? Things were strained. We made up, of course. I was sorry about what I had said at Mami's funeral and I told her so. She kissed me and said she understood that I was upset, so upset that I said things that I didn't mean. "You just don't understand how words can hurt, Cristi. You're like a little girl. You say things without thinking, without considering the consequences." And then she smiled at me as though I were a naughty baby who hadn't understood a word she'd said.

They were both unbearable. Both she and Diego. She was pregnant again and he wasn't one bit happy about it. He was already in a bad mood because of the awful experience he had had in the States and because he hadn't wanted to come back to Mexico. In spite of everything, he was a star up there, and being a star in a rich country is not the same as being a star in a poor one. The Depression dragged on, but the elite partied more than ever; at least, that's what it sounded like to me. In Mexico the government had commissioned some murals, but still, he was depressed. Besides, the diet he had been on in Detroit left him drained, listless, and bad-tempered. He was sick all the time. He had lost weight too fast, which affected his this, this that, his everything. His stomach hurt. His intestines were screwed up. His glands were a mess. Or maybe none of it was true and he just wanted to belly-ache. The fact is that he complained all the time.

And then Frida made it worse by going and getting pregnant

again. It was bad enough that she had made him come back to Mexico, he said, and that she did nothing but carry on about her foot, but now, on top of everything else, she had gone and gotten herself knocked up. Why did she do that when she knew he didn't want a baby? And when she knew she couldn't carry it to term? She just wanted attention, he said. She had already tried and failed twice before, and still, she insisted on putting herself and everyone else through the agony of another miscarriage. "It's not fair," he kept moaning. "What that woman is doing to me is just not fair."

I felt sorry for him. He was such an infant, he couldn't take care of himself. And now, Frida was all wrapped up in her womb once again. She had no time or energy left for her husband.

For weeks Diego wouldn't work. He just couldn't bring himself to pick up a brush. He sat around sulking, or else he flew into a rage for no reason at all. He'd throw things—paints, dishes, boots, Antonio's wooden toys. Once he threw a birdcage against the wall with the parakeet still in it. It wasn't his fault, though. He was miserable, and Frida irritated him with her constant groaning about her foot and her morning sickness.

Diego had a couple of big government projects he couldn't get started on.

"Come on," I said to him. "At least do something. Try a small painting or two just to get back into the swing of it. Even if you're not ready to tackle the Medical School mural, at least get out your easel." He didn't answer. "I'll pose for you!" I whispered, trying to sound enticing.

"I don't know how to paint anymore," he said. "I've never known how to paint. Everything I've ever done has been garbage."

I just laughed.

"I'm glad they tore up the RCA frescoes. They were shit. And the Detroit stuff. Shit. All shit."

"Look," I said, "stop it. You're acting like a two-year-old."

He just sulked. "Why do women always tell men they're acting like children?" he said finally. "You don't take me seriously. I'm telling you that I'm a fraud, Cristina. I'm not a great artist, I'm a fraud, and I'll never paint again because I refuse to go on living a lie.

I can't stand it. I'm going to kill myself."

"Look," I said, "just a little something to get going again. Something easy. Not the history of the planet, just a mango or a watermelon or whatever. Or me in my birthday suit."

But he wasn't paying attention. He had turned his back to me and sat facing the wall.

"Come on," I said gently. I put my hand on his shoulder. "Come on, give it a try."

He was crying. Tears dribbled down his cheeks in slow-moving little streams. He wasn't pretending. He wasn't putting on a show. He was really miserable. Poor Diego. I patted his jowl dry with the corner of my shawl.

"You'll feel better if you start to work again," I whispered. "You're not happy unless you're busy."

"Maybe you're right." He placed his head on my hip, burying his face in my skirt, and I caressed his hair lightly.

"Poor Diego. Poor, poor Diego. ¡Pobrecito!"

"Under one condition," he said without moving. His voice was muffled. I could hardly hear him.

"What?"

"You pose for me."

"Of course! I said I would, didn't I?"

I didn't think anything of it. I had posed for him so many times before. I had been his favorite model, and I was looking forward to being his favorite model again. I loved posing for Diego. It made me feel special, womanly. Anyhow, I had nothing else of importance to do. Nothing was going on in my life. Antonio was about four. He didn't need me there every minute of the day, and besides, Polinesta, his nanny, and the other maids took good care of him. I liked to have fun, go to parties, visit friends, just like Frida, but between the problems with Pinedo and Mami's illness, I never got to do any of those things. Posing for Diego would be fun. It would make me feel like a person again, I thought, a person with a life and somewhere to go once in a while. I would be like old times.

"I'd love to pose for you, Diego. Just tell me when and where."

"Tomorrow," he said, "at my house." His tone was matter-of-fact.

Diego and Frida had a kind of strange living arrangement. On the corner of Palmas and Altavista in San Angel, Diego had built two boxy houses connected by a bridge. He lived in the larger one, painted pink, and Frida lived in the smaller one, painted blue. His had a huge studio. Hers had a studio in the bedroom, which was bathed in light thanks to a perfectly positioned picture window. Frida loved that room. She had a bed with posts and a wooden canopy that she hung crepe paper ornaments from. The flowered bedspread, she had embroidered herself. She had her quarters decorated *a lo mexicano*, with gilded mirrors, native ceramics, papier-mâché parrots, flower wreaths, and colorful tiles. She also had a few skeletons hanging here and there, the kind they sell in the streets for the Day of the Dead. The room was just like Frida—bright, gaudy, and beautiful, but also a bit morbid. Anyhow, the arrangement allowed them each their own working and living space. In other words, it prevented them from killing each other. Often they ate together. Sometimes they slept together, but not often, because the doctor had told Frida not to have sex so she wouldn't lose the baby. That bothered Diego, but not too much, because girls still lined up to sleep with him.

I showed up at Diego's about noon. He had been up for hours. When he was working on a mural, he would start at the crack of dawn, so he was used to rising early. He had his easel all set up and his paints spread out in front of him on the old kitchen plate he used for a palette.

He hardly greeted me. He seemed anxious to get started, so I put down my things and asked for instructions.

"I'm doing some studies for the Medical School murals," he said. "We'll start with the allegory of health. You're the perfect model for it, Cristina. You know, fitness, vigor, well-being. Take off your clothes and stand here."

I did as he asked.

He explained the pose to me. Raised arm, firm step. As he demonstrated, his knuckle brushed against my breast. I tensed slightly, but he turned away as if he hadn't noticed. After about a half hour I began to get tired. I hadn't posed in a long time. I was out of practice, and besides, it was a difficult position to hold. I asked for a break.

"All right," he said, "but you can't be taking a break every ten minutes. I have a lot to do this afternoon."

I threw on the light robe I always wore when I posed and went into the kitchen to make us some coffee.

"Wait," he said suddenly. "Don't do that." He was standing in the doorway, looking at me. There was something different about his gaze. His eyes radiated an immense tenderness. I had never seen him look at anyone that way, except for Frida.

"Don't you want coffee?"

"Take that thing off," he whispered, nodding at the wrap. "I want to look at you. I want to watch you move." His voice was thick. I knew what was on his mind. It was obvious. I turned and faced him. Looking him right in the eye, I threw off the robe and let it drop to the ground. He smiled and stared, examining my body as though he had never seen it before. Centimeter by centimeter. I didn't care. I wasn't embarrassed. It had been a long time since anyone had looked at me that way. I was savoring the moment.

He moved toward me. I watched him come without recoiling. I was excited. Every nerve in my body stood at attention. He placed his fingers gently on my breast and circled the tip with his thumb. Then he drew me toward him. I felt a shiver from my arches to the peak of my crown, and I closed my eyes and let him put his hands where he wanted. His touch was delicious, and his body was sensitive and responsive. He slipped off his clothes. No, that's not right. That's what you might say if you were describing an art movie, but that's not what happened. Diego couldn't slip out of anything. He was too bulky. He could hardly see over his paunch to the bottom of his shirt to undo it. He had been gaining weight, since his doctor had told him that if he didn't inflate again, he would die of bad temper. He kept fumbling with the buttons until finally I pulled his hands away and put them on my hips, then ran my fingers down his chest and undid the last button on his shirt. We both burst out laughing.

"I'm a pig!" he chortled.

"Yes, you are!" I teased.

The skin underneath his clothes was soft and white like a baby's, with a few scattered graying hairs on his oversize bosom.

"You look like a girl!"

"So do you, Cristi."

He kissed me on the forehead. "A young, sensuous, beautiful girl." He had become clinging, breathy. "I need you so much," he kept whispering. "I need you so much."

"You can't have me until you take off your pants!" I whispered back, poking him in the stomach.

"Ah, that's going to be a problem, unless you help me with this belt buckle!"

I struggled with the buckle, but it was buried under rolls of stomach fat, making it difficult to release. I kept pushing at his spongy middle. "Pull in! Hold it in! Otherwise, I can't get the metal tongue out of the hole."

"Ha! I know all about tongues in holes!"

"You *are* a pig!" I kissed his bloated belly. "How do you get undressed when I'm not there to help you?"

"Frida does it."

Frida. The mention of her name. A kind of dull thud in the—where? In the brain? The gut? The conscience? Frida, my sister. I was about to make love with her husband. Ah yes, Frida. A dim image of Frida floated somewhere in the atmosphere . . . laughing . . . crying. Then it disappeared. But her voice, I could still hear her voice, distant, faint, disembodied. "Cristi! My own darling little sister!" An accusatory hiss. Diego heard none of it.

Frida! So what. Frida! She was there, I was here. She was here sometimes, but so what. Diego didn't seem to have a problem with it, and I was having too much fun to stop.

He led me to the couch at the far end of the studio. Making love with Diego was like drinking honey. Satisfying, satiating. A sweet taste lingered afterward. I don't know what I thought about. I can't remember. I didn't think of anything.

That's how it began. Innocently. Diego had had so many affairs. What difference did one more make? Frida knew about Lupe, she knew about Tina. She knew about the Wills woman and the students. She said she didn't believe in those stupid bourgeois ideas about marriage. "You don't die when you get married," she once told me. "You keep living, breathing, wanting." Even though she ranted and raved for a while when Diego slept with somebody new, she always came around. I mean, she always wound up accepting it, conceding that Diego needed variety and that his affairs meant nothing at all as long as he loved her best. She complained, yes. But she didn't leave him, did she? "Diego is a man who craves," she explained to me when she was in one of her tolerant moods. "He can never get enough of anything. Diego is a man who rejoices in the world and its pleasures, who thirsts after every kind of gratification. You take that away from him, and what do you have? One more fat, boring, ascetic draftsman. You take that away from him and you kill the exuberance! You kill the artist! Do you know what *ascetic* means, darling?" Anyway, most of the time she made friends and allies of her rivals, and it was she, not Diego, who had the last laugh. So, to tell you the truth, I didn't worry too much about what Frida would think.

I can tell you this: Diego was a wonderful lover. He not only fucked like a prince, he talked to me. And he listened to me. He described his student days in Spain. He said he hated the Spaniards because they had no imagination. The few good ones like Picasso and Gris went to France. Besides, the Spaniards decimated our native people. He told me things like that when we were lovers. He took me seriously, you see. He told me about his trips to Italy, about the Ravenna mosaics. "I traveled with just a knapsack," he told me. "All I carried with me was my brushes and paints, a few pairs of socks, and a change of underwear. I stank like hell after a week!" That's what he said to me, and I believe it, because Diego wasn't so fond of bathing. He trudged on. He made sketches in Milan, Verona, Venice, who knows where else? So many years have passed since I lay in his arms and listened to those stories. I do remember something he told me about Picasso, though. Diego knew that Picasso was a genius, but he didn't really like him. "I learned a lot from the son of a bitch," he would say, but Picasso got on his nerves. He was too imposing, too much the master who expected younger artists to kowtow to him. "The fag never let you forget that he was the leader and you were the follower," Diego told me. But Diego wasn't a follower, and that's the real reason he detested Picasso, if you ask me. They were too much alike, two strong men, two bulls in a perpetual pissing contest. Maybe he was just a little bit jealous. After all, Picasso was already a star, and Diego was just, well, he wasn't a star yet. When he left Europe for Mexico to paint murals for Vasconcelos, he told Picasso, "Cubism is dead, *viejo*. Your warped demoiselles say nothing to the people. You call yourself a communist, but you don't speak the language of the masses." "You've always been a *cabrón* and a liar," said Picasso without looking up from his work. That's how they parted company. Diego told me all those things. It was an education for me. Cubism, Lombardi painting, Franz Hals. I learned about those things from Diego, from listening to him. I'm, well, exaggerating. We didn't lie in bed talking about Picasso and cubism. Of course not! Diego was so hefty. It took tremendous energy for him to make love. Afterward, he'd just collapse, sort of like a rubber blimp that you punch a hole in, and it deflates . . . whoosh! That's how Diego was: inhale, come, snore! Inhale, come, snore! One two three, one two three, inhale come snore! But he never treated me as though I was stupid. He talked to me, although not while we were lying in bed. At other times.

And he listened. I told him everything—about how they teased us on account of Papá's being Jewish and a foreigner, about how Frida always managed to get her own way. I told him about Pinedo, and how miserable I felt when he left me. Even though Pinedo was a slimy, whoring slug and Frida said I was better off without him, being left like that by someone you once loved and who you thought loved you, it's like losing an organ. And I talked about my children, about how sometimes I thought that Isolda loved Frida more than she loved me because, after all, Aunt Frida was so glamorous, with her flowing Tehuana costumes and her hair done up in braids. I didn't talk about the kids too much, though, because Diego wasn't interested in children, and besides, Frida's pregnancy was a sore point.

Diego was generous, you know. He gave me things. At first, small things, things Frida wouldn't notice. A gold pin representing the god Chac Mool. A book of French impressionist paintings with soft colors and little girls dancing ballet. A typewriter. Why did I need a typewriter? At the time I didn't know that Diego was thinking of making me his secretary. That's right. I became his official secretary. That way we could go everywhere together. After all, an important man like Diego couldn't be without a full-time, rain-or-shine secretary, could he? Even in public. Even right in front of her, I was always with him. Cristi, write down Mr. Pérez's phone number, please. Cristi, check my appointment schedule for tomorrow, please. He needed his Cristi, see? But when he gave me that typewriter, I thought it was just something Diego found beautiful, with its big black frame and shiny keys with white letters stamped on them. A modern-day sculpture is what he called it. A poem to technology. Diego loved machines, all kinds of machines. Afterward, he gave much larger presents, but for the moment, just little things. Things I could hide in my room in the house in Coyoacán, where I was still living with Papá.

Frida visited that house all the time. She went to visit Papá and to play with Toñito and Isolda. She would dress Isolda up in beautiful Tehuana costumes with ruffled headdresses, and they would put on the phonograph and dance in the patio. But she rarely went to my room. She never saw the typewriter.

How did she find out? I'm not exactly sure. Maybe Petronila, Diego's maid, told her. Petronila came and went freely during the painting sessions. Or maybe Diego told her. After all, he wasn't ashamed of it, at least, not at first. For him, it wasn't a moral issue. For him, the man has one part, the woman has another part his fits into, and when they both feel like it, he sticks his into hers, and what's the big deal? So maybe he just said something like "You know, Frida, yesterday while I was screwing Cristi, I happened to think of a good theme for the left panel of the Medical School mural." Or maybe she just realized it. She had an eye like an eagle's, that Frida, and besides, she had a kind of sixth sense.

What happened is that one day she just popped in on one of the sessions. Just popped in unannounced. It was her house too. Why shouldn't she just pop in? After all, she and Diego usually had their dinner together around two or three in the afternoon in his enormous kitchen, and, of course, she had access to all the rooms. But lately, she hadn't even been coming over for the main meal. She had had her appendix out a couple of months earlier, and the incision was still bothering her. Besides, the pregnancy wasn't going well. She was tired all the time, and her foot hurt her, her back hurt her, everything hurt her. Sometimes it was hard for her to get around. Sometimes she couldn't even get out of bed, she'd spend the day under the covers feeling sorry for herself. And she was nauseous a lot of the time because of the baby. She spent most of her time in her own quarters, in the blue box on the other side of the bridge.

She had a strange look on her face. Nothing was going on between Diego and me at the moment. I was just posing and he was just painting. It wasn't as though she had caught us "in the act," as they say, but her eyeballs were spurting fire and her tongue flicked like a snake's.

She didn't utter a word. She was wearing gray trousers and a lavender shirt. She looked stunning. She stood right in front of me, very close, so close I thought she'd singe my cheeks. She didn't need to say anything. I knew that she knew, and I knew that she cared. What do you want me to say? I had hurt her. That was obvious. Her look was like bolts of lightning. I felt myself reduced to a pile of filthy ashes.

"Frida . . ." I murmured.

She turned away from me. Diego just kept on painting as if he didn't know what was going on, as if Frida were a fly or a gnat—annoying but unimportant.

She stood there staring at him.

"It's too early to eat," he said finally. "I'm not ready yet."

She didn't answer. She turned and faced me again. Then she took a step backward and looked me up and down, looked at my body as though it were a pile of dung. She walked around me, still staring. I felt like a slave on the block, a naked Indian slave. I felt like a whore on display. That's how she made me feel. My sister. Then she turned and left.

I waited for Diego to make a soothing remark. "It doesn't matter, Cristi." Or even "We've wounded her, Cristi. We've got to put an end to this affair." But he didn't. He just went on painting as if nothing had happened.

After that day, I didn't want to have sex with him anymore. I didn't even want to pose anymore. I made up excuses not to show up at the studio. "I have to take Toñito to the doctor, Diego." "I have to help my friend Ana María Quintano prepare two hundred burritos for her daughter's First Communion."

He begged. He had to get done with the preliminary studies in order to get going on the Medical School mural, he said, and he couldn't switch models in the middle of an assignment. Please, Cristi, just a few more days. Please, Cristi, just till I get myself together. Please, Cristi, otherwise I won't be able to paint at all. Please, Cristi, you were the one who said I had to start painting again, and now you're throwing me off the boat in the middle of the ocean. Never a word about Frida, though. Never a word about what we had done to her. Well, he wore me down. I wanted to stay away, but he wouldn't let me.

"All right," I said finally. "I'll pose, but I won't make love with you ever again, Diego. I can't bear what's it's doing to Frida."

"Ah, yes, Frida," I expected him to say. "We have to talk about Frida."

But instead, he said: "Just pose. That's all I ask."

Frida was playing the martyr. She was good at that, you know. Saint Justina, clutching the cross while the flames scorched her toes. But instead of carrying on like a madwoman, which was what I was prepared for, she looked out at the world through the eyes of a flogged puppy. Her foot was worse than ever. She was going to need an operation, and now the doctor said that she couldn't go through with the pregnancy because her health was too fragile. She was going to have to get an abortion. She didn't say it was all my fault, but the way she looked at me, I felt that it was. To make matters worse, Diego hadn't started the Medical School mural yet, and they had no money.

"Shit, you bitch!" I said to myself. "Call me slut! Call me traitor! Just spare me that mournful mask."

I couldn't bear it. The flogged puppy. The sacrificial lamb. I wanted to die. I couldn't stand the way I was feeling. But it wasn't her fault. It was Diego's. Why had I let myself get trapped in his web? An unwitting fly, that's what I was. An unwitting fly that suddenly got sucked into a sticky, silken maze and wrapped up in fatal threads. I could feel myself being squeezed to death, squeezed and smothered. I vowed never to let him touch me again.

But who could resist the great Diego Rivera? At first he behaved.

He painted. He didn't talk. He was cordial but professional. He built up my trust, and I let down my defenses.

One night, as we were finishing up, he took my hand and led me into the kitchen. I was dressed already.

"Just stay and have a bite with me," he pleaded. "Petronila prepared some *empanadas*."

"Diego . . ."

He looked like a rejected schoolboy. I didn't have the heart to go.

We ate in silence. He seemed not to be able to find words. I took his hand in mine.

"Poor Diego," I murmured.

"I'm so lonely, Cristi."

"Forlorn little froggie," I said, trying to sound sarcastic.

"I need you so much, Cristinita."

I didn't want to get caught again. "I can't betray Frida," I said firmly. I think I said it firmly. "We've hurt her once. Please, let's not do it again."

I was still holding his hand, but then he shifted positions slightly, so that he was holding mine. I felt him subtly tighten his grip.

"She's had an abortion," he said.

"I know. Poor Frida. She suffers terribly."

"Yes." He paused. "But why does she keep on getting pregnant? She knows she can't carry a baby to term. It seems stupid to me. Stupid and selfish."

"Why selfish? She wants to give life to a baby."

"She'll never give life to a baby, and now she can't give life to me, either. The doctor says no sex. Not for a long time. She has to recover, and then she has to have an operation on her foot. Whenever I go to her, it's the same. She can't have me. She won't have me. She's too wrapped up in her own pain. She loves to suffer, Cristi. That's the real reason she keeps on getting pregnant. So she can be miserable and make everybody else miserable with her. It's her greatest pleasure. But you know what, Cristi? It really doesn't matter, because you're the one I want. I need you, Cristi I need *you*. I've always loved you, from the very beginning, from the first time I saw you, when I went to visit Frida at your parents' house."

He was kissing me gently. He was unbuttoning my blouse, pulling it off my shoulders, massaging my buttocks, leading me to the bedroom.

How long did it go on? Maybe a year. Maybe longer. What I can tell you is this: I never felt more like a woman than when Diego and I were lovers. He was completely devoted to me. He talked to me. He painted me. He took me places with him. He wasn't ashamed of me. Whenever he had money, he bought me things. He set me up in a beautiful apartment on Florencia Street, in the best part of Mexico City. He even bought me a car. In those days, there weren't that many Mexican women who knew how to drive. I was special. When I went out in my two-tone Packard, I turned heads. I would let my hair down so it flew in the breeze. I was a sight to see. That's what everyone said. I would go to see Papá in Coyoacán every weekend, and I would take him for rides in the country. He loved it. I was a good daughter. I was even a successful daughter, because I was the favorite model of the great Diego Rivera! When Diego painted his *Modern Mexico* mural in the National Palace, he put me in the center of it. There I am, looking round and sensuous, leaning slightly forward to show the curve of my hip, my two children by my side. There I am, holding a communist something or other, a document, a declaration of the rights of the worker or something. I'm in front. Frida is there too, but she's in back of me, looking like a Girl Scout, no, excuse me, a Young Communist.

Frida was enraged that Diego and I were back together. Once in a while she spewed venom: "You've hurt me, Cristina! How could you do this to me! You little snake!" But most of the time it was just the cold shoulder. The I-don't-even-know-you're-here treatment. She'd walk into a room and kiss Diego, kiss Papá, kiss Toñito and Isoldita, even kiss Petronila and pretend I was invisible. At a party, if someone asked about me, she'd shrug as though she didn't know who they were talking about. Even if I was standing right there. Well, what did I care? I had Diego. She had a broken back, a sore foot, and an empty uterus.

She moved out of her house next to Diego's and into an apartment on Avenida Insurgentes, in Mexico City. "I'll help you pack," I told her. Instead of answering, she sniffed and turned her back. I was sick of her moods, sick of her hysterics, sick of her operations, her pain, her whining, her pregnancies and her abortions. I was the successful one, that's what I want you to understand. I was Diego Rivera's woman. I was the favorite, the pretty one, the one who had borne children. She couldn't even conceive a baby and carry it to term.

Diego still loved Frida. I knew that. I knew he went to see her almost every day. I knew because he told me.

"She's feeling better," he'd say. "We made love today. We made love savagely. She was magnificent!"

He said those things to upset me. They weren't true. They couldn't have been true, because Frida was sick. But he loved to get me riled. He loved to play one against the other. He was in heaven when women fought over him. He did everything he could to fan the fires. He bought me some beautiful red leatherette furniture for my apartment, then turned around and bought Frida the same set in blue. He knew we'd find out and would be at each other's throats.

"I'm just trying to be fair!" he said with that goddamn innocent grin of his. Fan the flames, fan the flames, keep the sisters clawing at each other! Was he taking bets on which one would destroy the other? Well, I didn't care. I was enjoying myself.

And what do *you* think? Do you think I was selfish? Do you think I was cruel?

I guess I was. Of course I was. Poor Frida. She was going through hell, and she needed me. But I was too busy zipping around in my new car, showing off, flirting with every pair of pants that came into my field of vision. I was enjoying my status as Diego Rivera's current favorite. Was that so wrong? All I wanted was a little happiness, a little fun. After all, hadn't she been running around to parties for years, hobnobbing with big shots and eating caviar? Well, now I was doing it! I was meeting movie stars, people like Dolores del Río! I was meeting famous politicians! Even Lázaro Cárdenas. And so many others! I would stand real close to them at parties and say outrageous things, fluttering my eyelashes at them right in front of their wives, just like Frida did. Just like I imagined she did. All I wanted to do initially was show Frida that I was somebody, that a man could really love me. Yes, I was hurting her, but so what? Let her take a little of what she's been dishing out. That's what I thought.

But then I began to think about it more. It began to sink in. I had betrayed my own sister. I had driven an awl into her gut. Who knew if I would ever be able to put back together what I had ripped apart. I began to think that things would never again be the same between us. I couldn't bear it. I began to stay home from the parties. I began to sit in front of the window, drinking and sobbing. Sometimes I'd hide in the bathtub. I'd sit and soak for hours. I'd lose track of the time. All I have to do is slide down under the water and breathe in deeply, I'd think. Then it would all be over. I wouldn't be an obstacle to Frida's happiness anymore. I would imagine myself slitting my wrists and watching the blood trickle out of my veins and into the soapy water. I'd imagine myself walking into the sea, Isolda's little fingers in my right hand and Toño's in my left. I'd just walk and walk, the gentle waves shrouding first the baby's tiny form, then Soldita's, then lapping around my neck, my ears, my eyes until at last they covered me entirely. I could hear Frida calling from the shore, "Cristi, please! Don't go! Don't leave me all alone! At least don't take the children! They're all I have!" Bitch! They're all *I* have? Even in my dreams she thinks only of herself!

I had finally realized what a mess I'd made of things. How did I realize? First there was the apartment. Frida's apartment, I mean. To move out of Diego's house and into her own place was a pretty radical step. She was trying to break away from him, that was clear. I'm not a psychiatrist, a professional like you, but I could see she was struggling to break bonds. She was going to try to support herself with her painting, she said. She didn't need him anymore. She was lying, of course. Lying to herself and to all of us. Because she saw him all the time. Every day! She didn't cut the cord at all. But she didn't want to depend on him financially, and to prove it, she set up a studio in her apartment and got busy working. She even went to see a lawyer, Manuel González Ramírez, one of the Cachuchas from her days at the Prepa, about getting a divorce. I never dreamed she would go so far. I was scared.

Frida was changing. What happened between us made her change. It made her more independent. It was as though Frida wasn't just divorcing Diego, she was divorcing *me*. I couldn't sleep at night. I'd lie awake, staring into the blackness, thinking about how I had ruined everything. I was miserable.

But there was something else that happened that made me realize what a shit I had been, how horribly I had hurt her. It was a painting she did around that time called *A Few Small Nips*. It was inspired by a newspaper story about a man who viciously murdered his girlfriend. He stabbed her all over her body, then left her in a pool of blood. When the police arrested him, he said something like "What's the big deal? I just gave her a few small nips!" Frida's picture shows the assassin holding a bloody knife over a woman lying on a cot, her body covered with gashes. It's brutal, incredibly brutal. But, this is awful, I'm embarrassed to tell you this. The first time I saw it, I burst out laughing! I mean, it was so gruesome, it reminded me of a Mexican melodrama. You know, those movies where the wronged husband shoots his wife, her lover, her mother, her father, her sister, the kids, the family dog, and all their cattle to boot! I couldn't stop laughing. Tears gushed out of my eyes. I tried to stop, but what could I do? "It's all right, Cristi," Frida said softly. She had that hurt little smile on her lips. "It *is* funny, in a way." She was in such pain. And the murderer in the painting was me. I knew that. Diego and me.

I loved her. So did Diego. We both loved her. We loved her more than we loved each other. Diego made her suffer, but afterward he was miserable, really, sincerely. We hated hurting her. Hated it. And yet we kept on doing it.

Diego and I didn't separate. I had learned how to type, not very well, but I kept on working as Diego's secretary, and I kept on posing for him. Frida knew we were still lovers. What was it about Frida that made you hurt her even though you didn't want to? Why did I treat her so cruelly? It was as though I were trapped . . . trapped in some kind of zombielike state where I couldn't control my own actions.

Did Frida ever forgive me? She said she did. Eventually, after it was over, she told me that she had put it all behind her. Her love for me and Diego was greater than anything, she said. But I knew that things would never be the same between us.

Frida didn't go through with the divorce, but she took a lover of her own—a famous Japanese sculptor—and then another and another.

Some were men, some were women. An art student. One of Diego's assistants. A waiter at Sanborn's. A young political activist. A dancer from a visiting *zarzuela* company. A nurse she had met at the hospital. She was drowning her sorrow in sex, and she was getting even. Diego didn't care about the women. He thought lesbian affairs were interesting. All the women in their crowd were having them. But the men, that he couldn't take. He couldn't bear the thought of Frida in another man's bed. That's why, every time she did it, she made sure he knew. Once she convinced her sculptor-lover Işamu Noguchi to take an apartment with her. They ordered some furniture for it, but Frida had it sent to Diego's instead. "Oh!" she told him. "The delivery man must have made a mistake and delivered it to the wrong address!" She did things like that to hurt him, you see.

Why do people who love each other torture each other so? You figure it out. That's your job. The only thing I know is this: I never stopped loving Frida. No matter what terrible things I did, I loved her. Write it down: Cristina Kahlo loved her sister Frida.

CHAPTER 18

Turning Point

DOLORES DEL RÍO WAS THE MOST GLAMOROUS WOMAN I EVER MET. I'D seen all her movies, including her first, *Joanne*. She just had a bit part in that one. But even in that tiny role, you could see she was so mysterious, so graceful. You just knew she was bound for stardom. She was just our age, maybe a year or two older. But I looked up to her as though she was a more mature, experienced woman. There was something fine about her, something left over from her education in a fancy French private school. You could tell she was raised in a house where they ate roast beef on porcelain and had pictures of great-grandmothers in ruffled collars in the vestibule.

Her father was a banker, she herself told me. He was the director of the Bank of Durango. During the Revolution, he hightailed it out of Mexico and settled in the States. Of course, we had been Zapatistas, but by the time I met Lola—that's what we called her—none of that mattered. We could laugh about it. We could be friends, and we *were* friends. I adored her. Her real name was Dolores Asúnsolo y López Negrete. Del Río was her husband's name. She had married very young, at fifteen. Her husband was Jaime del Río, her first husband, I mean. These aren't things I read in some movie magazine. These are things she told me herself.

Imagine this scene: We're in a *trajinera* in Xochimilco. Diego and Frida and a bunch of friends had decided to have a picnic in the floating gardens. I think Lola Alvarez Bravo was with us—the famous photographer who took so many beautiful pictures of Frida—her

husband, Manuel, and Lucienne. Let's see, who else? Jean van
Heijenoort, the French mathematician who became Trotsky's secretary. All kinds of famous people. Nicolasa Larrubia de la Barca, the
dancer. And there I was, right in the middle of everything.

We were in one of those big canoes they have at Xochimilco, you
know, the *trajineras*. An adorable young oarsman with brown skin and
luscious green eyes like mint candies, probably the descendant of
some horny conquistador and an Indian princess, this boy . . . this
young man was punting smoothly, so smoothly over the poplar-lined
canal. The arches of the boat were decorated with every kind of
flower—orchids, chrysanthemums, hibiscuses, carnations. The perfume made you heady, mixed with the tangy aromas of chile and
moist earth. I was giddy from happiness, drunk with the moment,
the fragrance, the luxurious vegetation, the delicious, lukewarm
breeze, and Lola. She was intoxicating. Her smile made you feel ine-
briated. A couple of guitarists dressed like *charros*—Mexican cow-
boys—sat in the back and played "La Paloma," "La Ciudad de Jauja,"
"Cielito Lindo," things like that. It had rained earlier in the day, and
drops of water still shimmered on petals and leaves. Along the canal,
the vegetation was so dense you could hardly see beyond the *álamos*,
but you knew the forest was alive. You could feel it . . . you could hear
the concert of invisible birds, crickets, frogs.

We had packed a spectacular lunch in huge metal containers,
chile, *mole poblano, enchiladas rojas, enchiladas verdes*, tamales, refried
beans, and rice with saffron. There were stacks of tortillas, tomatoes,
tart black olives, guacamole, and bottles of wine, tequila, rum,
whiskey. I had made *sangría*: sweet, potent *sangría* full of fruit that
retained the alcohol. The alcohol concentrates in the fruit. You can
get drunk just by eating the fruit. I was sitting next to Lola—Dolores
del Río—right next to her, my head resting on her shoulder while
she talked about Hollywood. It was so strange to hear her speak.
Practically all the pictures I had seen her in were silent, *All the Town
Is Talking*, with Edward Everett Horton, *Upstream*, with Walter Pidgeon,
and *What Price Glory?*, in which she played a French peasant girl
named Charmaine. There were so many.

"In Hollywood they don't think I look Mexican, they just think I

look foreign," she said. That's exactly what she said. Well, something
like that. She wore deep purple lipstick, and her lips seemed to be kissing the air as she spoke. They were so sensuous you almost wanted to
reach out and touch the corner of her mouth. "So, up to now, I've
been getting away with playing little French girls. But now, with the
talkies, who knows what will happen?"

Who knows what will happen? We all knew what would happen. It
was already happening. She would make the transition beautifully.
They would bill her as Spanish, which was more glamorous than
Mexican, and put her in films where her accent wouldn't be a problem. She had just made *Flying Down to Río*, with Fred Astaire and
Ginger Rogers. *Who knows what will happen?* No, I'm lying. I didn't
know what would happen, but I should have. I should have seen it
coming.

We were all fascinated with Lola. The first Mexican actress to
become a real Hollywood sensation. There were a few others who
almost made it. Ramón Novarro and Antonio Moreno before him.
But the one to really dazzle the gringos, the one to become a legend
was Lola. She was lucky, though. Just like Frida, she hooked up with
a man who . . . I'm not saying they didn't have talent. They had phe-
nomenal talent, but to have a powerful man behind you, it helps. You
can't deny it. I was never smart that way. Lola's father took off for the
States and left Lola and her mamá in Mexico. Lola learned French
and also flamenco dancing, which was very popular with the daughters of the wealthy. Of course, her mother was anxious to marry her
off. A pretty girl in a household is like a honey pot at a picnic. It
attracts pests. So, at fifteen, she married Jaime Martínez del Río, and
that's how she became Dolores del Río. He was almost twenty years
older than she was, a lawyer, a landholder, a great catch! They went
to Europe on their honeymoon. They visited London, Paris. They
basked on the seashore in Cannes. They were gone for two years in
all. Jaime was well connected. Once they were back in Mexico, his
friend the painter Adolfo Best Maugard introduced him to some
American movie people, including the director Edwin Carewe, and it
was smooth sailing from then on. Carewe got Lola her first role, the
couple moved to Hollywood, and you know the rest.

I was sitting in the boat with my eyes closed, listening to her talk,
her voice like a marimba. She was in ecstasy. She had divorced Del
Río years before and had just married the art director Cedric
Gibbons a couple of months ago. They were on a sort of belated honeymoon in Mexico. It's tough being a movie star. You're always so
busy, you have no time to do what ordinary people do, take honey-
moons, go drinking, whatever. We had just finished eating, and the
maid, who we treated as one of the group but who still had to clean
up, was gathering dishes. We had brought Frida's favorite earthenware with us, heavy, rustic earthenware with Indian designs. The
cups were clinking against the saucers. Another maid was serving
rich, delicious coffee. The aroma mingled with the scents of hibiscus
and wild orchids. The birds warbled on, the crickets were out in full
force, everything was alive. It was divine. Frida's pet monkey Fulang-
Chang chattered incessantly in his cage. She had locked him up so
that he wouldn't latch on to a branch and swing his way to freedom.
It was heavenly. The *trajinera* glided along, swishing against petals
and fragments of plant. The bright pinks, purples, and greens of
daylight were deepening into the muted shades of evening. And
there I was, right in the middle of it, my head on Dolores del Río's
shoulder! I can hear her. She's talking about Gene Raymond, her
costar in *Flying Down to Río*. "The film just opened at Radio City
Music Hall . . . you must all go to see it, darlings."

Frida doesn't know where to rest her eyes. She is flirting
unabashedly with Lola, showing her pretty teeth, biting suggestively
into a banana, taking discreet little swigs from a flask she carries with
her everywhere. She drinks cognac. Constantly. Frida drinks constantly now. At the same time, she is fascinated with the punter's
crotch, and every so often calls his name so that he will have to adjust
his position and she can watch the shifting of the bulge between his
legs. Now she has finished her banana and takes out a thin little cigar,
very fine and stylish. She lights it and sucks on it while looking Lola
straight in the eye.

Diego wriggles off his seat next to Jean van Heijenoort and carefully, carefully makes his way to the bench across from Lola and me.
He doesn't stand. If he did, the canoe would rock and pitch like a

reef in a storm, and Diego would go crashing overboard, causing such a seaquake that the fish would come flying up in waves like birds. So he crouches and moves warily across the space from one bench to the other, then sets down first one enormous cheek, then his whole ass. Finally, he shifts his feet so that he's facing me . . . no . . . facing Lola. He smiles at her, a big, wet smile, a perverse smile. She smiles back. Her husband isn't with us. He stayed back at her mother's house. Montezuma's revenge, maybe.

Diego leers at Lola. I catch the eye of the gondolier. I simper suggestively, and the young man winks and smiles, then looks away. He is nineteen or twenty. His work has made him muscular and taut. His thigh contracts as he pushes the oar. Diego jerks his head toward me suddenly—he moves in little froglike twitches—and discovers the game I'm playing with the boy. It's nothing, really. A sly grin. A provocative pout. Suddenly, Diego's face becomes mean. His mouth twists into a kind of sneer as he pulls his foot back sharply then shoots his boot into my ankle. The pain is so intense I have to clamp my teeth together to keep from shrieking. Like a bolt of electricity, the pain surges up my leg to my hip, my side. My eyes fill with tears.

Lola seems oblivious. Jean is telling her about how Trotsky has been misunderstood by the Stalinists and how wonderful it would be if he could find refuge in Mexico. Trotsky has always wanted to come to Mexico and finish the biography of Lenin he began years ago. Now it looks as if it might happen. That's why Jean is here, to make the arrangements. He tilts his blond head toward Lola. He is so intense, so passionate, when he talks about Trotsky. Lola listens as though she's thinking about her next film assignment.

Frida has seen everything.

"¡Imbécil!" she hisses at Diego, but he just smirks, then runs his tongue over his upper lip.

Frida gropes her way to the other side of the gondola. She sits next to me and puts her arm around my shoulders. Then she takes my hand in hers and kisses it. I want to bury my head in her bosom like a little girl, but I can't, so I bite my lip to keep from crying and pretend to listen to Jean chatter on about Trotsky.

Diego is interested, because Trotsky is one of his heroes. He asks

Jean questions about where Trotsky will stay once he gets to Mexico and offers the Casa Azul—Papá's house, Frida's house, *my* house—as a safe haven, should they actually find a way to smuggle him into the country. Suddenly I hate Diego, and I love Frida more than ever.

It's well after dark by the time we're back in town. Diego and most of the others have slept in the car and now they want to go out dancing.

"I'm too tired," I announce. "I'm going home." But nobody will hear of it. They stuff me into the car, my car, and make me drive to a place in a working-class barrio, a dimly lit cantina where sweaty laborers drink *pulque* or beer and smoke sawdust cigarettes. They watch us with expressionless faces, their mustaches wet and their hats pulled over their brows. They speak in low voices, as if conspiring. Once in a while, a gold tooth cap glitters in the light of the lone bulb. This is a scene from a third-rate Mexican movie, I think. In the center of the room there's a small space without tables—maybe two meters by three—which serves as a dance floor. But none of the customers are dancing. They're all men.

Diego decides where we will sit—a table near the counter where the heat is stifling. Lola sits across from him, and he looks at her with eyes like a beast's. They're going to spend the night together, I think. Frida looks at me as if to say "Now you see what it's like," but I ignore her.

Why was I surprised? Everyone knew that Diego slept with every female he could get his hands on. Why did I think he would be faithful to me when he was never faithful to the one woman he really loved?

Let's see. Jean van Heijenoort sat next to Lola, and I sat across from him, next to Diego. Frida sat on the end. She ordered a rum, and while they brought it, she took a couple of swigs of cognac from her flask.

Jean wanted to dance. He said to Lola, "Let's dance," and he tugged on her arm. Diego got up and pulled me toward him.

"I don't feel like dancing," I said. I pleaded to be left alone, but he dragged me out onto the splintery floor.

"Isn't Lola beautiful?" he whispered in my ear. His breath was heavy and rank with liquor.

"Very beautiful," I answered.

"Doesn't she have a magnificent ass?"

I had been on the verge of tears for hours, and now I felt as though the dam was bursting, but somehow I managed to hold myself together.

"Yes, magnificent," I whispered.

"Should I make love to her tonight?"

I didn't answer.

"Should I?" he insisted, crushing me against him.

"Go ahead. Enjoy yourself."

"Yes, I will. Of course I will. I'll enjoy myself more than I ever have with any other woman."

I tried to push away from him. I was suffocating.

"Maybe Frida will sleep with her too. What a delicious thought, the two of them together, both so beautiful, so sensuous. Two female bodies entwined, the possibilities are dizzying!"

I said nothing.

"You know, I'm glad that Frida loves other women. It keeps her busy. It gives her an outlet."

I continued to dance in silence. I wished he would let me go back to the table. I wanted to sit down.

"Who are you looking at?" he said suddenly.

"Looking at? No one."

"Yes, you are. You're looking at that boy over there."

"You're nuts, Diego. *Estás loco.*"

"Don't talk to me like that, you bitch! You're humiliating me in front of all these people!"

I knew he was drunk.

"Calm down, Diego," I said. "I'm not looking at anyone. Don't be silly, *mi amor.* I don't have the energy to flirt right now."

"On top of everything, you're making fun of me," he snarled.

I pried loose enough to glance around the room. Lola and Jean were lost in the rhythm of their bodies, but Frida was watching us, her smirk changing to concern.

"Don't be silly," I whispered again. I tried to sound soothing.

"You bitch! Don't pretend you're not coming on to that little shit in the checked shirt." He hissed when he said *ese pedacito de mierda.*

"No, Diego. I swear, I'm not." I was fed up with his carrying on, but I was trying to keep him calm. I was afraid he'd whip out his pistol and shoot up the place. I'd seen him do it before.

We danced a while longer, and then he started up again. "You're looking at the guy behind my back. I know it, I feel it!"

I lowered my voice as much as I could. "What do you care what I do?" I whispered. "What difference does it make if I look at other men? After all, you're going to fuck Lola."

The rest I remember in a kind of nauseating slow motion. I saw his hand move up behind his head as though it were an animal, an independent creature, then pause in preparation for the attack. Poised, fierce, vicious. I saw it fall hard and fast, but somehow I didn't make the connection between that and the horrible crack, then the ache in my jaw. My mouth was full of blood. I could taste it. I was afraid I was going to throw up. I felt myself wobble, lose my balance, and then suddenly Frida was there, holding me, sustaining me.

"*¡Bruto!*" she snapped at her husband.

She took me back to her apartment. Beyond that point, the images get blurry. Compresses—hot? cold? I can't remember. A swig of alcohol . . . a deluge of tears . . . and Frida holding me in her arms like a baby.

"Poor Cristi, poor poor Cristi," she kept saying. "*Pobrecita Cristinita. Pobre muñequita.*"

She stroked my cheek with her knuckles. "Just because he smacks you around a little bit doesn't mean he doesn't love you, Cristinita," she said gently. "And just because he sleeps with other women doesn't mean he doesn't love you. That's the way he is, Cristi. He's just, well, he's an artist."

Since my relationship, my affair, with Diego, Frida had started to grow more detached. It wasn't that she didn't still love him. She did. She loved him more than anything, but she was struggling to become self-reliant. Diego had so many friends. He was always entertaining celebrities at his house, politicians like the Trotskyite bigwigs and the president, Lázaro Cárdenas, writers like the American John Dos Passos. And then there was the movie star crowd. But Frida was developing her own group of friends, and besides, she was becoming a successful painter. More and more people were getting to know about her. The newspapers wrote about her, not just because she was the wife of the great Diego Rivera, but because she was an artist. That's what she wanted, control over her own life. She didn't want to be just Diego Rivera's little woman. She had to have her own individuality. Even when she moved back to her own house, the blue house next to Diego's big pink house, she kept her life separate. She remained in control. Her pain had made her strong. The pain I caused her when I had that affair with Diego. It was a kind of turning point, not only for her, but for me, too, because once it was over I was so sorry, so filled with guilt and remorse, that all I wanted to do was make it up to her. I spent the rest of my life trying to make it up to her.

But I'm getting ahead of myself.

I think Frida really wanted to forgive me, but I had hurt her so horribly. She was angry. She tried to keep it inside, but she showed her hostility in a million different ways. Yet, at that moment, there in her apartment, I felt that things were all right between Frida and me. I thought that she *had* forgiven me. From then on, I did everything I could to make her love me. I took charge of her medicine. I counted out her pills. She took so many of them. Pain pills, pills to make the swelling in her foot go down, pills to help her sleep. I gave her massages and I prepared her medicinal baths. I loved her so much, and I felt so terrible about what I had done to her. That night, lying there in her arms, hearing her try to calm me, trying to make me feel as though Diego still loved me, I felt that Frida cared so much about me. I vowed to do everything I could to make things easier for her and to heal the wound. And maybe the wound would have mended if it hadn't been for Trotsky.

Diego adored Trotsky. Trotsky was his hero. Trotsky was this romantic figure who had fought for an ideal and had been misunderstood and rejected by his own people. The Stalinist communists hated him, and I think that Diego, who also had been spurned by the more—how can I put it?—the more orthodox communists, identified with Trotsky. He had painted pictures of him. One was in New York, in the Trotskyite office there, and one was in the Rockefeller Center mural. Now that Jean and the International Communist League were working to get Trotsky out of Europe, Diego saw his chance to be his savior.

Trotsky couldn't stay over there because he had too many enemies. In Mexico, also, the Stalinists attacked him, and Siqueiros, who was a fanatical supporter of Stalin, criticized him every chance he got. He threw shit not only at Trotsky, but also at Diego. He accused Diego of selling his paintings to rich American tourists, to selling out to the gringos. When they snuck Trotsky into Mexico in . . . let's see, it must have been in 1937 . . . Diego brought him and his wife, Natalia, to the Casa Azul in Coyoacán. It was dangerous to harbor Trotsky, and that made Diego all the more anxious to do it. Diego loved excitement. He loved risk! Poor Papá. He was so confused. He didn't know who Trotsky was. He kept saying, "Is that poor man involved in politics? It's dangerous to be in politics these days!"

What can I tell you about Leon? He had incredible eyes—eyes like vast, unfathomable lakes. You could lose yourself in those eyes. You could disappear into their blueness. They swallowed you up and made you forget everything around you. He wore glasses, and their tortoiseshell frames were like a shoreline, where everything turns to brown and gold. On some people glasses look ugly, but Leon's grabbed your attention and drew you into those mysterious eyes. They seduced you and paralyzed you. Then they would suck you in and consume you. He had an intensity about him. He walked like a soldier, looking straight ahead, with measured steps, all the same length. Head high, chin out. Sometimes you'd think he hadn't even seen you, and then suddenly, he'd turn and wink, and his white beard and the tips of his mustache would quiver. He was obsessive about everything. He worked all the time. He was preparing a biography of Lenin, and he would sit for hours dictating to his secretaries. He was also preparing a deposition for a kind of mock trial in which he answered the charges brought against him by the Stalinists. When he was writing, he never looked up. The only one who could disturb him was Frida.

Trotsky was the one who brought Frida back to Diego. Trotsky and the civil war in Spain. The Spanish conflict was something we all cared about. The republicans and communists against the fascists. Frida got involved in propaganda and also in getting help for war orphans and the children of antifascist soldiers. The war got her involved in politics again, and that was a bond between her and Diego. Once Trotsky came to Mexico, Diego needed her more than ever. He had been seriously ill because of all that dieting. He had problems with his kidneys, his eyes, who knows what else. Frida's foot bothered her, but she was in better shape than he was, so it became her job to look after the Trotskies.

That suited her just fine. Charming Frida! Witty Frida! The glamorous hostess, the brilliant conversationalist. She stepped right back into the limelight, just where she loved to be. Once the journalists found out where Trotsky was staying, the photographers couldn't get enough of her. Here she was, posing in her frilly Tehuana dress, and there she was, posing in her chic new Chanel-inspired suit. She buzzed around Leon, waiting on him, making sure the meals were to his liking. "Do you have enough writing paper, Comrade?" and "Do you need some more blankets, Comrade?" and "Shall I have the cook prepare you an herbal tea and some *pastelitos de almendra*, Comrade?" She couldn't do enough for him. Since security was an issue, she had to be very careful about servants, and she brought in her own girls to clean up after him. "Eusebia has made you the most delicious *chiles rellenos*, Comrade! Just for you. Just because you like them." Natalia was ill with malaria, so she was out of the way a lot of the time. How convenient, right? So it was up to Frida to entertain Comrade Trotsky. She could talk to him about politics. Their secret language was English, because Trotsky didn't speak Spanish. Most of the time, I didn't know what was going on. In fact, most of the time, Frida treated me as if I weren't even there. She'd translate only the most stupid, insignificant things. "Don't worry, Cristinita. We're not talking about you. I just asked Leon if he'd like a cup of tea." It was like she was alone with him. I was hurt. After that incident with Lola, I thought Frida had really forgiven me and things were going to be just like before. But now Frida was up on her high horse again, acting like some Aztec princess and treating me as if I were her goddamn slave. But I didn't just cower in the shadows while she was putting on her

show. You see, I was Leon Trotsky's chauffeur, and that meant that I
spent long hours in the car with him.

He fell for me first. That horny old guy with the beautiful eyes.
You should have seen the way he grinned at me when he crawled into
the car and sat by my side. I mean, it wasn't as though he sat in the
backseat like a tycoon or a movie star. He sat right next to me, as close
as he could get. I'd ease out onto the road and we'd be cruising along
when, all of a sudden, I'd feel a hand on my knee. Once he squeezed
my thigh, right here, on the inside right below my crotch. *Virgen
madre,* he startled me! I lost control of the wheel, and for a second I
thought we were going to ram right into a cactus the size of a telephone pole. But somehow I regained my composure enough to
brake. Then my insides turned to jelly, and I felt sort of damp, if you
know what I mean. It was awful, but it was also funny.

He was so direct about the way he approached women. I realize
that he was practically a god to the International Communist League
and everything, but he was crude. The truth is, I felt sorry for his
wife. Poor Natalia, she was sick so often. She was in her fifties. I was
just in my late twenties, and I thought fifty was old. Natalia was all
wrinkled. She'd look in the mirror, and tears would well up in the
corners of her eyes. Then she'd look at me with that sad, sad face, as
if she were going to die of despair. "You're so young," she'd say with
a sigh. "No wonder he . . ." And her voice would trail off. Frida always
used to say, "People should do what they want. You, too, Cristi. Just
do what you want and don't worry about what others think." But it
didn't seem right to me, the way old Trotsky would tweak my ass or
make lewd gestures right in front of his wife.

I didn't know what to do. On the one hand, I really didn't want
to make love with him. But on the other hand, he was so important,
so brilliant, and so famous. I have to admit it, there's something exciting about the idea of going to bed with a man that millions of people
worship. It's hard to turn down a man like that!

He came up with the strangest schemes. One day, right out of the
blue, he said, "You know, in case of fire, I wouldn't know what to do. We
should have a fire drill." He said it in English, and Frida translated. The
minute the words were out of her mouth, she burst out laughing.

"A fire drill, Leon! What are you conjuring up?"

Everybody was laughing except Natalia and Leon.

"This is a very serious affair," he said. "In Russia I was in a potentially devastating fire. Stalin's men tried to burn down my house with me in it. It happened there, and it could happen here. I have many enemies. We must have a plan."

Jean spoke up. "I don't think this is such a good idea, Leo," he said. "We can't have you running down the street in the middle of Coyoacán. That would be as dangerous as a fire."

But Trotsky was a stubborn old guy. He insisted over and over again. Like a fountain dripping on stone, drip drip drip. He finally wore you down. "Look," he kept saying, "we should try it just once. Just to make sure we all know what to do in the case of an emergency."

The plan was that we'd all escape over the garden wall.

A few evenings later, Leon suddenly dashed through the house screaming, "Fire! Fire!"

We all ran out into the patio. It was dark, and we could hardly see where we were going. Frida kept stumbling until she finally grabbed on to Diego and he hoisted her up over the wall.

Once we were on the other side, Leon grabbed me by the hand.

"*¡Vamos!*" he murmured. It was one of the few Spanish words he had learned.

"What? Where?"

"*¡Vamos!*" he kept saying. "*¡Vamos! ¡Vamos!*" He signaled for me to keep running, but in the middle of the street I stopped.

"Wait a minute," I said. "What's going on?"

"Your house," he panted. "*¡Vamos a tu casa!*" Then he made a gesture, and I realized what he wanted. The whole fire drill was a ruse to get us away from the others, to get me to take him over to my house on Aguayo Street so that we could make love.

I stood there laughing. But he wasn't laughing. He was trying to hustle me down the street. "*Vamos,*" he said over and over. "*Vamos, vamos a tu casa.*" He kept patting my behind, slapping it gently as though I were a pony that he was intent on moving down the road.

I didn't know what to do. I was tempted, I can't deny it. After all, the way Diego had been treating me, it made me feel terrible. Even though Lola had gone back to the United States by that time, and I was pretty sure that she never went to bed with Diego, that it was all just a stupid flirtation, things had changed between Diego and me. I was no longer Diego's woman. I was just one of the many women whom Diego had had affairs with. Going to bed with Trotsky would be a coup. And it would be fun. Let's face it. I was a young, single woman, and I liked to have fun. Trotsky was a character! And he had charm. But then there was poor Natalia. I had already betrayed my sister. How could I betray Natalia now? I stood there, wavering.

But then it was too late. Jean and the security men were closing in. They were running toward us, lanterns in hand.

"Leon! Is that you?"

"Comrade Trotsky!"

As it turned out, I never did make up my mind. I didn't have to, because Frida decided for me. Helpful Frida. The next morning she hovered over Trotsky like a hummingbird over a honeysuckle. "Leon" this and "Leon" that. She flashed her sharp little cat teeth and wiggled her ass. She brought him tea and tortillas with mashed avocado, a dish he had learned to love. She brought him fruit and sweets. She couldn't do enough for him. The two of them chattered endlessly in English. Of course, I felt left out. She wanted me to feel left out. I didn't know English. Natalia and I just watched. We both knew where it was going.

She was getting even. With Diego and with me. I thought she had forgiven me, but all she was doing was biding her time, waiting for the right moment to thrust in the dagger. She wanted to punish me for having an affair with Diego, and the best way to do it was to lure away Trotsky. *She* would be Trotsky's woman, not me. She had to be the star. She had to have the place of honor! And she wanted to punish Diego too. She could forgive him his other affairs, but she couldn't forgive him for falling in love with me. And what better way to hurt him than to betray him with the man he idolized?

Frida and old Leon, they were like schoolkids. He would pass her notes. He would slip them between the pages of a book and shove it into her hands when they said good night. But then Frida started to get brazen. Much more brazen than I would have been. She would

giggle and flirt and blow Leon kisses across the dinner table. They
even held hands and kissed, tongue and all, right under Natalia's
nose. He'd pinch Frida's ass, she'd call him *mi amor.* And then she
asked me if they could use my house to make love. My little house on
Aguayo Street! What could I say? I could never deny Frida anything.
Still, I hesitated.

"It will be our way of getting even with Diego," she told me. "The
way he hurt you, carrying on with Lola like that."

I just looked at her. By then, I was convinced that nothing had
ever happened between Diego and Lola. Diego had taunted me with
Lola that night in the cantina, but Jean told me that after Frida and
I had left, he took Lola back to her mother's house.

Frida realized that she wasn't getting anywhere, so she changed
tactics. "He hit you, Cristi," she said. "He's an abusive man! Why
should we put up with his tantrums, Cristi? We'll show him he can't
control us."

So I gave in. That's the upshot of the story: I gave in. I would
drive Frida and Leon around for a while, then drop them off at my
house so they could be alone. It was just like when we were kids. I
would do whatever Frida wanted. I would slump down in the seat of
the car and imagine Trotsky making love to Frida, just as I had once
imagined Alex making love to Frida. What was the old man like in
bed? There was something perverse about it, old Trotsky and Frida
not yet thirty. And yet it was tantalizing, the idea of making love to a
man whose ideas had galvanized the world. In my mind, I would see
him cup her breasts, then run his hands down her body . . . her back,
the curve of her waist, her hips . . . It could have been me.

What was my role in this drama? I was the chauffeur. The extra.

It didn't last long. By July it was over. Frida didn't love him.
She wanted only to prove that she could do it. She wanted to seduce
the great Trotsky in order to punish her husband and sister, but
soon the affair got stale, and she lost interest. After the initial thrill,
how exciting can it be to sleep with an *abuelito* with arthritis and
rancid breath?

"I'm leaving, Leon," she told him. Just like that. "I'm leaving. I
have to get away. Some friends of mine in Veracruz have invited me

to visit." She wasn't even graceful about it. Just good-bye and screw you. She was done with him. She was pretty much done with all of us for the moment.

Was he upset? I don't think so. I thought that maybe after Frida was out of the picture, he would come back to me, but that didn't happen. I didn't care. By that time, I was bored with Trotsky and the International Communist League, the investigations, the commissions, the reporters who hovered around the door at the Casa Azul. I was bored with everything. Leon missed Natalia. After Frida left, I would see him walking with her, hand in hand, in the garden. If you ask me, she was the only woman he ever really loved.

Diego found out about the affair. That's what Frida had wanted all along. She had gone out of her way to make it obvious. Diego blew up at Trotsky. He called him a Judas and a slime bag and a *chingado de mierda*. But Diego couldn't really afford stay mad at Trotsky. What I mean is, he was already in trouble with the Stalinists, and he couldn't have Leon Trotsky for an enemy too. In the end they wound up, if not friends, at least on speaking terms. In November Frida sent Leon a gift. It was a portrait of herself. What else? In it she looked as brazen as she had behaved in the Casa Azul. Beautiful Frida. Seductive Frida, with bright red lipstick and painted nails, a purple carnation and a red ribbon in her black hair. A memento, perhaps, of the passion they had felt for each other. Or maybe just a tease.

CHAPTER 19

My Sister, the Artist

HER BODICE HAS BEEN RIPPED—NOT NEATLY CUT, BUT RIPPED—FROM shoulder to waist, revealing—guess what! A luscious, round breast? No. What do you think this is, a penny romance? No, the subject's insides, her viscera. Because the flesh has been severed as well, slit to expose a living, pulsating heart. Pulsating, pumping blood in spite of the fact that the arteries have been sliced open, tubes or hoses lopped off in the middle, gaping orifices, mouths without tongues, pipes leading nowhere, except for one—a long vein that wraps around her back, working its way along the outside of her frilly blouse, down to her skirt, where it falls gracefully under her elbow like a thin red ribbon. Then it extends under her wrist and continues beyond her hand into the folds of milky cloth, where she catches it with a surgical pincer and snips it off. Snip! And the blood from the vein pours onto the fabric and forms a pool. Some of it seeps into the fibers, but some of it flows into rivulets that trickle toward the floor. Globs that seem still to be pulsing, streamlets that impel themselves forward with the rhythm of heartbeats, only now the viscous liquid has nowhere to go, so it gathers in a crimp in the material and drips down toward the hem, smudging the cloth. The stains blend in with the embroidered floral pattern. You can hardly tell the crimson flowers from the bloodstains. Petals, droplets, ribbons, stems, leaves, all part of the delicately woven design.

Well, you asked me to describe my favorite painting, didn't you? It's funny you should ask that now, after all this time. We haven't talked much about Frida's work. For me it's hard to talk about *liking* or *loving* a painting by Frida, because I know when they all were painted, why they were painted, what they mean. They're all wonderful, but a lot of them are hard for me to look at. The one I'm describing to you is called *The Two Fridas*. It's a large painting, a square painting. It was done about the time we're talking about, 1939 maybe. Before Leon died.

It shows two images of Frida. Frida alone with herself: one Frida is holding the hand of the other Frida, because Frida has only her own hand to hold. Does that make sense? At that time, she and Diego had begun to grow apart, although Diego was completely supportive of Frida's painting. "She's the best portrait painter alive," he would say, but then he'd treat her like garbage. He'd stop talking to her for days, or else he'd go over to her place and hole up in the bathroom. She'd make a wonderful lunch for him, and he'd refuse to eat. *Nopales* salad, roast pork, guacamole with *chipotles*, and for dessert, those little butter cookies we call *lenguas de gato*—dishes that Diego loved. But he'd just go sit on the toilet.

In the painting, both Fridas are sitting up straight as a rod, but those expressionless faces are just masks that hide pain. That's how she wanted to portray herself, you see. Strong. Moving on with her life, pushing ahead in spite of everything. Invincible Frida! But you know she's suffering, because she's split in two. One Frida is wearing a Tehuana costume with a lacy ruffle. That's the Mexican Frida, her authentic self. In that image, her heart is whole. "That's the me that Diego loved," she said. The other Frida, the one with the open heart, is wearing an old-fashioned gown, maybe a wedding dress. "That's the me that Diego abandoned," she said. The Tehuana Frida holds a tiny portrait of Diego from which a vein shoots out and joins the hearts of the two Fridas, but the unloved Frida snips it off. They're both Frida, Frida trying to get free, trying to cut herself off. But even though she's severed the vein, it continues to drip. Diego's love, it just won't be stemmed.

Sometimes I think that *The Two Fridas* is not about just her. It's about her and me. *I'm* the other one, the unloved one—the pretty one—because one of the figures is prettier than the other. She holds my hand, and I sit there, looking strong and brave. Invincible *Cristina*! I think my sister painted a picture different from the one she thinks she painted. Is that possible?

What do you mean, why is it my favorite painting if it causes me such pain? I didn't say it was my favorite painting, did I? I did? Well, I guess it's because I see my own feelings in it. What I mean is, it expresses not only Frida's pain, but also my own, not only how sorry I felt for my sister, my twin, but also the sense of abandonment that I was experiencing. That painting makes me feel sad, just like old photographs of dead people make you feel sad, whether you liked those people or not, because it helps me relive the times when I lived life so intensely. It hurts, that's true, but the thorn that those images drive into my heart reminds me that I was once alive.

Frida's career was taking off. After her fling with Trotsky, it was as though she had to paint to lose herself. And even though Diego treated her horribly, he pushed her to exhibit. She had never wanted to show her stuff, at least that's what she said. But Diego started making contacts with galleries, and before she knew it, she had a show going up right here, in this cesspool we call Mexico City. She was lucky that way. She had Diego. Even after her betrayal with Trotsky, she had Diego. What does a woman have to do to make a man that devoted to her?

Her foot tortured her. "Devil's hoof," she called it. "The devil's got me on the rack again," she'd say. "You know, he gave me his own hoof to punish me. He sneaked into my bedroom one night and stuck it onto my scrawny leg. Too bad he didn't screw me while he was at it! That'd be a hell of a fuck, wouldn't it, Cristi? I mean, the horny old goat! Horns growing right out of his skull! He must fuck like . . . he must fuck like the devil!" And then she'd burst out laughing. But it was a forced laugh, because she wanted you to know that she was suffering yet putting on a brave face.

Even though she complained all the time, she kept on painting.

"I don't know why anyone would want to buy my paintings," she told people. "I'm sure everyone would rather have one of Diego's. But Diego's are so expensive, they settle for buying one of mine."

The devoted wife content to paint for fun. Art for art, not for money. It was just a show. I mean, what if she really didn't sell? What then? She could always just say, "Oh, I was never a serious artist. Painting has always been a hobby." How could I not see through it? I'm not as dumb as people think, you know. I knew Frida like the palm of my hand, and I knew it was all an act to preserve her pride, just in case. Silly, isn't it? What I mean is, how could she not sell? After all, she was the wife of the great Diego Rivera.

Diego blamed Frida's affair with Trotsky on Trotsky. Afterward, he and Frida got back together again, at least for a while, and Diego arranged for the sale of four of her paintings to the American movie star Edward G. Robinson. Did you see him in *Little Caesar*? I did, but I never got to meet him in person. Robinson's real name was Emmanuel Goldenberg. Did you know that? A Jewish name: Goldenberg. Why do movie stars always change their names? I guess because in Yankeeland, people are so prejudiced. Anyhow, the sale got into the newspapers, and people started to pay more attention to Frida's paintings.

Around then André Breton came to Mexico. You know, the French poet. I did get to meet him. Breton was a big shot, the father of surrealism. Frida and Diego took Breton around everywhere, and Breton said that Frida's paintings were the essence of surrealism. That's what he said, the *essence* of surrealism. He said her combination of Mexican folk motifs and fantasy made her one of them, one of the surrealists.

But Frida hated Breton. He was full of himself, she said, always spouting out ideas that sounded profound but were actually just bullshit. "Surrealism unites the conscious and unconscious realm of experience so completely that dream and everyday reality become indistinguishable from each other. Reality becomes a surreality." That kind of stuff. I heard him say it so many times that I know it by heart. "Surrealism unites the conscious and unconscious realm . . ." What's that supposed to mean? For us Mexicans, death and ghosts and dreams are all just part of everyday life, so what's the big deal? The

Virgin of Guadalupe and the corner florist are both real. The skeletons that dance for the Day of the Dead and the clerk who stamps your identity card are both real. "Pompous ass," Frida called him, and she was right. But we both adored his wife, Jacqueline. She was a pert, smart, warm woman. A painter, just like Frida.

"Cristina, *chérie*, you must come to Paris with your sister!" she told me. You see, André had agreed to arrange an exhibition for Frida in France.

But I couldn't go. The plan was for Frida to go first to New York, where she would exhibit at the gallery of Julien Levy, a friend of Diego's. Then she would leave for Europe.

It was the publicity event of the decade. Maty, Adri, and I had planned a going away party, but Frida would have none of it.

"Diego wants something really lavish, darlings. We're inviting absolutely *everybody*, from the Trotskies to President Cárdenas." Lázaro Cárdenas was Diego's new hero. Instead of living in the presidential mansion in Chapultepec, he lived in his own little house. No more taking orders from the political bosses, he said. Instead, he would listen to the people. He would return Mexico to its revolutionary ideals. Can you ever really believe politicians? I don't know, but Cárdenas won Diego's trust, and it's true he had the balls to nationalize all the oil companies, and to do that, he had to take on the Americans. Well, *you* probably won't appreciate that part of the story, but the fact is, in Mexico he was the new hero, the new god. We all adored him. Even I did. In those days I believed everything they told me. Anyway, you can't give a party for the president of the Republic and serve enchiladas made by your sister, even if the president of the Republic says he's just a *campesino*. They handed the matter over to Lupe Marín, the great Lupe!, the most acclaimed party planner this side of the Río Bravo. Lupe hired a professional cook with a whole kitchen crew, which was fine with me.

Lupe and her hired hands outdid themselves. Endless platters of stuffed *chayote* peppers, chicken in peanut sauce, *enchiladas verdes*, *enchiladas rojas*, pork stewed in *pulque*, *mole poblano*, Mexican flags of green, white, and red rice, every kind of dessert you can think of— quince paste, almond cookies, coconut balls, fruits, cheeses—what else?—tequila, grenadine punch, *sangría*, wine. I went to Frida's party, even though I felt awful and still couldn't eat normally. I had just had an operation myself, you see. A gallbladder operation. "Really, darling, you look as droopy as a limp dick," Frida whispered in my ear. "And you look as mangled as a modernist sculpture, with your deformed leg and crooked back," I cooed in hers. Or maybe I didn't actually say it. I may have just thought it.

Society ladies and politicians fell over themselves to get close to the honoree. And the place was crawling with actors and actresses. Armendáriz, who was in *María Candelaria* and *Flor Silvestre* with Lola, María Félix, Sara García, Carlos López Moctezuma, who was in *El gendarme desconocido* with Cantinflas, Paulette Goddard. (Paulette was going to turn into something of a problem later on, and so was María Félix.) And me, right in the middle of it all, sharing recipes for *mole poblano* with Sara García. You can imagine, the place was buzzing with reporters, all hovering around Frida. Frida, the Star. She had prepared a huge list of guests that she had invited to her show in New York—the Rockefellers, the Luces, Alfred Stieglitz, Lewis Mumford. She was dropping names like horses drop turds.

"You know, I'll be painting Clare Boothe Luce's portrait when I'm in New York. And the artist George Grosz has promised to show me his studio. No, Diego doesn't hold grudges. Both of us want John and Nelson to be there. Oh, Fallingwater! I've already accepted an invitation from Frank Lloyd Wright and Edgar Kaufman to see it. Nikolas Muray the photographer blah blah Meyer Schapiro the art historian blah blah (it helps to be part Jewish, darling) Conger Goodyear blah blah Dorothy Hale blah blah (I'll be painting her portrait, darling) Sigmund Firestone blah blah blah blah blah."

Both she and Diego put on quite a show at the train station. Again, the baby talk.

"My precious Froggie, how will you manage alone?"

"*Mi niñita chiquitita.* If you need anything—anything at all . . ."

Tears, tears, and more tears. "Oh, my darling Dieguito. *Pobue bebito, pobue ranita.*"

"Fridita, Friduchita. I know you'll be a huge success. My *bebita linda.*"

Only a few of us knew how close these two buffoons were to a divorce. When the spotlight wasn't on them, when no reporters were watching, they hissed at each other like alley cats.

At last she was gone. She didn't write to me during this trip, either, not once, although she did write to Maty and Adri. What did I have to do to make her happy? I kept asking myself. What did I have to do to make her forgive me?

CHAPTER 20

Fragments

DOROTHY HALE IS DEAD. SMASHED TO SMITHEREENS IN FRONT OF THE Hampshire House, her luxury apartment building in New York City. Hairpins in place, seams straight, corsage of tiny yellow roses neatly fastened to her black velvet dress, right side of cranium shattered—a gooey mess of blood, bone, and filth. Sticky splinters of skull stuck to her cheek, her bodice, the concrete, the stones of the elegant structure she had called home. What would it be like to jump off a ledge and feel yourself falling falling, falling into space? Did she repent suddenly and try to undo that fatal step? Did she flail? Did she struggle to grab on to a ridge or a balcony? Did she pray? *Thy kingdom come, thy will be done, on earth as it is in heaven* . . . Thy will be done? Did she ask herself if this was God's will? Communists don't believe in God, you know. They say that religion is the opiate of the people, although a Jesuit priest once told me that they've got it all wrong, that communism is the opiate of the intellectuals. Was Dorothy a communist? I don't think so. Most of Frida's New York friends weren't communists. Just the opposite. They were rich jackals who spent their days partying and licking their paws. Oh, they made communist noises. They talked about exploitation of the proletariat. But they were really just *comunistas de salón*, armchair communists. Anyhow, I think Dorothy was just a society girl, used to having money, who found herself in a real stew when her husband died. Her husband, Gardiner Hale, was a painter. He did portraits of people who were dripping with money, and he charged them an arm and a leg for a painting.

Dorothy was a knockout. I met her when she was in Mexico. She had been a showgirl in the Ziegfeld Follies. That's why Gardiner married her. She was really stunning, with black hair, skin like vanilla cream, and sculpted features. They bought a house in southern France, on the beach, and they entertained in high style. All the bigwigs came to visit, all those guys that Frida called the *cacas grandes*. But then Gardiner was killed in a car crash, and there was Dorothy. Gorgeous face, gorgeous figure, but no dough. And after she had spent all that time entertaining Picasso and the other pashas of High Art on the Riviera, she couldn't take it. One moment he's here, the next moment he's dead, a mangled mess of guts and metal. I'm talking about her husband. She didn't want to go to work. She didn't want to be poor, so she blocked it all out and went looking for *la pelona*. Did she squeeze her eyes shut, or did she stare straight ahead? Did she wind up lying on the sidewalk, irises front and center, blood trickling out of her ear, the way Frida painted her? What would it be like to plunge through space, knowing that you'll crash and shatter like a crystal vase? Shards of your crown flying off every which way. Blood spurting onto the sidewalk. Blood gushing from your smashed body, dirtying pedestrians' shoes and hems. Do passersby spring aside so that your body fluids won't mess up their outfits? Do they run in terror? Do they even flinch? Does anyone ever try to pick up the pieces?

Dorothy Hale gave a party the night before she did it. Everyone was there—Bernard Baruch, Isamu Noguchi, Constantin Alajalov, who did covers for the *New Yorker* . . . everyone. Frida left early because she was supposed to begin a portrait of Dorothy the next morning. They had met in Mexico a couple of years before, and Frida had promised to paint her someday when she was in New York. Now Frida was there, and they had decided on that day in October 1938, that day after the party. There was a problem, though. Dorothy couldn't pay. Since Gardiner had left her without a penny, she was begging from friends, paying the rent on her fancy penthouse with the money Clare Boothe Luce grudgingly gave her. At first Frida planned to drop Dorothy. "She's such a bore, darling, always whining about her tough luck." Frida wasn't so interested in hearing about other people's suffering. But Bernie Baruch said he'd pay for the portrait, and Frida was anxious to be in with that crowd, so she suddenly remembered she was a good communist and didn't care anything about money. "You don't have to pay me, darling." "No, I insist." "No, really, darling." "I insist!" "Well, all right, darling, but only because I really need the bucks." Frida was trying to become financially independent. She didn't like to have to ask Diego for money. That day, I mean the next day after the party, Dorothy was going to sit for Frida. They had it all arranged. I see Dorothy pushing aside the curtain, opening the window of her fancy New York penthouse. Frida knocks at the door.

"Can I come in, darling? I've come to paint you."

"Sorry, darling, I'm busy killing myself."

Dorothy is standing on a chair in her strappy, high-heeled shoes. She's balancing on the sill, looking out over the city, the skyscrapers, the office windows, the haze, and down below, the cars, the cabs, the vendors, the bustling shoppers and office workers—all doll-house size. She's taking a deep breath, she's stepping forward into nothing, she's dropping . . . dropping, faster, faster . . . She's yielding to the sweet darkness of death, to the sweet, sweet darkness.

Have *I* ever thought about it? Yes, I've thought about it. Hasn't everyone? Frida used to think about it all the time. She was still reeling from her separation from Diego, from the business with her foot. She'd be suffering horribly, and she'd mix herself a cocktail of liquor and painkillers to put herself out of her misery for a few hours. She was beginning to do it more and more often.

"Someday I'll plop all these little candies into a pint of vodka and drink the whole thing down," she told me more than once. "Then *adiós*, Frida. Good-bye, you little bitch. No great loss to the world. You never could paint anyway!"

After Dorothy Hale died, Clare Boothe Luce asked Frida to go ahead and do the portrait anyway. She supplied a couple of photographs so that Frida could do a nice painting. Ms. Luce was going to pay for it and give it to Dorothy's mother as a gift, you know, as a kind of memento. Mrs. Luce wanted to give Dorothy's mother something beautiful to remember her daughter by. But Frida did a scandalous thing, a really scandalous thing, and cruel. It was just like Frida. She could be so cruel. She painted a picture of Dorothy Hale's suicide! I mean, of Dorothy actually committing suicide. That's right. It shows Dorothy tumbling head first through the air, enveloped in a whirl of clouds that extend onto the frame, her shoe flying off her foot, her arms stretched forward above her head as though to break the fall. And then, in the foreground, it shows another image of Dorothy, already dead. Dorothy lying on the ground, her dress wrapped around her legs, her eyes open, blood spilling off the side-walk and onto the frame, blood everywhere, blood dripping onto the banner that borders the scene, the banner that originally said that Mrs. Luce had commissioned the picture, but which Mrs. Luce made Frida change, blood that seems to splash onto the floor, the very floor where you're standing and looking at the painting. It's as though you're right there, right there in the same space as Dorothy, you can almost smell the flowers in her corsage, you can almost reach out and take Dorothy's foot in your hand.

It came out in all the Mexican papers, not the suicide, nobody here cared about *that*, but the painting Frida had done. We were all embarrassed. At least I was. How could she do something like that to a poor mother who had just lost her child, a beautiful daughter? Frida, you bitch, why did you do it? Why did you paint that picture? Was it an act of pure meanness, or did you do it just to get attention? Like when we were kids and you stole my little blond doll with the porce-lain face and the cloth body, and you left her on Mami's bed, naked, with her legs open. And then you put my little rag donkey on top of her, with his mouth on her . . . you know. Maybe that painting wasn't about Dorothy at all. Maybe it was about you. That would make sense, wouldn't it? You always were the star of your own drama, the tragic heroine, the victim. Is that woman falling through the clouds Dorothy Hale or is it Frida? Frida's pain, Frida's despera-tion—Frida's—Frida's . . . I'm . . . I'm sorry. I don't know—I don't know what came over me. Wait . . . I have a hanky here somewhere . . . It's just that—She never wrote to me. She never wrote to me the whole time she was away. Not even a postcard. Why didn't you send me at least a postcard, Frida? I know you were still mad at me because of Diego, but I loved you so much, Frida. I missed you so much, and I was so alone here. Why couldn't you forgive me? Adri and Maty got letters—a few letters. They showed them to me. You talked about your new lover, Nikolas Muray. He was a photographer, you said. Very handsome, you said. And Hungarian. But he didn't spark my interest. I wasn't interested in meeting him. No, not at all. I didn't want any more rivalries with Frida. Anyhow, I could never really compete with her.

Frida was going to exhibit at Julien Levy's gallery in New York. It was all set for the end of 1938, the year before the war in Europe. She left for New York in October, and from there, she would go on to France. I remember that people were edgy because nobody knew what was going to happen with the Germans. There were rumors. Papá had Jewish relatives in Germany, and there were stories about bombs going off in people's living rooms. There were a lot of Jews coming into Mexico then, Jews who weren't able to get into the United States because the Americans had quotas. Someone told Papá that German soldiers had grabbed a toddler out from under the skirts of a cousin of his, a little girl, and they threw her in the air the way you toss a mamey up over your head and shoot it for target prac- tice, over and over again, up and down, up and down. The baby is screaming, I can see it in my mind. The baby is screaming, and the mother too, and then they give her one final toss, very high. She seems to float up forever in slow motion, and then one of the Nazis pulls out a gun, all the time the mother is watching, and the Nazi pulls out his gun and aims right at the baby. When the mother sees what he's going to do, she grabs his arm and tries to yank it away. He pushes her down. She's on the ground struggling to get up, and he points his gun at her and fires. The instant before, she was alive, and now she's dead. The baby is not traveling slow motion anymore. The baby is plummeting. She crashes and smashes her head. The instant before she was alive. And now Frida was off to where those things were happening. First to New York, but then to Europe. There was no danger of—what I mean is, Mamá was Catholic, and since Jewishness is transmitted through the mother, there was no danger that some Nazi would grab Frida, because Frida wasn't Jewish.

Anyhow, Frida was an important painter, a celebrity, not just Mrs.
Diego Rivera. So there was no chance at all. Nobody bothers you if
you're famous.

Frida left for New York in October. I remember it was October,
because we were getting ready for *el día de los muertos,* the Day of the
Dead, when we celebrate those who have gone on before us—*Jesus
Christ, triumphing gloriously over death, rose the third day, immortal, never
to suffer again.* I remember that we were preparing sugar-candy skulls
for the festivities. Skulls, skeletons, crossbones, all decorated with
sugar flowers of every color. My kids just loved to suck on those luscious little skulls. They loved to chew on those sugary white fingers
and ribs and femurs. Ha! I bet you thought I didn't know that word:
femur. How could I have a lame sister and not know it?

Frida was getting ready to go. As for her and Diego, their marriage was as wobbly as a top, so I didn't expect Diego to take such an
interest in Frida's show. After all, both of them had been carrying on
with other people for months. But all of a sudden, Diego started running around like he had a firecracker up his ass. Everything had to
be perfect for Frida, darling Frida. He put her in touch with important people, helped her put together the guest list for the opening,
that sort of thing. André Breton wrote a piece for the brochure, and
the gallery publicized the event as though Frida were a movie star.
Newspaper articles, a spread in *Vogue.* Frida was everywhere, just like
the Holy Ghost. Frida in her Tehuana outfit standing in front of *What
the Water Gave Me.* Frida dressed like a movie star next to *Fulang-
Chang and I.* Frida holding a cigarette in a long, elegant holder and
sipping champagne by the self-portrait she did for Trotsky. Frida
laughing boisterously and pointing to Papá in *My Grandparents, My
Parents and I.* So you see, not only did every painting contain a portrait of Frida, but every publicity shot contained *two* portraits of
Frida, the photograph itself and the painting inside the photograph.
Two Fridas for the price of one, see? *Frida, Frida everywhere! By the windows! On the chair!*

My Grandparents, My Parents and I did include a portrait of Papá.
But at that moment it was okay to bring up Papá. In fact, in that particular New York crowd, it was quite fashionable to be Jewish. What

with the war coming on and everything, Jews were the new political cause. Such terrible things were happening to them, more terrible than anybody knew at the time, and Frida knew how to milk a situation. A lot of the American leftists were Jews, and a lot of the people who were active in the art world, people who bought paintings, people with dough, people Frida needed as friends and allies. So Frida just suddenly became one of them. Very exotic, very Mexican, and yet one of them. The best of two worlds. They were enchanted that they could count this alien creature as one of their own, this bird of wondrous plumage, so familiar, yet so foreign. And that made selling them paintings so much easier, didn't it? Clever Frida. She *was* clever. She was shrewd at selling. Signs and announcements were going up all over the place. They all read *Frida Kahlo (Rivera)*.

I asked her why she used Diego's name in her publicity. "You always say you want to be recognized for your own work. You don't want to be known as *la señora de Rivera*."

"It was Levy's idea," she said. "Levy's and Breton's." That's what she told me when she returned home. "They insisted on including Diego's name in the publicity."

"Ah? And you couldn't do anything to prevent it? You couldn't talk them out of it? Couldn't you have just told them, Look, it's a matter of professional pride?"

"No, darling, of course not. Julien is in business to make money, and Diego Rivera's name sells."

"Yes, but your stuff is good. Diego says you're a better painter than he is. You didn't need to latch on to his name like that!"

She looked at me like she thought I was trying to steal her silk stockings. "You know how these gringos are, darling," she said finally. "Everything is money."

"But what about the Mexico City exhibit, Fridita? The one you had before you went to New York? Every piece of publicity mentioned that you were *really* Frida Kahlo de Rivera."

She was beginning to snort and paw the ground, so I didn't insist. After all, what was the point? What I wanted more than anything was to make peace with her.

She wrote to Maty that the New York show was a huge success,

that she had sold every single painting. "Look at this!" Maty
shrieked. She had just burst through my front door and was clutching Frida's letter in her hand. "Our baby sister has taken New York
by storm!" Actually, *I* was the baby of the family, but never mind.

I read the words, written in turquoise ink, on a page that Frida
had decorated with fruits, flowers, and cactus leaves.

*Maty darling, you won't believe it, but everyone here is in love with your
Friducha. They love me so much that they bought absolutely everything. Alfred
Stieglitz even wanted to buy a lock of my hair, and Mrs. Rockefeller wanted to buy
the dress off my back! Ah no, I told her. My Tehuana dresses are not for sale! I
hate it when gringas use Indian clothing. They don't understand the meaning, the
symbolism of our designs. They cheapen our native culture, don't you think so,
darling? But in the end I did offer to have one made just for her. I had to, darling. She has been so nice to me.*

"She's done it again!" I said, laughing. But maybe not, I thought.
Maybe she's exaggerating. It wouldn't be the first time. Still, if one of
her goals was to break loose from Diego, then the trip certainly was
a success.

*Darling, I've seduced all the men in New York. Well, maybe there's a police-
man or a butcher or a schoolboy or two I've missed, but really, almost all. Listen
to what happened at Fallingwater. You've heard of Fallingwater, haven't you,
Maty? It's a magnificent house designed by the famous American architect Frank
Lloyd Wright.*

Everyone in Frida's life was a famous something or other. A
famous photographer. A famous movie star. A famous philanthropist.
A famous architect.

*This house is in Pennsylvania, in a perfectly wonderful place called Bear
Run, full of trees and streams and animals (even human ones, kid, wait till I tell
you!). Wright's idea was to blend nature and architecture—I'm sure you can
understand this, Maty, Cristi never could, she's awfully slow, isn't she, darling?—
so he built the house on a cliff, perched over a waterfall. The house consists of*

several terraces cantilevered (that means hanging, kid) over the ledge. It's right in the middle of a forest, so you can imagine that when Eddie Kaufman, the owner, first invited your poor Friducha to visit, she was just terrified. I mean because there you are, right in the middle of all the ACTION—chipmunks scrambling around, foxes springing out from behind bushes, I swear, Maty, you can hear the bunnies screwing from the guest house! [Look, here she drew a picture of one rabbit leaping on top of another.] *At night you fall asleep to the crickets' song, the whisper of soft breezes nibbling at the leaves, and best of all, the steady rush and gush of the waterfall. In the morning, you look out the window, and suddenly you're seeing the world for the very first time—a branch twisted into an exotic sculpture, a drop of rain (left over from when Saint Peter peed the night before!) glistening on a trembling petal, a tree like a priest with arms outstretched toward a perfect sky. The fantastic thing is how Wright combined concrete, glass, and steel, creating a sculpture that you can live in. The cantilevered slabs clutch the boulders and produce such a sense of power! You feel so sheltered. It's like lying snug with a man you're truly in love with.*

She went on to describe sections of the house, the concrete pier, the terraces, the living room with its enormous picture windows, the tangled, tricky stairways. The tangled, tricky stairways are significant. Here, I'll read the next section.

Darling, you won't believe what happened. First, let me tell you that Edgar Kaufman, his son (whose name is also Edgar), and Julien are all madly in love with me, and I flirt shamelessly with all three at the same time. Well, one night Julien and Edgar Sr. decided to face off once and for all. Each was waiting for the other one to go to bed so that he could sneak into my room via the double stairway. And me, I was just relaxing in bed, placing bets with myself to see who would win. Really, Maty, it was hilarious. First I'd hear Eddie open his door and pitter-pat up the steps. Then Julien would open his, and Eddie would scamper back down to his own room, but instead of going in, he'd linger in the hallway so that his rival would know he was watching him. So Julien would go back and shut the door, and the whole comedy would start all over again. Well, Julien finally threw in the towel. But what do you think was waiting for him when he got back to his room? Me! While he was on the staircase trying to outsmart Eddie, I sneaked into his room, took off my clothes, and jumped into his bed!

Soon I'll be leaving for Paris. Believe me, kid, I would be really having a good time here if it weren't for my spine. It's like having the devil ride you piggy-back everywhere you go. He just hangs on with those pointy little claws of his, which he digs into you deeper and deeper.

I'll write to you from Paris. Do you want me to buy you some perfume?

Now, doctor, look at this:

The American Hospital
Paris, February 15, 1939

Dear Maty:

I arrived here in the underworld last month, and Satan (disguised as Breton) has been showing me off to all his little incubi and succubi (I mean, of course, his surrealist playmates) like a new toy. It's not as though they don't love me, darling. Quite the contrary. They adore me, but only because they think I'm one of them. André calls me a surreal-ist par excellence, a quintessential surrealist. Quintessential. Got that, kid? He thinks because I cut myself open and show my pain that I was influenced by his stupid doctrine. The painting he loves best is *What the Water Gave Me*. He thinks it's full of birth and life symbols that came to me in a dream, when actually it's just the way I see things: floating in the pool of my own reality, what do I perceive? My ailing foot. Mamá and Papá. Lovers and corpses. Skeletons and embryos. My body. Chac Mool. A skyscraper shooting out of a volcano. My cast-off Tehuana dress. Gnarled vegetation. What these morons don't understand is that we Mexicans see things differently. For us, death and life are all rolled up into one. This shit-filled little planet and nirvana, darling. All one and the same. For them, that's odd, you see, whereas for us, it's perfectly normal. The *grandes cacas* of surrealism can't get it through their little heads that we move between the material and the ethereal as easily as a frog goes from land to water.

You wouldn't believe what a fuss they're making over me, and even though I think they're full of shit, darling, I must admit I'm having a wonderful time. Pablo has been just outrageous, showering me with gifts and introducing me everywhere. They're having a big Picasso exhibit in the spring, and he wants me to stay, but I'm anxious to get back to New York to see Nick, so I probably won't. But I *have* met the most fascinating people—the poet Paul Eluard and the painter Max Ernst (you've probably never heard of them, darling, but over here, they're very famous)—and, of course, Elsa Schiaparelli, the designer. She was so taken with my Tehuana dresses that she's designing a version for Parisian women! I've seen the sketches. The frock is scrumptious, of course, but the idea of a Tehuana wardrobe *à la parisienne* is sort of silly. I've gone to a few Trotsky meetings here. (Please don't tell Diego. I know he's mad at Leon.) But I've hardly had time for political activities, precious Maty, because my exhibit goes up in March. And now I can't even attend to that because I'm sick again, this time with a kidney infection. So here I am, holed up in this awful American hospital. As hospitals go, it's the best in Paris, and the doctors are wonderful, they hover over me constantly, but all I want to do is get out of here.

The truth is, I miss Nick so much. You remember him, don't you? Nikolas Muray, the photographer. Well, we've become *very* good friends. He's the most dynamic, beautiful man I've ever met, with those volcanic Hungarian eyes. What a lover! And what an artist, Maty. You should see some of the pictures he's taken of me. He understands me as no man ever has before. He photographs my very essence, Maty. My very soul. What I mean is, he captures my inner core. My pain, my passion. He knows how to look at me. Oh, my darling Maty, my sweet sister, can you imagine what it's like to pose for an artist like that? Diego would be very jealous if he knew how much I love Nick.

Maty, dearest, please forgive me, but I won't be able to get you that perfume you wanted. In the first place, I have so little money. I had to move out of Breton's apartment and into a hotel because I really need a nurse, and there was no room there to put an extra person. I was so ill that I couldn't even stand up, never mind go shopping, and when I leave the hospital, I'll still need to be attended to. You understand what I'm saying, don't you, Maty? I have to save my money—the few cents that I have—to take care of myself. I haven't bought anything at all, nothing, except for two dolls for my collection. They're lovely, really. One has blue eyes and blond hair. The other one is dark. Those are the only things I bought, precious Maty. Just two baby dolls to keep me company. Your poor little sister will be so lonely in Mexico without her dear Nick.

Kiss everyone for me, and don't fret too much over your little dog. It's better to die than to suffer so much. Poor thing. If you get another one, don't let Isolda roughhouse with it. *Escuincles* have such fragile bones.

Hugs and kisses,

Your Frida

She didn't mention me even once. Not once did she say "give my love to Cristi" or "say hi to Cristi" or even "don't tell that bitch Cristi that I wrote to you." No, not a word. Not a single word for the sister who pampered her and nursed her and loved her. Not a word.

One more letter came from Paris, this one addressed to Adriana. I don't have a copy, but it was dated March something. In it, Frida talked about her exhibition, which had just finished. They included other stuff in the show besides hers, she said, mostly junk—*cachivaches*. She led Adri to believe that she was definitely the star. I had already begun to suspect that the gallery-going public wasn't as enamored of Frida as she had said. Why? Because Frida always exaggerated her own success, and also because articles had already come out in the Mexican press about the New York show. She hadn't sold all her paintings, as she claimed. In fact, the show wasn't a financial success at all. Later it came out that the Paris exhibit was a real disaster. Breton called it *Méxique*, which means Mexico in French. According to *Novedades Mexicanas*, the French are so damn nationalistic that they look down their noses at foreign artists. If it had been someone from Germany or Italy, at least, that might have been a little different, but a Mexican painter? Half the French probably don't even know where Mexico is. Couldn't even find it on a map. Well, that's what *Novedades Mexicanas* said, but who knows. Maybe being Señora de Rivera doesn't mean anything over there. Or maybe Frida's work just isn't that . . . Another thing you have to take into consideration is that the war was about to start. People were nervous. I mean, you're not going to be interested in looking at pictures of Aztec gods and dead birds floating in the bathtub when you're scared shitless that the Germans are going to drop a bomb on your house and blow you and your kids to bits. Frida was supposed to exhibit in London after she left Paris, but she decided not to. She was sure that Europe was going to explode any minute, and besides, she was anxious to see Nick. That's what she told us when she got home. By the end of March she was on her way back to New York and her beloved Nick.

I close my eyes, and what do I see? I see a beautiful, spacious kitchen. I see walls of glistening blue and white Mexican tiles. I see kettles, huge kettles, bubbling on the fire. I hear the glug glug glug of their cooking, and I smell the aromas of *mole*, of *albóndigas con chipotle*, of *caldo de camarón*. I see a wide, sturdy wooden table laden with read and white hand-painted bowls from Guanajuato, red and yellow platters from Puebla, scalloped, earthenware crocks from Oaxaca. Avocado salad. *Nopal* and tomato. *Chilaquiles*, pork rinds, stacks of tortillas wrapped in loosely woven red napkins embroidered in blue, yellow, and green with intricate Indian designs. I see two women, young, slim, nearly identical. Twins. They could be twins. They work together without speaking. One chops chiles, the other stirs *pipián* sauce. Both are somber. Each labors with her back turned slightly toward her sister. One has betrayed the other. A shadow falls across the floor. There is no laughter in this room.

But then, as the onions crackle and the caged parakeet in the patio begins to twitter, as butter melts in the *baño de María* and a fly darts drunkenly from sill to table, one sister begins to hum, ever so softly, and the other sister listens, smiling slightly. It is time to begin the desserts. It is time for sweetness. One sister mixes the batter in a huge, flowered bowl, and the other stirs the chocolate, catching the rhythm. The shadow lifts gradually, as though someone has eased open the shutters. Sugar dissolves into syrup as they chant a nursery rhyme.

Arroz con leche,	Sweet rice pudding,
me quiero casar	I want to marry
con una señorita	A nice young lady
de este lugar . . .	From around here . . .

One sister giggles. A high-pitched titter; a tinkle, like a tiny bell. The other sister tilts her head toward her and smiles.

Arroz con leche,	Sweet rice pudding,
me quiero casar	I want to marry
con una señorita	A nice young lady
de este lugar	From around here,
que sepa coser,	Who knows how to sew
que sepa bordar,	Who knows how to stitch
que sepa la tabla	Who knows how to multiply
de multiplicar.	The eights and the nines.

The first sister lays down her spoon and turns to face her twin. She smiles a warm, forgiving smile. She holds out her hand, and the second sister takes it. They stand there a moment, squeezing hands. The first sister draws the second toward her and holds her in a firm embrace. The other sister lays her head on her sibling's shoulder. A tear materializes on her eyelid. The shadow is gone. The kitchen is filled with light.

But that didn't happen, did it, Frida? It was just a fantasy. A fragment of dream that I held on to my whole life. Now it's time to let it go.

CHAPTER 21

Slave and Master

I WAS MY SISTER'S SLAVE. THE MOST GROVELING PEON COULDN'T HAVE served his master as devotedly as I served mine. I was her charwoman, her drudge, her secretary, her chauffeur, her nursemaid. I was her everything. Let me tell you what happened after Frida left Paris, then you'll understand.

Imagine you're alone and very frail, in a strange place, a place you hate, where you don't speak the language and the people are slimy. You force yourself out of your room. After all, you're a star, and your audience is waiting, but you're so feeble that it's only by an act of will that you pull on your clothes and stuff a flower into your hair. They've planned a party for you. You've got to go. It's the opening of your exhibition, *Méxique*. You collapse into the car and let yourself be driven to the gallery. Everyone is there, all the glitterati—the intellectuals, the society ladies, the movie stars, the politicians—all the huge *cacas* who can make or break a career. Artists and would-be artists oil their way around, ogling the fat cats who look like they might be willing to bankroll a show. They smile, their well-lubricated jaws tightening into a mechanical grin. You retreat into a corner. You're in pain, and your French is poor. You can say *salaud, conasse, ta gueule*, your favorite swear words. But you can't carry on a conversation, so you don't try. You lose yourself in your thoughts. Soon you'll be leaving this nasty city. You'll skip London and head right for New York.

New York is where *he* is. You're not so young anymore, you're a woman of thirty-two, and who knows if you'll live to be forty. Seize the moment! Run to your lover! Such an exquisite man, all fire and incandescence. Just close your eyes and conjure up his angular jaw, his wide forehead, his cologne, his tangy breath. You think of him, and your body turns into hot wax. Imagine him whispering in Hungarian: *Let's fuck, darling. Let's fuck.* To you it sounds like an exotic poem or an ancient chant. Even in your illness, or perhaps especially in your illness, the memory of his fingers on your thigh sparks a bonfire.

You haven't seen him for three months, your Bohemian sweetheart, your beautiful gypsy. But you've been holding him, caressing him tenderly, in your mind.

And now, finally, you're flying to him, borne across the Atlantic . . . and no matter that your back feels like a mangled spire, no matter that tiny fiends cling to your hip with claws as sharp as hunger, your spirit is free and dashes back to him.

Then you are there, in his apartment, brimming with love and passion. Everything is as you remember it. The Lalique ashtray is on the coffee table. The mint-colored curtains are slightly faded from the sun. The photograph he took of the two of you is on the wall. His Olympic Saber medal is in the display cabinet. Pictures of friends line the hallway—Martha Graham, Edna St. Vincent Millay, Eugene O'Neill, T. S. Eliot. Copies of *Dance Magazine* and *Vanity Fair*—with his articles—are piled on the floor. Everything is exactly as it was, except this: He doesn't want you anymore.

He doesn't want you anymore.

You're an invalid with a twisted back, a stunted leg, and an ugly disposition. The pain makes you irascible. You find fault. You pick fights. You're fragile. You can't make love like an acrobat. Nick wants a young, healthy woman. A nimble, nubile filly. One who can experiment and play games. He's marrying someone else. Good-bye, Frida.

She didn't see it coming. It caught her by surprise. He was engaged, and he wanted her out of the picture. All she could do was pack her bags and come home.

In April 1939, Frida returned to Mexico.

"I couldn't stay in New York any longer," she told me. "I missed you all too much."

She was lying. She didn't miss all of us. She missed Diego. I mean, if she missed anyone at all, it was Diego. But now she was going to have to face a new disappointment. Diego wasn't at all happy to have her back. He had gone back to Lupe Marín, and soon he would be involved with Paulette Goddard.

Yes, *the* Paulette Goddard. The movie star. But wait, I'm getting ahead of myself again.

Frida was sobbing softly, patting her eyes with an embroidered hankie that had been Mami's. We were in the kitchen of the Casa Azul, seated at the same table where we had eaten tortillas with guacamole as kids. She was being melodramatic and annoying, but I let her get away with it. She needed me. And I owed Frida. I had done something terrible. I wanted to make things right again between us.

Why didn't you write to me the whole time you were gone? I wanted to ask her, but I didn't.

"Even when I was with Nick," she was saying, "I was thinking of Diego. I mean, I loved Nick, I admit it, but Diego was always on my mind. I never stopped caring for him, Cristi."

I knew it was true, because I still loved Diego too. No matter what I was doing—preparing Papi's medicines, mending a skirt for Isolda, playing cards—Diego was there, in my mind. If I woke up at night, I'd be thinking about him. If I was typing a letter, I'd be thinking about him. Even when I was shaking my ass on the dance floor of some dimly lit dive—something that didn't happen too often those days—Diego would fade in and out of the shadows.

Once in a while I'd run into him at Lola Bravo's house, or Maty would ask me to take him some clippings Frida had sent her from the New York press. Or sometimes he'd need me to do some work for him, secretarial work, or driving. We'd sit and chat a while, and he'd tell me about news he had received from his Fridita. He'd recount her latest exploits—not those involving other men, of course—or else he'd tell me about the arrangements he was making to get her stuff seen by some influential New York critic.

"Simon Weintraub will do a piece on her. He won't say no to *me*! He owes me money!"

You see, even though they couldn't live together, even though they fought all the time, even though he treated her like shit, he still loved her. There was this deep affection between them, and nothing could destroy it. Diego didn't care anything about me anymore. He was kind to me. He bought me gifts—a silver candle holder, a papier-mâché piñata for the children, a silk scarf, a silver comb. Once he brought Isolda a movie poster showing Tito Guízar in *Allá en el Rancho Grande*. But things weren't the same. The shadow of Frida had fallen between us. Our betrayal of Frida. It was like some hideous ogre, always there. At least for me, maybe not for him. I don't think it bothered him as much as it did me. For him, sex was just fun and games. It was natural for him to sleep with whatever woman he happened to find in his path. Some people can't pass a dog without petting it, and some people can't pass a flower without sniffing it. Diego was like that with women. So that's why I think he didn't feel as guilty, as miserable. Maybe he had just lost interest in me. There were so many other flowers to pick along the path. But what I do know for sure is that he still cared for Frida.

And yet, when Frida came home, Diego wasn't waiting for her with open arms and a warm bed. No, Diego was living with Lupe Marín.

There was no doubt where Frida would stay when she returned. She was too weak to be alone. She looked like a heap of pulled-up tree roots, and she could hardly walk. Even though she hadn't written to me, we both know that there was no one to nurse her but her loving twin. Maty could have taken her in, but she was having problems at home. Anyhow, Frida wanted to be with me, or maybe she wanted to be with her darling niece and nephew. She needed a nursemaid, and I was already taking care of Papá, so what difference did it make if I had one more chamber pot to empty? I had gotten to be an expert at mixing medicines and counting out pills. I could give shots as well as a professional nurse, and I was as quick as lightning when it came to sticking a thermometer up an ass. I took her to the Casa Azul and put her in her old room, with her collection of dolls, her papier-mâché skeleton, and her canopied bed.

Diego came by the day after she arrived. Not alone, but with Lupe and Irene Bohus, his new assistant. And Paulette Goddard.

Lupe and he were holding hands like kids.

"Look, darling, we brought you this," Lupe said. She pulled a brightly colored wooden necklace out of an envelope. It was made of painted beads and little carved parrots, pink ones with green wings, blue ones with yellow wings, red and purple ones. Frida grabbed at it greedily and slipped it around her neck, pretending to be delighted. But out of the corner of her eye, she was watching how Diego played with Lupe's fingers, how he pressed her hand against his haunch, pretending he didn't want Frida to see, yet clearly wanting her to see.

Irene stood by demurely. At the time, I didn't realize that Diego was cheating on Lupe with Irene.

Paulette Goddard sat on the arm of a chair and smiled her radiant smile without saying a word. She didn't speak much Spanish. Maybe she felt out of place. On the screen she was a cut-up, but in person, she was as quiet as a sleeping kitten, at least until she got to know you. Yes, I'm talking about *the* Paulette Goddard, the blond Hollywood goddess, star of a bunch of comedies. I saw them all. Let's see, *Modern Times, Ghost Breakers, Second Chorus*—that was a musical—and then, a few years later, *Diary of a Chambermaid, An Ideal Husband*—what else?—*The Torch* . . . You like her films too? Which one's your favorite? I loved *An Ideal Husband*, it was so funny. Believe it or not, Paulette visited me at my house. We got to be friends. Stood right there in my kitchen, serving herself coconut cookies and coffee. So you see, I've known quite a few movie stars. I may never have been a famous artist like Frida, but I had important friends. Before long, Diego would be cheating on both Lupe and Irene with *Paulette*!

It was cruel the way Diego showed up that day with his gaggle of women. He kissed Frida on the lips and fussed over her a while, but he hardly asked about the shows. He already knew they had been flops, so maybe, in that sense, he was kind. He didn't want to make her admit that she had had to back up most of her paintings and ship them home again. He didn't want to bring up the fact that instead of making money, she had lost it. It was cruel of him to show her that he was now with Lupe. But that's how he was.

Frida caught on right away. She saw that he was with Lupe, and she probably even suspected that Irene was in the picture too. It was around that time that she painted a portrait of herself with a necklace of thorns, a kind of fallen crown, like Jesus. Holy Frida, suffering on her cross.

That's not fair of me. She really was suffering. Suffering horribly. First she lost Nick, then Diego. And that's why I decided I really had to take care of her. She was such a wreck, and both of us were so lonely. We needed each other. I needed her as much as she needed me.

I never resented waiting on Frida. Maybe I did, just a little, because, after all, it's normal to feel put upon, but I realized how much she needed me. At that time in my life I was fragile too. My health was poor, I still hadn't completely recovered from that gallbladder operation, and I still had two young children to take care of. Isolda was about ten, and at that age, girls get rebellious. We were always arguing about something, Isolda and I. If I told her to wear the blue dress, she wanted the yellow one. If I told her to stay with Grandpa, she wanted to play in the park. And whenever she got mad at me, she went running to Frida, who let her do whatever she wanted.

Tía Frida Tía Frida Tía Frida . . . all day, *Tía Frida*. Aunt Frida is funny and smart! Aunt Frida paints like a dream. Aunt Frida is beautiful and modern. Aunt Frida smokes American cigarettes. Aunt Frida knows important people. Aunt Frida cooks better than you do. Aunt Frida lets me wear her makeup. Aunt Frida gave me this ring. Aunt Frida *really* loves me. Poor Aunt Frida, her back is killing her. Her leg is killing her. Her hip is killing her, her kidneys are killing her, her foot is killing her her head is killing her her eyes are killing her herankleiskillingherherpelvisiskillingherherfingeriskillingher. I couldn't stand hearing it anymore. Not from Frida, and not from my own daughter!

Although I have to admit, if I was in purgatory, Frida was in hell.

Let me tell you about Irene Bohus.

She was not a spectacular woman. She was one of the girls Diego slept with because she was *there*. She was Hungarian, large-boned, with shoulder-length hair pulled back tight around her face and fastened in back, with billows of brown curls lying softly on her neck,

like Andrea Palma in the movie *Distinto amanecer.* Only Irene wasn't as
pretty as Andrea. She had come to Mexico to study muralism and was
staying at the studio.

The day that Diego showed up with Lupe and Irene and Paulette,
Frida's back began to hurt, so she went into her room to lie down.
After a little while, we followed her in there. It wasn't unusual for
Frida to receive people lying in bed. Toward the end, she did it all the
time, especially after the amputation. After she lost her leg, it was
awfully hard for her to get up, but I'll tell you about that another time.

Lupe, Diego, and I were standing on one side of the bed, which
was pushed up against the wall, and Irene was sitting at Frida's feet,
looking at her adoringly. Frida captivated people. Even though Irene
was sleeping with Diego, she loved Frida and wanted Frida to love
her too. The great Frida Kahlo! She was like a movie star to a girl in
her early twenties.

Lupe looked devastating, in a burgundy off-the-shoulder blouse
and loose white trousers. Her chocolate-colored eyes were luminous.
Her chin was slightly raised, giving her an arrogant air. She looked as
though she were posing nude for a worshipful schoolboy. Frida, not
to be outdone, had put on her frilliest Tehuana dress and adorned her
hair with red and white roses. On every finger she wore a glittery ring.
Mostly they were junk, false emeralds, false rubies, false diamonds,
false sapphires, and the like, but the overall effect was one of opu-
lence. Frida used two gold incisors, but that day she had popped dia-
mond-encrusted gold caps over the originals, giving her the appearance of some sort of Aztec potentate. She had taken off her heavy
orthopedic shoes, but aside from that, she was fully clothed and
decked out in all her finery, lying on top of the covers and talking
about Paris.

"They think they're such marvelous cooks, but they eat mostly
snails and ants in greasy sauces. Really, *mi amor,*" she said to Lupe,
"you can't find decent tortillas anywhere."

"You see? I should have gone with you! I would have made you
a delicious *mole poblano.*"

"Don't be silly, darling. I had a kidney infection. Besides, you
were too busy fucking my husband." Frida laughed and took a drag

on her cigarette.

Lupe chuckled, but she had been caught off guard.

Diego and Irene exchanged a quick glance. I would have missed it if Frida hadn't made a crack. "You know, darling, the fountain that fills too many flasks runs dry."

I didn't get it.

Diego burst out laughing and laughed with gusto for a long time. "The pitcher that pays too many visits to the fountain winds up breaking."

"Don't worry about me, darling. I haven't broken yet, and I plan to take a tour of fountains of the world." She flashed a broad, menacing, diamond-studded smile. She reminded me of an exotic and ferocious animal. An imperial jaguar.

Diego's expression changed. He looked at her with a face like sour milk. He didn't like to be reminded that Frida slept around as much as he did.

Irene began to fidget.

"Precious girl," Frida murmured. "Why don't you come over tomorrow without all these boring people, and I'll teach you how to make *enchiladas tapatías*? You shouldn't go back to your country without acquiring some real art." Actually, Irene didn't go back when we all anticipated because the war broke out.

That's when I figured out that Diego was sleeping with Irene. Because that's when I saw that Frida was up to her old tricks. Remember, I told you? She always made friends with Diego's girlfriends. That way, they were less of a threat to her. Sometimes she could even pry them away from him. She was so nice to them that they began to feel guilty and stopped fooling around with Diego.

But what Frida and Irene and Lupe hadn't counted on was that Paulette had moved into the sumptuous San Angel Inn. And guess where it was: right across the street from Diego's studio!

Instead of Irene coming over for a cooking lesson the next day, Frida planned an elaborate lunch for her and Diego and had me take it over to the studio. Frida didn't actually make it, Graciela did. Oh, Graciela was a servant, a kitchen maid. Inocencia had died years ago. I drove it over there.

I put the basket into the car. It was a warm day, but overcast. The air smelled of rotting vegetables. There were fewer pedestrians than usual in the street, and things didn't seem to be in their customary places. I mean, the laundry was on the corner, with its sign, *Lavandería Olmedo,* and next to it the mechanics' shop, with greasy tools scattered all over the floor. The mechanics were taking apart an engine in front of the same sleazy pinup that had been hanging on the wall for years. I recognized the newspaper vendor by the fountain and the lottery ticket vendor leaning against the side of the building. And yet I felt disoriented, as though I were in a different city at a different time, or as though I were going in the wrong direction. Everything was the same, but nothing looked familiar. I felt I should turn around, go back to Coyoacán, and start out all over again. When I got to the intersection, I didn't know whether to go left or right, even though I had made that trip hundreds of times before.

When I got to Diego's studio, I parked the car too far from the walk. I just couldn't get it right, so I left it as it was and tucked the lunch basket securely under my arm. I kept feeling that I was going to drop it, and then everyone would be furious with me—Diego, Frida, maybe even Irene.

A servant opened the door—an old Indian woman I hadn't seen before. Where was Petronila, the maid I knew? This woman was a tattered rag. She didn't look like she was expecting me, although she let me in anyway. Diego must have forgotten to tell her I was bringing over the midday meal, I thought.

There they were, the master and his assistant, so lost in their work they didn't even hear me come in. They were both painting the same model. Stretched out nude on a sort of divan in a pose identical to the one in which he had painted me as the goddess, the blond Chimalma. The sacred mother of the most revered Aztec god, only blond, long-legged, white and rich as cream, and exquisitely buxom. In other words, perfect.

"Hello, Diego," I said.

Diego turned to face me, but as he did, he exchanged knowing glances with the other two women. He looked as sheepish as a man who has just farted at his own wedding.

What was going on there? What did those glances mean? On the surface, it was a routine scene: artist and disciple painting a nude. But volcanoes erupt and fish devour one another beneath the smooth surface of the ocean.

Paulette eased herself off the divan but didn't seem in a hurry to throw on a wrap. She moved like a dancer, buttocks tucked under, abdomen tight, arms undulating in fluid movements, tiny, controlled steps. Diego watched her, hungry but not ravenous. It was clear that he had enjoyed that body already, that he had satisfied his most immediate cravings. He had taken the edge off his appetite. Later he would want more, but for now he wasn't starving.

On the other hand, Irene's eyes were gluttonous. She surveyed Paulette's body as a child might survey a display of meringues. Were they both in love with Paulette? Did Diego watch as the women went at it? Or was Irene the spectator? Or perhaps it was a sort of unconventional triangle. Obviously, Diego and Paulette were lovers, and Diego and Irene were lovers, but what else? And how did Lupe fit into the picture?

Driving home, I was even more disoriented than before. I took a wrong turn somewhere near San Angel and wound up circling around the same neighborhood for hours. How could that have happened? Normally, I could have driven from there to Coyoacán with my head in a sack. But that day everything was out of kilter.

I kept asking myself: Should I tell Frida about Paulette? Now that she's decided to win over Irene, should I tell her that what she needs to do is begin working on Paulette? How can Frida keep up with Diego? He seduces them faster than she can lure them under her protective wing. I decided not to tell her anything.

I had more immediate problems to deal with. How was I going to explain why I was an hour and a half late getting home? And that I had gotten lost going from one familiar place to another on a road I knew as well as my own bedroom? And that I had forgotten to prepare the afternoon's medication?

As it turned out, I didn't have to explain anything to anybody. Papá was still gaga from the sedative I had given him in the morning, and Graciela had fed him his midday meal and put him to bed. He was, she said, in for a nice long siesta.

Frida was too drunk to know what time it was. She had been boozing all morning. As Graciela chopped onions for Diego and Irene's *comida*, Frida sipped from her flask. Her head got heavier and heavier until she tumbled into bed. She had been taking more painkillers than usual, for her back, her leg, her foot, and now she had a fungus infection on a finger. Dr. Ovando, a specialist, gave her some pills and told her to cut down on the painting because it was bad for her to hold a brush all day. That's why Frida wasn't chopping onions herself. Instead of painting, she lay around drinking and popping pills until she got mean, then hysterical; then she was dead to the world.

I thought the Paulette Goddard affair would just slip by. What difference did it make whether Frida knew about it or not? It was just another one of Diego's escapades. And Frida was in such bad shape physically and emotionally.

But then the rumors started. Diego loved to flaunt his women, and he had shown up at the opening night of the movie *Sólo para ti* with Paulette on his arm, all lovey-dovey and goo-goo-eyed. There were tons of reporters. Diego's picture came out in all the papers and his name was in all the headlines: FAMOUS MURALIST AND AMERICAN STAR TURN HEADS . . . RIVERA AND GODDARD TOGETHER AT OPENING . . . BLOND, BEAUTIFUL, AND IN LOVE WITH DIEGO RIVERA! . . . THE HOLLYWOOD-D.F. AXIS!

Under other circumstances, Frida would have been able to handle it, but after the breakup with Nick and the disappointment of her shows in New York and Paris, this was just too much.

No sooner did the news hit the papers than Lupe was at the door. "I don't mind if he sleeps with *you*!" she exploded. "After all, you're his wife. But that American slut! He's thumbing his nose at both of us."

Frida started to cry. Not melodramatically, not hysterically, just softly, dabbing her eyes with Mami's old embroidered handkerchief. It was clear that she was really hurting. There was nothing phony about it. She wasn't just putting on a show. I know you're going to say that the whole thing was Frida's fault because, after all, she had betrayed Diego with Nick. But running off to New York and falling in love with Nick, that happened because Frida felt so desperate and abandoned.

And when it was all over with Nick, she came home to her husband, isn't that true? Sick and broken, she came home to Diego. But instead of offering her his affection and his moral support, Diego was behaving like a shit. Yes, he came over and brought presents, but he never gave himself. And this affair with Paulette was just too much for Frida. Paulette was too beautiful, too sexy, too blond. I think Frida felt that she just couldn't compete. She couldn't be the contortionist lover for Diego any more than she could be for Nick, and it killed her to think she wasn't able to meet her husband's physical needs. It was destroying her. And now that Diego was broadcasting his relationship with Paulette, Frida just felt beaten down. Irene was a different story. Irene wasn't important, she was just a studio assistant. But Paulette, who could compete with Paulette Goddard?

Frida began divorce proceedings on September 19, 1939, and by early the next year, the divorce was final.

She cut off all her hair. She always did that whenever she had a serious rift with Diego. It was her way of expressing pain, and you might even say it was a way of punishing him, because Diego loved her hair.

So, you see, Frida was all alone, all alone except for her loving twin. Who could take care of her better than I could? Who loved her as much as I did? I had to be there for her. Cristina, her sister, her sidekick, her slave.

CHAPTER 22

Connections

HIS NAME WAS RAMÓN MERCADER. HE MADE ME FEEL LIQUID, LIMPID, light. Like a jellyfish floating in warm water, free, bobbing, yielding to the whim of gentle currents. When he smiled at me, I remembered something I hadn't thought about in years. A tiny beach we once visited somewhere near Cozumel when I was a child, sitting in the sun, heady from the briny vapors. But now I wasn't a child. I was a jellyfish, formless, crystalline, compliant, trusting my fate to the powers that be. Kindly gods, gracious gods.

No other man has ever made me feel like that. It was the way he talked to me, and more than that, the way he listened to me. As though he actually cared about what I had to say. He asked questions. He wanted to know what I thought, what I knew. He was one of Frida's friends, of course. A Spanish communist. She had met him in Paris, and now that he was in Mexico, he came over every once in a while, not nearly as often as I would have liked.

We weren't lovers. I wished we were. I thought that he was the prince I had been waiting for, the Spanish *conquistador* who would carry me, the beautiful Aztec maiden, off into the sunset. Together we would form a new race, the mestizo race. But Ramón didn't seem to have time for love. He was too tied up in his politics. And yet, when we talked, it was as though we were making love. He gave himself to me the way none of my other lovers ever had.

He was a man who grappled with things. We talked about the Party, of course. That was his passion. Trotsky, Diego, the future of

Stalinism. Whether the Soviets would survive the Nazi offensive, whether or not the Americans would get involved. He never talked down to me, and he never spouted clichés the way Diego and Frida did. With Ramón, you had the feeling that everything he said came from the gut, from the soul. He had pondered the issues and come to his own conclusions. Every word he dredged up from the fathomless ocean of his soul.

Pretty poetic, huh? How did you like that? "The fathomless ocean of his soul." That's the way Ramón talked, with words like that, I heard him use that expression once. "Ah, Cristinita, these are truths I have dredged up from the fathomless ocean of my soul." He seduced you with words. He was a Spaniard, and he had that beautiful Peninsular accent. *Grathiash* for *gracias*. *Cothesh* for *coces*. Ha! He made me giggle, with his Castilian pronunciation. It was so titillating. To tell you the truth, sometimes I didn't even know what he was talking about, but it didn't matter. Just to hear him talk made me feel like I was dying.

Frida was never alone. She needed to have people around her, adoring her, praising her. After the divorce, she sent out invitations by the truckload. The house became a grand hotel, with celebrities crowding through the door for an audience with the empress. Fascinating people. Stars as glamorous as Frida herself. Well, almost as glamorous. After her hair grew back out, she would receive them in her frilly costumes, a ring on every finger, a crown of hibiscus on her head. Brave Frida. The wronged woman. The suffering victim. Limping, masking her pain. Now, not only her health made her the object of admiration—"What courage, to face guests in such a state of affliction!"—but also her new status—"What courage, to go it alone without Diego!" She was a phenomenon in Mexico. The divorced woman. Not just a woman who lived without a man, plenty of us had done that. But a working woman, a true comrade, a woman who looked out for herself and made her contribution to society.

She played the comrade bit to the hilt. Chin up, eyes front, a smile on her lips, and a quip on her tongue. Sometimes, during her parties, she sat in the kitchen with the servants, cracking jokes. "See, *compañeros*? I make no distinctions!" "Where's Frida?" someone would ask. "Husking corn!" "Peeling potatoes!" "Stirring the pudding!" Whatever the answer, the brigade responded with appreciative oohs and ahs.

I have to admit I loved the parties. I loved to be in the middle of the whirl, even if I was only there because I was Frida Kahlo's sister. Sometimes I'd forget. What I mean is, sometimes I'd stop thinking about it and enjoy myself. After all, everyone was nice enough to me. And I *was* someone. I was part of the group. I belonged there. Yes, I did. But why did I keep feeling as though I had to prove it?

The one person I didn't have to prove it to was Ramón Mercader.

"Your sister," he once said to me. "She's quite the little political dilettante, isn't she?"

I didn't understand, but I was embarrassed to say so.

Ramón realized I didn't know the word, but instead of making some nasty crack the way Frida might have done—"My God, Cristina, don't you even know what *dilettante* means!"—he just went on.

"Actually, Cristinita," he said softly, "I prefer people like you . . . people who don't make a spectacle of their politics."

I caught on. "Frida isn't making a spectacle. She really believes in communism."

He ran his fingers over my cheek and smiled. I wanted to kiss his hand. He was talking about living one's creed, about expressing one's beliefs through one's day-to-day existence, about the monumental contributions of ordinary people. I didn't care about those things. I just wanted him to touch me. His words were like a warm, perfumed bath.

And then one day, Ramón Mercader disappeared. I looked for him at every social gathering, at every communist powwow, but he seemed to have vanished. I felt as though I were drying up on the sand. No one could tell me anything. I couldn't find his address. He didn't have a phone. Political assassinations were not uncommon in Mexico, and I checked the newspapers, half hoping, half dreading I would find his name. I braced myself for the expected headline: SPANISH COMMUNIST FOUND SHOT. But if Ramón had died, it hadn't made the papers. Frida didn't seem even to notice. She had plenty of friends. One Spanish communist, more or less, was hardly worth making a fuss about. It's true that in spite of her parties and her gaiety, Frida was in bad shape, but that had nothing to do with Ramón. That had to do with the divorce. Not being married to Diego was more than my sister could abide. I knew what I had to do. I had to forget that I was in love. I had to push Ramón out of my mind and attend to my sister. I sniffed back my tears. I bit my lip. Good old Cristi.

I went to see Paulette Goddard. In spite of what they say, in spite of what you think, I loved my sister, and I couldn't stand to see the way Diego's affairs were consuming her, causing her health to decay, corroding her stamina as a fungus rots living flesh. It was horrible.

In spite of the divorce, Frida still doted on Diego. She fretted over him constantly. All day long, she'd say things like I wonder if Diego's watching his diet, I wonder if Diego got those new shirts from New York, I wonder if Irene gives him enough pussy. I'm sorry, but that's the way Frida talked. I wonder if he really loves Paulette, and what about Modesta? Modesta was one of his models, an Indian. She was an incredibly sensuous woman. He painted her in the nude, braiding her hair.

Diego and Frida still saw each other. In fact, she did his books. I know it's unbelievable, but it's true. Diego had no head for accounting, so Frida handled all his business—who paid, who owed money, how much came in, how much went out. She went on doing it for him just as though they were still together. And when she wasn't by his side, she was dizzy with anxiety. What was Diego doing now? What was he eating, painting, thinking? She was obsessed with him.

On the outside, she was as spirited and sassy as ever, but not on the inside. That's why I went to see Paulette. I was going to tell her what she was doing to Frida. Not that I expected her to care, but I was going to tell her anyway. Paulette was one of those women who was always involved with somebody famous. She had lived with Charlie Chaplin, and eventually she married him. I just loved Charlie Chaplin. He was so fabulous, so adorable, especially in *Modern Times*. That was my favorite movie of his. Well, I thought, since she's had guys like that, why does she need Diego? Why doesn't she just leave him alone? She had everything—money, looks, fame. She even tried out for *Gone With the Wind*. She wanted to be Scarlett. She didn't get it.

I understand it wasn't all her fault, that *Diego* was the one who was running after *her.* But my sister was beginning to look like a rag, all droopy and washed out, and I had to do something. When Frida went out on the street, she behaved like a movie star, a regular movie star, just like Rita Hayworth. She would wave at her admirers, *¡Hola, cuate! ¡Hola, mi amor!*, flirting and winking, licking her lips as though eyeing a luscious mango whenever she'd see a cute boy, or girl, but then she'd get back home and hit the bottle, and before you knew it, she'd collapse like a pile of puke and wine-soaked laundry. Oh, she'd glue herself together for parties and for her public appearances, but once she was alone, she'd just crumple. The only time she was okay was when she was painting. Fortunately, she painted a lot that year. Self-portraits, of course. Frida with her monkey, a red ribbon running around her neck like bloody gashes. Frida in a man's suit, all alone in the middle of nowhere, with her hair cropped short. She has a scissors in her hand and scattered around her are clippings of hair, swatches of hair, on her knees, on her hands, all over the chair, on the ground, as far as you can see. That picture frightened me when I saw it. It was an image of self-destruction. Scraps of Frida strewn everywhere, limp, dead, shreds of Frida flung around like garbage.

I went to see Paulette. For reasons I didn't understand at the time, the road was closed off in front of the San Angel Hotel, so I parked on a side street. The receptionist announced me.

"Señorita Kahlo," he said. And then, as if the name had struck a chord: "Are you related to Frida Kahlo, the wife of Diego Rivera?"

"She's my sister."

"*The* Frida Kahlo?"

"Yes."

"She's your sister?"

"Look, I'm in a hurry."

But there was no reason to rush, because Paulette took her time answering the door.

"*¡Un momento!*" she called from inside. Not once, but several times. "*¡Un momento! ¡Un momento!*"

She's got somebody in there, I thought. Some guy. While Diego's cheating on Irene and Frida with *her*, she's cheating on Diego with some up-and-coming movie producer. But when she finally let me in, I didn't see signs that anyone else had been there. No ashtrays brimming with butts. No wineglasses stuffed hastily behind sofa pillows. No telltale odors.

I thought Paulette might not recognize me, even though I had been announced. At parties she had never paid much attention to me. What if she thought I was some movie buff who had found out her address and come to hound her? But she smiled and showed me in. I thought it was strange that she didn't have at least one maid attending her. After all, a famous movie star like Paulette Goddard.

She was diaphanous, celestial. I half expected to catch her hovering a few centimeters above the floor. She was wearing a powder-blue sweater. Her eyes were wide and moist, and her lips—the color of begonias—were painted on perfectly. Her fragrance made me think of jasmine and honey, of ambrosia. It must have been French.

She kissed me on the cheek, but I didn't love her the way I had loved Lola. She didn't make me feel as though I was her friend. I was just an extra person who sometimes tagged along. She lacked Lola's Mexican warmth. She seemed to be an angel floating up there somewhere—distant, untouchable. I know I said before we were friends but we weren't really.

She went to the window and looked out. That seemed strange as well. After all, I had just gotten there. I mean, if someone had just come to visit you in your hotel suite, would you walk away from her and go look out the window? It occurred to me that she was spying on Diego, trying to see what he and Irene were up to. And yet, like Frida, Paulette had never shown jealousy toward Diego's assistant. Irene was just a minor annoyance—like a mosquito or a fly.

Paulette bit her lip, but she didn't mess up her lipstick. Me, whenever I bite my lip, I always leave my makeup a disaster.

She said something in English that I didn't understand. I just smiled. How was I going to explain why I had come? I wondered.

"¡Un momento!" She flitted around the suite like she was looking for something. She seemed nervous. She kept glancing out the window. I walked over to the window myself, but there was no one in the street. At least, I didn't see anyone.

"Look," I said in Spanish—the only language I speak. "I'm not making a social visit. I came to talk to you about something very important."

She nodded as if she understood. *"¡Un momento!"* she said again.

She picked up the phone and spat what sounded like an order into the receiver. Again she spoke in English. A few minutes later, a waiter knocked on the door with a serving table laden with coffee and sweets. It was a strange time to be serving dessert, I thought. In about an hour Graciela would be putting our *merienda* on the table at home. Paulette took hold of the table and wheeled it into the room herself, signaling the uniformed servant to leave. "Some Yankee custom," I said to myself.

She smiled at me.

"Look," I began again. "I'm not paying a social visit. I need to talk to you about my sister. Do you understand what I'm saying?"

"Sí, sí," she said. *"Comprendo perfectamente."* But she was obviously preoccupied with something else.

I was annoyed. She thinks she's too important to talk to me, I thought. She thinks I'm one of her admirers, one of those drooling fans who break windows to get close to her at premiers. I opened my mouth to explain about Frida, how miserable she was, how hurt she was, but Paulette motioned for me to be quiet.

I waited in silence, my eyes glued on Paulette, my anger swelling.

All of a sudden, a look of terror crossed her face. She moved toward the window, then back to the phone.

"¿Qué pasa?"

She whispered into the receiver. I heard "Diego," "danger," "Trotsky," "police," "murder."

I moved toward the window and looked out. The street had been transformed. Suddenly, my fingertips felt icy. What had happened? Police were everywhere, scores of them, and they were cordoning off Diego's studio. They were preparing to take the house! Some of them had their guns drawn. Who did they think Diego was? Pancho Villa? It's true that he walked around with a pistol and shot off his mouth as though he were Lenin's grandmother, but Diego never killed anyone. Oh sure, he bragged that he had fought in the Russian Revolution and downed dozens of Czarists, but that was all bullshit.

"I was hiding in a cellar when I spied the sable cloak of Count Alexander Kaminoff, so I cocked my gun and bam!" but it was nothing but bravado, what do you call it?—braggadocio. So what was this all about?

"¿Qué pasa?" I said again.

"Trotsky."

At first I didn't get the connection. I mean, I knew that someone had tried to mow down Leon and Natalia, but I didn't see what that had to do with what was going on outside Diego's studio. Paulette was trying to explain, gesturing crazily. "Diego," "danger," "Trotsky," "police," "murder." For an actress, I thought, she's not very good at getting across a message. The same five words kept surfacing and resurfacing in different combinations. Finally, I began to piece it together.

I don't know much about politics, but I do know that Leon had a lot of political enemies. That's why he came to Mexico in the first place; they had expelled him from the U.S.S.R. He didn't get along with Stalin. Leon thought Stalin wanted to have the final word on everything, but that he didn't really understand issues like industrialization. Stalin didn't like it when Leon pointed out his mistakes, so he had him thrown out of the country. Only now, Leon was living abroad and spreading his anti-Stalinist ideas around. Back home, Leon's enemies accused him of a huge anti-Soviet plot, and they sent out their agents to get him. Diego was mad at Trotsky for other reasons. He still blamed him for going after Frida, so when the anti-Trotskyites in Mexico began talking about getting rid of Leon, Diego started shooting his mouth off. "I'll blow that son of a bitch's brains out! That bastard is a traitor to the cause!" At the time, Diego was trying to pass himself off as a Stalinist.

I wasn't that interested in politics, and besides, Ramón Mercader said that when it came right down to it, Diego didn't know what he was talking about. Diego was a political opportunist, he said. He went along with whoever was winning. And it's true that when the winds began to blow against Stalin, Diego became a Trotskyite all over again. I've said this before: He was a great artist, but when he started talking politics, he reminded me of a great big inflated balloon farting hot air. And when it came to Leon, I knew the bone he had to pick with him was personal, not political. Or, at least, not entirely political.

But it was a big mistake for Diego to go around threatening to feed Leon to the vultures, because when someone actually did try to mow down Trotsky, and Natalia too, Diego immediately became suspect. What better suspect for an attempted murder than a man who has announced for months that he is going to commit that murder? That's why the police had come to arrest him, and that's why Paulette called the studio. To warn Diego.

But the real culprit wasn't Diego at all. It was the painter David Alfaro Siqueiros, the man with whom José Orozco Clemente had helped Diego launch the muralist movement. For David, politics was always more important than painting. He painted to spread the message but for him was never an end in itself. He was more a fighter than an artist, and when he opened fire on Leon and Natalia, I'm sure he didn't care whether he made it through the ordeal alive or not. In fact, dying for Stalin would have been a triumph for David. A martyrdom, like Saint Martin's. As it turned out, David didn't die trying to murder Trotsky. The police caught him, but he was pals with President Cárdenas, and before the year was up, he was out of jail and on his way to Chile to paint murals. But wait, what I want to tell you is what happened with Paulette.

I went to stand next to her by the window. She was trembling. She was frightened. She was no longer the precious angel, aloof and inaccessible, floating up there far away in the heavens. She was a real woman who cared about Diego. I put my arm around her waist and we stood there together, joined at the hip like Siamese twins, waiting for something to happen.

Finally, a car pulled out from behind Diego's studio, only Diego wasn't in it. Irene was at the wheel.

A uniformed officer forced her to stop and get out of the car. He appeared to be asking questions. Irene looked composed, even indifferent. The policeman walked around to the back of the car and pulled open the trunk. He poked at some canvases, then slammed the hatch. He opened the rear door and repeated the operation.

Finally, he signaled Irene to move on. She drove slowly past the band of policemen and out of sight.

Seconds later, the law stormed the building. There was a volley of gunfire. Smoke poured out the windows.

I let out a scream that could have split stone. *"¡Virgen santísima! ¡Diego! ¡Diegooo!"* No one could have survived that barrage.

Paulette burst out laughing.

I turned to look at her, confused.

"Diego es . . . está bien," she said. She was laughing so hard she was gulping air. She looked like the Paulette I had seen on the screen, the comedian, the clown. *"Está en el coche."*

I didn't get it.

"En el coche . . . el automóvil . . . con Irene." She walked the index and middle finger of her right hand over the palm of the left, as if to represent someone escaping.

What did she mean, Diego was in the car with Irene? No one was in the car. I had seen the officer search it myself.

"Under the canvases!" she hiccuped, trying to catch her breath. She made her hand into an animal that scrambled under a pile of napkins. "Hiding! Hiding! *¡Ocultándose!"*

I couldn't believe it. They had pulled it off! Thanks to Paulette's warning, Irene had saved Diego's hide.

Where had they gone? I wanted to know. But Paulette wouldn't tell me. She ran into the bedroom and threw a few things into an overnight bag. Then she hustled me out of the suite.

A few days later, she turned up in Coyoacán. Diego was fine, she said. He and Irene were in hiding, but she took them food every day. Not just tortillas and frijoles, but delicacies—caviar, pâté, *boeuf bourguignonne,* champagne and pastries. And she had supplied Diego with fresh clothes. Not to worry. Diego was in paradise. Two women to wait on him and all the éclairs he could eat. Paulette giggled. Diego had friends in high places, and they were going to arrange for him to sneak out of the country. He had been commissioned to paint a mural at San Francisco Junior College, Paulette said, and both she and Irene were going with him.

Frida was thrilled and devastated at the same time. Diego was safe.

That was something to celebrate. But not only was he leaving Mexico, he was going to California with Paulette and that pesky Irene Bohus.

Not long afterward, pictures of the three of them landing in San Francisco appeared in the Mexican newspapers. "Beautiful Paulette," Diego gushed to the press. "She saved my life. She is my guardian angel, my goddess. It was worth going through hell just to be able to take refuge under her exquisite wing."

What sort of hell had he gone through? the papers wanted to know. What had caused his sudden departure? But Diego wasn't telling. "Diego Rivera refuses to elucidate the circumstances leading to his escape from Mexico," trumpeted *El Pregonero*. How much more enticing his adventure was made by all the mystery, don't you see? Diego, the hero, the mystery man.

Two years later, Paulette divorced Charlie Chaplin, and before the ink was dry on her papers, she had taken up with Burgess Meredith. Didn't I tell you that some women always manage to hook up with the right guy?

After Diego left, Frida's health took a turn for the worse. Just breathing became a chore. The doctors thought her twisted spine was crushing her lungs, and they put a gadget on her to straighten out her back. "If the disease doesn't kill me, these bastard doctors will!" she fumed. "This damned thing hurts like hell!" There was talk of another operation. With what money? I wondered. And with what energy will I attend to her? Papá's condition was also deteriorating. He needed me as much as Frida did. And Isolda and Toño needed me more than ever, especially Toño. He was such a little dynamo. It wore me out just to watch him.

The summer was just getting under way. The days were long and comfortable, but Frida was in a perpetual snit. She had written to Diego, a long, weepy letter filled with baby talk and detailed descriptions of the torture devices the doctors had invented just for her, illustrated with lurid sketches of contraptions with fangs and claws that tore apart human flesh. He had answered her, but instead of oozing compassion, his letter was a chirpy account of how well his mural was going. He was painting in public for the Golden Gate International Exposition's "Art in Action" program, and he was surrounded by young admirers, "bright young people," "adorable gringas," "delightful aficionados," "promising students." Irene had moved out of his studio, but there were plenty of other young girls roaming around. And, of course, there was Paulette. The theme of his work was going to be Pan-Americanism, he said, and it was going to feature portraits of himself and his guardian angel gazing adoringly into each other's eyes. She, fair and arctic as a snow queen, he, dark and passionate as the horny old man he was, symbolizing the love between the Americas. At the time, Diego had given up trying to figure out whether he was pro or anti-Stalin and was promoting the idea of inter-American solidarity. An easy cause. A crowd pleaser. After all, everybody loves a lover. Only, Frida didn't want to hear about Paulette. She wanted Diego to tell her how much he missed her.

"Sounds like a beautiful idea. Friendship between peoples and all that," I said to Frida. I was trying to cheer her up, make her see the bright side.

"Sounds like shit to me. Give me a drink, will you, kid?"

I didn't want to. I had just given her some Demerol, and I was afraid she'd have a bad reaction. The evening before, she'd had a very bad reaction. She'd passed out on the floor, and Graciela and I practically broke our backs trying to get her into bed. She had lost weight, it's true, but it was still a job. The torture device clamped to her neck complicated things.

"You've already had a couple, Frida. Plus one of those little vials of God knows what."

"Come on, Cristi Kity Cristi Kity. Come on, be nice."

"I don't think so."

"Come on, you bitch. Or else give me a shot of morphine."

There was a sharp knock on the door. Graciela came out of the kitchen wiping her hands on her apron.

"Your admirers think they can just pop by all night long," I hissed. I was exhausted, and I wasn't in the mood to be charming to Frida's guests.

But Frida wasn't interested in who was at the door. "Shoot some morphine into me, you bitch! I can't stand this pain! Come on, Kity

Kity Kity. Don't you love me? Give some morphine to your little sister. Come on, Kity, candy for the baby, candy for the baby."

She was already beginning to doze off. Her words were slurred, liquid.

"Open up!" thundered a man's voice from the other side of the front door.

Then the banging started. Deafening thuds that sounded as though they were made with the butt of a gun. Graciela was trembling.

"Open up!"

"Open the door before they break it down!" I yelled to Graciela. But she just stood there, paralyzed.

Isolda stuck her head out of the kitchen, where she had been rolling dough with Graciela. More than the pounding, her apprehension made me tremble.

"*¿Qué pasa, Mamá?*" She had the pleading look of a drowning kitten.

Frida unglued her eyelids, two long, narrow slits. Her face was screwed up like a fist. She opened her mouth to say something, but her tongue was too heavy, her words a blur.

I didn't know what to do. I'm not usually the one who makes the decisions.

Graciela came out of her daze. She unlatched the door. A pack of men shoved her aside and stormed into the house. Policemen. Six or seven of them, with clubs and guns. Graciela let out a shriek that smarted like a gash on the head. A squat cop with a broad, scarred nose elbowed her in the stomach, and she clamped her lips together to keep from whimpering.

"Frida!" I pleaded. "Frida!"

Frida's eyes were wide open. She had pulled herself to her feet and was facing down the uniformed thug who had hit Graciela. The commotion had slapped her awake.

"What's this all about?" she howled. Her words were a little slurred, but considering the state she had been in moments before, her composure was amazing.

"You're under arrest!"

A huge, meaty man with tawny skin yanked her toward him and slapped a pair of handcuffs on her. She winced.

"What's this all about?" This time her voice trembled ever so slightly.

I stood there crying. The stocky man who had hit Graciela grabbed my wrists and twisted them.

"Leave her alone and tell me what's going on!" commanded Frida.

"*¡Puta comunista!*" snarled another policeman, this one a wiry guy with curly hair. "Communist whore! You're under arrest for murder!"

"Murder!" Frida burst out laughing. "Who do you think we murdered, you moron? Us! Three women who spend our time making enchiladas and *chiles rellenos*. Take a good look, kid. Do you see murderers?"

The cop whacked her across the lip. Blood spurted over her chin, then rolled onto her neck brace.

"You mean they had to send seven of you goons to arrest three women, one of whom is an invalid? You cocksucking cowards!" This time the cop raised his fist and took aim. The jab caught her right below the eye and knocked her onto the floor. Frida convulsed wildly for a moment then lay quiet. But she was only stunned. As soon as the cop turned his attention to me, she began to wriggle, struggling to sit up.

"Leave her alone!" she stammered. "Leave my sister alone!"

A surge of love swelled my breast. Feeble as she was, she was struggling to protect me—a mother fox, wounded yet snarling at the hunter who menaced her cub. And yet, at the same time, I felt a pang of resentment. Why did she always have to put on a show? Why did she always have to play the heroine?

The policeman made a move to kick her in the mouth. "Frida, for God's sake, shut up!" I screamed.

"Good thinking," the man grunted.

"Shut those brats up!" snarled the tawny-skinned policeman. The terrified squeals of Isolda and Antonio were making him edgy. I remembered the stories I had heard about Nazi soldiers murdering children simply because their crying got on their nerves.

"It's okay, darlings!" I called, trying to pull myself together. "Everything's going to be all right. Just be quiet now. Try to be very quiet." But then, in spite of my efforts to sound calm, I was overcome by a spasm of tears.

The wiry cop clutched my arm and rammed me against the wall with one hand while he opened the door with the other. Then he propelled me outside and toward the patrol wagon. I could still hear Isolda and Antonio shrieking hysterically. Within seconds, Frida and Graciela fell on top of me, shoved into the car by a hand I couldn't see. A pudgy man with a thick neck got behind the wheel and started the motor. I noticed a mole on his neck—ugly and irregular, like a spider with outstretched legs.

"My children!" I cried. "I can't leave them alone!"

"Take me and leave her here!" begged Frida. "There's no one to take care of the kids! She's their mother! Leave her here!"

But we were already pulling out into the street.

"At least leave Graciela here!" pleaded Frida. "She can't possibly know anything about this. Let her stay home to feed the children!"

Again, a spasm of conflicting emotions. She was an angel, I thought—at least, that's what I knew I should think. That's what any reasonable person would expect me to think. After all, she was sacrificing herself. "Take me! Spare her!" And she was doing it for my children. And yet there was something of the martyred saint in her manner that irritated me.

I was sobbing, sobbing, shaking so violently I thought I would shatter. I felt as though a storm had come up within me, and everything was flying around every which way. Frida's pills, Diego's paintings, Graciela's rolling pin, Isolda's doll. All swooshing around inside me.

"I need to pray," I whispered, when I finally caught my breath.

And even though Frida was a communist, she said, "Go ahead and pray. I'll pray with you."

Dios te salve María, llena eres de gracia . . .

I admit it. During those terrible years I prayed all the time. I know it went against communist teachings, but somehow I needed to do it. It made me feel not so alone. It calmed me. Now I'm an old lady, abandoned by everyone, even by God. Now I don't pray anymore. What's the point? God wouldn't listen. Why should he?

When we got to the station, we were led into a dark room. They left us there a long time, who knows how long. I kept thinking about the kids alone in the house. Graciela hadn't left anything ready for supper. What would they eat?

Three police officers came in and turned on the light. They took Frida and Graciela into another room then returned. A man in a black suit joined them. I was drenched in sweat. I needed to pee. The man reminded me of my maternal grandmother. He also reminded me of my kindergarten teacher, Señorita Caballero. Mean and authoritarian. I knew he wouldn't let me use the bathroom.

Leon Trotsky had been murdered, he said. What did I know about it?

I started to shiver. Leon, dead? I knew there had been an attempt on his life, but that was three months before. And he had escaped unharmed. He and Natalia had rolled behind the bed and evaded the salvo of bullets that came through the window. I thought that with David's arrest the matter was closed.

"Where were you last night?"

"Who were you with?"

"Who saw you?"

Someone had ambushed Leon Trotsky, the man said, and stabbed him in the skull with an ice pick. Driven it into his head, deep into his brain. Someone had buried an ice pick in the soft flesh of his temple, deep, deep in his gray matter. That beautiful, brilliant brain, that brain that spouted theories and ideologies. That night it spouted blood like a geyser, a spray of blood all over his face, his collar, his beard, his funny tortoiseshell glasses. Leon, who had run through the street yelling, "Fire! Fire!" Leon, who had loved me, who had loved Frida. Leon who had betrayed Diego. Leon Trotsky, the man who had sat next to me in the car. Leon Trotsky had an ice pick lodged in the very core of his brain.

I felt weak, nauseous. I felt rivers of vomit churning, churning. I wanted to retch, I wanted to pee. I felt like I had an ice pick in my own skull, in my throat, in my gut.

"We have reason to believe you were in on the plot."

"Why?" I whispered.

"Because you were a friend of the murderer. We know you have connections."

"Who was the murderer?"

"You mean you don't know?"

"No, I don't know."

"Someone who often had dinner at your house."

"Lots of people have dinner at my house."

"Ramón Mercader."

I didn't respond.

"Ramón Mercader."

I felt a warm stream trickle down my leg. I sensed a pool forming at my feet. My shoes were wet. The smell of urine permeated the room. Everything seemed to be going dark, as though someone was turning off the light slowly.

I don't remember anything after that, except I kept crying for my children. "Who will feed my children! Who will take care of my children!" They kept us there more than twelve hours. Then they let us go.

Frida was unbearable. She wailed. She moaned. It was as though she was the only one who had lost a friend. As though she was the only one betrayed by Ramón Mercader.

"This is Diego's fault!" she screamed.

"How is it Diego's fault?"

"Because if Diego hadn't brought Leon to Mexico, this wouldn't have happened!"

She called Diego on the phone. "Idiot! Moron!" she screamed into the receiver. Then she collapsed onto her bed, weeping.

In the days that followed, Frida plunged into a profound depression. Her health was deteriorating faster than ever. The doctors thought she had tuberculosis, aggravated by her spinal injury. They insisted on an operation. But Dr. Eloesser, her old friend from California, wrote to her that it didn't sound like tuberculosis. Why didn't she come to San Francisco? He was sure she could get better medical treatment there than in Mexico. Anyhow, Diego missed her, and he was worried sick about her. "Come! The change will do you good," he urged.

I hoped she would go. I was too worn out to take care of her.

Leon's death had left me drained, and Papá was in a terrible state. It was enough to be a full-time nurse for one, I thought. I just couldn't attend to Papá and Frida, too.

Before the end of the summer, Frida left Mexico. She couldn't go on any longer without Diego, she told me. She needed him back. She knew he wouldn't change, that she would always have to share him with other women, but she was willing to pay the price.

Diego and Frida were remarried on December 8, 1940, in a small, simple ceremony in California. I didn't go. I wasn't invited, and to tell you the truth, I didn't care. I was growing bored with the antics of Frida and Diego. They were like two spoiled children, and I was worn out.

CHAPTER 23

Broken Dolls

WHEN YOU'VE LIVED THROUGH A WAR, YOU NEVER FORGET. MEMORIES haunt you. A child lying in the street with his head blown off, a mule with its guts flowing into the dirt, its eyes eerily open, blood gushing, rushing. Children screaming, shrieking, squealing like pigs being slaughtered. Blurred images. Solitary fingers, a footless leg, a disjointed arm, crushed skulls . . . I was overcome with nausea.

"Frida! What did you do? Frida!"

A torn torso, a ripped, sexless crotch, a smashed shoulder.

"Frida! Why did you do this? What's the meaning of this?"

Bits of hair, scraps of lace, a tiny parasol, a ruffle.

I could hear her in the bedroom, sobbing. I picked up a tiny hand and buried it in my fist.

"Poor baby," I whispered. "Poor baby." Who did it belong to, this delicate little hand? The blond baby with the sad blue eyes? The brunette baby with the crinoline dress?

"Frida!"

The entire collection, smashed or torn to smithereens. The Mexican revolutionary rag doll with her strap of cartridges, the French adolescent with her pretty bonnet, the Indian with her braids and her baby on her back, the painted porcelain babies with their perfect smiles and unmoving eyes, all of them in pieces. And those terrible scenes of real babies shot to pieces rushed into my head. The Revolution, and now, the war in Europe. It was happening again, only somewhere else. Sweet young girls in organdy dresses hanging like tatters on barbed wire fences. Girls that seconds before had had moist cheeks and quivering mouths. Dolls. Real live dolls. And here, now, plaster dolls with lacquered lips, brutally dismembered. How could my sister be capable of such violence? What monsters could have driven her to destroy her brood of beloved dolls? I felt like I was losing my mind. I was weary.

"Frida!"

She'd been unpredictable ever since Papá had died. One minute she would be all joy and laughter. "Hey, *cuate*, come here and give me a hug! How 'bout a tequila and a game of cards?" "Hey, *manita*, let's go shopping. Let's buy rings for every finger or a pretty, painted piece of junk!" But then she'd start to drink, and no one could stop her. If you tried, she'd get mean. "You bitch! You don't want me to have any fun!" She'd throw things, smash things. You just couldn't control her. The booze combined with the painkillers, that's what made her crazy.

And after Papá died, things went from bad to worse. I was the one who cared for him, who measured out his medicine and forced it through his parched lips. I was the one who read him letters from old friends to keep him distracted. Some distraction! Jews were decaying in the camps. The Mexican papers didn't say much about it, but the letters told it all. Jews were streaming out of Germany and into Spain, where Franco was giving them safe conduct through the country. Why? Diego said Franco was a monster, an ally of Hitler and Mussolini. But Franco was saving Jewish lives. Why did he do it? Papá didn't know, but he blessed him for it. Not that Papá was Jewish, I mean really Jewish. He no longer considered himself Jewish, but still. Most of the refugees went to the U.S. Those who couldn't get in went to Argentina or else came to Mexico. Papá agonized about relatives, people he hadn't seen in decades, and about people he had never seen at all, and he wondered when the U.S. would get involved in the war. Papá died in 1941, and during those last years, Frida was off in New York screwing Nikolas Muray or in Paris cozying up to the surrealists or in San Francisco being the new Señora de Rivera. I was nursing our father. She was busy with her own life, yet when Papá was dying, it was Frida he asked for, and after it was all over, it was Frida who went berserk.

I'm not being sarcastic. She was the favorite, and his death affected her horribly. And don't forget, we had just gone through the ordeal of Leon's murder. One thing right after the other. It was too much. And her own health was going downhill. Everything was wrong—her spine, her foot. After she got back to Mexico from the States, she moved back to Diego's house, but she spent most of her time with me. She wrote to Dr. Eloesser constantly. "My shank is better, but my stomach is in shambles. My neck is better, but my plumbing doesn't work at all. My head is better, but my spine is like one of those gadgets invented by the Spanish Inquisition." Sometimes she called him long-distance on the phone.

"What a jerk I am! I forgot to tell you something very important in my last letter! My digestion is as clogged up as the Mexican sewer system. I constantly need to burpted."

"Burped!" Diego corrected her. We were sitting in the living room holding hands, Diego and I. It was the first time in ages that he had shown me any physical affection, but I suppose he thought it was okay because Frida was right there, not three meters away. I mean, how could there be anything naughty about it? We were both listening to Frida's side of the conversation, although I didn't understand most of it. I asked Diego to translate the good parts, but he said there weren't any good parts, they were just talking about burping.

"Burping?" I asked.

Diego just laughed. "I'm an artist, not a translator," he pretended to growl. In the end, he did translate a few sentences although his English was still pretty bad.

"I feel pain in my belly all the time," Frida was saying, "and if I don't burpted, I feel like a firecracker ready to explode."

"Burped, not burpted!" snickered Diego. "I already told you!"

"And whose English is better, yours or mine?" she snapped. She scowled. She thought her English was perfect.

"Burp!" shouted Dr. Eloesser over the phone, so loud that even I could hear it. He was laughing hysterically. "You're both wrong! It's not *burpted* or *burped*. It's *burp*! If Frida doesn't *burp*, she feels awful!"

As I said, I don't know much English, but after their conversation, well, I knew *that* word. *Burp burp burp!* How could Dr. Eloesser bear it? I mean, hearing her carry on about burping. How can doctors stand to hear about people's gas and vomit and shit all day? It sounds like the worst job imaginable.

But you're not that kind of doctor. You don't have to deal with bodily functions.

Anyhow, the day she smashed her dolls, she was in such a black mood. It was as though God had turned his back on her and walked away. And just watching her, I felt as though I were lost in an underground tunnel with no entrance and no exit.

"Frida," I whispered, caressing her hair. "Friducha, your beautiful babies."

"No more babies!" she sobbed. "No more babies. I'll never have a baby."

We both knew it was true that Frida would never have a baby. She had come to terms with it a long time ago. Now she didn't even pretend to want a child. She had no time for motherhood. She was too busy and too famous. Trotsky's assassination and her divorce and remarriage to Diego had made her a superstar. She was interviewed by all the newspapers. The commissions were pouring in.

"You should get divorced and remarried more often," I told her. "It's good for business."

She didn't think that was funny, but she certainly smiled for the camera every time a reporter showed up at the door. She was in demand, and I wasn't complaining. Frida's good fortune was my good fortune. She was generous. She gave me money. She bought me clothes. She bought toys for Isolda and Antonio. She was thrilled to be the successful, noble, charitable sister.

That's why the doll episode took me by surprise. I thought things were going better, that she was pulling herself together. She had just been asked to paint a series of portraits of the five Mexican women who were the most significant in the history of our people. "Cockroaches," Frida called them. She was sure, she said, that ordinary Mexican women were more interesting and had "bigger teeth," that is, were tougher. But she was going to accept the assignment anyway, because no matter how many commissions she was getting, we always needed more cash. The women she had to paint were Josefa Ortiz de Domínguez, who, as every schoolchild knows, was a heroine of Mexican independence, Sor Juana Inés de la Cruz, the famous nun-poet who did scientific research, women like that. The portraits were going to be for the Dining Hall of the National Palace. Frida wrote to Dr. Eloesser, asking him to get her some information about the "cockroaches." The thing is, Frida was the provider. You see, we were a family, Frida, me, and the children. I was the mother and Frida was the father. Diego was a randy uncle who showed up on the doorstep once in a while.

I'm just an uneducated woman, and a stupid one at that, but I don't think this business with the dolls had anything to do with babies. Maybe it was the pressure of having to do those portraits combined with everything else. Or maybe it was that Diego was still screwing every skirt he could get his hands on.

"I know I have to accept the presence of other ladies in his life," she told someone, I can't remember who. But it was probably someone important, because she said "other ladies" and not "other women."

But then, later, when we were alone, she exploded. "His goddamn serial fucking is killing me, Cristi! It's killing me! I can't stand it anymore!"

"Serial fucking," she said. Those were her exact words. Because, you see, that's what he was, a goddamn serial fucker. A goddamn serial fucker! I'm sorry. I didn't mean to be crude.

I don't know if you can understand. When a man hurts a woman like that—when he says he loves her, then humiliates her—because it wasn't so long after they remarried that Diego started fooling around with María Félix. He painted her, he showed up at openings with her. Their picture was in all the magazines, and before we knew it, Diego was talking about getting another divorce.

"Of course I love María," he told an interviewer. "Everybody loves María." And it was true. Ever since María starred in Fernando de Fuentes's *Doña Bárbara,* people saw her as a savage, sexy Jezebel. All Mexico was in love with María. María the temptress. María the man-eater. It wasn't until later, when she played a courageous schoolteacher who stands up to the town bully, that María Félix became a national heroine. You know, a great patriot, a champion of the Revolution. All that.

And what about Frida? the reporters asked. "I have to leave her,"

Diego said simply. "I'm bad for her health."

He was making himself out to be a hero. A man willing to make sacrifices. Yes, he was going to leave Frida, but it was for her own good. He added stress to her life, he explained, and her doctors insisted she avoid stress.

The truth is, he was bored with her. Her drinking was getting worse, and she wasn't much fun to have around. After all, a woman who smells of vomit and death can't be much of a vamp. Puke is no great come-on. But Diego was right about one thing. He was bad for her health.

She had promised me she'd stop drinking, and she even wrote to Dr. Eloesser that she *had* stopped. But I found empty glasses and bottles everywhere. She drank to deaden the pain in her body. She drank to deaden the pain in her soul. Diego's behavior was killing her, and she was killing herself, destroying herself. The dolls were a kind of extension of her. They were little Fridas. She was killing the babies that represented a dream for the future. I think, at this point, Frida began to see that for her, there wasn't much future.

For a while, I thought La Esmeralda would make a difference. You've heard of La Esmeralda, haven't you? It was an art school started by the Ministry of Education sometime in the forties, 1942, I think. My God, over twenty years ago. They made Frida one of the teachers. Diego taught composition there—a lot of famous artists taught there—and he thought it would do Frida good to be around young people. Because she always loved kids.

She did love children. She painted them all the time. Well, maybe not all the time, because mostly she just painted herself, but, yes, she liked kids. Yes, absolutely.

I went with her sometimes, just to help out. I was there on the first day of class, tagging along, lugging canvases. It reminded me of that day so many years before when I had hauled Frida's paintings from Coyoacán to the city so she could show them to Diego. The school was on Esmeralda Street. Frida had prepared nothing, brought no books or reproductions to show the kids. I didn't have much education, so I'm no expert, but I would think that a teacher would have to do something to get ready for her class. At least figure out what to do on the first day. But Frida didn't seem to attach much importance to the whole business.

The place was so new that it was dizzying. The vapors from freshly opened containers of rosin and turpentine and tempera made you light-headed, giddy. They created a terrible but wonderful perfume. Acrid and intoxicating. I felt slightly nauseated, and yet so excited. The place was exhilarating! Every space held a secret: the room where they made mosaics, tiny tiles of brash colors spilled from a sack like an Aztec chieftain's cache of jewels. Trompe l'oeil cupboards of wooden inlay, so cleverly worked that the doors appeared open even though they were shut. A beautiful altarpiece with shellacked papier-mâché figures in bright pinks, yellows, turquoises, and lavenders, very Mexican, very lively.

The kids were huddled in clusters, buzzing like a motor in low gear. They were mostly from working-class families, the sons of street vendors and maids. Tuition and supplies were free. Some of the kids were peasants. They were young, mostly about sixteen or seventeen, but one or two looked about fourteen. There were a few girls, but not many.

Frida caught them off guard. She sashayed in wearing a white ruffled Tehuana outfit with pink and red ribbons. Her hair was done up with red, yellow, and pink roses, and she wore a ring on every finger. She looked like anything but a woman whose job it was to teach youngsters about the messy business of painting.

One of the girls approached Frida and looked her up and down. She must have been about sixteen, but she had the air of a petulant four-year-old showing off a new pair of shoes.

"I've only had men teachers, never a woman," she announced. She spat out her words as though they were wads of tobacco.

Frida threw her head back and laughed.

"You're no teacher!" hissed the girl. "Even my landscape instructor, Feliciano Peña, says that you're no teacher!"

Frida looked at the girl with affectionate eyes. "You're right!" she said gaily. "What's this business about teaching, anyway?" Frida's laughter fell at the girl's feet like a shower of diamonds. "I swear, I have no idea what it means to give classes! Will you teach me?"

The child stood there, dumbfounded.

"What's your name, darling?"

"Fanny."

"Fanny what?"

"Fanny Rabinovich."

Later, when she became famous for her portraits of children, she would be known as Fanny Rabel.

"Ah, well, Fannycita, you will be one of my *muchachitas*. You will be my student and you will teach me how to give classes, because really, darling, I have no idea. Will you do that for me, my precious Fanny? Will you teach me how to give classes?"

Frida had completely disarmed the girl. You see, she had that talent. She was so funny and warm. She left people defenseless.

Fanny was still standing there, paralyzed.

"No? Well, then, who will teach me how to give classes?"

No one answered, but some of them started to twitter shyly.

"If that's the case, I'll guess I'll just let you all do whatever you want. How would that be? Because I'm certainly not going to tell you what to do." Once again, she burst out laughing. They stared at her in amazement. A boy in a ragged white shirt shifted his weight from one foot to the other. A boy with a poncho and a surprisingly healthy mustache for one so young pulled at his ear nervously. Then, one by one, they joined her in laughter.

She didn't break her promise. She actually did let them do whatever they wanted. I mean, she didn't teach them to draw, really. Instead, she taught them to open their eyes and see the world around them. She let them paint the stuff that was lying around their homes, jugs, flowers, brooms, scraps of cloth. She taught them to appreciate the beauty of their surroundings, the *mexicanidad* of their surroundings. She let them pick their own subjects and work at their own pace. She never said, "Draw it this way. Copy from the book. Use my work as a model." She never said, "Trace this page." She let them develop their own styles. "Draw what you see," she told them. "Draw what you feel." She just wanted them to create images taken from their own world.

"All I want is to be your friend," she told them. "So let's get to work, and you'll teach me as much as I teach you. More, in fact, because I really know nothing about teaching at all."

None of those kids had ever heard an adult talk like that before, and especially not an adult in authority. They ate it up. They adored her. The great Frida Kahlo was going to be their friend.

She did love them. She had a way of teaching them that was different from anyone else's. They'd be painting in a classroom when all of a sudden she'd say, "Oh, this is too boring! Let's go out in the street. That's where the true beauty and color of Mexico can be found. Let's go, kids! Take your sketch pads!" And they'd all troop out to the slums and look for hours at the wash hanging from a clothesline—colorful cotton skirts, *rebozos*, underwear, shirts—or a dog urinating by the side of a building, or a cactus in a pot.

Sometimes they'd go to a *pulquería*. They'd drink and watch other people drinking, and they'd listen to the guitar music and sing songs with the drunken ex-revolutionaries Frida called her comrades, even though she didn't invite them to her fancy dinner parties with guests like Dolores del Río and President Cárdenas.

Sometimes she'd show up at the school with basketfuls of snacks—*empanaditas, flautitas,* plantain chips, coconut cookies.

These were poor kids. A basketful of snacks went a long way. A basketful of snacks meant something.

After a few months, Frida got tired of going to La Esmeralda. She and Diego were both living in the Casa Azul in Coyoacán, and it was a long ride into the city every day, exhausting and hard on her back.

"Fine," said Diego. "Don't go anymore."

"And my *muchachitos*?"

"Have them come out here!"

Did she really love them, or was she addicted to their devotion? Guillermo Monroy called her a walking flower. He was a poor boy. His father was a carpenter. I think he was overwhelmed by Frida's presence. By the fact that Frida Kahlo, *the* Frida Kahlo, was paying attention to him.

Ha, I thought. He should see his walking flower when she's puking in the toilet. He should see his walking flower when she's so sloshed she slumps into the *arroz con pollo*. But then I thought about it. "Why am I being such a bitch?" I said to myself. "Why am I being so unfair?" Because I knew, deep down inside, that even though

Frida was a selfish woman, she gave these kids what she could.

"I can't abandon them," she told me. "They need me. They adore me."

And it was true. They adored her. But did they need her? *She* needed *them*, but did they need her?

"You're so beautiful, Frida. Pose for us!"

"Teach us a song from the Revolution, Frida!"

"Come with us to the Communist Youth Organization tonight, Frida!"

Fridita, Friducha, Fridísima all day long. They called themselves the Fridos.

At first about ten or twelve Fridos came out to the house every day. They set up their easels in the garden and painted all morning. She fed them. She supplied paints and canvases. While they created images of swelling hibiscuses, exploding watermelons, cavorting monkeys, and exuberant jugs, Frida painted more Fridas. She painted her emotions, her physical pain. Frida beset by demons, Frida with a skeleton plugged into her brain, Frida with Diego in the middle of her forehead like an all-seeing eye, Frida in desolation, Frida with roots growing out of her gut, Frida with a crumbling spine, Frida in tears, Frida pierced with nails, Frida disemboweled . . . Frida the goddess, Frida the Christ, Frida the lord of all things seen and unseen.

My God! My God! Fridos and Fridas everywhere. It was like a shrine to our most holy lady Santa Frida. They even wrote music for her. Really! Guillermo Monroy wrote a *corrido* with fifteen verses. "Doña Frida de Rivera / our revered teacher . . ." la la la, and so on and so forth. Don't ask me to sing it! A shrine attended to by devoted priests and priestesses. And I was one of them, don't you see? I was the mistress of the cult, I was the chief priestess, the pope, the goddamn pope of the religion of our most holy lady the divine Saint Frida Kahlo de Rivera, because I was the one who took care of her, who medicated her, who fed her and bathed her. I was the one who listened to her, who soothed her and put up with her shit, her temper tantrums, her drinking, her vomit all over the bathroom floor, her whining, her depressions. No priest of any religion ever devoted his life to his beloved god the way I devoted mine to Saint Frida.

Go away. I don't want to talk about it anymore. Please, doctor . . . please just go away.

Well, all right. I'll finish the story, but then, for the love of Jesus, go away.

One by one, the students stopped coming. Coyoacán was too far away. Most of them weren't willing to make the trek. Anyhow, Frida didn't really critique their work. Oh, once in a while, but not very often. Sometimes she and Diego would go out into the garden and throw out a comment or two, like princes throwing scraps of meat at dogs, but it wasn't enough for some of them. They wanted a real teacher, so they left. Or maybe I'm wrong. Maybe it wasn't that way at all. Maybe they stopped coming because they just couldn't pay the bus fare or couldn't spare the time or didn't have the energy. I don't know why they stopped coming, but they did. Only four remained— Arturo García Bustos, Guillermo Monroy, Arturo Estrada, and Fanny Rabinovich. In addition, there was another one who came once in a while. He was about fifteen. His name was Carlos Sánchez Ahumada. A scrumptious boy, a young Aztec warrior, with an aquiline nose and a high forehead. You could just see him in a loincloth and feathers, lifting his arm as if to hurl a lance, flexing his muscles. He had a beautiful body. He was a mason like his father, and he was used to lifting stones.

Frida took an interest in him right away.

She used to bring him into her bedroom. That's where she had her easel set up.

"Carlos, come see the portrait I'm doing of Doña Rosita," she said to him one morning. The others pretended not to notice. "I want your opinion of it. Honestly, darling, tell me what you think. I learn as much from my students as they learn from me!

No one said a word. The others all knew that Frida had unconventional tastes. That's one of the things that made her so fascinating to them—her absolute disdain for traditional morality. The morality of their peasant mothers. Catholic morality. They took Frida's unusual preferences as an expression of her commitment to communist ideals. To hell with the middle class and all that. Only these kids weren't middle-class, they were poor, and the morality she was thumbing her nose at was the morality they had been raised with. Even so, they accepted her. They loved her. Santa Fridita.

Still, her interest in Carlos came as something of a surprise. Everybody had thought she had her eye on Fanny. And maybe she did. But one thing didn't rule out the other.

"Carlitos, *mi amor*, come and see the portrait I'm doing."

"*Sí, Doña Frida.*"

"How many times do I have to tell you, Carlitos! Don't call me Doña Frida! I'm your friend, darling, not your maiden aunt."

"*Sí, Doña Frida.*"

She put her arm around his waist and nestled against his shoulder. She giggled, and her laughter floated up to the treetops and mingled with the chirping of the birds.

She winked at Carlos and ran her tongue over her lips.

"*Carlitos, mi amor!*"

The boy looked down at his sandals. Frida took him by the hand and led him into her bedroom. I watched from the kitchen door.

He emerged an hour or so later, his hair a mess, his shirt open, and his white homespun trousers askew. The others kept on painting. Carlos, back at his easel, kept his eyes on his work.

Frida was leaning against the patio wall, a malicious smirk on her lips, her eyes dancing.

"He's impossible," she told me that night. We were sitting in the kitchen, shelling peas. "He thinks his *mamacita* is watching. Whatever he does, he thinks his *mamacita* can see him. Her and the Virgin of Guadalupe. You touch his crotch, and you have the feeling the whole assembly of saints is right there with you, Santo Tomás, San Ignacio, Santa Teresa, Santa Rosa. The whole gang, and the whole choir of angels. Everyone from Doña Hortigosa, the next-door neighbor, to the goddamn pope is scrutinizing your every move!" She burst into gales of laughter. "Shit, the rubbish they pump into these kids' heads!"

I was annoyed. She had used the word *scrutinize*. I didn't know what it meant.

She looked as me as though she expected me to express sympathy. I kept on shelling peas.

"But eventually, he came around." She chuckled. Then she stuck her index finger in her mouth and sucked on it wickedly. "When they're young, they'll do whatever you want."

I was overcome by a sudden fit of nausea. Carlitos wasn't that much older than my own son, Toñito.

She must have seen the look of disgust on my face. "Is something wrong?"

"No," I lied. "Nothing."

"You're happy for me, aren't you, Cristi?" She sounded heart-breakingly sincere.

"Of course I am, Frida."

"I love you so much, Cristi."

I knew she meant it.

"I love you, too," I whispered.

My heart was in shreds. I bit my lip and got up and left the room. Why couldn't I just accept her the way she was? Why did her stunts drive me so crazy?

Not long after that, Carlos Sánchez Ahumada disappeared. He not only stopped coming to the Casa Azul, he abandoned La Esmeralda altogether. Why? I don't know. No one looked for him. No one went to his house to inquire.

What? No! Of course not. I had nothing to do with it! I never said anything to anyone about it until now, and now it doesn't matter anymore.

So many years have passed. Anyway, nobody ever mentioned him again, not ever. Carlos was a taboo subject, like babies. You just didn't talk about certain things with Frida. It was as though they didn't exist. They had been erased by virtue of her wanting to forget them.

I'm old. I'm older than old. I don't want to remember anymore. All I want is for you to go away.

All right, I'll go on, but only for a little while. You have to understand, I'm tired.

I know I've been selfish. All the times I judged Frida harshly. All the times I resented her success. I admit it. I was horrible, cruel. I hate myself for that, but sometimes I just couldn't help it. Sometimes she was so annoying, so self-centered, I just wanted to kill her. No, I

don't mean that. But she was full of herself, like a clam that fills its
shell so tightly there's no room for anything else. For example, at the
opening of La Rosita.

You don't know La Rosita? It was a *pulquería* on the corner of
Aguayo and Londres, right down the street from our house. A sorry
little place, dirty floors, a few stools. Some of the Fridos had studied
mural painting with Diego, and so Frida got permission for them to
decorate the outside walls. It would be good practice for them, she
said. It wasn't such an original idea. What I mean is, *pulquería* walls
were usually painted. Simple stuff, graffiti almost, drawings of things
suggested by the name of the place. *Pulquería El Cacto* had a lot of cac-
tuses painted on its walls, for example. Or sometimes the pictures
were political—revolutionary heroes, that sort of thing—or had
something to do with the history of the town. For example, in San
Pablo Guelatao, in Oaxaca, all the *pulquerías* had pictures of the
famous president Benito Juárez because he was born there. At one
point the government decided that the *pulquerías* had to be cleaned
up, and so the walls all had to be whitewashed. But Frida and Diego
objected to that. The paintings were the people's art, they said, beautiful, authentic, and unconstrained. Frida's idea was to give her students practice painting murals by giving them a crack at the walls of
La Rosita. Just an exercise, she said, but at the same time, these kids'
paintings were going to revive the kind of folk art that had produced
the original *pulquería* murals.

So they all trooped down there. The Fridos and some of Diego's
students too, the Dieguitos. They painted for days. Fanny did a little girl
and a lot of roses. The name of the *pulquería,* Rosita, could be a girl's
name, or it could mean "little rose." Frida and Diego would visit every
once in a while and offer their comments. Anyhow, by June it was done.

The year? I think it was 1943. I'm almost sure. It was the year the
movie *Distinto Amanecer* came out. Well, when the *pulquería* was ready
to show off its new murals, Frida had these broadsides printed up,
very funny broadsides with pictures of roses and people drinking
pulque, and the announcement of a spectacular lunch, a barbecue of
meats sprinkled with the best *pulque* in Mexico. She made it sound
like she was announcing the opening of a very important exhibition.

She had these broadsides distributed everywhere, in the central market, in the plazas. She had them pasted to church walls, she sent them
to the newspapers, she sent them to the most important and influential people in Mexico City.

As you can imagine, it was a circus, a parade of celebrities.

"¡Dios mío!" said Frida. "I never suspected it would be anything
like this!"

But of course she did. I mean, she's the one who made it happen.
After all, when Frida and Diego Rivera gave a party, the reporters
came running. And Frida made sure they had plenty of advance
notice. She made it into an *event*.

Concha Michel, the famous folksinger, sang "Delgadina," about a
girl who refuses to become a big shot's mistress, and Guillermo sang
his damned *corrido* about his beloved art teacher. Salvador Novo,
Frida's old friend from Prepa days and now a famous poet, recited
verses. Padre Esteban, the parish priest, kissed Frida's cheek, and the
mother of one of Frida's students kissed her hand. All the reporters
kissed her ass.

Everywhere the lively sounds of guitars, blithe adolescents, spirited children. A toothless old lady was dancing a *jaranda* with her
grandson, moving her hips and throwing her head back in joy. Even
the dogs seemed to bark in time to the music. One chased another
into a group of dancers, and a crew of little boys howled with laughter. The girl students were dressed in Tehuana costumes with full,
colorful skirts, lacy blouses, and roses and ribbons in their hair.
Miniature Fridas. Next they'll all be limping, I thought.

The air was redolent with barbecue, as well as poached guavas,
quince paste and cheese, and sugar cookies. And the best *pulque* from
Ixtapalapa. You could get drunk just on the fragrance. Frida the
bountiful. People thought she had paid for the whole thing, even
though Diego and several other generous fat cats had footed the bills.
Everyone ate and laughed and rejoiced in the exquisite *mexicanidad*
of the moment, and Frida was the queen of this fairy-tale kingdom,
where for one afternoon everyone was in a good mood and everyone—from the governor to the carpenter's son—had enough to eat.

Lola del Río, my old friend Lola, who had held my hand and

stroked my hair in Xochimilco, stood up on a chair and congratulated Frida on her great contribution to Mexican culture. Then she jumped down and hugged Frida. Diego applauded. Frida beamed. The photographers went snap snap snap. The pictures would be in the morning's paper. I smiled at Lola, and she looked right past me. "Lola," I whispered, but it was like I wasn't there.

They were all dancing. I was dancing too, but as though in a dream. Floating, bobbing up and down like a balloon on a string. I was there, yet I saw the scene from afar, in muted colors, soft reds and yellows and greens, grainy, like a poor-quality film. I felt as though I were on the outside, as though I were watching from some place in heaven, where I hovered like a quivering, feathered creature.

The only one who wasn't dancing was Benjamin Péret, a French teacher at La Esmeralda. He was a slight man with dull hair, droopy eyelids, and a limp wrist. He had just arrived from Paris and made it clear that although he shared Mexicans' revolutionary zeal, he had no intention of ever touching a real Mexican. He was a good communist, he loved humanity, but he washed his hands with disinfectant whenever he shook hands with a *campesino*.

Diego signaled him to move into the dance area. "*Vamos, compañero*. We're going to do a *zapateado*."

Péret looked horrified. "*Mais non!*" He twitched. He looked like a scrawny rooster who had just swallowed a foul-tasting worm. Or maybe a string he had taken for a worm.

"*Mais non!*" His head jerked around oddly. His eyes were enormous and round. "I do not know how to make those dances, Diego."

Diego was drunk. "*Vamos, Benjamín*," he coaxed. He winked at him and beckoned as though the French teacher were a coy young girl.

"No, Diego. I do not know how. I do not!"

Suddenly, Diego's face turned mean. "Then I'll teach you!" he snarled.

He yanked out the gun he always carried at his hip. Bystanders moved to the side. Mothers grabbed their children by the hand and snatched them away. Diego aimed at Péret's feet.

"*Non!*" whimpered the Frenchman. "*Non, Diego!*" He was almost in tears.

Diego fired, and Péret hopped onto one foot. Diego fired again, and Péret shifted his weight again. Diego fired over and over, and Péret sprang from one foot to the other, suddenly agile.

"Now you've got it!" Diego roared. He kept on firing, and the dancer kept on *zapateando*. The patio of the *pulquería* exploded with laughter, but poor Benjamin was sniffing back snot.

Frida came up behind Diego and slipped her hand gently around his waist. "Come on, darling," she coaxed. "That's enough."

Diego let himself be wooed.

Frida took the gun out of his hand and snuggled against him. Then he took it from her and slipped it back into the holster, and the two of them started to dance.

They both made me sick. How many times can you sit through the same film? It was time to change reels. It was time to change roles.

Frida danced for hours that night. How did she do it? I knew she was upset over Diego's behavior and that her back and leg were killing her, but somehow she managed. Was it the liters of *pulque* she poured down her throat or simply the excitement? Or was she too aware of other peoples' eyes on her not to put up a good show? Or had she taken an extra dose of painkillers before the spectacle began?

She was dying. Her body was decaying, wasting away before my eyes. And yet there she was, dancing.

"Pour me another drink!" she'd call out every once in a while, and someone would come running with another glass of *pulque*. All she had to do was ask. All she had to do was open her mouth, and someone would do her bidding. The whole world groveled at her feet. Frida the empress. She played her part like Bette Davis.

I was angry, I admit it. Her self-centeredness, her brave-little-invalid act. All of it disgusted me, but at the same time, I felt guilty because so much of Frida's pain stemmed from what I had done to her. I just couldn't put it out of my mind. I had betrayed my own sister. I loved her more than anyone in the world, yet I had betrayed her. Of all the horrible things that had happened to Frida, my treachery was the one that hurt her the most. It's because I was family. That's how it is with us Mexicans. One thing you learn from the time you're born is that you can't trust anybody except the members of your own family. So, you see, I had betrayed a sacred bond. Maybe things would have been different. Maybe she would never have gotten a divorce. I felt I had to do something to relieve her suffering, even if it meant being her slave for the rest of my life.

I watched Frida twirl around faster and faster, her face flushed, her chest heaving. She was laughing gaily. She was spinning from one partner to the other, stamping, clapping, swinging her hips. And yet, she was dying of a crushed back, a rotting leg, a broken heart.

And then I saw her gradually transform. Unexpectedly, without warning, Frida was no longer Frida. She was her skeleton. Instead of her face, her body, her feet, I saw her fleshless carcass, still in her Tehuana costume, whirling, laughing, its bony frame moving to the rhythm of the music, tapping, swaying, a skull sticking up above a ruffled blouse which hung limply over a mass of bones.

I looked from one to the other: Diego, Lola, Guillermo, Fanny, Salvador Novo, Concha Michel, all of them skeletons. Diego, who moments before had been stomping and pirouetting, graceful in spite of his tremendous girth, a supple giant. Now, a skull grinning ghoulishly atop a clanking, fleshless cadaver. Lola in her chic purple dress and sandals, Lupe Marín in her off-the shoulder white cotton blouse, the *campesinos* in their homespun shirts and trousers and huaraches. All skeletons. Even delicate Fanny, with her fine European cheekbones. Even Benjamin, jerking roosterlike along the edge of the dance area. All skinless skulls and torsos.

I wanted to scream, but why bother? Who would hear me? I was invisible.

Well, the La Rosita project was so successful that Frida got a lot of new projects for her Friditos. They did a mural in a public laundry with portraits of all the laundresses—a huge success. They did an exhibit at the Palace of Fine Arts in maybe 1945 or '46 that made a lot of people mad because of its leftist themes. I can't remember all the projects, but she helped those kids out a lot, getting them jobs, arranging shows. They came to think of her as a kind of second mother, and that was a big mistake. That was the beginning of the end.

As you know, I guess you know, in Mexico we celebrate Mother's

Day on December 8, the Feast of the Immaculate Conception. One year Frida's students decided to give Frida a Mother's Day gift. They put together a collection of their paintings. Fanny did a maternity scene, a mother and child, but not *the* Mother and Child. One of them did a family of the Revolution—father, mother, son, and daughter—all poor in peasant clothes and huaraches, all with cartridge belts slung across their chests. Another did a birth scene inspired by Frida's *My Birth*, painted more than a decade earlier. They were all small paintings, almost miniatures. The idea was that Frida would hang them together in her studio, on one wall, a tribute to her from her spiritual children. They came over early in the morning with their gifts and a huge bouquet of flowers—roses, orchids, daisies, carnations, hibiscuses—a huge bouquet, all done up in colored ribbons.

They had made a little card to go with the flowers. On it they had written: *To our second mother.* They had all signed it.

Obviously, they thought it would please Frida. They knew how much she had wanted to have children, how much she said she had wanted to have children.

Fanny presented the bouquet, a wide grin on her lips.

"*Maestra . . .*" she said breathlessly.

"Our *adorada maestra,*" Guillermo Monroy echoed her.

Frida stood staring at the youngsters, paralyzed. Only her lips moved, but no sound came out of her mouth.

Monroy seemed not to notice. He sat down and began to strum his guitar. He had written Frida another *corrido*. He started to croon. *Segunda madre,* "second mother," are the only words I remember. They were part of the chorus, which he kept singing over and over. "You're a second mother / to the kids who love you." Something like that.

Frida's lips were trembling. I expected her to make a biting remark, to light a cigarette and stare into space, as though she couldn't possibly be bothered with their stupid little gifts. I expected her to adopt a bored look and a cynical tone. Instead, she thanked them graciously and told them that she was feeling ill, they would have to come back another time.

"But *maestra,*" they said. "We took the bus all the way from the city."

"I'm sorry, darlings," she whispered. "I'm sorry, but I just can't."

"Those idiots!" she howled the instant they had left. "Those stupid little morons! What do they think they're doing calling me their
mother? I'm not their mother! I'm nobody's mother. I don't want
their presents! I don't want their sympathy! I don't want to be anyone's *second* mother. Get this fucking shit out of here! Get it out of
here right now."

She took a knife and stabbed Fanny's beautiful mother and child.
She shredded each and every painting, then she attacked the flowers.
She attacked them as though they were people, children. She ripped
off their delicate heads, she yanked off their little leaves, she tore up
their fragile stems. Crazed, she snatched pieces between her teeth,
chewed them to shreds, then spat them out. Her eyes were white, out
of orbit. She was screaming and sobbing. "Morons! Asses! Idiots!
Imbeciles! I'm not your goddamn mother! I'm not your fucking
mother, you fucking little dimwits. Take back your fucking posies.
Get your shitty paintings out of here! I'm not your mother, do you
hear me! I am not your mother! I have no children, and you are *not*
my children!" She was shrieking, carrying on like a madwoman. I
imagined she had ranted and raved the same way the day she
smashed her dolls. She was hoarse from hollering. Finally, she collapsed onto her bed and sobbed.

So you see, I couldn't abandon her. Sometimes I said to myself,
"I just can't stand this anymore. I've got to get out of this house." But
Frida needed me. I had to be her slave until the end.

CHAPTER 24

Agnus Dei

MONDAY, JULY 12, 1954. 11:07 P.M.: THE NIGHT IS AS BLACK AS A SHROUD, but outside, children are scampering. Perhaps they're bringing home *pulque* for the old man or tortillas from Auntie's house. There's no moon, although there should be. Señora Mayet, the nurse, has just given Frida some carrot juice. Frida gags. She hates it, but she has to ingest something. Mayet moves quietly, her expert hands propping up Frida's head and pressing the cup gently against her lips. In the street, a shriek of laughter slashes through the darkness, then silence—viscous and sticky, like tar. "Come on, Friducha," coaxes Diego. "Drink it all up." No one else speaks. Señora Mayet insists on the juice, tipping the cup so that the liquid trickles into Frida's mouth. I get up and massage my sister's shoulders. Outside the window, the shuffle of footsteps that soon disappears. Someone is going about his business. Close your eyes, Frida. Close your eyes. Soon it will be time. She closes her eyes and sleeps.

Last week she went to a communist demonstration, even though Dr. Farill told her not to on account of the bronchitis. "My lungs are rocks, Cristi, sharp rocks that cut into my chest." "Then use your head, Frida. Don't go!" But she pulled herself into her wheelchair anyway. "It won't be long, *Pelona*." She grimaced into the mirror, then jabbed a wilting red rose into her hair. It fell to the floor, a heap of loose, melancholy petals. A few strays fluttered away, forming isolated drops of blood on the floor. I looked away. "I can't do my hair, Cristi." "Well, I won't do it for you. You don't have to go out, you know." She pouted. "It doesn't make any difference whether you do it or not. It's going to rain anyway. It's already raining." She tied a kerchief over her dingy hair, giving her face the look of a mass of cobwebs framed in white cotton. It was a pathetic afternoon, cold and wet. I felt as though I were a clump of sand wrapped in a soaking sheet. But Frida had to go. It was a major event, a must performance. Frida had to be seen clenching her raised fist and shouting ¡Americanos! ¡Asesinos! We were protesting the CIA, how the CIA pushed Jacobo Arbenz out of power. Arbenz, the Guatemalan president, champion of the people. He refused to kowtow to capitalist interests. That's what Frida said, although it seemed to me that she and Diego kowtowed plenty to capitalist interests when they took money from the big shots in Chicago and New York. Anyhow, there was Frida shouting slogans. "Down with the gringos! Yankees out of Guatemala! Murderers! Butchers!" She looked like a little sparrow, so fragile and popeyed, so weary, so wan. Her voice barely carried past the tip of her kerchief, but it was the image that counted. She had so little time left to create her legend. People fell all over her. "What a show of solidarity!" "Valiant Frida, just like Joan of Arc!" "Just like Benito Juárez!" "Just like La Güera Rodríguez!" The reporters were lapping it up. I could imagine the headlines: FRIDA KAHLO DEFIES ILLNESS TO SHOW SUPPORT FOR THE MASSES.

Who? La Güera Rodríguez? She was a heroine of the Independence from Spain. You've never heard of her? In Mexico, every schoolchild knows her. Anyhow, we went to the protest, but I wanted to stay home. What I mean is, I wanted Frida to stay home. Why? Because I loved her, of course. Because she was dying. If you keep interrupting me, I'll never get through this story, and I want to get through it, doctor, because I want you to go away and leave me alone.

When it was all over, she collapsed on her bed and begged for Demerol. I pretended not to hear. She was sobbing hysterically. "Demerol! Demerol!" That seemed to be the only word she could articulate. I went into the bathroom and washed my face. I was exhausted myself. When I came out, Frida was lying on top of her bed, grasping her cane, thrashing the air. "Demerol!" I didn't have the energy to argue, but Mayet intervened. "No," she said firmly. "I gave her medication at the demonstration. No more painkillers. No injections. No pills." "Yes, Señora Mayet," I said. As soon as Mayet left Frida's bedroom, I gave Frida a shot of Demerol.

11:29 P.M. Isolda tiptoes in. She is a young woman now, slim and feathery. "Does Tía Fridita want some broth?" "No, darling, she dropped off about a half hour ago." "I'm going to read a while." "Yes, go and read. Tomorrow she'll be better." A drunk stumbles down the street crooning "Amapola." A dog barks once, only once. Somewhere in the direction of La Rosita, two men are laughing. The nurse has returned and is dozing in a corner, her breathing like dust flurries over the desert. Diego straightens Frida's sheet and kisses her on the forehead. "You should get some sleep." "No, Diego. You sleep. I'll watch over her." I push aside the curtain and gaze at the night sky. A greenish moon gleams faintly behind the clouds. A pair of lovers caress outside the window. I sense rather than see them. I suspect they will create new life tonight.

Tuesday, July 13, 1954. Midnight. Tuesday the thirteenth is a bad luck day, doctor, like Friday the thirteenth in your country. Frida wheezes like rusty bellows, but she is sleeping. Diego's head sinks into his chins, spongy pillows resting on a babyish chest. I have returned to the window and once again pulled aside the curtain. I'm not going to sleep. No, not tonight. I'm waiting for the right moment. An old man hobbles by. He doesn't lift his eyes to look into mine. He's lost in his own thoughts, unaware that inside our house, the very house he is crossing in front of, someone is dying. I leave the window and sit at the foot of the bed. "Diego!" He nods and grunts softly, like a piglet. "Diego, she's sleeping. It's okay for you to go now." He opens his lids as though there were salt under them. "What?" His breath is rancid. "Go back to the studio, if you want. She's sleeping." He's trying to focus, trying to make out Frida's silhouette. Her hand lying slack on the sheet, her chest rising and falling spasmodically. "You can go back, Diego. I'll stay with her." "You think she'll sleep all night?" "She'll be peaceful . . . yes." He pulls his legs under him and thrusts his bulk into an upright position. "You don't mind?" "Mayet and Isolda are here with me. Manuel's in the other room." You remember Manuel, don't you, doctor? Papá's old servant. He came back to stay with us sometime before Papá died. Diego stoops and kisses Frida on the forehead. *"Adiós, mi amor."* He looks doubtful. He doesn't want to go. He lingers by the bed, caressing her fingers. At last he gathers up his jacket and his hat. "It may rain before you get back to the studio." He shrugs. In the doorway he presses my hand to his cheek as if my flesh against his can somehow keep him from crying. He looks haggard. His lips are trembling. A tear forms in the corner of his eye, then swells and bursts into a rivulet that flows via pappy furrows to his chin. His pain pierces my heart.

But I harness my feelings. I remember things. What right has he to slobber in remorse now, when seven years before he had been carrying on with María Félix?

Río Escondido came out in 1947. Oh, it was a glorious movie. The communists loved it. María Félix became the darling of Mexico after she played Rosaura Salazar, the spirited schoolteacher who takes on the big, powerful bad guys and wins. Soon people who saw the film began to take María for Rosaura. They thought she was a saint. They bought images of her and even prayed to them.

María Félix was a stunning, curvaceous woman, a woman with a lot of everything. She went to parties in strapless evening gowns that showed it all off. She lounged by swimming pools in tiny bathing suits, her long, smooth legs dangling off the chaise longue. She wore her hair loose, disheveled, chocolate and licorice—an irresistible invitation to run your fingers through it. The crowds loved her because she was the Virgin Mary and Eve all wrapped up into one. God and the devil. In the portrait Diego did of her, she looks as though she could be thinking or she could be praying. Her eyes are slightly downcast. And yet she's so alluring, her hair falling over her bare shoulders. The light catches it right on the crown. She looks like a Magdalena.

And everywhere María went, there was Diego, attached to her like some sort of an appendage. And the newspaper photographers snapping away. Always. At the parties, at the openings, at the press conferences. María laughed and blew kisses and talked about patriotism. And Diego talked about divorcing Frida.

And Frida? She cracked jokes. He'd been saying for a while that he was going to leave her, so she had had time get together her script.

Once a reporter asked, "What's this about Diego and María Félix?" "Ah," said Frida, "so he likes screwing her. What's the big deal? I wouldn't mind screwing her myself!" You see, she was showing them all that she couldn't be hurt by Diego's womanizing, not because she didn't love him, but because she shared his passions. They were still a team, only instead of he and she, they were two macho guys on the prowl. Look at her self-portraits, doctor. They get more and more manly. "What's the idea? You look like a guy in this picture," a young newspaperman said to her. "Really? You think so? Well, you know how Diego and I met?" she quipped. "We were dating the same girl!" Another time, we were at a reception at the American embassy, and she pulled aside a silver-haired society lady who was impressed as hell to be meeting the great Kahlo. "Listen," Frida whispered in her ear. "I'm going to tell you a secret. Diego isn't the father of Lupe Marín's daughter, Lupita." The woman looked delighted to be let in on a naughty secret. "You know who the real father is?" Frida said with a wink. "It's *me*!"

"Listen," Frida told a crowd at Eddie Kaufman's hotel. Eddie was visiting Mexico and had invited us all to a huge reception at the Moctezuma. "Listen," Frida said. "Did you all know that Eddie, Diego, and I were all on the *Titanic* when it started to go down? Kaufman, a real gentleman and hero, shouted, 'Save the women and children! Get all the women and children to the lifeboats!' But Diego rushed off in the direction of the lifeboats himself, screaming 'Screw the women and children!' As for me, I stopped and pondered his words a minute and asked, 'You think there's time?'" Gasps. Whoopies. Catcalls. Gales of laughter.

My heart was breaking. My sister was performing like a marionette, the kind of dancing skeleton that amateur puppeteers dangle and jerk on the Day of the Dead. Jerk jerk step-to-the-right, jerk jerk step-to-the-left. Wherever we went, she allowed the crowds to pull her strings. She had lost weight, and her face had become sharp and bony. She was so drunk or drugged most of the time that she couldn't even put on her makeup straight. She'd paint on a macabre ghoul's mouth. I wanted to take her in my arms and say *Stop, Frida,*

stop! I couldn't stand to see her become their toy, their amusement. I
wanted to kiss her, to take her home, to put her to bed. My poor, darling sister. I wanted to say *Make them leave you alone, Frida. Let me take
you home to die in peace!* But she had to play the role. Even then, she
had to be the star.

The night she told the *Titanic* joke at Eddie Kaufman's party,
Diego and I took her back to Coyoacán afterward. On the way home
she was hysterical, weeping and laughing almost at the same time.
Her face was screwed up in pain, like the face of a rag doll that someone had washed and wrung out. Diego left for San Angel right away.
Her nurse—Señora Mayet wasn't working for us yet—her nurse had
prepared her medication, and just as she was bending over to give it
to her, Frida reached out and grabbed her crotch. The woman just
snorted. "Come on, Miss Frida, take your medicine." "Yeah, give me
those pills, and give me some pussy too, you little bitch!" The nurse
just laughed and slapped her fingers as though she were a naughty
child. Frida took her cane and tried to work it up between the
woman's legs. "Come on, darling," she cooed. "Lift up your skirt for
Frida." We could never keep nurses very long, because Frida always
went after them. They all ran away after a week or two. All of them
except that one, because she shared Frida's inclinations. I'm sure that
in addition to Demerol and barbiturates she gave her a hand job once
in a while. But eventually, even she couldn't take Frida's temper
tantrums anymore, and she left too. I can't even remember all the
nurses we had, doctor. Women who came and went. Came because
Diego offered a good salary and because it was an honor to empty the
bedpans of the great Frida and left because the canings and the
crotch grabbing just got to be too much. Then it was up to me to
smooth Frida's brow and hold her hand. "Give me a shot, little Kity!"
she would beg. "No, Frida. It's not time yet." "Come on, Kity. Give
me some Demerol. Give me some codeine, some opium, some
atropine. Anything!" She couldn't take straight morphine, only
Demerol, because it's a synthetic. "Please, Kity. Come on, Cristi Kity.
If you loved me, you'd do it!" "I can't, Frida. Try to go to sleep." "I
can't sleep without drugs. Come on, Kity, give me a jab." I couldn't
bear to look at her body. But she would maneuver herself onto her

stomach and hike up her nightgown, and what could I do? "Find a spot!" "There is no spot!" "Find one!" She'd be trembling and screaming, and I'd be afraid she was going to have some kind of an attack, so what could I do? I'd find a tiny patch of clear skin and inject her, and in a while, she'd calm down.

2:51 A.M. Her eyes are open, wide open. I've pulled the curtain back a bit because it frightens me to sit alone in a pitch-black room. Her pupils catch the moonlight and flash like knives.

"Where's Maty?"

"Maty left hours ago, Frida. Go back to sleep." But she can't sleep because her leg hurts, the leg she doesn't have, the leg they cut off. A piercing pain, she says. A dagger in the calf. "Demerol!" But it's not time yet, and I can't break the rules because Mayet is in the doorway. She's come to check on her.

"Why aren't you sleeping, Miss Frida?"

"You know why I'm not sleeping, you cunt! I'm in pain, terrible pain! Give me Demerol!"

Señora Mayet turns on a lamp and takes Frida's temperature. "Why don't you go to bed, Miss Cristina? I'll stay with her the rest of the night."

"That's all right. I'll stay with her."

She doesn't trust me. She suspects I break the rules. She suspects I disobey her when she's not looking. I try to allay her misgivings.

"I'm not sleepy, Señora Mayet. I'll just sit here a while longer. You go on to bed."

"Yes, Señora Mayet. You go to bed. My sister will take care of me." Frida's voice is more robust than you'd expect. The nurse vacillates, but only for a moment.

"Don't give her any medication, Miss Cristi."

"No, Señora Mayet."

"Just a compress on her forehead, if she needs it. But no more drugs."

Frida doesn't say a word.

"Promise you'll call if you need me."

"Of course, Señora Mayet."

The nurse turns out the light. We hear her footsteps in the

patio. We hear the toilet flush. Silence. Two, four, five, ten minutes. "Cristi, I can't take any more." Her voice, barely audible, is pleading, desperate. "I know, darling." I fill the syringe and inject her. Her hand brushes mine, and she tries to squeeze my fingers in gratitude. In a moment, her eyes close and she is quiet.

Five years ago, Frida spent nine months in the Hospital Inglés. That's when they started talking about amputation. Her circulation was bad. Two of her toes had turned black, and the doctors said gangrene had set in. Gangrene. That means your body starts to disintegrate slowly, so slowly you don't even notice it, until one day you wake up and part of you is dead. They had to cut off two of her toes.

Maty and I went to see her every day. Adri went every other day. Diego took a room in the hospital and stayed there with her. By then, his romance with María was over. But even while it was going on, and this is one thing I want to make absolutely clear, he loved her. He always loved her, just as I did. We hurt one another, but we loved one another.

They operated on her back. I can't remember all the details. They decided Frida needed a bone graph, but it turned out to be disastrous. They put a horrible corset on her after the operation to keep her from moving, but it kept her wound from draining properly, and before long an abscess formed on her back. The whole thing was infected. It stank so badly you could vomit. Maty said Frida smelled like a dead dog. I thought she smelled like a pig's fart. It's a horrible thing to say, but I'd gag every time I went into her hospital room. Imagine how she felt, poor Frida, so finicky about her clothes, her hair, her jewelry. Imagine how she felt when the stench from her sores starting driving people away. "Do it, Cristi," she pleaded. "An overdose of Demerol." But instead, I begged the doctor—his name was Juan Farill—to save her, to give her something stronger for the pain, and I prayed. I admit it, I prayed. Because even though Frida said the Catholic Church was full of shit, that Catholicism was evil, I just didn't know what else to do, so I prayed.

I never pray anymore, although sometimes I want to.

They made a new plaster corset with a hole in the back so the filth could ooze out. But her body was a cesspool. The wounds didn't heal.

She still stank like a rotting carcass, and yet . . . I couldn't . . . I knew she wanted to die, but she was my sister, after all, and I loved her.

They set up an easel in her room and fastened it to the bed so she could paint lying down. People came in to watch her. Diego brought in a Huichol Indian in an elaborate costume to pose for her. A hand-some young man with perfect features and long hair, copper skin, even white teeth. What a vision he was, with his wide-brimmed, ban-gle-edged hat, his embroidered shawl, his short red cape, his exquis-itely worked cloth belt. He wore a slew of bracelets and an ornate, woven shoulder-strapped bag. Frida was in heaven—her with a ring on every finger, her painted corsets, her dangling earrings, and him with his trinkets and baubles. Between the two of them, they were a frenzy of color and design. For a while, he was her favorite toy.

But she had other toys. She had a collection of skulls, which she trimmed with flowers and ribbon and labeled with our names. Mine was a smiling sugar skull with colored jellies. Hers had a hammer and sickle and pink bows and flounces. Cristina dead. Frida dead. Life and death. The gay and the macabre.

She liked to have people in. I was there all the time, of course, and so was Maty. Diego too. But this wasn't just a family affair. The doctors and nurses would congregate around her, and guests flooded the room. María Félix—who, of course, had become Frida's good friend—Lupe Marín, Isolda and Antonio, Fanny and the other Fridos, old buddies from the Prepa. Adelina Zendejas was one of the pals from the old days who came all the time. Politicians and poets, actors and neighborhood children. Even La Reyna dropped by once or twice. Diego got ahold of a projector and showed Laurel and Hardy movies. Sometimes he would dance and Adelina would play the tam-bourine. I brought food, baskets and baskets of it. Frida would laugh and tell dirty jokes. "Why did the widow wear a black tampon? Because that's where she missed him most!" She oozed joy and hope, as long as she had an audience. But when there was no one around, it was *Polish my nails! Do my hair! Bring me my mirror! Find my ring!* She had a silver ring with a turquoise quetzal bird on it, and she got it into her head that if she lost it, another part of her body would rot and fall off, another toe, perhaps, or a finger, or an earlobe. If I said,

Your nails, Frida? I think you need to rest now, she'd get nasty. *Don't tell me what I need to do, Fatso. My friends will be here soon, and they can't see me like this!* She was horrified by the prospect of abandonment. She had to be surrounded by people. She had to be in the limelight. Her health depended on it, so I'd polish her nails, comb her hair, decorate her braids with silk bows and flowers. And then she looked beautiful. I have to admit it. She looked beautiful, in spite of the disease that was consuming her body, eating her alive. Beautiful, like the ornate plaster skulls that filled her room. Once the crowd materialized, it was an ongoing party, pure *alegría,* except for one thing: Frida was dying, and everybody knew it. Yet they allowed themselves to be comforted by her fake high spirits. After they all went home, she would squeeze my hand and plead, "Do it, Kity, my darling Kity. Put me out of my misery."

And still, when they finally sent her home from the Hospital Inglés, she was glad to be alive. In spite of her wheelchair, in spite of the plaster corset that crushed and bruised her flesh. She threw herself into everything. She partied constantly, a smile on her face and a cigarette dangling from her fingers. She surrounded herself with stars. Josephine Baker. Concha Michel. María Félix. Not Lola. Frida and Lola had had a falling-out. Frida had sent her a painting out of the blue, a painting Lola hadn't asked for, along with a bill. That's what Frida sometimes did when she needed dough. She sent her friends unsolicited paintings and then billed them. Only Lola refused to play that game. Lola refused to write a check. Instead, she returned the gift. She was through with Diego, and she didn't need either one of them anymore. The end, but so what? Who needed Dolores del Río? We had poets like Carlos Pellicer, painters like Dr. Atl, photographers like Lola Alvarez Bravo. And movie stars galore. Because Frida needed stars. She needed to be the star of stars.

Frida had to do everything in a big way. How do you say it? With pizzazz. She partied with pizzazz, she suffered with pizzazz, she even mourned with pizzazz. When Stalin died, she went into spasms of suffering. You should have seen her wail and weep for the reporters and photographers. I don't want to imply that her commitment wasn't sincere. It was completely sincere. She had always wanted to meet

Stalin, and she had missed the chance. She felt that something precious had slipped through her fingers, that the world was somehow drifting away from her. But even if she never got to meet him in life, at least she could be with him through art. She painted a double portrait. Frida and Stalin. It was a portrait within a portrait. One side showed an easel with Stalin's picture, very large, very dominant, and the other side showed Frida seated and dressed in a red Tehuana costume. He's large, she's small. He's a piece of art, she's a live woman. He's her creation, but she's his creation too, because without him, she wouldn't be the devout communist, the enlightened thinker, that she is. He's turned away from her, and she looks out at the viewer as if sitting for a photograph. Frida and Stalin, together and not together.

Art was what kept her going. Creating beauty out of pain helped her make sense of things. It gave her suffering a purpose. She would decorate her plaster casts, those instruments of torture, turn them into things of beauty. She painted hammers and sickles on them, stars and flowers, birds and babies. She painted a fetus on one of them, so when she wore it, she felt as though she were carrying a baby.

3:47 A.M. How much longer until dawn? Every muscle in my body tingles. My mind is bubbling like a pot of *mole*. I'm pure electricity. Tonight I'll atone for my sins. My darling Frida, you'll soar like an eagle, like an *águila!* Someone's in the street. I push the curtain aside. It's Marco Antonio, the baker. I can barely see him, but I recognize his stocky body, his straggly, shoulder-length hair, his limp. As a boy he caught a bullet in the ankle. Now he stands on his disfigured foot all day, baking crusty rolls and egg bread. For the *Día de los Muertos* he makes Dead Man's Bread, and for Epiphany he makes *rosca de Reyes* with cinnamon, anise, and raisins. Like all of us, he learned young to lick his wounds and keep on living. His sombrero is pulled down almost over his eyes to protect him from the damp air. How can he see where he's going? I can't make out his feet in the darkness, but I can hear his sandals scraping against the moist ground. Soon Ana Teresa, the tortilla maker, will come hustling along. Her step will be light, like that of a chicken in a hurry. Before long the shadows will fade, and morning will creep over the rooftops. It's already tomorrow.

April 1953. Last year. It seems like centuries ago. Frida was lying in bed, just as she is right now, except that the sun had been up for hours. Her eyes closed, her face pasty.

Yes, it's the first week in April 1953. Her jaw has lost the taut smoothness it once had. She's forty-six years old, not twenty, but the servants still treat her like a spoiled child. The paintings are gone. They were packed up and sent days ago. Her hand hangs limply over the side of the bed. She holds a cigarette, but she isn't smoking. Soon it will be time to dress her, but not yet. Dr. Farill limps in and sits down by the bed. Frida loves him because he's lame like she is. He uses crutches. He's bald, with heavy eyebrows, a round face, and a sense of humor. "Hi, beautiful," he says to Frida. "Hi cutie," she answers without opening her eyes. How can she be sure it's him? Frida knows everything. "Did my tubby sister give you something to eat?" "Not yet, but she will. Cristi always takes good care of me." "Not too good, I hope," Frida's voice is tinged with sarcasm. Just tinged, not dripping.

The room smells of chili, lilacs, alcohol, and urine. I leave when Farill starts to examine Frida, although she hasn't asked me to. She doesn't care if I watch him thump and manipulate her bruised body.

The phone rings. It's Maty. She's at the gallery. She says reporters are already there, hugging the entrance. Like bees, she says. Like bees swarming around a hive.

Dr. Farill says that Frida is running a fever. It would be better if she didn't go. "The wound hasn't healed," he says. "It's infected." The bone transplant, was a failure, and Frida's spine is a mess. She cries all night from the pain.

"She can't go," says Farill. "She can't walk. She can't even stand up."

"Go fuck yourself," says Frida. "I'm going."

Diego is standing in the doorway. "Go fuck yourself," he says. "She's going."

She has been looking forward to this forever—her exhibition at Lola Alvarez Bravo's Galería de Arte Contemporáneo. The only individual show she has ever had in Mexico, and only the second of her entire life. "Listen, doc," she says to Farill. Her voice is softer now, more playful. "I can't die today. Keep *la pelona* out of here, at least until after the vernissage." But Farill shakes his head. The pain has been excruciating, and he would have to administer a dangerous dose of drugs. Even then, standing for hours would be unthinkable. Even sitting for a few minutes might be impossible. "No, Frida," he says. "I can't permit it." He is standing about a foot from Frida's canopied bed, one hand on the post.

"Get out of here, you fucking bastard!" She throws her lighted cigarette at his face, but she has no force in her arms. The cigarette hits his jacket and falls. Diego signals the doctor to follow him into the corridor. "Come on, Juan," he says. "There must be a way." "No!" screams Frida. "You're not going to decide this without me! You're not going to treat me as though I'm already dead! Keep your asses right here, and we'll work this out together!"

Another call. It's Maty again. The phones are ringing off the hook at the gallery, she says. Everyone wants to know if Frida will be there. The pictures have all been hung. The staff is putting up labels. Deliverymen are bringing in fresh flowers and champagne. Lola Alvarez Bravo has planned the whole thing, and with her usual artistic flair, she's made it into a gala, a Hollywood event. "But people want to know if Frida's well enough to come," says Maty. "Without Frida, well, everyone wants to see Frida."

Weeks ago Frida sent out invitations, the kind of little booklet poets make to hand out to their friends. Poor poets who have no money to pay a printer. Booklets fastened with ribbon or string, with handwritten verses on colored paper. Frida made a bunch of them, hundreds. "This is my party! My party!" She's screaming at Juan Farill, her beloved doctor, screaming like a hawk diving in for the kill. But he's not budging. He's used to it. We all are. All of us except Diego. He can't take Frida's hysterics, which is why he comes by less now. These days he's spending his time in his studio with Emma Hurtado, his art dealer. Beautiful Emma, with her rich chocolate-brown hair. Who knew he would eventually wind up marrying her? "Get that fucker out of here," shrieks Frida. "I don't need any prick of a doctor to tell me what I can do and what I can't do!" Actually, she loves for Juan Farill to tell her what she can and can't do. It's just that today, today she just can't give in.

The episode has left her exhausted. She's quiet now. Farill and Diego have gone, but Diego promised to return within the hour. I'm fixing Frida's hair, combing out her dreary locks and pulling them back and up into a braid, which I pin to her head and decorate with ribbons and roses. I insert the wires of long, dangling earrings into her ears. She's wearing a colorful blouse, with brightly embroidered geometric designs.

Adri bustles around the house. Every once in a while she glances into the street. The phone rings every few minutes, and now it is ringing again. "It's Maty!" she calls. "Maty says that hundreds of people are there already. She can hardly control the reporters. They want to know if Frida's coming." "Tell her to hold them off!" I tell Adri. "Tell her to say she just doesn't know yet." Frida smiles. "Bring me a mirror," she commands. I hand her a mirror, but she's so weak she can hardly hold it. Adri comes in with some ox-tail broth. "Eat this, then sleep a while," she says. But Frida can't sleep. She can't relax. Adri spoons broth into her mouth, and I massage her hands. "What's taking Diego so long?" Frida asks every few minutes. "He's getting everything ready. It's complicated," I answer. Actually, Diego made tentative arrangements days ago.

"They're here!" Isolda calls from the other room. Diego and two male nurses come in and ease Frida onto a stretcher. "Gently . . . gently . . ." "Where's Juan?" Frida wants to know. "He'll be traveling with you in the ambulance when it gets here." The hospital personnel place the stretcher in another room. Several hefty men materialize and lift up Frida's canopied bed as though it's a toy. Without dismantling the canopy or the posts, they carry it outside to a truck, then drive off. "Splash some cologne on my neck," begs Frida. "You're already as perfumed as a hothouse flower." Adri laughs. "Just a bit more," Frida insists. "I smell like death." Adri and I exchange glances. It's true. She smells of death.

Now the male nurses return. They lift the stretcher and carry it outside, then place it in the back of the ambulance parked in front of the house. The motorcade is waiting to roll. It will be a Hollywood production—lights! camera! action!—a hospital ambulance with screeching sirens and a full motorcycle escort. Frida smiles. "Lola would be jealous!" she whispers.

The ambulance pulls out. The cycles rev up. Frida Kahlo, accompanied by her adoring husband, Diego Rivera, her sisters Adriana and Cristina, zoom through the streets of Mexico City to Lola Alvarez Bravo's famous gallery in the fashionable *Zona Rosa*. The place is packed. Reporters are elbowing one another in the struggle toward the entrance. Photographers are fumbling with their lenses. But when the nurses unload Frida from the ambulance, the newspapermen drop their equipment in astonishment. The great Kahlo has done it again! She has made jaws drop and eyes pop! She's arrived at her vernissage on a stretcher! Diego grins. Farill hobbles along, tight-lipped. Frida greets her guests in the horizontal, beaming through teeth clenched in pain. A martyr's smile, yes. But Frida is genuinely happy. This is, perhaps, the happiest moment of her life. The nurses hoist her into the gallery and place her on her bed, which has been set up in the middle of the room, canopy and all. Her adoring fans form a receiving line, filing by, kissing her fingertips, gushing praise. Some are speechless, paralyzed by her majestic presence. Lying there, surrounded by admirers, celebrities, reporters, and photographers, Frida is the sovereign, the grand Aztec empress. And I am overcome by a deep sense of joy, an inner satisfaction. No one is looking at me, no one is talking to me. No photographers are taking my picture, and no reporters are asking me my opinions. But at least I have helped give this to Frida.

4:05 A.M. The first shimmers of light grope the horizon like an insecure lover. Somewhere a bird chirps gaily, celebrating the dawn. Today will be different. It's not going to rain. Three or four workers stride down the street with purpose. Some carry tools. I suppose they have to be at work by 6:00. Perhaps they have to go all the way to the city. Tired men who lift and pull all day long for a peso or two, not enough to feed their families. Frida's right. It's not fair. I feel sorry for them. They don't see me. They don't even know that I exist, or that Frida exists. They don't know about Frida. They know only about their aching backs, their leaky ceilings, their children's empty bellies. They are absorbed in their own thoughts. I wonder if they would like to die. I hear voices in the street, men's voices, but I can't make out words. What are they talking about, these workers whom we love so passionately but can't understand? What is it like to be them? "Cristi!" She's awake. Her tongue is heavy, sticky. "Cristi!" "Yes, darling. Try to sleep." "The pain . . ." "I know, darling, I know." "Don't let her come back." But it's too late. Mayet is already standing in the doorway. "She's awake, Señora Mayet." The nurse turns on the dim lamp on the dresser and takes a vial of Demerol out of a locked case. "Give me double this time, Mayet. It hurts too much." She chews her words. Mayet pretends not to understand. She fills the syringe and injects. "Can't you increase the dose, Señora Mayet? She's suffering." The nurse looks right through me. She turns out the light and leaves the room.

Last year they cut off her leg, not long after the magnificent exhibition in Lola Alvarez Bravo's gallery. Poor leg. It was so crippled and shriveled, it reminded me of Diego's limp penis. Dr. Farill was the one who told her they had to do it. "Not just a toe this time, Frida, but the whole leg, up to the knee." Adelina Zendejas was with us. Adelina, Frida's old friend. Frida let out a scream so shrill, so deafening that traffic stopped, planes dropped out of the sky, church bells shattered, and wildcats in the desert fell dead. "No!!" Walls trembled all over Coyoacán, and in the *pulquería* on the corner, all the paintings fell to the ground. "No!!!" Gongorina, the *escuincle* dog, miscarried her litter, and in the church in the plaza, a plaster statue of Our Lady turned away from the congregation and wept real tears. "No!!!" But there was nothing to be done. Diego sat on the bed and smoothed her hair. "Friducha," he whispered. *"Mi Friducha."* Adelina bit her lip. "It'll be okay, Frida," I kept saying. "You've come through so much already."

She closed her eyes and was quiet a long time. Then, suddenly, she opened them. "What's this crying?" she snapped. "What's this sniveling? Haven't I always been Peg-leg Frida?" She started to chant that old song from our schoolyard days. *Frida Kahlo, pata de palo, un pie bueno, el otro malo.*

I cried. I cried more than she did. Frida painted. She painted Fridas with wounded feet, but also melons and bananas and mameys bursting with life. But since I couldn't paint, all I could do was cry. Frida comforted me. Yes, doctor, *she* comforted *me.* "What do I need that miserable paw for anyway?" she said. "It doesn't work anymore! It doesn't take me where I want to go! Let them chop it off!" But it was an act. Underneath it all, she was screaming, screaming in silence, screaming at the miserable fate that prevented her from doing what she really wanted to do: soar, dance, paint, love. "Don't worry, Cristi," she told me. "As long as I'm here, I'll love life, and when it's time for me to leave, I'll go joyfully." I looked into her eyes. "Just promise me one thing, Cristi. If *la pelona* drags it out, help her along. Give her a little push so that I don't suffer . . . needlessly." I didn't answer. "Promise," she whispered, drawing circles on my palm with the tips of her fingers. "Promise . . ." I stared at my trembling wrists and said nothing.

"She's going to die," Diego said to me.

"Yes," I said. "She can't take anymore. This time she really is going to die." When it was time for the operation, I went to the hospital with her, as I had so many times before.

The doctor had an artificial limb made for her. "I won't wear it," she said. "It hurts, and it's ugly." "Wear it, *mi amor*!" coaxed Diego. "I'll take you out dancing!" "Go dance with Emma Hurtado, you fucking son of a bitch!" By now, Diego was living openly with Emma.

But instead of taking his new girlfriend dancing, he had a pair of boots made for his wife—dainty red boots with bells on them, boots she could wear with her fake foot. When visitors came, she lifted her skirts above the ankle and showed them off. "They're dancing boots," she told everyone. "Diego is going to take me to the clubs!" And she would laugh and wink. "I'm going to wiggle my ass and flirt with all the young boys. I'll make him good and jealous! And while I'm at it, I'll flirt with the young girls too."

But Frida didn't dance. In fact, she could hardly stand. Instead, she sat in her wheelchair and painted, on good days, although her work was growing sloppy. She no longer had control. On bad days she sat and drank brandy out of a bottle and smoked cigarettes that made her breath fetid. It got so that the only one who could stand to be around her was me, and even I sometimes had to spend a night in my apartment in the city.

One morning I was sleeping in my room in the Casa Azul when

Manuel woke me up, banging on my door and howling like a wounded wolf, "Something's wrong with Miss Frida! I can't wake her up!"

She was lying in a lagoon of vomit and shit. Her tongue was hanging out of her mouth like a small, independent animal. Her bed-clothes were crumpled and piled on the floor as though she had thought they were attacking her and thrown them off in desperation. The stench was unbearable. Empty pill bottles were strewn all around. She had stashed them under her pillow and emptied them in an orgy of self-destruction during the night. I called Farill at home. "Frida's committed suicide!" "Where was the nurse?" "How do I know where the hell she was? Get over here right away!"

But she wasn't dead. They rushed her to the hospital. They pumped her stomach. They saved her. That's when we got Mayet, because Diego decided that she needed a full-time, live-in nurse—not like the others who came and went. Someone had to be with her all the time. All the time. But even after we got Mayet, that someone was me. Her sister. Because, to tell you the truth, no one else could stand to be around her day and night, not even for money.

I've told you this before: only one thing interested Frida. No, not communism or the plight of the workers. Not art, not muralism as an instrument of education, not creativity or where to buy the best oil colors. And no, not sex, not even sex. The only thing that really fascinated Frida was Frida. People said I was stupid. They said I never really understood what was going on. But I'm smart enough to know this: Frida Kahlo had a lifelong romance with herself, and nobody, not Diego, not me—nobody could ever replace Frida in Frida's heart. During those days and months after they amputated her leg, Frida was heartbroken. Part of herself was missing. She felt ugly, broken, shat-tered, flawed. And what she wanted most was to tell you about it. She was enthralled with her own suffering. She was mourning for her lost limb, and she wanted you to mourn with her. But who would listen? Everyone was tired. She wore everyone out. Who would listen to her analyze every twinge and spasm? Who but her doctors? After all, they got paid for listening, didn't they? And so she surrounded herself with doctors, the only people who shared her fascination with her decaying body. She called Dr. Eloesser long-distance all the time. She had dreamed of being a doctor, and now, at last, she could devote all her attention to medicine.

And then, finally, there came a doctor who really wanted to hear her talk, a new kind of doctor, an innovative plaything, a psychiatrist. *A psychiatrist!* One of your colleagues. And so Frida became a new kind of star: the first woman in Mexico ever to be psychoanalyzed.

And now I'm being psychoanalyzed too, right? That's why they sent you here, isn't it? To dig into my mind, to find out why I did what I did. Right, doctor? But this doesn't really count, does it, doctor? I mean, to be the eighth or the tenth or the fifteenth person to be psychoanalyzed in Mexico, that's not important. What matters is to be the first. But me, I didn't set any record. I'm just another patient.

Have you really been listening to me all this time, doctor? If you have, you know why I did it. I did it because I loved her. And I still love her.

4:30 A.M. It's now, in the stillness that precedes dawn, that God works his magic. Strangely, as I retreat into myself, into the secret castle of my own soul, I become intensely alert. My senses—fine-tuned, wide awake—take in everything, the soundless scampering of an insect, the buzz of a mosquito helicoptering over live flesh, the silhouette of the bedpost, an eerie sculpture formed by the twisted leaves of a wilting bouquet, the stink of emptied but still foul bedpans, blood coursing through my veins, Frida's ratchety breathing, my own cadenced inhaling. Frida moans and mumbles unintelligibly. She's still alive. I sit on her bed. I sense movement under the lids of her closed eyes. Dawn struggles to be born. A feeble sliver of light hugs the sides of the drawn curtain. Frida mumbles: "pain" . . . "misery" . . . "unbearable" . . . "dance" . . . dance?

Dear God, grant us peace.

"Cristi . . ." "I know, darling." "Cristi, you'll never guess who I just saw." "Try to rest, darling." "I saw Princess Frida Zoraída!" "Don't try to talk, darling." "Princess Frida Zoraída, Cristi! I haven't seen her for years!" Frida's forehead is on fire. I reach for a compress and place it above her eyebrows. "She had the same sweet, high, bell-like voice as before, Cristi. 'Is that you, Princess Frida Zoraída?' I asked her. And she sang to me, the same way she used to: 'I'm hiding in your mind! / Now open the door! / Don't ask me how / I'll tell you no more!'

"So I tiptoed to the window and breathed on the pane, and when the glass got all steamed up, I drew a door in the mist. And then I flew out that door and across the plain. When I got to the Pinzón Dairy, I zoomed right through the *O* of Pinzón." "Were you wearing your gingham pinafore, darling?" "I was wearing a nightgown, Cristi. This same nightgown, high bodice, white lace, this same one. And my red boots with the bells." "And what did Princess Zoraída have on, Frida?" "She was an old woman, Cristi, just like I am. But she had on the same frilly white bow she used to wear when we were little girls, and a long red-orange robe adorned with round, peso-sized mirrors, sequins, and beads, and a purple-braided rope trim, just like before, Cristi, just like before. Only instead of those felt boots with upturned points that she used to have, she wore red boots with bells, just like mine. 'Dance,' she said. I didn't want to. 'I can't,' I told her. But she insisted, and I started to hobble around, first this way, then that way. She danced with me, following my movements as gracefully as a balloon." Princess Frida Zoraída told her how graceful she was and how much she loved her lacy nightgown, and Frida cried with joy. "I want to go back to her, Cristi. I want to stay with her forever. She'll take care of me, darling, and then you won't have to." "I don't mind taking care of you, Frida." "It's too much of a burden for you, darling. I'm wearing you out." "No, Frida, no. I don't mind at all!" "I love you, Cristi, but now it's time for me to go to be with Princess Frida Zoraída. Help me find her. Please help me find her. I'm in so much pain . . ."

I get up and pull aside the curtain. At last the dawn has elbowed aside the darkness, and I can see Frida's eyes, those beautiful brown eyes whose brows form a bird in flight. "I can't stand the pain, Cristi. There's a bottle under my pillow." I reach under her pillow and find a small brown bottle of laudanum and a medicine dropper. I twist the cap off the top and fill the dropper. Frida smiles, and we kiss one last time. Then calmly, lovingly, I place the nib under her tongue and squeeze, releasing the medicine drop by drop.

Author's Note

FRIDA IS A WORK OF FICTION. ALTHOUGH EVENTS IN MEXICAN HISTORY and in Frida's life provide the general framework, many incidents and characters portrayed here are the author's inventions. For example, I have found no evidence that Frida destroyed her doll collection or that she seduced a fifteen-year-old Esmeralda student (or any other minor). Although Frida's bisexuality is well documented, Leticia Santiago is my own creation. Although many of Frida's biographers mention her younger sister, Cristina, I have reinvented the youngest Kahlo girl to make her a perspicacious witness to Frida's life. Frida's last hours have long been shrouded in mystery. In 1953 she tried to kill herself, and some of her biographers entertain the possibility that her death in 1954 was, in fact, a suicide. However, there is no evidence that Cristina played any part in that event. She died February 7, 1964.

My intention in writing *Frida* was to capture the essence of Frida Kahlo's personality, not to document her life. I was particularly interested in what it might be like to be the unexceptional sister of such an exceptional woman. The rivalry between Frida and Cristina for Diego's attention is factual, and the psychological repercussions of the affair leave ample room for conjecture. More broadly, I was concerned with some of the underlying issues in human relationships—in particular, our seemingly limitless capacity to do harm, even to those we sincerely love.

I have relied on a number of primary and secondary sources for information about Frida Kahlo. Frida's letters (*Cartas apasionadas,* compiled by Martha Zamora, San Francisco: Chronicle Books, 1995) and her diary (*The Diary of Frida Kahlo: An Intimate Self-Portrait,* New York: Harry N. Abrams and Mexico, D.F.: La Vaca Independiente, 1995) provided me with insight into the painter's character. (However, the letters included in this novel are all fictional.) I also garnered information from Hayden Herrera's stellar biography (*Frida,* New York: Harper and Row, 1983), as well as from studies by Raquel Tibol (*Frida Kahlo: Una vida abierta,* Mexico, D.F.: Oasis, 1983; English trans. Albuquerque: University of New Mexico, 1993), Rauda Jamis (*Frida Kahlo,* Mexico, D.F.: Diana, 1987), Martha Zamora (*Frida Kahlo: The Brush of Anguish,* San Francisco: Chronicle Books, 1990), Sarah M. Lowe (*Frida Kahlo,* New York: Universe, 1991), J.M.G. Le Cézio (*Diego y Frida,* Mexico, D.F.: Diana, 1995), and Terri Hardin (*Frida Kahlo: A Modern Master,* New York: Smithmark, 1997). Another source of data was *Frida's Fiestas* (New York: Clarkson Potter, 1994), a collection of Frida's favorite recipes compiled by Guadalupe Rivera (daughter of Diego Rivera and Lupe Marín) and Marie-Pierre Colle. *Drawing the Line* (London: Verso, 1989), by Oriana Baddeley and Valerie Fraser, and *Textured Lives* (Tucson: University of Arizona, 1992), by Claudia Schaefer, broadened my general understanding of Latin American women artists. Many books on Diego Rivera are available. I found Diego's own *My Art, My Life* (New York: Dover, 1960), and Bertram D. Wolfe's *The Fabulous Life of Diego Rivera* (Chelsea, MI: Scarborough House, 1969) particularly valuable.

I wish to thank my husband, Mauro, for his encouragement and undying faith in this project. I am also indebted to Hermann Lademann, of The Overlook Press, for his brilliant editing; to the novelist Janice Eidus, for her excellent suggestions; and to my agent, Anna Ghosh at Scovil, Chichak, Galen.

READERS GUIDE ONLINE
www.penguinputnam.com/guides
OR AVAILABLE AT YOUR LOCAL BOOKSTORE

A Member of Penguin Putnam Inc.
www.penguinputnam.com

Available wherever books are sold